ANGELS OF WAR
TALION

PREVIOUSLY IN THE SERIES:

Angels of War: Veritas

CHECK OUT THE *ANGELS OF WAR VERITAS & TALION* TIE-IN NOVELLA:

Jezebel: An Angels of War Novella

GET READY FOR THE EPIC CONCLUSION TO THE *ANGELS OF WAR* SERIES:

Angels of War: Terminus

ANGELS OF WAR

TALION

BOOK 2

A Novel by D.J. Thompson

MASTERLESS
P R E S S

www.masterlesspress.com

Masterless Press
www.masterlesspress.com

Angels of War: Talion
Copyright © 2019 by D.J. Thompson
Cover design by Hampton Lamoureux

First Masterless Press print edition: April 2019

Printed in the United States of America

ISBN: 978-1-7323064-3-1 (print)
ISBN: 978-1-7323064-4-8 (ebook)

AUTHOR'S NOTE

To all of the awesome readers who made it to book two, thank you and welcome back to the *Angels of War* Universe and to Dion Johnson's journey! As a gift to you for supporting my work, if you haven't had a chance to read the tie-in novella, *Jezebel*, you can download the first seven chapters for free at MasterlessTribe.com if you join my mailing list! Those chapters occur during the same time period as Dion's journey in *Angels of War: Veritas*. The last six chapters fill in the gap between *Veritas* and *Talion*, concluding early on in this book. If you want to read the complete Jezebel story after finishing this, it is currently available on Amazon!

If it's been a while since you've read *Veritas,* here's a short recap.

After embedding sleepers in key positions of power and manipulating soldiers to fight against their own nations, Richard 'The Architect' Thomas and the Deciders plunged the world into chaos and he became humanity's overlord. And during Richard's takeover dubbed the Annex, the masses were reeducated through Veritas, a collection of truths long hidden from the public that exposed the corruption perpetrated by shadowy elites, megabanks, and governments.

Early in the Annex, Dion Johnson avoided being captured and herded into a Decider reeducation camp. And because he resisted, his friend Hope met her end. That loss drove him to rebel against the Deciders. He and his friends banded with a group of former soldiers nicknamed Renegades and they formed the Angels of War

Militia. The AOW waged guerilla warfare against the Deciders, acquiring allies and weapons of war along the way.

During a mission to avenge his best friends Stefan and Dave, Dion learned his nemesis was Anne 'Ice Queen' Buckingham, a Decider founding member who wanted to end the hell she helped unleash. The former enemies bonded, developing feelings for each other during their quest to destroy the Deciders. And, with Anne's help, Dion was able to end Richard Thomas and the Angels of War freed the Vanguards (soldiers forced to fight against their countries), sparking a global rebellion known as the Disintegration. Before suffering absolute defeat, the Deciders vanished into the shadows without a trace and the war ended.

One year later, Dion, Anne, and their son are living in peace, thriving off of the riches seized from the fallen Architect. Panic kicks in after Anne divulges to Dion that Decider-like chatter was intercepted by the new military branch, USAW (United States Angels of War). And then, a figure it white appeared outside of Dion's home ...

If things weren't dark enough for you in *Angels of War: Veritas*, get ready for a whole new level of bleak ... Talion is retributive justice—eye for an eye style punishment. "*Saving*" humanity and murdering the leader of a world dominating army has its consequences ... The new antagonist will employ some pretty vile tactics to get back at Dion and friends in the midst of reclaiming what was taken from him. And those sinister, unmentionable crimes he commits to claim revenge, I do not condone. It's all purely for the story to not only break our hero in every way possible but also to make you feel the level of hate and disgust our heroes will experience.

This one goes to you, mom,

You taught me how to read and write
before I even began kindergarten, so I'm
not sure I would have even been a writer if it
wasn't for you. And I'm not sure I would have
worked as hard to make my books reality if you
hadn't gotten sick. Though you aren't here to
witness the rest of my journey as an author, I know
you'd want me to keep strong and continue
on. Everything from here on out is not only
because of you, but now it's all for you
[and of course for dad, too].

Thanks for everything.

GLOSSARY

A.E.——Asiatic Empire

A.O.——Area of Operation

AOW—— Angels of War

AWB——Angels of War Base

BDU——Battle Dress Uniform

Deva-AM——Deva-Aegis Model

Deva-FHOM——Deva Full-Face Hazardous Operations Mask with tactical goggles attached

Deva-HF——Deva Half-Face gas mask

ECO——Executive Command and Overwatch

HUD——Heads up Display

LMTV——Light Medium Tactical Vehicle

LZ——Landing Zone

MR-Deva Farsight Variant—— Magnetorheological liquid armored Deva helmet

OP—— Outpost

OPFOR——Opposing Force

OPSEC——Operational Security

POS——Position

POW——Prisoner of War

PR-1 Terah drone— Penetrating Radar One Terahertz Drone

PROXCOM——Proximity Communications, an encrypted frequency invisible to TARSEN

RP——Rendezvous Point

SERE——Survival, Evasion, Resistance, and Escape; a training program

STF——Shear-thickening Fluid (liquid armor technology)

TARSEN—Total Area Sensory Field— a rapid, pulsating Wi-Fi emitter for sonar imaging and detection

TATCO—Threat Assessment and Tactical Command

TSI-Icarus—Tactical Stealth Insertion Icarus wingsuit

UAV—Unmanned Aerial Vehicle

UGV—Unmanned Ground Vehicle

UFR—United Federation of Russia

UNE—United Nations of Europe

USAW—United States Angels of War

WISC—Wolf in Sheep's Clothing

PART ONE
REEMERGENCE

1
PARANOIA

September 2, Two Years After Deliverance
8:06 A.M.

SWEAT'S DRIPPING DOWN my face. I block the oncoming back kick, but it sends me stumbling back. Before I can catch my breath, the combos start coming again. I expect nothing less from my opponent.

Deadly. Fast. Relentless. Those three words describe her best.

I slip the first punch, parry the second, and block a kick. Now I strike with a jab. She knocks it away, attacking simultaneously with a hammer fist to my abdomen. I take a low kick to the thigh followed by a punch to the ribs. She maneuvers around me and somehow gets me in a chokehold, bringing me down to the mat. Her legs wrap around my torso and she squeezes like a boa constrictor. I try breaking free, but the more I fight, the more winded I become.

I'm losing again.

Of course I am—she's my toughest opponent and I can't help holding back because I'd never want to hurt my fiancé.

I tap out.

Anne releases me then lies panting on the mat, smirking. The coldness that was in her eyes when we first met on the battlefield has melted over the last few years into a faint glint. The sorrow and emptiness are gone now too, both from her eyes and from her voice. Her glacier blue eyes now radiate happiness.

"What's that? Three to two for the week?" she teases in that British accent I love so much. "One more win and you're on house cleanup and dinner prep all next week, my king!"

I remove my gloves as I stand. "Nope. I'll tie it up tomorrow."

Hand-to-hand combat training has been a part of our routine almost every morning for the past year. We always begin with a full body workout. After that, we practice tactical room clearing and then we run knife and gun disarmament drills. Sparring follows. It's a mash-up of Krav Maga, Muy Thai, Judo, kickboxing, and military CQC techniques. It doesn't end there. Before hitting the shower, we head to our vast backyard and practice some run-and-gun drills with suppressed weapons.

For most, Deliverance Day celebrated a new era of peace. For me, its first anniversary was the day when Anne broke the news that our fallen enemies were becoming active in the shadows. The doorbell had rung shortly after, and as I descended the stairs to let Sam and Dave in, I saw something white out in the distance. *A White Coat,* I thought, drawing the Glock 19 from the holster nestled in the small of my back. Jeremy and Karla, who were at the base of the stairs, stared at me in horror and confusion.

"There's someone in white at the edge of the woods!" I shouted, surveilling the area through the bulletproof window as I unlocked the door. "I'll secure the perimeter. Arm up!"

Before opening the door, I caught a glimpse of Anne at the top of the steps. She too had a pistol in hand. "Dion, wait!" she cried.

"Hey!" Dave said as I bolted past him and Sam.

"Get inside!" was all I said.

With my weapon pointed ahead at the white fabric fluttering from behind the pine tree, my eyes darted side to side in search of more enemy combatants. There was no movement in the woods. Aside from Anne and my friends running up behind me, the only other person outside was the target ahead.

At the tree line, I came to a stop, then slowly sidestepped around the pine until my target came into view at the other end of my sights. "What ...?" was the only word that escaped me.

The white fabric fluttering before me didn't belong to a trench coat. There was no helmeted figure looming in the shadows. The threat was nothing more than the damn grill cover I had drunkenly forgotten to tie down the night before. It had blown off, somehow found its way into the front yard, got turned inside out and caught on a tree.

Standing there with my fiancé and my friends staring worriedly at me, I felt like a complete idiot. I couldn't even explain myself, not without letting them know about the intercepted chatter. And at that moment, I realized that I hadn't come out of the war as mentally unscathed as I thought I had. In the year after the War of Annex, I was a bit paranoid, but that was the first time I hallucinated a threat, or anything for that matter ...

Considering that it's been two years since the War of Annex— two years without an appearance by the Deciders—it might seem excessive to keep training as hard as we do. But shooting and sparring are both hobbies that we dearly enjoy. And it doesn't hurt to keep our minds sharp and our skills honed, especially since the economy is still in shambles and violent crime rates remain at historic highs.

Anne jumps on my back, kissing my sweaty cheek while I carry her to our nineteen-month-old son Dean's room to check on him before hitting the "range." The door opens with a squeak and she dismounts. We tiptoe inside and stand over the crib, smiling as we watch our boy sleeping peacefully. Nothing makes me happier than knowing that after everything we went through, after everything we sacrificed two years ago, my kids can live in a world where their lives aren't in constant danger.

But how long will it last?

Recently, I've been trying to convince myself that the Deciders won't return. The United States Angels of War's interception of that Decider chatter was a one-time thing; they've fallen silent since. So far as I know, anyway. I'm not in the loop these days. I tell myself that if anything were to happen, there'd be no need for me to get dragged into it this time. All U.S. agencies involved in national security are up and running at full capacity, preventing anything like Richard Thomas's reign of terror from even getting started. And even if they did, the Army, USMC, Navy, and USAW, are more than prepared to deal with them. The Angels of War have become a behemoth whose sole purpose is Anti-Decider/Antiterrorism Operations domestically and globally.

Not only is USAW a fully functioning army with bases spread around the country and territories across the world, and just under two-hundred-thousand active duty soldiers, it also has thousands of federal agents who work tirelessly in information-gathering fusion centers across the nation using a surveillance grid that would frighten Joseph Stalin. Hell, it frightens me. There are measures in place to keep them from abusing their powers of surveillance, but I'm still wary.

Despite how vigilant USAW is, I can't help but feel I'll wake up one day to a world on fire. If there's one thing I learned during the Annex, it's that safety is an illusion. Hundreds of thousands of uncaptured Decider sleepers are still living among us, and our security and lives could be threatened at any given moment. That's why I train daily. That's why I used Richard Thomas's funds and my military connections to amass an arsenal of weapons. That's why I purchased multiple safe houses while I built up my real estate empire. It's the reason why I said yes when Commander Todd Finley contacted me a few months ago to see if I was interested in taking part in the Special Forces Operation training, training that I had asked about the last time we met. He knew damn well that I wouldn't enlist after training, but since he was in charge, he allowed me to take part in it off the books.

Of course, Anne insisted on signing up too. Our morning training routine is proof that she can't let go of her inner soldier either. So, at the beginning of summer, we left Dean with my parents and headed down to Fort Bragg for training. And to my surprise, I wasn't the only one of the original Angels of War militiamen there. Among the unfamiliar faces were college friends and former Delta Squad soldiers Ken Nguyen and Abby Snyder, USAW soldiers of almost two years. Andrew Steele, the rookie soldier who I fought alongside during the War of Annex, and my college buddy and Renegade Sung Seo were there as well. Each of them claimed to be participating in order to advance their military careers, though I suspect that wasn't the whole truth.

Anne and I were late to the party, so we started during Phase II, which was small-unit tactics and SERE. The first part consisted of physical training (conditioning and CQC techniques), advanced marksmanship training, mission analysis, military decision making, small-unit tactics, and Special Forces tactics. During the second part, we learned survival field craft skills and techniques for evasion, resistance to torture, and escape. In the last part of the training, we had to put all of our skills to the test, evading Finley's men and their search dogs over the course of five days. Other than being tortured and shot during the War of Annex, that SF training was the most brutal thing I've ever put my body through.

After changing into tactical clothes, we head to the armory on the first floor. Today we both decide on HK416s for rifles and an assortment of pistols. With the duffle of weapons and ammo hanging from my shoulder and baby monitors attached to our duty belts, I follow Anne to the backyard. Right before I reach the door, the encrypted Galaxy smartphone in my pocket begins vibrating. I fish it out of my cargo pants and find JESSICA STEWART on the screen with a picture of her and our son in the background.

Jess gave birth to our kid two years ago, on December 28. We named him Marshal Stefan Johnson after Aaron Marshall, the man who sacrificed his life to save mine as well as Stefan's, my oldest best friend who died at the hands of my fiancé during the war.

I always snicker when I think back to the day Marshal was born. During labor, Jess, grabbed me and shouted, "You don't know how much I hate you for doing this to my body then leaving me for another bitch! I hope you know I'll never forgive you for any of this! But I'm glad you are here!" Despite those words, I can safely say we're friends again, even though she's still somewhat bitter. She denies it, but I hear resentment in her voice whenever we speak and see it in her face every time I visit. Had she never been pregnant with my child, it's likely that we never would've spoken again. So, I guess I'm grateful for knocking her up …

I hit the volume key to end the vibration before sliding the phone into my pocket. "I'll call her back later …" I mumble to myself. *If it's something important, she'll call right back.*

I get my revenge for the sparring match by showing Anne up on the range. I only hit two more bull's eyes than she did, but hey, a win is a win. On the way to the shower, I hear Dean crying over the monitor.

"I guess we're not showering together today," Anne pouts, removing the hair tie from her shoulder-length ponytail.

I kiss her. "I guess not. You go first, I'll feed Dean."

He's already standing in his crib and crying when I walking into his room. He has Anne's blue eyes and hair, but his complexion is closer to mine and he has my features.

After changing his diaper, I carry him down to the kitchen and sit him in the highchair. He gets a sippy cup of OJ and a bowl of oatmeal while I start on breakfast for Anne and me. In a couple of minutes, the ham and cheese omelets are finished and I put the sausages on to cook. My phone goes off again and I swipe to answer. "Morning, Jess."

"Hello, Dion," Jess says with attitude. "Thought that you were avoiding my calls."

I sigh. "I was working out."

"Oh ... sorry ... Well, um ... I was just calling to see if you would be able to attend my family's Labor Day barbeque. I would really appreciate it if the father of my child came to at least *one* family function, this one especially."

"And why's this one so special?"

"I have family coming by that haven't seen the baby yet and I'd like it if they could meet the father of the child—America's savior!"

I roll my eyes. "I'm out of town this weekend, and Monday we're going over to Eric and Casey's. Maybe I'll swing by for a bit. It has been a while since I've seen little Marshal ..."

"Mmm. It's been a while since we've seen each other too ..." she says. Silence follows.

I check to see if the call dropped. She's still on the line.

"I miss you ... a lot."

I groan. "Jess ...."

"I'm just sayin' it's been a while. You know I moved on …" she mumbles. She has a boyfriend now, whose name I can't remember. "Despite how it all ended, you're still a big part of my life. Hell, every day I'm alive, I owe to you!"

I sigh again. "I know."

There's more silence. "Alrighty, just call me before you show up on Monday. See ya!"

The call ends before I mouth the first syllable of "goodbye."

"Who was that?" Anne asks.

I turn to find her strutting toward me while drying her brown hair, her robe half open, her body glistening wet. "Jess."

"Oh, her again," she huffs, picking up the glass of orange juice. She takes an elegant sip. "Say the word, Dion, and I'll get rid of her." She smiles devilishly. The scary part is she's serious.

I slap her ass. "You know I love it when you talk assassin to me in the morning, babe."

While we eat, we debate what time we should leave for Virginia Beach and Anne surfs channels on the wall-mounted flat screen across from the table.

"What time are your parents coming to pick up Dean?" she asks.

"Around three. We can leave right after that." I drink some juice. "We'll be back in time for Eric and Casey's barbeque, right?"

"Mmm," she hums, mouth full of omelet. "Why?"

"Jessica wants me to stop by her family's barbeque."

She stares at me, a tinge of bitterness in her eyes. "Are you asking for my permission?"

"Yeah … I told her I might swing by for a bit since we'll be in the area."

"Fine by me." She looks to the TV. I'm about to say thanks when she interrupts me. "Um, Dion ..." she says, lifting her chin to the screen.

The news is showing footage of a building I know all too well going up in flames. Thick black smoke rises up from the deep orange flames shooting out of the windows. A crowd of employees in lab coats stand watching behind the police tape. The chyron reads "EXPLOSIONS AT COEUS LABORATORIES, INC."

"What the hell?" I ask, looking at Anne.

She shrugs with a concerned look on her face.

Coeus Labs is the first of several businesses I opened with the funds I'd claimed from Richard's Legacy. Named after the Greek Titan god of intellect, Coeus is a biotechnology and pharmaceutical company specializing in the research and development of the medical advancements long hidden from the public. Drugs such as Cascade, a gel that speeds up wound healing, life extension research, and new, natural alternatives to cancer treatment are among the things that are developed there by some of the brightest, scientific minds that Richard cataloged in the Legacy laptop.

The reporter is saying that the explosion was due to an accident in the lab, speculating that there was a gas leak somewhere on the ground level. *Bullshit.* I had strict safety protocols in place and the building was engineered to contain fires to the source of ignition.

"Dion ..." Anne says, holding my hand. "Relax, love. It's probably nothing."

"Come on ... This is obviously sabotage. Look, the west wing is on fire ... That's where the security room is. There aren't even gas lines there! It's gotta be them ..."

"Even if it is sabotage, it could just be a Decider sympathizer group. I told you they have become active in recent days."

Though the Deciders have disappeared, their ideals are still alive and well. In the past year, the aftereffects of Richard Thomas's brainwashing during Act II's Purge became evident. In his final words, he promised that he'd made everlasting alterations to the minds of humanity. With a world exposed to Veritas, I didn't doubt it. Those high school students and college-aged kids who were subjected to Richard's reeducation program had formed clubs, some secretive, some overt. Those clubs led to organized rallies promoting the foundations of the Deciders' ideology. Most rallies were peaceful, but others bordered on aggressive. Sympathizers were detained and questioned by USAW. None were found to have any Decider involvement so they were released and placed under strict surveillance in case they happened to make contact with the sleepers we all know exist.

Anne still works as a senior level analyst for the Angels of War under the alias Annabel Myers, so if there was anyone I should listen to on the matter, it's her. "Yeah, maybe you're right," I say, scrolling through my phone.

For security reasons, there's only one person at the company who has my number—my good friend Carmela Discala, the Coeus director of operations and my tutor during my freshmen year at Penn State. It worries me that she didn't call before the news media picked up the story. I can't call her because the call might be traced.

Once the fire is extinguished, they start carrying out bodies. Now following the story online, I watch the body toll climb to eleven, with six wounded. Nearly a hundred more employees are unaccounted for. Seeing how the building hasn't collapsed, there should be no problem locating the missing.

Something's not right here ...

2
INSTINCTS

September 5
2:02 P.M.

THE TRAFFIC ON I-95 North isn't bad. The sky is cloudless and the weather is warm, but nice. Perfect, actually. Our weekend at the beach was everything we wanted it to be—romantic, peaceful, relaxing, fun, full of mind-blowing sex. But the explosion at the lab and the specter of a hundred dead scientists and staff haunts me.

Before leaving for the beach, Anne's work contacts assured her that there was no evidence of foul play in the Coeus Labs explosion. But as we were preparing to head to the Wilsons' for their Labor Day barbeque, Anne received a call from Sergeant Sung Seo saying that she needs to go to work to "help review some new material." That's strange, considering she only goes to Quantico on Mondays and Thursdays, and she's never called in on her days off. Most days, she just works from home using a secure connection to the USAW network.

Currently, I'm obsessing over what sinister plot might be underway at this very moment. It takes everything to restrain myself from asking Anne what she thinks she's being called in for. Of course, if she knew anything, she'd tell me without waiting to be asked. Also, obsessing about potential Decider-related events and connecting them to the smallest of events is one of her pet peeves.

So, rather than badgering her with questions and getting scolded, I keep our conversation as far from the topic as possible.

The ride from our beach house to Fort Sanctum, Quantico, takes two hours and thirty-five minutes thanks to my lead foot. As I round the bend of AWB-3 (formerly MCB-3) toward the gate, a black BAE Systems JLTV Valanx armored truck parked beside the guard's station comes into view. My new model Cherokee's armored plating and bulletproof glass probably rival its durability.

"Pull up behind the Valanx," she says.

"You got a VIP escort to take you to the office? This material you have to review must not be very important at all ..."

Her eyebrows rise. "Don't."

A soldier approaches the driver's side of the Jeep, his M4 at the low ready. He's wearing the black and dark gray Angels of War combat uniform with a camouflage pattern reminiscent of snakeskin. On the left shoulder of the uniform is the new insignia composed of a dark gray circle "A" with three blocks on both sides for wings and a black background.

The old one was better. This one looks like something out of Avengers ...

I roll down the presidential tinted window and Anne flashes her credentials. He examines them then eyes me suspiciously. I'm wearing a black hood over my head and aviator shades, so I don't blame him. Protocol or not, he's not seeing my face. He'll recognize me, and I don't want anyone knowing that I'm here.

"He's fine," Anne assures the guard.

The guard nods and returns to the booth, giving the Valanx driver a thumbs-up.

As the window rolls up, Anne and I kiss.

She opens her door. "I know you'll need a buzz to deal with Jessica and her family, but try not to drink *too* much. I'll probably need you to pick me up in a few hours."

I smirk. "Bet you twenty bucks I never leave Eric's."

"I'm not taking a losing bet, dear." She smiles and gets out, slamming the door behind her. I sit there until she climbs into the Valanx and it drives out of sight.

Upon entering the town of Warrenton, I'm hit with a wave of flashbacks—being attacked by the Deciders on the way here from Pennsylvania, Hope's death, Han getting shot, venturing into the hostile controlled hospital, all of it. The memories are so vivid, the road before me vanishes. I shake my head to refocus and realize that the cars ahead have stopped. I quickly slam on my brakes. The tires screech and the Jeep stops just a few inches from next car's rear bumper. The driver glares at me through his rearview mirror and flips me off.

Panting, I rub my face. *Relax, Dion. Relax.*

Warrenton, like most towns in America today, has been rebuilt from the ruins it was reduced to during the Annex. Pell's aggressive, nationwide reconstruction program is to thank for that. So is my charity-funded home construction company. Though smaller towns are back to what they once were, most cities are barely starting to shape up. Forty percent of them are still uninhabited mounds of rubble.

There are a bunch of cars parked outside the Wilsons' million-dollar home, so I park across the street, half a block down. When I get out, I can already smell grilled meats and charcoal. I slam my door and walk around to the backseat to retrieve the cooler full of beer sitting on the floor. When I shut the door, I catch my reflection in the Jeep's glossy black paint. With my black hoodie pulled over my head and sunglasses, I look like an undercover cop.

As I walk down the street, I scan every car I pass. I do that everywhere I go to ensure that I'm not under surveillance. It's not paranoia, it's situational awareness. Directly across the street from their house, I spot a black GMC Terrain with two white male passengers chatting and staring at the house. They look suspicious to me, but everyone does these days so I chalk it up to guests not yet ready to enter and proceed to ring the doorbell.

Casey opens the door, her daughter Hayley in her arms. "Yay! Dion!" she shouts, half-hugging me with her free arm. She cranes her neck and scans the street. "Where's your *queen*?" she teases.

"Working," I sigh, pulling back my hood. "She'll be here later, though."

"Ah, poo …" she pouts. "So … when are you and Miz Buckingham going to tie the knot? You've been engaged for a year already!"

"When they're good and ready, honey," Eric interjects as he enters the foyer.

"Exactly." I smile. "We're in no rush. Love doesn't need a ceremony."

A woman calls Casey from the rear of the house.

"Coming!" she shouts. "Well, my guests beckon!"

"Let's get you some food and drink," Eric says. "I have a new beer you need to try."

Eric hands me a stout made from the barley he grew in his backyard, then leads me outside so I can fix a plate. I load up my burger with all of the essentials, get some macaroni salad and some hot wings, and then we retreat to his man cave. With a clink, we cheers then immediately get to talking about beer since we both recently began brewing. The topic then shifts to our kids, comparing stories and all of that. After complaining about how being a surgeon is cutting into time with his daughter, he asks about Coeus Labs. As I tell him what I know, I glance at the TV behind the bar. The CNN anchor has just mentioned something about President Pell's upcoming Labor Day speech from the University of Richmond. The broadcast then shifts to a story about SpaceX and how they're entering the final phases of completing the ODESA satellite system.

ODESA, or the Orbital Defense Satellite, has been in the making for the last three years. I remember first hearing about it just before the Annex, but I still don't know what they're doing exactly. Based on what I've learned from Anne, the satellite system will somehow use high-powered, direct energy lasers to divert or vaporize asteroids and meteors that are on an Earthbound trajectory. Sounds like it'll get turned around on Earth eventually.

By the time I finish eating, President Pell's speech is just starting up.

"Hey, hey," Eric says. "It's Kenny Washington! Didn't know he was still working security detail for the president."

I nod. "Yeah, he's one of the only original members of the protection detail. Everyone else reenlisted with USAW."

Pell is in the middle of giving one of his awe-inspiring speeches about how America is growing toward an ideal nation. Extolling the progress of the reconstruction program, he says, "It's not the government that's responsible for the recent economic boom and the nation's recovery. It's the American workforce—the American spirit."

I can't help but smile. Ever since the war's end, I can finally watch a presidential speech and know that I'm not watching a politician run by shadowy elites. And I put him in power ...

An explosion rocks the camera and a cloud of dust blows across the room from the left. The camera is tilted slightly downward, showing reporters ducking and covering their heads. Kenny Washington and two other Secret Service agents are shielding the president.

Eyes wide and heart racing, I stare frozen in disbelief. *It's them. It's definitely them …*

Some reporters run for the exits, but they don't make it very far. Automatic gunfire barks off camera, dropping them two at a time.

"What's happening?" Eric gasps, eyes wide and beaming fear like they were when we first met in the hospital.

"I have no idea …" I reply, looking back to the TV.

Eric walks backward toward the door behind him, his gaze fixated on the flat screen. "Casey?! Casey, get in here now!" he hollers.

Several Secret Service agents are gunned down. Kenny's taking cover behind the bulletproof podium, firing at the unseen assailants. Pell's ducking behind him, looking around frantically. Just as Kenny begins reloading his pistol, an assailant steps into view.

"What is it, babe?" Casey asks as she enters the room with a group of guests.

Eric just shakes his head.

The assailant is dressed in slate gray tactical gear with a black balaclava, tinted tactical goggles, and a next-gen mask. There's no trench coat or no Deva helmet like I expected, but those are standard Loyal colors.

Two remaining agents engage the shooters and Kenny signals the president to move. Kenny lays down cover fire and Pell scrambles for the exit stage left. A second later, the agents are dropped and Kenny is hit. The assailant steps on stage and kicks the podium over. Two more masked men dressed identically to the first drag Pell back to the center stage. Someone off-screen fixes the camera and zooms in.

"My god, they're going to execute the president!" a woman behind me gasps.

The two hostiles stand on each side of Pell, forcing him onto his knees and holding him in place. The third man walks up behind Pell, letting his FN P90 submachine gun hang from its sling while drawing a gray 1911-style pistol from his drop leg holster. He puts the muzzle to the back of Pell's head. There's no speech. There's no threat. He just pulls the trigger.

Everyone in the room gasps. Whimpers follow.

For the first time since Kennedy, a U.S. President was assassinated live on television.

My heart rate spikes like I'm at the peak of one of my workout routines. *This can't be happening! Not after everything I've done ...*

The assassin then shoots the camera and the transmission ends, immediately switching back to the newsroom. The anchors sit there in silence.

I swivel the barstool to face Eric and Casey.

"What. The. Hell," Casey says through clenched teeth.

"Were those ... the Deciders?" Eric asks.

I shrug.

Some wide-eyed girl behind Casey points at me. "Hey, that's the guy who stopped the Deciders the first time. That's Dion Johnson!"

Everyone bursts into a clamor.

"Are the Deciders back?"

"Did you know this was going to happen?"

"It's happening again, isn't it?"

I stare blankly while Eric works to herd them outside.

Baby Hayley starts crying as Casey approaches me. "Dion, what do you know?" she asks.

"Nothing," I whisper. Then something clicks. "Anne getting called into work today, and then this ... It can't be a coincidence. It can't be ..." I let my words trail off as I stand. "I've got to go."

She follows me to the door and gives me a hug. "Keep us posted, Dion. Let us know if we need to do *that thing* we've talked about."

I don my shades and pull on my hood. "You know I will," I say, opening the door.

As I descend the steps, my eyes lock onto the GMC. When the two men see me, they pretend they weren't looking at the house. Everything in my gut tells me they're trouble.

Coolly, I stroll toward my Jeep. Once I'm out of their sight, I lift my gray shirt and draw the SIG P226 MK25 tucked underneath my belt in the small of my back then swiftly slip it into my hoodie's pocket. There's a Glock 26 in an ankle holster on my left leg if I need it. Anne and I never leave the house without a pistol or two.

Once across the street, I crouch and slink back up the block. I manage to sneak right up to the passenger side window. Now I rise slowly, then tap my pistol against the glass. "Out of the car," I growl.

Both men stare in shock, raising their hands. The passenger is a bald man, maybe a few years older than me. The other is slightly younger with a manbun and has some facial hair.

I pull the handle and the door opens. I step back, aiming at them. "Out ..."

The men exit slowly.

"What's your problem, dude?" Baldy asks.

I push him up against the truck and step back. "Why are you two watching that house?"

The driver scowls, his hands lowering.

"Keep your hands where I can see them!" I command, shifting my aim to him.

Out of nowhere, the passenger's hand shoots down to his side. He brushes his burgundy button-down shirt away and grabs the pistol tucked in his pants. Manbun raises a pistol of his own. Time slows to a crawl as I enter a hyper-focused mind state.

My eyes flick back and forth and I assess that the driver is the most imminent threat. I then aim center mass and depress the trigger twice. A split second after the second shell casing is ejected from the pistol, my sights are on Baldy. Before he punches his pistol out, I double-tap him. His back hits the truck and he falls, the Springfield XD-9 clattering beside him. I kick the pistol away and scan the area. No more threats are present, but people are coming out of Eric's house and neighbors are peeking out their windows.

I search Baldy for clues. "Who are you? Why are you here?" I don't find anything. No ID, no wallet, no badge, no dog tags, no tattoos. Just a cell phone, a lock pick kit, a suppressor, and a pouch filled with syringes ...

He coughs up blood then falls limp.

I hoped I'd never have to take another life ever again ... Not that it bothers me. I'm just as numb as I was after the first life I took ... and the forty or so that came after it.

I pocket the phone then check on the driver. He's dead too. On his body, I find a phone and magazines for the pistol. Then I check the vehicle. There's a bag in the back with duct tape, zip cuffs, and two MP7 submachine guns equipped with suppressors inside.

"What the hell?" I mumble to myself. Looks like they were planning a kidnapping. *Did they know I was going to be here?* I take pictures of their faces with my phone to send to Anne.

"Dion!" Eric shouts from across the street. He's staring nervously at the scene. "Who are those people?"

"I don't know! They drew on me when I asked them why they were watching your house!" I shout, taking a picture of the license plates. "Call the cops! But don't mention my name! As soon as they arrive, you and Casey take Hayley and get to that place we talked about! I'll fill you in when I figure out what they were here for."

I haul ass back to Fort Sanctum. The fact that Anne doesn't answer after I call her three times makes me antsy. A flood of texts from family and friends comes in before I can call her again. I don't answer any of them. There's no point until I have more intel.

The president's assassination and the hit squad I just encountered have to be related. Or maybe they're not. Maybe those men were staking out the Wilsons to rob them later. Submachine guns might seem like overkill, but they're not exactly hard to get your hands on. Many military-grade weapons weren't repossessed after the war.

I reach the gates of Fort Sanctum in just over twenty minutes. My window goes down as I pull up to the security booth. At the same time, a group of three Black Hawk helicopters rumbles overhead, flying south.

"Sir, I need to see your identification please." the soldier orders. "Sir?"

I snap out of my trance. As I pass him my USAW visitor badge and license, I finally recognize him. It's Eddie Franco, the once rookie soldier who guarded the gates of Quantico during the War of Annex.

"Damn, still on gate duty, huh, Sergeant?" I tease, removing my shades.

"Holy shit, it is you, Johnson! How the hell have you been, sir?"

"I've been great, Franco. You have any idea what the hell happened with the president?"

He shakes his head. "No, sir. I don't think anyone does."

"Gotcha. Well, can you let me in? I need to go pick up Anne, pronto."

"Of course!" He salutes me then runs to the booth. The gate opens. "I'll call HQ and have her sent down."

I give him my two-finger salute. "Thanks, Franco!" I speed off.

This is the first time I've been to Quantico since early last year and it's unrecognizable. A twenty-foot-high wall now surrounds the base. Beyond the wall lie brand-new buildings redone with a more modern and militaristic look. The barracks have been rebuilt and extended and the training grounds were revamped. There are troops running laps through the base wearing a darker navy blue and charcoal variant of Eddie Franco's black and dark gray USAW uniform.

The USAW Central Command Complex is smack-dab in the middle of Fort Sanctum. Two massive satellite dishes and a radio tower sit atop the roof. There are biometric scanners on every door and motion-detecting cameras all over the place.

I don't even look for a spot in the packed lot, I just park outside the building and put my flashers on.

Just as my boot hits the steps, the door swings open and Anne appears. We greet with a kiss and hug. As I pull away, I notice someone up on the third floor looking down on us. I can't really make out a face, but I can tell that it's an older man. He watches us for a second then walks away.

"What happened with President Pell?"

She holds my hand and starts walking. "We will talk once we're in the car."

En route to the Jeep, I tell her about the hostiles I encountered outside of the Wilsons'.

She looks surprised and worried at the same time. "Odd ... No one could have possibly known we'd be there. Perhaps they wanted hostages to hold as ransom to get money from you."

I nod. "That would make sense. They're the only non-soldiers of our group who could be easily tracked down and be taken without much of a fight ..."

Once we're in the Jeep, Anne takes both of our smartphones, powers them off, and places them in a tin box that will prevent any signals from being received or sent. Then she pulls out the broad-spectrum signal jammer she keeps in the car and turns it on.

"That serious, huh?"

Anne purses her lips. "It always is ..."

I let out a short involuntary laugh. "So, was Pell's assassination why you got called into work today?"

"Yes. A USAW fusion center intercepted a message on a deep web site they've been monitoring for some time. The message was coded, but after running it against a cipher, it roughly translated to 'Omega Anax.' Anax is Greek for 'king' or 'military leader.'"

"And omega is 'the end' ... End the leader?"

She nods. "But we didn't crack the message until minutes before Pell was assassinated."

"Do you know where it came from?"

"The message originated from a server in China ..." She scans my face. "And before you say the 'D' word, we have no reason to suspect that *they* were behind the assassination. Our intel indicates that a foreign radical group, most likely one in the Chinese government, was behind it. I told you before that they hold America responsible for the Deciders' reign."

I scan her face. She seems to be telling the truth. "I guess it's not really their style, is it? A single attack that doesn't immediately affect the rest of the world?"

"That's the point I made ..." She stares into my eyes. I can see the worry in hers, which is concerning because she's never worried. She removes her phone from the box then takes the hostiles' phones from me. "I'll run these inside. We should be able to pull some prints off of them and, if we're lucky, we can find out who they were talking to." She exits the Jeep.

A sinking feeling hits as I power my Galaxy back on. The air begins to feel heavy. Bad vibes radiate through me like static. This feeling ... it's the same sensation I had two years ago. It's the feeling that something horrible, something earthshaking is going to happen. And for some reason, it feels like whatever's coming will be much worse than it was before.

3
PHOBOS

Date Unknown ...

I WAKE UP lying in rubble, coughing my lungs out from the acrid smoke surrounding me. I know this smell. Gunpowder, burning wood, and metal—the smell of war. I fan the smoke away with wide swings of my arm and, eventually, it dissipates. Some buildings are burning, others crumbling. Plumes of black smoke rise like towers into the sky over the structures they replaced. Ashes fall from above like snowflakes. The sky has an eerie, reddish-orange glow as if the atmosphere itself is on fire. None of the street lights are on. The only source of light is the flames. The only sounds are crackling fire and my coughing.

I rise and dust myself off. For some reason, I'm wearing tactical gear, but I can't recall why. Maybe my sore head has something to do with why I can't remember. Something that sounds like wheezing catches my attention. I do a full turn and find no one.

"Hello?" I call out.

Silence.

"Still standing, huh?" a menacing voice responds, the last word echoing as if I'm in a large, empty hall.

I frantically look around. I don't see anyone, but there's an M4 on the ground ahead.

The labored breathing grows louder as I approach the weapon. A long, drawn-out breath passes by my left ear like a breeze. "Just when you thought you could let your guard down … I've returned to give you hell," the voice says, followed by a sinister laugh.

It can't be. I pick up the rifle. "Come out!" I yell, spinning in circles, staring down the iron sights.

"Here I am, kid …" the voice whispers from behind the crumbling concrete wall ahead. "I told you, Mr. Johnson, you cannot kill a god!"

A silhouette bleeds out of the shadows, dragging his feet. When the figure in white appears, my eyes widen. *Richard Thomas … it can't be.* He looks exactly the way he did the day I shot him dead—bloody and bruised, face still swollen, bleeding from his gut.

Richard unslings the white TAR-21 from over his shoulder and raises it. "It's time we ended this."

He opens fire.

I duck behind a burning SUV and return fire. "Where are all of your 'loyal' servants, Richard?" I shout. "You were never one to confront an enemy combatant on your own."

He laughs, sending a quick burst of rounds my way. "Don't you remember? You killed them all …" He fires another burst. "You've killed all of my men and, in exchange, I've killed all of yours. We're the last two standing!"

"You're lying!"

"Me? A liar? You must have me confused with a politician." Richard opens fire again.

A sharp pain flares in my side. I touch where it hurts and raise my hand only to discover my palm is covered in blood. *When was I shot?* Rounds begin passing through the SUV as if it isn't even there. Several bullets rip through my flesh like hot blades. I stumble backward, blood pouring from my wounds. At the intersection behind me, there is a black abyss. My boots hit the edge and I stop, trying to keep my balance. My footing crumbles and I fall. It feels like I'm falling forever but, eventually, I hit the bottom, crashing back-first on a cushioned mass. It smells of rotting meat down here. Beneath me are bodies—bodies of men wearing Angels of War BDUs. Most faces I don't recognize. Some don't even have faces, they're just skulls. But then I see faces I know.

Han ... Tommy ... Sung ... Ken ... Jeremy ... Abby ...

"This can't be ..." I mutter.

A cloud of smoke floats by. When it dissipates, Richard appears before me. He's holding someone by the collar and smiling darkly. "Couldn't let you die without your whore ..." he says, tossing the body at me. The corpse hits me and I fall on my back, face to face with ... *Anne* ... There's a bullet hole in the middle of her forehead. My eyes well up with tears and I bellow an almost feral roar. Richard presses the muzzle of his rifle to the middle of my forehead. "Matching wounds for the perfect couple ..." He racks a round into the chamber. "I win ..."

He pulls the trigger.

September 8
3:03 A.M.

A shout escapes me as I spring awake, my clothes drenched in a cold sweat and my heart beating like a jackhammer. The two-year-old scars across my body are burning as though they are freshly made.

Anne groans. "Another bad dream, my love?" she whispers groggily while rubbing my back. "You're breathing like a fat child who just jogged up two flights of stairs."

I snicker, rubbing my face. "I'm losing it, Anne."

It's been three days since President Pell's assassination. Three days since I gunned down the two spooks staking out the Wilsons' place. Every night since then, I've woken up in a panic. Each nightmare was different, but they all shared the same theme: the return of the Deciders. In each dream, everyone I know is dead and the world is in worse shape than before.

No one has claimed responsibility for Pell's death and no new intel has come in. As for the spooks, Anne's USAW operatives cleaned up the incident and began their investigation. The hostiles—Daryl Greene and Joshua Hilton—didn't strike a match on the list of known Deciders from Richard's files. They had no connection to any known Decider-sympathetic organizations either. As far as USAW is concerned, they were just petty burglars. Given the timing, I can't agree with their assessment.

Anne kisses my cheek. "You're just stressed." She wraps her arms around me and rests her head on my chest. "Your mind is stronger than this, Dion. Just relax." She caresses my abs. "Think happy thoughts. Think about making sweet, sweet love to me."

Grinning, I cuddle up to her. "Great. Now I'm excited in a different way ..."

I wake up to kisses on my face and a hand sweeping gently from my neck to my belly. Anne's lying beside me in her panties and bra. When she sees that I'm awake, she withdraws her hand.

"Good morning," she says, eyeing me seductively. "It's after nine. How about you help me out of my knickers so we can have a pre-workout warm-up?"

I smile so hard my face hurts. "Well ... warm-ups are important."

She smiles naughtily. "Excellent." She bites her bottom lip and climbs on top of me.

Anne's sexual appetite knows no bounds. There's rarely a day that goes by that we aren't going at. Not that I'm complaining ... it's just that chances are this is actually more for her than it is for me, which is fine.

After our "warm-up," we hit the gym. Our routine is cut short when Dean starts throwing a fit in the playpen. Anne tends to him while I head upstairs to shower. Halfway down the hall, I halt at the Shrine. It's a guest room I converted to a study/war memorial. In the past few days, I've spent more time than I should've looking through Decider Legacy files and Richard's journal, searching for something I missed, some hidden contingency plan to reclaim control. Anne forbade me to enter the room, saying that my obsession with their "unlikely return" is the reason for my nightmares. But I can't help it. I turn the knob and step inside.

In front of the window is a leather armchair behind a black oak desk. On both sides of the doorway are half-empty bookshelves with novels, old college textbooks, and textbooks about military history and strategy. Throughout the room, the mementos I collected during the War of Annex are exhibited in a museum-like fashion. On the wall to the right, encased in a large black frame above a white background, hangs the jacket I wore throughout the war. Beside it, Anne's old Deciders trench in the same frame. Underneath my jacket, my HK416 and Sig P226 are mounted on stands inside glass cases. On another pedestal is my battle-damaged Deva helmet, also housed in a glass case. Richard's bloody white trench coat is mounted in a white frame with a black background. Underneath the trench coat are Richard's Desert Eagle, tanto blade, and white helmet. A briefcase containing his laptop, codename Legacy, lies on a small table. Scattered across the walls are the photos taken during the war, medals awarded to me by

President Pell, and Marshall's dog tags. In the closet next to my gear are all of the Deciders' files we acquired along with a few weapons we probably shouldn't possess.

I sit behind the desk where Richard Thomas's journal has been left open at the middle. While Anne is at work, this is where I've spent my time studying military strategy and reading up on scientific research. But in recent days, it's been the site of my own private, counter-Decider operation. If there's one thing I know, it's that Richard always had a contingency plan. Even his backups had backup plans. He had to have something in place for potentially losing control post-Annex. The answer had to be here somewhere.

Watchdog, the libertarian alternative news guy on YouTube, has a new video up about Pell's assassination. He's a bit radical, but he has some good theories so I play that while I pick up where I left off yesterday, first skimming the journal and then reading some of Richard's plans on his laptop.

Who's pulling the strings now? There are still approximately fifty White Coats out there … it could be any one of them. Maybe Paul O'Brian … I turn to the page in the journal about him. O'Brian trained Richard and he was his brother Ryan Thomas's right-hand man.

There's a knock at the door. Anne's arms are folded and she looks irritated as hell. "Dion Johnson … when are you going to stop this?"

I close the book and the laptop. "After I find what I'm missing."

"You aren't missing anything. As a founding member of the Deciders, I would know. Even if the assassination and the Deciders are connected, it's not your problem—" She pauses. "It is not *our* problem anymore. Stop obsessing over this, and get your ass downstairs for breakfast." She stomps off.

In the kitchen, I find Anne setting the table. She's made bacon, pancakes, and eggs—my favorites. She's definitely trying hard to make me happy.

As she pours us both some orange juice, the sunlight from the sliding door window hits her in such a way that she just glows. Her beauty, her energy, her love for me—it all beams off of her. The whole world fades away along with all my Decider-related worries and I am in complete bliss. She's my answer to every problem, the cure-all to all my troubles.

I just sit there smiling at her. She sits across from me and cuts her pancakes into bite-size pieces. Then she looks up as she reaches for the syrup.

Anne smiles back. "What?"

"I just love you. That's all." I eat some bacon.

She blushes so hard her cheeks look sunburned. "I love you too." She stares at me for a moment. "Dion. Do me a favor?"

"Anything for you, sweetheart."

She reaches across the table and holds my hand. "By this meal's end, I want you to stop worrying about everything that's going on, all right? If the Deciders are back, so be it. This no longer concerns us. Dean and I—we are your world. We're the only things that should be on your mind. As long as we are okay, there's nothing for you to worry about."

"Okay. Just know that all of this obsessing I've been doing is for you two. And Marshal. I want to know that I've done everything I could to stop history from repeating itself. I promise I'll stop worrying." I finish a piece of bacon. "But if anything does happen, I will protect all of you with everything I have."

Her face lights up. "Good." She forks some of her bacon and feeds it to me. "I am so lucky to have you."

I lean across the table and kiss her. "I'm the lucky one."

Around four, my best friend of eleven years, Jeremy Tribble, calls to tell me he and Karla are going down to Warrenton for the weekend to do "couple stuff" with Jessica and her boyfriend, Keith, and asks if they can drop by for the night. Of course, I say yes.

"Good, because we're an hour away!" Jeremy snickers.

The next sixty minutes are a hustle and bustle to clean up and prepare dinner. Once they reach Winchester, Jeremy calls, my signal to meet him in town. I hop in the Jeep and head to the gas station rendezvous. I park in the parking space and watch as Jeremy pumps gas in his car. He has on a button-down shirt, khakis, and dress shoes. I'd say he looked like he was ready to go to a country club except his beard is thick and unkempt, and his afro has a pick in it.

When he's finished, I call him and direct him where to drive while I trail behind a few car lengths to make sure they're not being followed. Once I know they're clear, I pull up next to them, honk, and then lead them to our house. That's protocol for all visiting guests, not paranoia.

We have a four-car garage so they pull inside next to me. By the time I exit the SUV, Anne is in the doorway holding Dean. "Cheerio!" she says.

Jeremy and I bro-hug. "Long time no see!" I say, moving to hug Karla next. She's wearing a fancy pink blouse and white jeans and smells of berries. Her hair is tied in a ponytail that reaches the middle of her back.

"It's been too damn long," Jeremy says. The last time we were together was early spring.

"I've missed you guys!" Karla squeals, hugging Anne before kissing Dean all over his face. "He's getting so big! And so *cute!*"

After catching up over dinner, we migrate to the living room to drink and vibe out to some music. Beers in hand, Jeremy and I get to playing pool while Anne and Karla sit on the couch chatting and laughing, Karla almost spilling wine all over the place. Those two have become the best of friends since the Wilsons' wedding, a result of me always dragging Anne along on my visits to Jeremy. As for Karla and me, we haven't regained our closeness after I cheated on her best friend Jessica and left her for Anne, but we're getting there.

Jeremy and I are tied at three games apiece and are both three beers in. I cut the two ball right into the corner pocket and set myself up for a straight shot at the five. I take the shot and the cue ball follows it into the pocket for a scratch. Now I remember why I hate pool. As Jeremy is telling me which date they're thinking about for their wedding, Anne's work phone rings. Phone to her ear, she rises and fast-walks into the kitchen to escape the noise.

Who's calling at this hour?

She returns a minute later, laptop tucked under her arm. She looks slightly concerned, which worries me because nothing bothers her. She eyes me as she passes then sits and opens the laptop.

"Anne? What's wrong?" I ask.

She changes television to CNN and mutes the music. Her lips are curled into her mouth. "Just watch."

The headline reads: BREAKING NEWS: GROUP RESPONSIBLE FOR PRESIDENT PELL'S ASSASSINATION TO BE REVEALED.

My stomach tightens as I sit beside Anne.

No words are spoken. We just exchange looks. There's fear and past trauma bubbling to the surface of Jeremy's eyes. Despite the anxiety-inducing flashbacks I suffer occasionally, and that one time I hallucinated a threat, I came out of the war relatively unfazed. It's because taking lives didn't bother me—like Anne, my mind happens to be built for war. Jeremy, on the other hand, damn near fell apart after returning home. He started binge drinking alone, he couldn't sleep. The last time he shaved was before the war began. He had to see a shrink and take meds for his PTSD. It was only recently that he began getting himself together. I shudder to think what would have happened if Karla and I weren't there for him.

Bill Hayes, the main anchor, is at the news desk with Trish Childers, a hot blonde reporter who usually does field reports. Trish is one of many up-and-coming postwar reporters. Her career took off after she landed an interview with Steele. He was so hungry for fame that she didn't even have to sleep with him to get the story, but she didn't know that … and he didn't care that Trish nurtured their budding relationship just so she could use him to get an exclusive interview with me. A wasted effort since I respectfully declined when he tricked me into meeting her at a bar. My autobiography aside, I stayed out of the media.

"Good evening, Hayes says. "If you are just now joining us, we are covering the breaking story on the identity of the group claiming responsibility for the assassination of President Ron E. Pell."

"The news of this reveal comes to us from Twitter," Trish continues. "A tweet made at 6:29 P.M. by Twitter handle @The_Decaryan reads: 'We are responsible for President Pell's death. Identities revealed @ 9:00pm EST #live. Don't miss it. #TheReveal #PresidentPell.' The tweet also contains a hyperlink that leads to a blank screen on YouTube."

The word Decaryan sends a shiver down my spine. *Decarya* has appeared only a few times in Richard's journal and once in Legacy. The codename for the utopia he wanted to create was an amalgamation of *Deciders* and *Ryan*, the deceased older brother who put Richard on the path of global domination. Since I imagine Richard was the only one who knew the word Decarya, the thought crosses my mind that he's actually returned from the dead ...

I eye my watch. It's 8:57 P.M.—two minutes and forty seconds to go. Anne already has the YouTube live stream up on her laptop. Her leg is shaking nervously, something I have never seen before. I check Twitter on my phone to see what people are saying. The number four trending topic is #TheDeciders. I slam my phone back on the couch.

Trish is now blabbing a stream of speculations like she's some damn expert. "No information has been released yet regarding the investigation, but my sources indicate that this is, in fact, an organized terrorist cell, the first to surface since the Annex. Judging by the militaristic techniques displayed in President Pell's assassination, it's most likely rogue special operations units from within the Asiatic Republic or the Russian Union."

China and Russia were the first two nations to snatch up crippled, defenseless territories in the power vacuum the Deciders' defeat left behind. After they helped their neighboring nations fend off the Deciders during the Disintegration, they remained behind to help rebuild and defend them from an inevitable Decider reemergence. Months had passed and the Russians remained in Ukraine and the other former Soviet satellites and "convinced" their leaders to become semi-independent states tied to the Russian government, giving birth to the United Federation of Russia (UFR), essentially an Americanized version of the USSR. China scooped up the Asian countries, with the exception of Japan and the Philippines, in a similar fashion, forming the Asiatic Empire, or the A.E.

When Russia and China made a move for Latin America, Pell—despite being an anti-globalist—was forced to persuade the weaker nations unable to resist the new "megapowers" and to join the United States. Figuring that joining our freer-than-ever country was better than Russian or Chinese rule, the countries of Central and South America, along with the West Indies, Japan, and the Philippines joined us as our newest states. Now "USA" stands for the United States of the *Americas*. The new prime minister of Britain did the same with the Eurozone, forming the United Nations of Europe (UNE). The Middle East and North Africa formed a new caliphate, the Ummah Wāhidah. And with all the warlords who had terrorized the sub-Saharan nations of Africa wiped out by the Deciders, the United Africana Union was born.

"There have been no signs of tension or escalation," Hayes protests, "so how can we assume it was one of those parties?"

"Given how the perpetrators vanished without a trace, that leads me to believe that this group could very well be—"

Bill puts his finger to his ear. He holds up a hand, silencing her. "Okay. Fifteen seconds until it airs."

Suddenly, the TV blacks out. I grab the remote and start flipping channels. Every single one is out. A large white number fifteen appears and a countdown begins on the YouTube live stream and the television.

The air in the room is tense. Anne and I exchange looks and hold hands. Jeremy is kneeling on the floor, arms resting on the coffee table, twiddling his thumbs. Karla's rubbing his back.

There's a nauseous feeling in my gut because I know what's coming. The countdown seems to go on in slow motion.

5. 4. 3. 2. 1.

Both screens go from blackness to a distorted, pixelated image. There's a silhouette, but the video is still too choppy to make it out.

"Good evening, world," a male voice announces in American English, his voice sounding slightly modified like Richard's did during his debut.

Both screens flicker and blackout simultaneously. The image returns a split second later, clear as day.

My unblinking eyes stare in shock. Both hands are balled into fists. My heart's thumping. The sight before us is one we hoped to never see again—one the world never wanted to see again.

Standing in a dim, gray room in front of the Decider flag is a man in a white Deva helmet, its visor tinted silver. The helmet looks to be an upgraded version of what the Deciders wore in the past. A white trench coat with a white fur collar drapes his all-white attire. The white, gray, and burgundy Decider flag is stitched into his left sleeve. In the shadows behind him is another White Coat with tactical magazine pouches and MOLLE webbing sewn onto his trench coat. The subordinate White Coat is holding a rifle. Loyals stand in upright stiff postures like the Queen's Guard on each side of them.

I'm waiting to wake up in a cold sweat, but this time my nightmares are coming true …

4

REEMERGENCE

September 8
9:00 P.M.

FLASHBACKS OF RICHARD Thomas's debut following the attack on Rome replace the scene before me. Having both lived through the Annex and survived a war against the Deciders, I feel like I generally know what to expect this time around, but the unknown magnitude of the threat makes me anxious.

"I am the Dominus, the current Decider leader," the man in white continues. The video zooms out, showing a room full of the gray trench coat–wearing Loyals. There are no flag patches denoting country of origin this time, just Decider flags. "We are the Deciders!" he roars. The camera zooms back into the main White Coat. "And yes. We. Are. Back. Then again, we never truly left. We've been here all along, living in the shadows, planning, watching, recollecting ourselves after the defeat suffered by the former regime."

The Dominus turns left and places his arms behind his back. "Now that our house is in order, the time has come to *reclaim* what is rightfully ours. We have come to *reclaim* what was taken from us by the Angels of War and the world's militaries. There will be no forewarnings this time around. Our attacks will appear random in nature."

A clip of President Pell's assassination flashes on the screen. "They will come out of the blue." The headquarters for my nonprofit, the Angels of Earth Foundation, flashes on screen next and is set ablaze.

Wait, when did they attack that?

"They will seem like accidents." A video of the burning Coeus Labs appears next.

"I knew it ..." I whisper.

It's followed by a short clip of the wreckage of the British PM's Jaguar after his fatal car accident from two months ago. Then a screenshot of India's president dead in a hospital after a heart attack last week.

"And while we work to supplant the false leaders put in power, all parties responsible for the Disintegration will suffer for their actions ..." He tilts his head. "In the days to come, the world will witness a scourging like none it has ever seen. If you thought Richard Thomas's campaign was devastating, wait until you see what we have in store this time around! As the Architect once said, 'No amount of preparation can keep you safe.' This way of life, this illusion is coming to an end! A new dawn is near! To those who believe in the Deciders, make yourselves known! Seek us out and join our ranks, for those who cooperate will be rewarded with a place in the coming utopia and safety for your loved ones. Death awaits those who resist! So, get ready! The Reclamation—" he pauses for effect and raises a fist— "is upon us!"

The YouTube video blacks out and the TV flickers then returns to normal broadcasting.

My nails are cutting into my palms. *They set fire to my charity organization, my business ... Those threats were for me ... for Anne ... They're coming for us. They're coming for the Angels of War ...*

Beneath the rising fury, I feel another, unexpected feeling manifesting. Relief. The anxiety I've felt since President Pell was assassinated seems to be evaporating.

Anne and I exchange looks. I have no intentions of telling her "I told you so." I knew I was right all along and I think she did too.

Karla and Jeremy's nervous eyes rest on me. Karla looks like she wants to cry.

"Ugh," Jeremy groans, "I think I need to stop visiting you. Every time I do, someone wants to take over the world."

"Seems like it," I say, shaking my head.

"So, now what? We gonna suit up and shoot out again?" he asks, mimicking loading and firing a rifle.

"No. We get our group together and we go so deep underground not even the Angels of War will be able to find us."

"Bigfoot Protocol?" he asks. Bigfoot Protocol is the bug out plan that Anne and I developed for my family and friends and their families. Living off the grid in one of two safe houses stocked with a year's supply of food, we'd become as elusive as Sasquatch. And should the worst happen, each of them is equipped with bunkers, safe rooms, and enough weaponry to wipe out a full division of soldiers.

Anne and I both nod. "Yeah …" I mumble. "Mind housesitting for a bit? We have to swing by my parents' before we leave."

"Yeah. No problem," Karla says.

I head for the stairs.

"No phone calls, no texts, and no social media or email account logins while we're gone," Anne instructs as she trails behind me.

On the way upstairs, I pull out my smartphone and send Jessica, Ken, Han, Tommy, Eric, Casey, Dave, and Abby a message: "You ever see *Valley of the Sasquatch*? We should watch during our next reunion."

Late last year, I briefed them all on what to do if they received that message. The procedure was for everyone was to ditch their cell phones for the encrypted phones we provided them with last year. We were to meet up at a predesignated location near our home before heading to Casey's family cabin. It's located in Jefferson National Forrest, northwest of a small town named Clifton Forge. The cabin has been in their family for generations. It is so old that there's no digital trail connecting Casey to it. I even had Anne check the USAW database to make sure.

As for my parents, they're taking Dean to a more recently modified house turned shelter a few miles from where we're going. Like the cabin, there is no data trail connecting it to me or my family. Also, I had my parents declared deceased not long after the war, and Dean's birth certificate doesn't list Anne's name or my own. It's going to be hard being away from our boy for who knows how long, but since the Deciders will be coming after us, it's best that he is as far away from Anne and I as possible.

"Did you know?" I ask as I pack Dean's things into a duffle bag.

Anne gives me a pitiful look. "We had absolutely no intelligence suggesting the Deciders would resurface. But ... deep down, I always knew they'd return."

"Ha, and you called me the paranoid one."

She laughs, shaking her head. "I was in denial." She holds my hand. "I didn't want to believe that this life we built could be threatened. I wanted us to live happily ever after until we were both old and gray."

I pull her in and kiss her passionately. "We'll get our happily ever after, don't you worry. Whatever it takes, I'll make it happen."

As I drive the five miles to my parents' house, I'm feeling even more serene than before. Though I'm worried about the coming devastation, at least I know that I'm not crazy. Now that I know I no longer have to be the paranoid conspiracy theorist drawing connections where people say there are none, I can finally relax.

During the Annex, when cities around the world were burning, I was scared out of my mind, always worrying about not being able to protect my friends from marauders or Deciders. But somewhere between Hope dying and my first mission, Operation Debut, worry was replaced with a determination to rid the world of Deciders. The crippling fear diminished to levels that kept me alert and on my toes. I became more and more resolute, focused, and driven—like nothing could break me. And then after I was tortured, after I fought through a compound of Deciders alone, I began to feel unstoppable. That feeling persisted from Operation Deicide all the way to the war's end and into the months that followed. Then, on the first Deliverance Day, Anne told me about the Decider-like chatter that USAW had intercepted and I lost my resolve. Until now, that is. My unshakable resolution has returned. A faint smile creeps across my face as I pull into my parents' driveway.

On the way to the front door, I catch Anne smiling at me. There's a look in her eyes that reflects what I'm feeling, like my newfound fortitude has sparked something in her as well.

The next thirty minutes is a packing frenzy. Weapons, body, armor, clothes—it's all piled into bags and loaded into the Knight XV armored truck I gave to my parents after the war. I sense the anxiety in my mother as she packs. I can tell how worked up my dad is.

They shouldn't have to be going through this again …

When the truck's all loaded up, I hand my dad a backpack that contains encrypted cell phones, satellite phones, and chargers.

Then I hand my mom an envelope with the address, directions, and keys to the safe house.

My mom scowls. "You're not coming with us?"

Anne and I shake our heads. "They're coming for us," Anne says. Tears start running down mom's face so Anne consoles her. "It'll only be for a short while, Mum. We'll all be back together in no time."

After running a surveillance detection route that includes driving in circles for twenty minutes and zigzagging through town, we follow them out to I-81 for a few miles before heading back home.

Karla helps Anne pack while Jeremy helps me disassemble the Shrine. I grab the journal and a four-terabyte flash drive containing Richard's files and shove them into my black tactical backpack. We pack the clothes, Richard's Deva helmet, the pictures, and mementos into a fireproof case. The trophy weapons, Richard's Desert Eagle included, go into a duffle bag. Jeremy and I haul the fireproof case to the downstairs closet and stash it in a safe under the floorboards.

Once our belongings are packed in the trunk, I make one last trip upstairs to grab the three duffle bags from the Shrine closet.

"What's in here?" Jeremy asks as he takes a bag from me. "It's heavy as hell!"

"You know … just some extra weapons, body armor, magazines, ammunition, communication equipment—the usual," I say.

Karla eyes the bags. "Uh oh, you're planning on starting another militia, aren't you, Dion?" she jokes.

I smile, shaking my head.

"Well, here we go again!" Jeremy said as he tosses the bag over his back.

With the last of the bags in the Jeep, I tap the LOCKDOWN option on my phone's app and the metal door and window shudders drop and lock. No one's getting in now.

"What do you think is going to happen next?" I ask we climb into the Cherokee.

Anne sighs. "Honestly, I can't say. We both know what they are capable of. If they aren't stopped early, I don't think the world will be so lucky this time around."

"What do you mean?"

"Well, Richard's motive was to take over the world and make it a better, less corrupt place. For the most part, we accomplished that with Restore. The world is less corrupt now than it has ever been. And what do you suppose the Deciders' goal is now?"

My eyes widen. "Revenge and complete subjugation."

"And since it's unlikely they were able to insert their operatives into positions of power like before, the only way they can achieve dominance is through complete and utter global devastation."

Anne and I take the lead in the Jeep while Jeremy and Karla follow in Anne's armored BMW. As I leave my home behind, déjà vu strikes. Cryptic TV announcements by a man in all white, leaving home with those I care about, venturing to a place to hide out to avoid whatever's coming … But this time around, I also feel a sense of responsibility that I didn't before. It feels like it's my fault for not eradicating them completely. And staring at the dark road ahead, I have this feeling that I won't be able to sit idly by.

5

PEACE UNDONE

September 9
9:19 A.M.

OUR RENDEZVOUS IS a boarded-up, four bedroom, two-and-a-half-bath home at 747 Merrimans Lane five miles south of our home. Though there's a sign on the front lawn that reads FOR SALE, it is owned under one of Anne's aliases. As one of the homes abandoned during the war, it came pre-furnished with whatever the previous owners had left behind, family pictures and all. It has running water and power, courtesy of some clandestine tapping into the grid.

Yawning and wiping the sleep from my eyes, I roll over and notice Anne is gone. That's when I hear the showerhead spurting. For the first time since Pell's assassination, I slept for seven hours without one nightmare. Although, I did wake up once when my parents called to say they'd reached the bunker safely around 1:00 A.M. Yawning and stretching, I rise from bed, grabbing my SIG P226 MK25 from the nightstand and tucking it into my jeans.

The only light in the hallway comes from the flickering living room TV. Unsure of whether or not Karla and Jeremy fell asleep on the couch with the TV on, I gently close the bedroom door behind me and tiptoe across the creaky floor into the living room.

"Morning," I say when I see that they're sitting up on the couch and watching the news. "How's the world reacting?"

Karla just shakes her head.

"Feels like a repeat of two years ago …" Jeremy replies.

The chyron on the bottom of the screen reads: BREAKING NEWS: INTERNATIONAL TENSION RISES. I flop down on the loveseat and watch while Jeremy and Karla fill me in. In a nutshell, all nations are on DEFCON-2 or their equivalent. The world's armies are conducting exercises and patrolling the streets in preparation for the Deciders' attacks. Heads of states are slinging mud at the U.S. Despite the Deciders being composed of operatives from every nation, the world holds the U.S. responsible for them. *How could the most powerful nation with the most advanced security measures allow the Deciders to manifest within its own borders and then spread across the globe?* That's the question the world asked after the war. Now Russian head of state President Viktor Orlov and President Zhao Yu of the Asiatic Empire are calling for direct action in America, the United Nations of Europe, and India, supporting a motion for "a passive occupation to quarantine the spread."

Orlov is speaking from behind a podium in the rebuilt Kremlin with Zhao standing slightly behind him. Their plans for preventing another Annex include the U.S. and its allies allowing weaponized drones to patrol their airspace over the most likely attack zones and several dozen divisions of the UFR and A.E. armies on the ground alongside domestic troops. It sounds like they're using the Deciders as a Trojan Horse to invade without a fight. That makes me wonder if they have a pact with the Deciders or if their governments have been infiltrated … The Omega Anax message calling for President Pell's assassination did originate in China, so it is a possibility.

My encrypted Galaxy vibrates in my pocket. The call's coming from THE TANK, Tommy Valen's codename in my contact list. "Yo, Tommy," I answer. "You close?"

"Hey, hey!" he responds. "I'm squaring away the parents now. I'll be there for supper."

"Copy that. See you soon, brother."

Seeing as how he is the only person I've heard from, I scroll down the list and text the others for a SITREP. When I get down to Jess's contact, I press call. The phone rings six times then goes to voicemail. She's probably still pissed at me for not showing up on Labor Day. *Not the best time to play stubborn, Jess ...* Seconds after the call ends, I receive a text from Ken saying: "Red and I are unable to attend. Management won't give us a vacation." Dave, who's stationed at a USAW National Guard base out in Ohio, replies shortly after with: "I'll be holding my ground here, Chief. This is why I enlisted after all! My sister's secure at the base with my family so don't worry about her. Be safe, bro!"

I stare at the phone, waiting for a response from Han, but nothing comes through. I haven't seen him in a while. He's been busy running the chain of MMA gyms that he founded. As I'm about to call him, the floor creaks behind me. I turn to find Anne dressed in gray jeans and a black hoodie. She's vigorously drying her hair with a white towel stained with dark smudges.

"Good morning, sweetheart," I say with a smile.

"Morning." She smiles back, removing the towel. Wet, black locks fall down and cling to her shoulders and neck. Her smile widens. "What do you think?"

I grin. "So that's what you were doing in there all that time," I say, eyeing her hair. "I love it! Not that I hated you as a brunette."

"It looks great, girl!" Karla says. "But why the color change?"

"I'm not going out in public anytime soon so I thought I would restore my natural color."

Jeremy shakes his head. "No ... she just wants to look the part of the Ice Queen when it's time to fight." He laughs nervously, a tinge of panic in his eyes.

Anne rolls her eyes. "If there is another war coming, the Ice Queen will not be making an appearance ... I am a noncombatant."

Very grimly, Jeremy says, "We're already at war." He looks to the floor, shaking his head. "Somehow, someway, we'll find ourselves on the battlefield again."

He looks distraught as hell, just like he did during the war. *He's cracking ...*

Throughout the day, international tension continues rising. Pell's successor, President Gary Lewis, comes on in the late afternoon to addresses the world, calling for Orlov and Zhao to "look within their own borders for the threat instead of pointing fingers. This is not the time to turn our backs on one another and promote distrust. Now is the time for the world to unify against a common enemy!" He promises to share intelligence with everyone as it becomes available.

At 3:11 P.M., an unidentifiable foreign drone armed with four Hellfire missiles is shot down over Los Angeles. USAW is still working on figuring out who to blame for the unauthorized breach of airspace. A similar incident occurs in London. By 5:21 P.M., things between the USA., the UNE, and the Russian and Asiatic allies reach its boiling point after the FBI and USAW databases suffer a cyberattack that supposedly originated out of China. Zhao claims that a rogue group from within the state of China is responsible but President Lewis isn't buying it. Now Lewis is on

TV, furious, calling the security breach an act of war and threatening action if our nation's security is violated again.

Before my eyes, the peace I helped forge in the wake of Richard's Purge is being undone—hacked into a pile of tinder ready to ignite another world war. All it took for the world powers to descend into hysteria was a single announcement by the Deciders. After the Annex, their name alone is enough to cause chaos. *Instigating conflicts, turning nations against each other—this must be a part of the Deciders' plan.* Clearly, they're playing by Richard's Chaos-Purge-Restore handbook.

As Anne, Karla, and I enter the kitchen to prepare dinner, my secondary phone goes off. It's Tommy.

"Yo, bro!" I answer. "Almost here?"

"Yeah, but I think I may have a problem …" Tommy says. A long pause follows.

I check the phone. "Hello? What happening!"

Anne sets down a pot of water on the stove and eyes me with concern.

"Sorry. I'm here. There's this SUV behind me. I think it's tailing me. I saw it in my rearview back near Frederick then I saw it again in Charles Town. I just drove into Berryville and now I'm driving in circles."

"Just keep moving." I start brainstorming on where to send him. "When you hit a red light, set your map for 250 Costello Drive. There's an old firehouse there. Directly behind the first building is a parking lot. Get to it. We'll be in the second building."

"I can shake 'em!"

"No. Just get there. Call me if anything happens. And be safe."

"Alright, bud." The call ends.

"Dion?" Anne asks, scanning my face. "What was that about?"

I head toward the garage. "Tommy's got a tail. I'm going to ambush them."

She trails behind me with rapid steps. "Not without me."

I stop in the middle of the hallway. "Anne—"

She gets right in my face. "Don't waste your breath. If you're going to go protect your friend, I'm going to protect you, my king. 'tis a queen's job, after all."

Jeremy appears in the hall, the Glock 19 I gave him last night in hand. "I'm rolling with you."

"No you're not," I say, shaking my head. "Stay here and protect Karla and our gear. If we need help, I'll call."

I open the Jeep's trunk and we unzip the duffle bags. After equipping ourselves with body armor and throwing on our black hoodies, we each grab a set of black tactical goggles and a black Deva-HF gas mask. The Deva-HF, or Deva Half-Face, is essentially the lower half of a standard Deva air filtration combat helmet that locks in with the ballistic goggles, forming the Deva Full-Face Hazardous Operations Mask, abbreviated Deva-FHOM. Goggles on our foreheads, Bluetooth sets over our ears, and gas masks dangling from our necks, we select our weapons. I go with my P226, a suppressor-equipped HK416 A5 with an eleven-inch barrel, and an MP7. I grab another HK416 and pistol in case I need to arm Tommy. Anne partners her gray P226 with a suppressed MP7 and a KelTec KSG shotgun. Then she grabs a backpack containing flash grenades and electronically timed, egg-shaped TD6 fragmentation grenades.

"Go time," she smirks, eyes as fierce as a wildcat.

Someone's excited.

Ten minutes later, we pull into the parking lot. Anne drops me off in front of the rearmost building. While I get into position inside the building, she drives off and parks behind the structure.

Six minutes later, Tommy calls, saying he is two miles away. I pull the goggles over my eyes and fasten the gas mask in place. Once the seal fits snugly over my nose and mouth, I push the two pieces together until they click. Now my hood goes up over my head and I sight the parking lot through my holographic EOTech XPS3-0 scope. My finger slides slowly over the trigger and I let out a slow breath. My heart rate steadies. My mind is calm and clear.

Ready.

My phone rings. At the same time, headlights from the road ahead illuminate the billboard outside. Before the vehicle becomes visible, I hear a loud crash. Tires screech after. When I answer the call, there's just silence. I already know what happened.

I touch my Bluetooth. "Anne. Change of plans. Bring the car around front."

The Jeep pulls up a few seconds later, headlights off. She must have heard the crash and put two and two together. As soon as I climb in, she guns it toward the street. Right near the turn into the parking lot is a navy-blue Honda Pilot turned onto its side. The driver's side windows are shattered and the rear left panel is smashed in and crumpled like a beer can. The airbags inside are all inflated.

"That's Tommy's SUV," I say.

Parked along the roadside a few feet from his vehicle is a black Chevy Suburban. The Suburban shows no sign of damage, which means it is likely armored.

Five men emerge from the Suburban. They're dressed in civilian clothes and armed with P90 personal defense weapons. Aiming at the wreck, two hostiles shuffle quickly toward it while the remaining three hang back and form a defensive perimeter across the road. From the east comes a pair of headlights. A gunman aims at the source of the lights and fires a burst. I can hear the car rev up and crash into something out of sight. Another set of tires screech off in the opposite direction a split-second after and the road falls dark.

The gap between us closes rapidly. They still haven't noticed us. Window down, I stick my MP7 and head out the window and aim for the nearest target. A quick burst of suppressed, submachine gun fire drops him. Before his body hits the pavement, I'm already aiming at the second target standing at the SUV's rear.

"Contact!" he yelps as one of my rounds tags him in the arm. He scurries behind the Suburban before I can finish him.

Meanwhile, Anne's arm is out the window and she's firing her pistol at one of the men running for cover behind Tommy's Pilot. Before the first hostile reaches cover, his head snaps back and he drops.

The remaining three return fire. We quickly duck back inside and our windows go up as rounds ping and crack against the bulletproof exterior. Anne smashes the brakes and cuts the wheel, bringing the Jeep to a screeching halt, driver's side facing the attackers. I switch to my rifle then exit the vehicle and crouch-walk toward the front end. Shotgun in hand, MP7 slung over her shoulder, Anne slides over to the passenger side and climbs out then heads toward the rear. Now I start panicking. Just like during Operation Deliverance, the mission that brought down the Deciders and the first time we fought side by side, having her in combat with me makes me nervous. She and I have trained to operate as one, and I know she is beyond capable of handling herself. Still, I can't help but worry about her getting hurt or worse, and it's distracting the hell out of me.

I need to end this fast.

As I lay down suppressive fire on the hostile hiding behind the Suburban's rear, her shotgun explodes behind me and in the corner of my eye, I see one guy hit the pavement near the Honda's front end with half his face missing. After a brief pause, I lay down more fire. When my target ducks, I drop on my side and fire one round at his leg. He falls and I put another round in his chest and one in his head.

There's one guy left, and I want him alive. I pull the pin out of a flashbang. "Flash out!" I say to Anne as I toss it over to the Suburban.

It pops as soon as it hits the ground. Anne and I hurry toward his cover. I lay down fire while Anne flanks. When I reach the trunk, the hostile is squinting hard, firing random bursts in the direction of my fire. I bring my HK's barrel around the corner and peek out. Then I put a round in his shoulder. He drops with a thud and his weapon clatters on the concrete. As I move to clear the weapon, he draws his sidearm. At that moment, Anne puts a round in his head.

So much for interrogating him. I examine the body. The burgundy shirt underneath his black fleece catches my eye. I investigate the other corpses. They're all wearing burgundy undershirts as well. "They're wearing the same color as the guys staking out the Wilsons'," I say as we approach the wreck.

"Perhaps they are Deciders," Anne says. "Or a radical group the Deciders are outsourcing their lesser work to. Judging by their shoddy combat skills, the latter is more likely." She starts snapping pictures of the men on her work phone.

"Either way, we know for sure that the Deciders are tracking our friends. The question is: are they trying to capture them or kill them?"

"Or are they trying to use them to find us," she says, sliding her phone back into her jeans pocket.

Inside the Honda, the airbags are deflating and Tommy is stirring.

"Hey, are you alright? Can you move?" I ask, opening the door. Glimmering glass shards and chunks pour out, clinging and clicking against the ground.

Groaning, Tommy nods and unbuckles his seatbelt. "I'm alright." He works his neck and climbs out. Other than a few cuts on his left arm and forehead, he appears to be relatively okay. "I've been in worse accidents. Remember when I got shot down during Operation Deicide?"

"Yeah, I imagine that was much worse," I say.

Sirens start blaring in the distance. There's no time to deal with cops, not when our general location has been compromised. We need to get back to the safe house and head to the cabin ASAP. We help Tommy over to our vehicle as quickly as possible and speed back to the house.

As we pull into the driveway, my secondary phone goes off. So does Anne's work phone. It's Red. I tap my Bluetooth to answer.

"Hey, Abby. What's up?"

I'm greeted by labored breathing. "Ken and I ... we were just attacked by the Deciders."

6

A REASON TO FIGHT

September 9
7:56 P.M.

"WHAT?" I YELP. "Are you alright?" I follow Anne and Tommy from the garage into the house.

"Yeah, for the most part." Abby sighs. "Ken took a round to the arm."

"It was just a graze!" Ken shouts in the background. There's some rustling and Ken comes on the phone. "We're fine, D."

"Did this happen at the base?" I ask.

"No. We were with a team investigating a shots fired report at Hudson's place outside of Quantico. He hadn't come to the base and he wasn't responding to our calls so we suspected foul play. When we arrived, the door was blown open, there was blood all over the walls and bullet holes everywhere. Hudson was nowhere to be found. His fiancé was missing too."

Sergeant Joe Hudson was one of the ten Renegades who took us in during the Annex and trained us to become soldiers. He's a good friend of ours so the news hits hard.

"On the way out, we were ambushed by Loyals and a Decider in a black, leather trench coat. The guy in black ... he was as skilled as they come. He wiped out almost half our team on his own. The strange thing was it seemed like they weren't trying to kill me or

Red. Their tactics seemed to suggest a capture operation. And when they realized they couldn't, they just evacuated ..."

"We just tangoed with some Deciders as well," I say.

"What? I thought you were at the safe house!"

I explain what happened with Tommy. "They're all dead. We're all safe."

Ken sighs, blowing into the phone. "Oh, shit. Well, I guess there's no reason to warn you that we're all in danger ... That damn database hack stole all our personal data, including addresses and phone numbers." He pauses. "And there's something else. What happened to Hudson wasn't an isolated event. Several active duty and former Angels of War militiamen were hit. Denmark and Marquez are both MIA."

"Shit."

"Yeah, that's not all. A couple USAW National Guard bases were attacked not long ago. They were hit hard and fast by precision, direct action teams. When the attack was over, a dozen or so soldiers were killed and a number of them were captured ... The USAW base in Ohio was hit. Dave is among the list of missing soldiers ... Sam's missing too. Sorry to drop that on you, but we thought you should know."

"Appreciate it, brother."

"Listen, we're pulling back into the base now. Later, Dion. Be safe."

"You too," I say.

The call ends.

As I enter the kitchen, Anne sets her phone down, eyeing me with concern. "That was Sung ... I take it you heard the news?"

"Yeah ... I just spoke with Ken."

Tommy, Jeremy, and Karla appear in the hall. "Is someone going to fill us in?" Tommy asks.

Anne and I brief them. While I do, I try contacting Han. When he doesn't answer after the third call, I assume the worst.

"Goddamn ..." Tommy sighs.

Karla shakes her head. "Good thing we came to visit when we did ..."

"So, do we run to the cabin while we have the chance?" Jeremy asks.

Anne shakes her head. "The Deciders have Dave and Sam. Both of them know the cabin's location. Dave has SERE training, but you can only hold off against torture for so long. And Sam's a civilian."

"She's right," I say. "We'll need to work on a Plan C. In the meantime, let me get my other phone and see if I can reach Han. Maybe he couldn't get to his secondary phone and he's been trying to reach me on that number ..."

On the way to the bedroom, my mind starts racing. My heart rate throttles up and I break into a sweat when I come to the realization that maybe Jessica hasn't been ignoring me all this time and that maybe something terrible has happened to her as well. And if they have her, they have our son ...

I'm on the verge of panic. My hands are shaking as I reassemble my primary phone. When it boots up, I go to my messages and find a pair of new texts from Han. I click on the conversation, bringing up a photo of Han on his knees in some dark room. His face is bruised and sweaty, his mouth is duct-taped, and his arms are tied behind his back. There are a bunch of shadowy figures in gray trench coats and gray Deva helmets standing around him. *Loyals*. The one behind Han has a pistol to his head. The text below it reads: "Jai Han is unavailable to return your calls because he is all ... tied up. If you insist on seeing him again, stay tuned."

A hand falls on my shoulder and I jump. "Is everything alright?" Anne asks softly.

I show her the phone. "They're not just going after the founding Angels of War; they're capturing the people closest to me."

Anne takes the phone and disassembles it. "They're trying to lure you out by giving you a reason to fight. Don't let them. You did all you could to protect your friends. It's out of our hands now."

"I can't just do nothing. You know they're like family to me— we're brothers in arms. I've known Han for five years. If I was captured, they'd stop at nothing to rescue me."

"What are you saying?"

I stare into her eyes with conviction. "I need to help somehow. I'll leave the fighting to the soldiers, but I want to be there in Fort Sanctum helping them any way I can."

"First Special Forces training, now this …" she mutters.

"Huh?"

"First you do Special Forces training, and now you want to run to Fort Sanctum, the place you swore you would never go. You do know that this is exactly what the Deciders want. That's why they made it personal …"

"Yeah, I know, but cowardice is not a part of my code. And we're not getting involved. If we can't help, we leave. At the very least I have to try."

"You say that now, but you'll find a reason to get dragged into the fight."

"Anne, I—"

She puts a finger over my mouth. "I know you, Dion!" she yells. "I know you better than you know yourself … better than I know myself. And I know that once things escalate, you're not going to just stand idly by and let the world burn. And the closer you are to the chaos, the more likely you will get swept up by it."

"I won't fight unless I absolutely have to," I say. "You know that."

"Alright. Just swear to me that you're not looking for a reason to take to the front lines."

I hold her hands. "Anne, I swear. But I can't live with myself if my friends turn up dead and I did absolutely nothing to help." I kiss her forehead. "I have too much to lose this time around. The only world I need to protect is my own."

Her icy blue eyes pierce me, attempting to gauge my sincerity. Out of nowhere, she gives me a kiss. "Fine, then. Twenty-four hours. If we can't locate your friends by then, we disappear until this is over."

I nod. "Twenty-four hours."

We gather our belongings then head out to the living room. Jeremy, Karla, and Tommy are all standing by the couch with their things.

"Heh, we couldn't help but overhear everything …" Jeremy says. "We're going with you—no if, ands, or buts."

"You sure?" I ask.

He smirks. "We all wouldn't be alive today if we didn't stick together, would we?"

"It's not like we have anywhere else to go," Karla says. "The cabin's location is blown. We'll be safer at Fort Sanctum than here."

"She's right," Jeremy says.

I set down my duffle. "Alright, once we walk out that door, we don't let our guards down for a second." I pull out a Glock 19 and three magazines and hand them to Karla. "Trust no one other than Ken, Sung, Abby, Steele, and those of us in this room. If anything looks suspicious, don't hesitate to call it out or draw your weapons." I pick up the bag. "Let's go."

There's a checkpoint a mile up from the guard station that Anne usually goes through. Ten heavily armed soldiers are standing guard. I stop fifty yards away and flash my headlights in the pattern Ken instructed. Headlights from a car hidden in the shadows flash the return signal back. The guards then wave us forward. Once we're past the barricade, I pull up beside the black Humvee parked along the shoulder. I roll down my window and greet the Asian dude with a fauxhawk who's behind the wheel. His eyes are serious but his mouth smiles.

"Follow me," Ken Nguyen says.

Still a man of few words, I see. With a nod, my window goes back up.

Ken leads us down a dirt road toward the large concrete wall. The silhouettes of guards patrol the top. There are also antiballistic turrets that make up the missile defense shield known as Sky Guardian. From what Anne's told me, it's composed of anti-ballistic missiles and a laser system that intercepts threats before they enter USAW airspace.

A door big enough to fit a tank through opens, separating into two halves as Ken approaches. Once we're beyond the wall, they shut with an earth-shaking crash. The road takes us past several buildings then descends into a tunnel underneath the Central Command Complex. The thick blast door rises and we roll into a vast parking lot housing combat vehicles brandishing the USAW logo. Ken parks near a stairwell where two people stand waiting for us. I pull up beside him.

Ken emerges, dressed in the charcoal and black USAW BDUs, his right arm bandaged. We give each other a bro-hug and then he greets the others while I approach the freckle-faced girl who's dressed like an undercover CIA agent. She's sporting her favorite pair of aviator shades, a dark blue vintage jean jacket with a low-cut black shirt underneath, blue jeans, and black tactical boots. Her red hair is in a bun. A marksman's Mk 14 Enhanced Battle Rifle is slung in the scabbard of her black tactical backpack.

"Hey," Abby says softly. She's still as quiet as ever. Her once-innocent green eyes are now emerald steel, hardened by combat and made cold from taking lives. It's the same look Anne and I both have, the same look all soldiers have after carrying out unthinkable tasks.

We hug. "Good to see you, Red Death." I smile. My friend, the Renegade sniper Lloyd Gray, gave her the nickname Red during training back in the Annex. After obtaining well over eighty confirmed kills during the war, and more during her USAW "peacekeeping" operations overseas, she earned the codename Red Death, an homage to the Finnish sniper known as White Death.

She flashes a pitiful smile as we part. "Good to see you too. I missed you guys."

The corporal beside her extends a hand. "It's an honor to meet you, Mr. Johnson," he says. He's about my age, with a crew cut, dressed in the same uniform as Ken. I don't recognize him, but he looks familiar. "I'm Corporal Leo Hill."

"You're not related to—"

"Yeah," Ken says. "He's Garrett's younger brother."

"No kidding," I say. Garrett Hill fought alongside me in Delta Squad. He died during Operation Forestrike, the mission I led to stop a shipment of chemical weapons—or that's what everyone thinks, anyway. Forestrike was cover for a personal, secret mission to exact revenge against Commander Anne Buckingham—the enemy soldier I'd later fall in love with.

I feel a stab of guilt as I shake Leo's hand. It was my fault that his brother was dead. "Garrett was my squadmate. He was a good man."

"He's the reason I enlisted, sir."

Ken puts his hand on Leo's shoulder. "Hill is Steele's protégé. He's been assigned to your protection detail. Speaking of which, Steele's waiting for us upstairs."

We take the elevator up to the first floor. Everything is gray—charcoal walls and ash-colored floors. The room we stop at has large wall-sized windows. Leaning beside the door is the chisel-jawed Andrew Steele, who's talking to another soldier.

When Steele spots us, he dismisses the subordinate. "Ho-lee hell," he says in that southern twang of his, smirking like the smug sonofabitch he is. "If it isn't the old Delta Squad."

We pound fists. "How've you been, Rusty?" I smirk back, calling him by the nickname he acquired in SF training on account of how rusty he was during the first few days.

"That's Corporal Rusty to you." he jokes. "This way."

Steele ushers us inside the large conference room. There's a flat screen TV in the wall to the left with a USAW logo screensaver. In the room's center is a huge, smart glass–topped table with ten chairs around it.

"Where's Sung?" I ask as sit down.

Steele presses a button on the touchscreen panel beside the door and the windows gradually go ink dark. "Sung's probably with the general. They're on the way."

While we wait, we update Steele about our run-in with the Deciders. Anne and I offer our theory that the Deciders are behind the rising tension between the mega-powers.

After about ten minutes, the touchscreen panel beside the door flashes green and the motorized locks click and clank. Someone outside holds the door open while a silver-haired man with a bushy handlebar mustache strolls through. He's about six feet tall and barrel-chested, maybe one hundred and eighty pounds. My guess, late fifties. He's suited up in a black service uniform with a black tie and a navy-blue shirt underneath. The black barracks cover has a dark blue band around it. Even if he wasn't decorated with dozens of medals and those four stars, his stern, stoic face and authoritative posture would give away that he's the general.

The soldiers in the room salute him, as do I.

His dead, deep-set, brown eyes scan my group after he salutes us back. "For those of you who do not know me, I am General Bernard Walker, head of the United States Angels of War combat and special operations." His eyes shoot over to Anne. "Good to see you have decided to return to work, Ms. Myers …" he says, calling her by the last name of her assumed identity instead of Buckingham.

Anne bows slightly. "My apologies, sir. We went dark since intel suggested we were in danger."

"From what I gather, that danger hasn't passed … and it won't for quite some time." His gaze shifts to me and he extends his large, wrinkled, liver-spotted hand. "Dion Johnson, we finally meet. It is an honor."

I stand and shake his hand as firmly as I can. "It's an honor to meet you too, sir."

"Are you here to enlist?" Walker asks.

"No. I'm here to aid in the search for those who were taken."

"And your friends?" He glares at the others. "Jeremy Tribble and Tommy Valen, correct? Founding members of the Angels of War Militia …"

"They're here for protection, not to fight," I say.

Walker scowls. "I see … How do you intend to assist us then, Mr. Johnson? I'm sure Ms. Myers has informed you how skilled our analysts are. And with her back at the helm, we'll be more than capable of tracking down the captured."

"While Anne is a … specialist, I have a better understanding of the Deciders than any other analyst on your payroll. I think the way Richard did—that's partly how we brought him down. Also, I may possess intimate Decider knowledge that your people don't have."

"You wouldn't be referring to some sort of intelligence that you did not surrender after the war, are you?"

"All I have is Richard's journal, but I submitted copies of all relevant pages to Pell. However, the irrelevant information may now be relevant, and since I have it committed to memory, I can make connections to intel that your people can't, in ways they can't."

General Walker looks me over while stroking his mustache. "Considering what you have done for this country, and given what you know, I will allow you to assist us as a consultant of sorts …" He inhales deeply. "Anne will set you up with top-level security clearance and access to whatever we have."

"Thank you, sir. I'll do my best."

He nods. "I know you will. Come with me."

General Walker leads us down the east wing to a windowless metal door. He places his hand on the biometric scanner and gives his voice command. The door opens.

"Welcome to ECO," Anne whispers as we follow him inside.

Executive Command and Overwatch is Anne's department. It's a large room with a second level above the far end. The walls are dark concrete. The floor is black and lustrous enough to see my reflection in, maybe obsidian or black quartzite. Analysts fill the seats of the first level, using touchscreen panels and laptops.

Opposite the entrance are large monitors mounted in the walls. One screen on the top left shows Zhao giving a speech to Chinese soldiers standing in formation in Tiananmen Square. Another shows spy satellite footage. Beside it, a feed from a UAV scanning a city.

Analysts gawk at us as we walk in. Chatter and whispers follow.

Anne puts a finger to her lips. They instantly fall silent and return to their screens.

The general gestures to a conference room with blacked-out windows. "If you need to reach me, I'll be in TATCO," he grumbles. "Someone will be with you momentarily to provide you with temporary security badges." He disappears into the room.

"Abby and I have to debrief," Ken announces. "We'll be back soon."

Anne leads us upstairs past a few analysts and into a room with its blinds closed tight. "And here's my second home." She unlocks it with her badge's RFID chip. The lights come on automatically.

The office is large with an elegant armchair that sits behind an oak desk. A coffee table sits in front of a cushy leather couch. There's not much on her desk other than two monitors and a picture of us and Dean.

She extracts her laptop from her backpack and hands it to me as I pull up the spare chair beside her. "We have twenty-four hours," she says. "Let's get started."

Twenty minutes into sifting through camera footage from around the area of the attacks, our temporary badges come in. Tommy, Karla, and Jeremy leave to grab some food from the cafeteria. Five minutes later, Sung, Steele, Leo, a sergeant, and the general file into Anne's office. Walker's face is just as stoic as before, but Sung and the others look like they've just watched a city get nuked.

"Hey, Sung," I say, anxious to hear the bad news.

"Dion," Sung says, shaking his head. "I'm just going to come right out and say it."

Anne sighs like she knows what's coming.

He gestures to the sergeant. "Sergeant Hughes just returned from checking on Jessica and her family. And … they have her. And your kid …"

Hughes hands me two bent-up Polaroid pictures. "Found these in an envelope stuffed in the dead dog's mouth."

Sung glares at Hughes as I take the blood-speckled pictures. The first one shows Jessica lying on the floor of a van, her legs bound, arms cuffed behind her back, mouth taped shut. A Loyal is holding her head up by the hair. Her left eye is swollen and mascara-blackened tears stain her face. I can almost hear her screaming my name through the photo.

When I look at the second picture, my pulse accelerates to a blur. Everything but the photo fades from my vision and the sounds in the room are replaced by a ringing in my ears. A Hispanic female White Coat with a green-stemmed white rose on her shoulder patch is cradling my son Marshal. I can't make out her face with all that curly hair obscuring it, but I know who she is …

Rose …

I briefly encountered Rose when I was captured during the war. They'd put a sack over my head so I never saw her, but I heard my first torturer, Tyrone, call her name before she took over with her whip. From Richard's journal, I learned that she was an original White Coat. Before the Deciders, Rosa Ramírez was a soldier in the Mexican Army tasked with combating the cartels. Ryan Thomas met her during a training op in Reynosa and they bonded over their radical ideals. Richard speculated if Rose and his brother were intimate, but that didn't prevent him from cheating on Anne with her in the days before his death.

I feel Anne's hand on my back then the blackness fades as the rest of the world bleeds outward from the photo. Body trembling, I glare at General Walker. "I'm going to need some gear and a team," I growl. "Sitting behind a desk is no longer an option."

PART TWO

REPOSSESSION

7

THE ARCHANGEL

September 9
10:11 P.M.

"MR. JOHNSON," GENERAL Walker grumbles, "I understand you are upset, and I am truly sorry about what happened to your son, but you need to calm down."

"I may not be calm," I say, "but I am in control and I am coherent enough to know what I need. And what I need is for you to send me to the closest Decider cell currently under surveillance. Sir."

His eyes shift to Anne then back to me. "Ordinarily, I would never entertain the idea of letting anyone join our operatives and soldiers on the field without going through the proper channels, training, and former enlistment protocols, but considering your experience and the Special Forces training you have participated in, I will make an exception for you to be attached to a team. If that *is* what you want."

I look at Anne. Her eyes are steely, clearly saying no, but she nods anyway. "That is what I want, sir," I answer.

"I'll be joining Dion," Anne says.

I glare at her but say nothing. That's a conversation for later …

"Alright," Walker grunts. "Talk things over then head down to TATCO when you're ready to discuss your enlistment." He nods then exits the room, Sung, Hughes, and Leo at his heels.

The moment the door closes and auto-locks, Anne turns to me. "If it was our son, I would stop at nothing to rescue him," she says softly, "so I understand what you have to do."

"Thank you." I sigh. "I'm sorry I have to break my promise."

"No worries, love."

I hold her hand. "I can't have you going out there with me, though."

She smiles darkly. "Either I'm at your side every step of the way or I shoot you in the leg and force you to do nothing."

"No way. If things go bad, our son needs someone to come home to."

Her smile softens. "I'm enlisting to ensure that we both return to him." Her hand moves to her pistol. "If you don't like it—"

I know she's serious so I gently grab her wrist. "Shooting me won't be necessary, my queen."

The vibe Anne's giving off on the way down is one of frustration, not anger. I know there's nothing I can say to her so I walk in silence, trying to anticipate how the Deciders will use my son and friends against me. *They'll use my kid as bait, and that's when they'll kill me. No. First, they'll make me watch them kill Han, Jess, and the others and then they'll finish me …*

The door to the ECO opens and Ken and Abby rush in, Jeremy and the gang behind them. It's clear by their faces and Karla's tears they too heard the news.

"If you're going after them, I'm in too," Jeremy says.

"Same," Tommy says. In the years since the Annex, he's been working for Lockheed Martin designing next-gen helicopters. And in his free time, he trained on USAW's tiltrotor and regular helicopters. I imagine he'll talk his way into serving as our pilot once again.

"No. I'm not dragging you guys into another armed conflict, no matter how short the duration." Images of the friends I lost during the war flash in my mind. "I lost Mike and Stefan last time and we barely made it out ourselves."

Tommy folds his arms. "It's not your call to make, brother."

Jeremy nods with resolution in his eyes.

I sigh. *First I drag Anne into this shit, now them.* "Fine …" I say, gesturing for them to follow.

The only person in the room is Sung. "Walker is down in Throne," he says, rising from his seat.

"Throne?" I ask Anne as we follow him out. She shrugs.

Ken and Abby do too.

Sung leads us back to the main building and then toward the west wing. It's desolate here, and still under construction. When we get into the elevator, Sung inserts his ID card into the slot underneath the screen displaying the floor options. B2 and B3 appear beneath B1. He taps B3.

The time to get from B2 to B3 is much longer than B1 to B2, which suggests that we're deep underground, maybe deep enough to survive a nuke. I wonder if this sublevel was here in the Quantico days. When the doors open, we emerge into a brightly lit concrete hallway. On each side of the hall are gray doors with tiny windows. The first one on the left has racks of weaponry. Some rooms seem to be bunks. At the end of the hall, we make a left and there's a large steel door, the kind that parts in the middle. Sung swipes his card against the panel on the right side of the door and places his palm on the biometric scanner. The door opens, vibrating the ground.

The command center we stroll into appears to be a condensed version of ECO. There are TVs embedded in the wall, sleek monitors and workstations, and all of the other fancy bells and whistles. An Indian guy who's slightly older than me sits hunched over at one of the desks, typing away. At the head of the command center is General Walker. Steele's beside him, staring up at the main screen, a ninety-inch monitor. To our left is another large room with locker room—style benches and metal walls made of segmented panels.

The four metal steps clang as we descend into the main space. Walker turns at the sound. "Welcome to Throne."

"What exactly is this place, sir?" Anne asks as she looks around.

"As I was explaining to Corporal Steele, Throne does not officially exist. This place was created to serve as a top-secret Angels of War Special Operations Command for one of our SF units, the Seraphs. It is one of many facilities and units that have been blacklisted and compartmentalized so that, in the event of a mainframe breech, we can maintain OPSEC on our more sensitive operations."

I lock eyes with him. "So why are we here then?"

"Because you are the ones who did what even the best couldn't. Your team spearheaded the resistance that brought down Richard Thomas and the Deciders."

"No offense," I say, tilting my head toward Jeremy and Tommy, "but they aren't qualified to be on a Special Forces unit."

"True, but it seems I had to make an exception. Corporal Steele has convinced me that if your companions were joining up, you would probably demand that I place them on your squad so you could ensure their safety. He insisted that if I refused, you'd give me hell until I did. So, here we are."

"Let me get this straight," I say. "You're making us into a Special Forces unit?"

Walker nods. "Along with a few others. The Seraphs are the highest tier of Angel of War soldiers. You will be tasked with the highest-priority missions and will receive intel no one else will. Dion Johnson, come here."

I walk over and the general sticks a finger in my face. "An assessment of your leadership during Special Forces training and during Operations Deicide and Deliverance has been given to me by Commander Todd Finley. The commander has built quite the reputation for himself, even before the War of Annex, and I hold him in high regard, so I take his recommendations very seriously. I will instate you as team lead of the Seraphs. Your rank will be sergeant. Your codename will be Archangel. Do you accept this position and the responsibilities and duties that come with it?"

Steele scowls, side-eyeing me. He might be pissed about being passed over, but I need to accept the position if I'm going to see my son again. "Yes, sir."

Walker nods then turns to Anne. "Ms. Myers, will you serve as Johnson's second in command?"

"Without a doubt," she answers immediately. It sounds like we just accepted each other's wedding vows or something.

"Excellent."

A chart showing ranks and field uniforms appear on the main screen. Sung explains to us that the ranking system in the Angels of War differs from other military branches in two ways. The first is that soldiers are separated into tiers rather than commissioned and noncommissioned officers. Second, the uniforms differ from one tier to the next instead of having standard uniforms for everyone.

Next, he explains the USAW hierarchy. First up, the commander class. The commanders rank from general down to second lieutenant. As Seraphs, we are the top combat tier and work directly for the general himself and the president, along with the other SF units. Below us are the Vanquishers, experienced soldiers hardened through combat and training that rank from sergeant major down to corporal. Ken is wearing one of their uniforms— black and dark gray camouflage that looks almost like snakeskin. Below the Vanquisher class are the Saviors. They span from lance corporal down to private and they make up the bulk of USAW. The Saviors' uniforms are similar to the Vanquishers' camouflage BDUs with midnight blue colors mixed in the pattern.

When the lesson ends, Walker and Sung lead us to the armory, the room we passed when we entered Throne.

"As Seraphs, not only will you be granted top-secret security clearance, you'll have access to bleeding-edge tech," Walker says. "Tech the other branches don't have access to." He taps a touchscreen panel and the metal panels on the wall pop out and lifts up, revealing weapons and gear. In the middle section are empty lockers, probably the width of my body from shoulder to shoulder.

"And here, Seraphs," Walker says, "are your uniforms."

There are jackets, boots, helmets, gloves, pants and some sort of strange two-piece black bodysuit. Everything's black. I grab a jacket and examine it. Even though it's all black, you can still make out the camouflage pattern. On the shoulders of both sleeves, are hard rubbery USAW insignias in charcoal. The jacket is a tactical softshell made of a pitted, durable-looking material. Kevlar? The pants are made of the same material and have a similar pattern. There are kneepads embedded in them that can be removed through zippers on the sides. For footwear: tactical combat boots with high-performance grips.

For head protection, there are two choices. The first is the Deva Full-Face Hazardous Operations Mask. The second is a version of the Deva helmet that I've never seen before. It's matte black with small Angels insignia etched on both sides. The visors are mildly tinted and wider than the old Decider model, providing greater peripheral vision. On the sides of the helmet underneath the visor are thin gill-like slits for breathing and filtration; no more filters jutting out in this model.

Sung puts one on. "If you push the buttons on the side, pull forward then pull down, the filtration system detaches." He demonstrates and the piece beneath the visor comes off and hangs from straps attached to the helmet.

That's a relief. The old ones were stifling.

The general walks over as I turn the bodysuit over in my hands. "That there's the newest in body armor technology," he explains. "STF-Aegis body armor."

"It's lighter and more durable than traditional body armor," Sung says. "And as you can see, it covers more surface area than traditional systems."

"It was reversed engineered from the armor STF-Deva body armor worn by the Deciders in White you encountered in D.C.," Walker says. He looks to me. "The armor you provided us with."

He means the armor I found in Richard's briefcase containing Legacy. We couldn't even drop the White Coats with a 5.56×45mm NATO rounds from under thirty yards away. If it's anything like that, we'll be all right in combat.

Jeremy examines the armor. "Uh, this looks too damn thin. How's this supposed to protect us, exactly?"

"Our resident engineer can give you the gist of it," Walker says.

"Essentially," Sung begins, "in between the layers of spider silk fibers lies a composite shear thickening fluid, or STF. STF is a non-

Newtonian gel containing bits of ceramic particles and certain proprietary molecules. When the fluid is exposed to a fast-moving external force like a bullet, the molecules instantaneously interlock and solidify. Once solidified, the bullets energy dissipates across the armor. The armor then returns to its gel state, allowing for full flexibility."

"So what's wrong with it?" I ask.

"There are only a few drawbacks. One is that the segments covering the limbs are thinner, so they can't withstand as much force as the torso. It can only defend against high-speed rounds, so the armor is susceptible to knife attacks. Third, your joints aren't protected at all. As for the torso, the effectiveness of the armor depends on the distance traveled by the round, the number of rounds that hit a single area in a short time span, and, of course, the size and type of round. The results of our testing vary too much to be definitive, but we've established that the STF-Aegis armor outperforms any other armor system it was compared to, including the old White Coats' variant."

"Suit up," Walker says.

Anne and Abby grab appropriately sized armor and slink off behind a set of lockers on the other side of the room. The rest of us change where we stand. As we shed our shirts, I catch a glimpse of the original Angels of War insignia tattooed on Jeremy's left shoulder. It's the circle 'A' with three branched wings—the same one all the original Angels of War bear.

As we gear up, Steele explains that Seraph BDUs are made of a flame-resistant Kevlar and spider silk composite that will help resist high-impact damage and reduce our heat signatures to thermal cameras and scopes. As for the Deva 2.0 or Deva-Aegis Model, they are bullet resistant up to a certain point, depending on the caliber and the distance. The antifogging visors are bullet resistant to 9mm rounds at up to 20 yards. The filters are built for high airflow and filtration of the smallest chemical warfare agents, including the infamous Psycho Nerve Agent. It also contains a built-in battery-powered cooling system utilizing small water tubes.

Besides head protection, the Deva-AM has a built-in headset and microphone that allows for hands-free communication with radio or cellular devices. They are primarily designed to synchronize with the Angels of War–issued satellite phones dubbed Nexus. The Nexus communication devices are small, about the size of a smartphone, but thick due to its durable casing. It has a large touchscreen with a QWERTY keypad at the bottom. There are rear and front-facing cameras. The Nexus system will connect us directly to Central Command through the USAW Morningstar satellite, formerly a USMC communication satellite named Streamline.

In the mirror near the entrance, I catch a glimpse of the guys and myself. Everyone looks badass, like soldiers from a distant future—much more alien than the Deciders appeared when they first emerged. Despite the Aegis armor underneath my outerwear, I'm surprisingly comfortable. I squat and throw a few punches and kicks to confirm that I still have high mobility.

"You gents decent?" Anne asks.

"Come on over," I respond.

Anne and Abby round the corner. They both look lethal, but Anne somehow looks tactically stunning. She has a smile on her face and that same look she had before we left to rescue Tommy. Even though she gives me crap, she's hungry for combat …

Sung hands out watches. It's the same kind he, Abby, and the other soldiers are wearing. The face is just under five inches wide and the digital display is about four. There are three buttons on each side and one under the screen. The screen is black and the time is displayed with a faint blue glow. I press the main button and a display like the home screen of a smartphone comes up.

Steele resumes his lesson on the Nexus communication system. He explains that each Nexus comm is uniquely programmed for the soldier it's assigned to. This allows for a type of caller ID function. When one soldier calls another, or when a soldier contacts Central Command, that person's name and the name of their squad will be displayed on any device connected to the Nexus system, including our watches. Once synchronized with the Nexus satphones and the Deva-AM helmets, the watches can receive SMS text messages, make and receive calls, and control the helmet's cooling system.

The watch can also display a map of your immediate area of operation and the locations of friendly soldiers as they're transmitted from the ECO. Sung gives us a quick demo. A digital mini-map opens up of the base and shows us where each soldier with an active Nexus device is relative to our position with up and down arrows to show who is below and above the user. It basically functions like the mini-map in a game like Call of Duty. Blue dots are friendlies. Red dots, when the system can find them, are enemies. Hostile targets can be marked by locking on to the frequency of their signals from their communication devices and using it as a beacon. UAVs can also sight them visually and transmit their coordinates to the network.

The watch also monitors vitals of the soldier wearing it. When a soldier's heart stops, his or her dot will disappear from the map. Finally, it can be used to remote detonate explosives and stream drone or surveillance footage. The battery is powered by its wearer's movement and body heat thanks to a thermo-conductive backing. The Nexus satphones also have motion charging capability, but they're primarily kept charged by solar panels built into backpacks.

The tutorial ends and Walker waves for us to follow him back to Throne's command room. The general grabs a stack of black folders from the desk near the stairs. "There's paperwork for you all to sign. When you're finished, have it sent up to my office." He hands the stack to me, along with a set of keycards. "Until you receive your security badges, these master keys will access Throne and all pertinent areas of the complex. Mr. Rahman here—" he gestures to the Indian male at the computer station behind him— "will set up your Nexus devices and add you to the system." He eyes his Nexus watch. "Excuse me." He marches past us with haste.

Rahman stands. "Hello, Ms. Myers," he says to Anne.

"Abdul," she replies with a nod before turning to me. "Abdul here is my top analyst. He is an expert level programmer and overall technical expert."

I extend a hand. We shake.

"Sergeant Johnson, it is an honor to meet you, sir." He speaks with a very faint Indian accent. "When I graduated from MIT after the war, I came here because I was inspired by you. I wanted to serve my country the best way I knew how." He finally releases my hand.

"Welcome to the fight, Abdul," I respond, not knowing what else to say.

"If you need anything, I'm your guy. No questions." He nods suddenly then returns to his chair. "Gather around. I'll set you up on the Nexus system and give you a tutorial."

Abdul gives a crash course on how to use the phones, watches, and helmets. It turns out that he had a hand in developing most of the programs and security systems. At the end of the thirty-minute tutorial, we hit the armory to prepare a loadout so we can be ready to go the second we get the call. When we're done, I sit at a computer, log on with the credentials Abdul gave me, and click my way to the files about ongoing Decider operations and surveillance programs. Just as I start searching through the files, the Nexus watch vibrates with a faint buzz, startling me enough to make me jump.

The message on screen reads: "SERAPHS, REPORT TO THE HELIPAD. PRONTO! --GEN. WALKER."

8
ONCE A SOLDIER...

September 10
12:29 A.M.

WE PUT ON our preloaded tactical vests. Single sling, light assault packs go over our shoulders. On the way out, we grab our weapons—KM2000 combat knives, SIG P226s, and HK416 rifles for everyone but Abby, who brings her Mk 14 EBR instead. Anne and I are armed with the HK416s we brought from home, which we customized with an M320 grenade launcher on the underbelly of the barrel. We also opt to also carry two P226s each.

We follow Sung as he jogs through a series of dim service tunnels to an elevator. When the doors open on the ground level, the heavy thumps of helicopter blades become audible. It's a short trek down the hall to a ramp that leads to a metal door. We emerge twenty yards from the helipads. Two platoons of troops of troops are rushing to the MH-53J Pave Low IIIs and two of the three Blackhawks. Most of them are Vanquisher class soldiers. Another distinction between the two classes is that Vanquishers, for the most part, wear Deva-AM helmets. A few wear standard military helmets with Deva-FHOM masks. As for the Saviors, they all wear the latter.

Sung glances at his watch then banks right, jogging toward the Pave Low. The general's there waiting with a six-foot tall African American soldier dressed the way we are.

Walker takes a long puff of his cigar as one of the Blackhawks dusts off. "It seems there's been a leak!" he yells over the propellers. "Marine One was shot down over Williamsburg moments after airlifting President Lewis from the Executive Complex to a secure facility. He survived, but the acting VP didn't. Secret Service and the USAW security detail had to move through Williamsburg in undercover vehicles to a safe house since whatever air support we send from Norfolk is being shot down by something … undetectable. The hotel they're holed up in is being evacuated so you won't have to worry about civilian interference." He gestures to the soldier beside him. "This is Staff Sergeant Anthony Hall. He'll brief you on the details. Now go!"

Hall and I shake hands. "It's an honor to meet the brother who rid the world of Richard Thomas," he says as we board the helicopter. "I heard a lot about you from Finley."

"Yeah? How do you know each other?"

"We did a joint op pre-Annex back when I was Delta Force working under Walker. We worked together post-war too. Walker attached me to your unit to keep your asses safe out there."

"Thanks. Appreciate it!"

"You got it, Archangel."

Archangel. The chief angel. That's what Richard said my codename should be when he learned I was leading the Angels of War Militia …

When the last person boards, the gate closes and the bird lifts off. "All right, people!" Hall says. "The primary objective of Operation Priority Package is to extract President Lewis and escort him to Raven Rock in Pennsylvania. With the target being the acting president, we expect Decider elite to be heading the snatch and grab. Once the package is secure, we're to capture any key Deciders, if possible. This'll be our best chance to gather intel."

The secondary objective is the only thing I care about. Capture a Loyal. Get him to tell me the whereabouts of my son. And the others.

The watch buzzes with a message designating our squad's call sign: Royal-1. Scrolling down reveals a list of call signs for our squad members.

Hall nudges me then nods at the two Seraphs across from us. "These two will be joining our squad. The one on the left is Corporal Manny Monteiro, our field medic. He goes by Chiron, the name of some Greek centaur known for healing or some shit. The other is Corporal Joshua Hillman."

When we make eye contact, I recognize them from SF training. Manny seemed a bit arrogant, but highly intelligent. Hillman reminded me of Lloyd Gray, silent, deadly, and weirdly calm.

I look back to my Nexus at the list of call signs. I'm "King" and Anne is "Queen." Something tells me that's Sung's doing. As for the others, Sergeant Ken Nguyen is Khagan, the Mongol name for an emperor. Jeremy is Joker, Abby is Dame, and Steele is Rook. Anne, Jeremy, Ken, and I comprise Royal-1's Fireteam Alpha. Steele, Manny, and Hillman will be under Sarge Hall's command on Royal-1 Fireteam Bravo. As for the other squads, Royal-3 is our support squad. On the two Blackhawks ahead of us are Guard-2, led by Sergeant Jon Patterson, and Guard-6, which is under Sung's command. His second in command is Sergeant Scott "Gunner" Hughes. The only other member of Guard-6 who I recognize is Lance Corporal Oliver Hawke. Pretty sure Sung mentioned that Hawke was his protégé.

The Nexus watch vibrates again, this time with a video call from ECO. General Walker informs us that Decider forces have found President Lewis's location and engaged their security detail. Helicopters let off Deciders on the roof and trucks dropped off more on the ground level. Walker lays out the new plan of attack. Guard-2 Fireteam Alpha will land on the roof then rappel down to the seventh floor to aid the security detail. Meanwhile, Guard-2's Fireteam Bravo will lay down aerial support and defend the extraction point. Guard-6 will liberate the perimeter of Deciders, allowing us to enter from the main entrance. Royal-3 will breach through the parking garage to flank the Deciders from the rear stairwell then clear the secondary extraction point in case the roof is inaccessible.

Simple enough.

Forty minutes later, our birds descend. Word comes in that the Deciders have breached the first line of the protection detail's defense and are working their way to the seventh floor where President Lewis is taking shelter. Guard-2 reports that they've engaged Decider sentries on the rooftop. They are described as wearing burgundy trench coats. I think back to the spooks outside the Wilsons' house and the men who attacked Tommy. They wore burgundy too. Maybe the color represents a new Decider class.

Guard-2 lead Sgt. Patterson reports that all enemies were eliminated and they have boots on the roof and are preparing to rappel to the seventh floor. Our helicopter approaches a rooftop half a block up from the hotel. When the ramp opens, the ropes drop. Two by two, our squad rappels from the chopper.

I look to Anne, eyebrows raised. *You ready?*

She nods as though she hears my thoughts. Our helmets go on.

On the way down, I can hear gunfire popping off down the block. The lights from the cop cars in the intersection below flash blue and red. Police helicopters whir overhead, circling the perimeter with spotlights shining down on the streets. The second my boots meet roof, I run with my team toward the stairwell, leaving Abby to set up her vantage point.

Guard-6 is fighting the Decider sentries posted outside the hotel entrance when we emerge from the building. Staring through my scope at the targets ahead, I am as calm as I would be going grocery shopping. Anne is radiating something akin to excitement.

I take cover behind a sedan, pop up and fire a burst at the burgundy coat coming down the alley. He goes down. I shift to the next target and drop him. In my peripherals, I see Anne effortlessly eliminate the large Decider at the entrance. Jeremy, who hasn't been in the field since Operation Deliverance, even functions like it's just another day.

Once a soldier, always a soldier, I think.

It only takes five minutes to clear the entrance. "We got it from here." Sung radios to us.

"Copy, Razer," I respond, switching channels to the Royal squads'. "Royal-1. Royal-3. Move out."

I take point, leading Royal-1 through the front with Anne right behind me. Royal-3 breaks off toward the parking garage. Anne and I clear the targets near the entrance. When the last body falls, we toss flash grenades inside. And when they pop, we breach.

Pools of blood envelop bodies of friendlies scattered across the lobby. Dead ahead, a Burgundy Coat emerges from behind the concierge desk. There are a few more scattered through the area. Anne and I dispatch the one behind the desk then Royal-1 Bravo lays down fire from the entrance, allowing the rest of Fireteam Alpha to charge in and take cover.

From behind my cover, I stare down my sights at the next target. Inside the brightly lit lobby, I get a better look at the enemy. They're wearing tactical burgundy trench coats, gray pants, and black boots. *Are these the new Vanguard?* Like the USAW Savior Class, these Burgundy Coats wear standard military helmets, gray in color, with an armored mask similar to the Deva-FHOM. It also appears they are wearing a device of some kind on their wrists, something that has a faint glow to it. *Nevrons.* Those were the devices Loyals wore in the Annex to monitor troops and detonate the explosive belts worn by the Vanguards who were forced to fight for them.

Behind the ten Burgundy soldiers lurk five Loyals. The Loyals are wearing dark gray trenches with magazine pouches sewn into them, dark gray pants, black and gray tactical gloves, and black boots. For head protection, they too have a new version of the Deva helmet. Their visors are bigger, almost V-shaped, stretching down to their noses where it narrows to a rounded point. Their filtration system starts underneath the bottom of the visor and extends from ear to ear. Like Burgundy soldiers, they wear glowing rectangular devices on their wrists.

I drop another Burgundy Coat then duck back as rounds chip away at the pillar I'm behind. Royal-1 Bravo moves to flank left while Alpha suppresses the threat. Anne takes a TD6 grenade, sets the detonation time for seven seconds, then lobs it at the enemy. Two soldiers break out from behind their cover to escape. I pick one off; Ken downs the other. The grenade destroys the rest.

Loyals to the left begin dropping when Bravo fireteam finally flanks around to the elevator bank. That's when the power goes out. We click on the tactical lights on our rifles and reengage. The Deciders illuminate the headlights built into their helmets. *Fancy.* Moments later, dull, yellowish backup lights kick on. As Anne and I move to engage the last few Loyals and their lackeys, we receive an update from Guard-2 Alpha lead Sgt. Jon Patterson.

"Message to all units," Patterson begins. "Guard-2 Alpha has linked up with the package and his detail. Decider forces are closing in. The Secret Service and USAW outside are taking heavy losses. SITREP says there are two White Coats—one male, one female—eight Burgundy Coats, and five Loyals sweeping the floor to Lewis's room. We need immediate assistance from Royal-1 and Royal-3! Over."

White Coats? For this mission? I take cover and hit the button on my watch. "Copy that. Royal-1 is moving to the southern stairwell now. If possible, capture those White Coats. Over."

Cpl. Greene, Royal-3's lead, chimes in right after. "Royal-3 has just cleared the second level of the parking garage. We're making our way across the bridge to the hotel's northern stairwell. Over."

By the time the message ends, Steele puts down the last visible Decider.

"Area secure," SSgt. Hall reports.

"Lobby's clear," Manny affirms.

Our fireteams regroup at the stairwell entrance.

"I'll take point," I say. "Hall? Cover the rear."

Ken opens the door and I charge in. Things are quiet until we hit the third floor, where two more Burgundy Coats are making their way down. As Anne and I engage, another report from Guard-2 lead comes in over the Nexus.

"The protection detail has been KIA and Guard-2 Bravo has launched their ambush," Sgt. Patterson announces.

"Malloy's hit!" Sgt. Kunes, Guard-2 Bravo lead, howls.

Things go quiet. As I climb upstairs, I glance at the Nexus watch. One icon disappears from the map. Malloy's dead.

"They hit us with precision shots before we even touched the doorknob," Kunes says. "It's like they saw us coming!" It goes quiet for a little while. "They're tearing this room in half!" Break. "It's the White Coat! Ahhh!" His transmission cuts out.

The icons belonging to Kunes and corporals Donaldson and Becker disappear from the map. Only Sgt. Patterson and two of his fireteam remain. "We need to hurry!" I say, quickening my pace.

I take the stairs two at a time until I hear footstep from above. I drop the lead man then take cover to reload, leaving Anne and Ken to engage. As I slam a fresh mag in, I get to thinking, *if they see us coming, maybe they have tracking tech like we do.* I try scanning for the nearby Decider radio wave signals then I rejoin the fight. There is only one enemy soldier left. Steele takes him down and I look back down at my watch. Still nothing. *What gives?*

On the sixth floor, we encounter more enemy combatants that we eliminate with relative ease. Now it's a clear shot to the seventh.

"Taking heavy fire!" Sgt. Patterson reports.

"Almost there!" I radio back.

"Oh shit!" There's gunfire and then he goes quiet.

Two more icons disappear from the map.

Ken and I burst through the seventh-floor door. The hallway strobes from the flickering light above. The walls are spotted with bullet holes and spattered with blood. The floor ahead is barely visible beneath the mat of bodies. None of the corpses belong to the Deciders.

We approach the corner with caution. There are no gunshots, just rustling and multiple footfalls ahead.

Staff Sergeant Hall hands me a rubbery black ball pitted with six cameras. "Toss it out," he whispers.

I do so gently and it rolls along the wall next to me.

Hall then points to his watch. I check mine and I see an option for OSO. When I select it, live footage of the hallway comes up. Four Burgundy Coats at the other end of the hall are working to clear rooms. Just past them is the White Coat standing in the center of five Loyals. He's about six-foot-six with a large, stocky build and is toting an M249 LMG light machine gun in one massive hand. His trench coat has forest green accents on the seams and around the pockets. On his left shoulder, a picture of a white bulldozer. Slung over his shoulder is an unconscious President Lewis, who appears to be wearing a gas mask.

The White Coat suddenly turns in our direction and takes aim as if something alerted him to our presence. "We've got company, Ghost!" he shouts to the much shorter, female White Coat who's hurrying into the hall.

I trigger the camera to zoom in. Ghost wears a different type of white trench coat. This cape-like hooded version is made of a dull leathery material with purple accents along the seams. The hood is draped over her helmet. Long white hair flows out from underneath. Beneath her unbuttoned trench, she's wearing a white bodysuit that hugs her form.

I wonder why they aren't wearing pure white like the White Coats on TV or the ones we fought in D.C. Maybe they aren't part of the remaining fifty founding members. Another new class, perhaps? Either way, I'm determined to capture this Ghost.

Ghost turns, staring down the hall through her tinted visor, already aiming our way with a white Glock 18 as I emerge from cover. Before I can scope her, she sprays the wall with a storm of automatic fire. I barely make it to cover as her rounds rip through the drywall where my head was, sending up clouds of gypsum plaster.

More guns bark. On my watch, I see that four Burgundy Coats have joined in. The male White Coat hands his LMG to the Loyal beside him and disappears into the northern stairwell with Lewis and four Loyals. While walking backward, Ghost sends a hail of rounds from two Glock 18s and follows after him. Now the LMG fire starts coming.

I toss out a TD6 grenade set for six seconds. It bounces off the wall and rolls halfway down the hallway. After it explodes, Anne and I lean out to lay down cover fire while Ken and Jeremy bolt to the nearest open hotel room for cover. They make it, but then so many rounds start coming our way that we have to cease fire.

"Heads up," Hall says over his comm. "Royal-3, four Loyals, and two White Coats are heading in your direction, probably for the roof."

"Roger that," Greene responds. "We have visual! Engaging!"

"Brown's hit!" another voice cries out. "We're taking heavy fire!" Something explodes. "The White Coats are escaping with the package!"

Guard-2 Charlie team's lead reports from the Blackhawk circling the hotel that they are moving in to lay down suppressing fire to keep the enemy in the stairwell until we arrive. Just as the report ends, there is a massive explosion outside.

"We're hit!" Guard-2 Charlie's Blackhawk pilot shouts. The building trembles and there is another explosion.

I hit the button on my watch. "What happened out there?" I ask.

Abby radios in. "It's some kind of stealth helicopter. Came out of nowhere! It looks like the Goliath, you know, black panels and all of that? I can barely even hear it and I'm across the street!"

"Tell Tank to get out of there!" I shout.

"Already on the move," Tommy says.

The general radios in next. "There are two Apaches inbound to support you all!"

"The stealth chopper is landing on the roof," Abby announces. There's a shot over the comm. "I dropped a Loyal." Another shot. "They're boarding the helicopter with POTUS."

Outside, there's gunfire from the helicopter's machinegun.

"Damn!" Abby cries. "They've targeted me!"

There is another explosion farther off in the distance.

"Dame!" I shout into the mic.

No response.

"We have two Burgundy Coats trying to flank!" Steele relays to the team.

I guess falling back is out of the question now.

Bravo engages the flankers while my team keeps the Deciders at the other end of the hall from advancing. I toss a grenade out. It rolls halfway down the hallway and goes off, but the shots keep coming. Suddenly, a pistol fires twice and the LMG fire ceases. I peer out to find the Loyal is wounded on the ground and two of the four Burgundy Coats have turned their attention to the room where Ghost came out of.

"The Loyal with the LMG is down. Engage!" Sgt. Patterson groans. He's still alive, at least for now.

"King, on three," Anne says.

"Copy," I respond. "Khagan? Joker? Go low and lay down support."

"Roger," Jeremy responds.

"As you wish, bud," Ken snaps. Like Steele, he's been a bit bitter with me today, probably because he's used to being in command of his teams.

Ken lies prone and Jeremy crouches behind him. They fire down the side while Anne and I rush the middle. We drop one. Ken or Jeremy crosses out another. The third is wounded but manages to slink into a room for cover. The fourth ducks into another room and returns fire.

Right as we dive into a room for cover, there are four rapid explosions outside.

"The Apaches were shot down by the stealth helicopters," Abby reports. The entire building shakes like an earthquake just rolled through. "A helicopter hit the south side of the building! Get out of there!"

The fire alarm goes off. The sprinklers hiss and spit and then water showers us.

Great ... How can this get any worse?

9
CAPTURE, KILL

September 10
1:49 A.M.

THE GUNFIRE IN the hall starts dying down. During my reload, I notice beads of water roll off of Anne's helmet and clothing. That's when I realize my clothes aren't getting heavier. *Gotta love water-resistant BDUs.*

I lean out, targeting the soldier two doors down on the left. Before I depress the trigger, a burst fired by someone behind me drops him. Then, aside from the hissing sprinklers, there's silence.

"All clear back here," Manny reports.

"There's still one left up ahead," Ken whispers as I exit the room. "Third room on the right."

"I'm capturing this one. Cover me," I order, turning to Bravo fireteam. "Sarge, have your men clear the rest of the rooms. Manny, assist Patterson."

"Copy that, Archangel," Hall grumbles. He doesn't seem to enjoy taking my orders either.

I switch to my P226, press myself against the wall, and inch toward the room. Jeremy and Anne post up behind me. Ken goes wide and slices the pie. Rapid semiautomatic pistol fire starts coming through the doorway and the wall in Ken's direction as he dives for cover.

The comms buzz. "The Decider choppers are back!" Sung says. "They're providing air support for the remaining ground troops to evacuate! All units, fall back!"

I take a deep breath. *Time to put this Aegis armor to the test.*

Time seems to slow down as I push off the wall and dart into the room. There's a black rappelling rope tied to the bed frame that leads to the window opposite the door. And crouched on the windowsill is a slim, female Burgundy Coat.

The last woman I crossed on the battlefield killed two of my best friends and I still spared her. And proposed to her ...

She grips the rope with one hand and aims a Glock at me with the other. I'm already diving for cover behind the bed before she rings off four shots. When I poke my head back up, she's gone. I sprint toward the window and grab the rope then shoot where it's tied to the bed. She shrieks as the rope starts sliding through my gloved hand. When I get both hands around it, the weight at the other end of the rope pulls me. Skidding, I hit the wall knees first then lean back and pull. Ken and Anne run in and grab hold too.

Cautiously, I lean forward and see the girl staring up at me as she dangles above the next floor. She's lost her rifle, but her pistol is clutched tightly in her free hand. "Drop your weapon and I'll pull you up," I say as calmly as possible.

She takes aim. "Let go! I'll die before I let you capture me."

Anne releases the rope and it slides a bit through my hands. The girl gasps, hinting that she might be bluffing about opting for death after all. Then Anne marches toward the window, aims down with her pistol, and fires a single shot. Her round rips through the Decider's right bicep and her weapon falls six stories. "Pull her in before she unclips herself."

We hoist up the Burgundy Coat. When she reaches the window, I grab her underneath her arm and pull her in. As she comes through, she thrusts a knife at me. I grab her wrist and slam her to the floor, pinning her arm behind her back. Ken holds her down with a knee while I strip her of her combat knife and communication devices.

"All clear, Archangel!" SSgt. Hall shouts from the doorway. "Patterson's hurt bad. Gotta move!"

"Copy. We're coming!" I shout.

Ken fishes out his zip cuffs and works on binding her wrists. She squirms and struggles, shouting obscenities. I notice a patch under the Decider flag on her shoulder that reads JEZEBEL. Once she's been restrained, I turn the device on her wrist so it's facing me. It definitely seems to be a modified version of the Nevron. *We can track the Deciders with this ...* On the large screen are nine red blips in our immediate area—that's us. And in the southeast corner of the garage, there's a cluster of four yellow blips—some star-shaped, some circular like Jezebel's—moving west. In the distance, there are three large clusters inside a helicopter icon that abruptly disappears.

I try removing the device, but it won't budge. "How do I take this off?"

"*You* can't," she hisses. "But even if you could, it'd just be disabled." Her accent sounds a little southwestern.

Ken forces her onto her feet and I come face to face with the Burgundy Coat—well, more like helmet to gas mask. She's about my height. My eyes set on her chest, not to stare at her breasts, but to read another name patch.

LCPL. MONROE. *Jezebel must be a codename.*

Monroe's hazel eyes glare at me through her visor. "Capturing me is a waste, *Archangel*," she taunts. "I know nothing. Only the Loyals know where they're takin' your president."

"Everyone knows something, Jezebel," I say coolly. "And what you know is how to operate that device on your wrist."

She scowls. "Once my people clear the AO, their Gauntlets will stop transmitting data. And once they realize I'm still here, they'll consider me a liability and remote wipe mine."

"So we'll have to get to your extraction team before then," I say, shoving her toward the door.

As she stumbles forward, I see she's fidgeting, her fingers desperately trying to reach a button on her Gauntlet. Anne reacts before I do. She knocks off Jezebel's helmet then gun-butts the back of her head, just below where her honey-brown hair is pinned up. The girl drops. "Pick her up and let's go." Anne orders.

I smile thinking, *that's my girl.*

"Razer, here. Decider birds have cleared the AO," Sung's voice buzzes over his comm.

I eye Patterson while activating my comm. "This is Archangel. We need immediate evac for one critically wounded and one prisoner. Hotel roof. ASAP."

"Copy," someone responds. "Blackhawk inbound. ETA one minute."

"There are still enemy forces fleeing the area on the ground. Establish a perimeter and secure the LZs." I say, turning to my team. "Ken, get Patterson upstairs. Jeremy, go with him. Take the prisoner. Direct us to the nearby Deciders using her Gauntlet. Hall, escort them. Everyone else, on me."

Jeremy tells us that the blips have begun moving northbound toward US-60 just as Anne, Hillman, and I climb into an armored GMC truck. The doors slam and I screech off with Steele and Manny following behind us in a gun-mounted black SUV. Word comes through that three enemy SUVs have punched right through the roadblock that Royal-3 just established. We roar past the burning wreckage where the surviving soldiers stand on the roadside.

It takes a few minutes of speeding and weaving through traffic before I get eyes on the targets, who are driving just as wildly as I am. No sooner than I do, the vehicles split up. One cuts across the lane into oncoming traffic and takes the ramp onto VA-199 heading east. The other two continue down US-60.

"Rusty, that one's yours!" I shout.

"Copy!" Steele responds as the tires of his vehicle screech.

At the underpass, one truck makes a sharp right onto VA-199 heading west. "Joker, which direction did the star icons go?"

"There're two in the group moving west and one heading north!" Jeremy responds. "Shit! They just went off radar!"

I tap the brakes, cut the wheel left, and drift around the turn, barely missing an oncoming vehicle that honks and flashes their high beams in fury. The SUV is now four or five car lengths ahead. That gap closes quickly. As we blow through the intersection, a helmetless Loyal emerges from the rear left window with a rifle. Muzzle flashes flicker and rounds pelt the grille and the bullet-resistant window. Hillman leans out his window and returns fire. His rounds just spark and skip off their vehicle the way theirs do against ours. The Decider gunner slides back inside and reemerges with a rifle equipped with a grenade launcher. He fires a round yellow projectile with a red blinking device in the center and it sticks to the sedan ahead of us. A few seconds later, the sedan explodes in a blinding fireball. I swerve around the blast and plow through the smoke. Another glob-bomb sticks to the road ahead. It detonates almost as soon as I spot it, sending large chunks of concrete hurtling toward the windshield. I hit the brakes and drift around the blast cloud and crater, almost swerving out in the process.

Anne rolls down her window. "I'll return the favor," she hisses.

Another car blows up ahead of us before I catch back up to them. Anne fires a 40mm round and lands a direct hit at the back-right tire, lifting the Decider vehicle's rear off the ground. When it lands, it swerves and flips four times before settling on its roof. I mash the brakes and drift to a stop, parking in the middle of the street perpendicular to the sidewalk, driver's side facing the wreck. As we emerge from the SUV, rounds start coming, forcing us to shelter behind the vehicle. Through the GMC's windows, I see two sets of the muzzle flashes and one silhouette helping another from the wreck. Four targets in total. From the Gauntlet, I know two are likely Burgundy Coats. *Kill three, capture one.*

While Anne and I lay down suppressive fire, I signal Hillman to flank right through the trees bordering the road. A poorly placed flash grenade clatters to the ground near the GMC's rear a few seconds later. Still blindfiring, we shield our eyes. It pops and is immediately followed by the distinct *FWOOP* of a grenade launcher firing. Without exchanging words, Anne and I take off at the same time, but I lag behind a bit to absorb the following shockwave and debris. We only get a couple feet away before the entire area lights up from the blast and the concussive force sends me flying into her.

Unharmed but groaning, I roll off of her onto my back and aim at the burning SUV. A figure wearing a burgundy trench coat appears through the smoke. Simultaneous bursts from Anne and I end him before he targets us. Back on our feet, we keep a tight formation and move toward the Deciders' last known location. There's a Loyal up ahead dragging another Burgundy Coat into the woods. The still-conscious man being dragged spots us first and takes aim, yelping something to the Loyal as he does. I drop him with a double tap. Anne puts two rounds through the Loyal's head.

Three down ...

Rapid rifle fire barks in the wooded area to the right. Rifles pointed ahead, we cautiously rush into the woods. Halfway there, about forty yards in, the gunfire ceases. Our paces slow and I lead the way toward the estimated source of gunfire, Anne moving with her back to mine.

"Hillman, do you copy?" I whisper over the comm.

Silence.

A few yards later, we come to a house that has its backyard porch light on—probably a motion sensor spotlight. Then I see someone in the shadows posted up against the shed with what looks to be a pistol at high ready.

"Contact right," I whisper to Anne. "No kill shots. We're capturing this one."

"Copy," she whispers back.

I train my sights on the figure, as does Anne. Something that sounds like a twig snaps from the other side of the shed. The figure in the shadows steps out into the open and into the light, pointing his pistol in the direction of the noise. Hillman! A gray-sleeved arm appears from behind the shed and smacks the pistol out of the way as Hillman fires off a wild round. Anne and I advance hastily now. Hillman takes a flurry of punches and kicks before stumbling back and drawing his knife. The Loyal lunges into the open while drawing a black machete from a sheath on his back. As he joins Hillman in the halo of light, I see he's not wearing a helmet. Shoulder length, brownish-blond hair blows back behind him, revealing the face of a man with a large burn scar covering most of the left side. His face seems familiar, but I can't place it.

Hillman thrusts his blade at him but the Loyal swiftly steps to the right and hacks off Hillman's right hand all in one swift motion. As blood spurts from the stub, Hillman cries out in agony. The Loyal raises his machete, then turns to stare at us with his dead brown eyes. I have a clear shot at the target but I don't take it. Neither does Anne, probably for the same reason I don't ...

"No ..." Anne gasps.

Don Chambers? "It can't be ..." I say. He looks different now, but I know it's him.

Don was Richard Thomas's best friend—his right-hand man—a founding member of the Deciders and a former friend of Anne's. He and I first crossed paths in Fredericksburg during Operation Cage Breaker—the mission to liberate civilians from a reeducation camp. I stabbed him, put a round in his chest, and left him for dead, only to find him alive after I was captured. Last time I saw him, he was staggering from the burning wreck of Richard's downed Chinook while covered in flames.

Chambers puts the machete to Hillman's throat, using him as a shield as he points a gray 1911 at us. It's the same gun that was used to execute President Pell ...

"Don Chambers!" I call out. "Kill him and you die!"

Don's head tilts to the side. "Don Chambers?" he smirks. "Most people know me as Savage now ... And according to USAW, Don Chambers was reported dead ... So just who the hell are you to know me by face?"

"Archangel! Help!" Hillman sobs.

"Release him and we'll talk," I growl.

Don sighs. "You know, *Archangel*, there's a reason they call me Savage ..."

Chambers slits Hillman's throat while simultaneously firing a single round that clips my arm. The next thing I know, he's half-crouched behind Hillman, pivoting back toward the shed for cover. It all happens so fast. But not fast enough.

Anne's rifle barks. Her round tears through his calf and sends him crashing down on one knee. Don tries aiming at her, but I land a shot near his elbow, disarming him.

Don snarls, arm limp. I sprint forward and hit him with a flying knee to the head before he can dive for his weapon. He hits the ground, conscious but groaning. He puts up no fight as I roll him onto his back, strip him of his weapons and comms, and zip-cuff him. "You're a tough son of a bitch to kill, Chambers," I say. "Last time I saw you, you were burning like a campfire marshmallow."

He smirks. "Dion Johnson … So, you crawled out of hiding after all …"

I roll him over. There's a gray patch on his right arm. It's the face of a troll with wild hair and red spatters around its mouth. A symbol for Savage maybe? First a rose patch, then a ghost and a bulldozer, now this? I remove my helmet and stare him down. "Yeah. I had to resurface. You bastards took my son."

He starts thrashing violently. His crazed, hate-filled eyes are glaring furiously at me, a twisted smile stretched across his face. "When I get free!" He laughs maniacally. "Ooooh … I've been aching to kill you since you murdered Richard and Tyrone—my bothers!"

"Extraction is inbound, my love," Anne says. "Five minutes out." She turns to Savage. "Your killing days are over, Don."

Don's face goes blank. "… Anne?"

She detaches the gas mask part of the helmet and gives him a dark grin. "Greetings, Donald."

His eyes widen. "What the flying fuck? Richard said something about not trusting you before he died … So it was you who betrayed the Deciders? You fucking *bitch*!"

Anne smirks.

I punch him in the face. "Watch how you talk to my fiancé."

Don works his jaw. "Unbelievable …"

"What's unbelievable is that you survived," Anne says. "Your burn surgeon is rubbish though. You look like a wad of chewing gum."

Anne and I put our headwear back on. I lift Don to his feet and shove him forward, jabbing the muzzle of the HK416 into his back.

"Do you actually think you'll be able to get any information out of me?" he asks. "I'll never tell you where you kid or friends are, dipshit!"

My eyes go dead. "It only took one thumb for your boy Hawthorne to start talking … Maybe I'll start with by taking a hand this time."

"Now that is some savage shit, Dion. You wear our gear, use our tactics, torture people … You're becoming more of a Decider every second." He laughs. "Just wait till you learn what we're doing to your friends!"

I crack him in back of the head with the buttstock and he hits the dirt face first. "Where are they?"

"Don't," Anne says. "He's just getting under your skin. We'll make him talk back at base."

We hike back to the road in silence. It takes every ounce of willpower I have not to tie him to a tree and beat their whereabouts out of him. The only reason I don't is that there are more efficient ways to interrogate him other than beating him to death. After

Hawthorne, I'd sworn that I would never torture anyone again, but that promise isn't meaning much to me right now.

Back at the wreck site, I hear the whine of a motorcycle in the distance.

I tap my Nexus watch and contact Steele. "Rusty, how far out are you?"

"Another minute or two, Archangel. The Loyal we captured tried committing suicide so we had to put him to sleep."

Nice, another Loyal. One of the three prisoners is bound to talk. "Copy that."

The whining engine grows louder. A figure in all black on a black motorcycle appears in the streetlights ahead. He's speeding toward us with no headlight. As he closes in, he swerves into the lane we're standing beside and picks up speed. Both Anne and I take aim. Don Chambers kicks back into my knee, throws all his weight on Anne, and then quickly limps into the street. Before we can subdue him, the rider in black turns on an extremely bright headlight and opens fire with a submachine gun. Shielding Anne with my body, I tackle her out of the line of fire. One round hits me in the arm like a sledgehammer before I hit the dirt.

10

FALLEN ANGEL

September 10
2:35 A.M.

THERE'S NO PAIN. It just feels like the round slammed into a brick attached to my arm. *Thank you, Aegis armor.*

When I roll over, I see the rider. He's wearing a leathery black trench coat and black Deva helmet. On his back, a large riot shield. Anne and I return fire, but he disappears in a cloud of smoke before either of us lands a hit. Incoming rounds start ripping through the smoke, forcing us to scurry back behind the trees.

The gunfire ceases, and I hear Don shout over the motorcycle engine, "What took you so damn long, Fallen One!"

"Quit bitching, Savage," the Decider in black yells back. "Get your ass over here!"

The smoke clears and I see through the upside-down Chevy's windows that the rider is off his bike. Don staggers to his feet while holding the riot shield in front of him with his good arm. The Fallen One shields himself behind Don, aiming his P90 our way.

"Hold your fire!" Don commands.

"What the fuck for?" the Fallen One snaps.

"You'll want to know who that is before you kill 'em!"

"Tell me later! I don't want to piss around playing guessing games!"

"But it's him ... Dion Johnson."

"Johnson?" the Fallen One calls out. The way he says my name sounds oddly familiar, but I can't connect a face to the voice. He attaches his P90 to something on his back. "Hold your fire, neophyte!"

Neophyte? No one's called me that since the early days of the Angels of War Militia ...

The Fallen One removes his helmet and I'm in shock.

"Dion, who is he?" Anne whispers.

He's smirking at me through the riot shield. His greasy black hair is almost as long as Don's. The look on his face is twisted, warped in some way. "It's been a while, Johnson!"

I'm too stunned to respond.

"Not going to say hello to an old friend?"

"Stevenson ..." I manage, practically speechless.

Staring at him from behind this tree, I can't accept that it's him. Corporal Andras Stevenson was a Renegade, one of the original Angels of War militiamen. He trained me in hand-to-hand combat. He fought valiantly alongside us to end the Deciders right up until we thought he died during Operation Cage Breaker. His last words to us were, "Keep fighting the good fight ..." Then radio silence followed.

I mourned him. We all did. Then I read in Richard's journal that Stevenson was the prisoner who divulged the location of our Quantico base, exposing us to an attack that would've killed us all if Anne didn't warn me it was coming. I always imagined they killed him after they got what they needed, but, clearly, I was wrong ...

"Dion, who is he?" Anne asks again.

"That's Andras Stevenson," I say loud enough for him to hear. "He's a former Angel of War."

"Oh, I remember. He's the one who sold you out."

Stevenson dons his helmet. "Once an Angel of War, always an Angel of War."

"You lost the right to call yourself that—"

"What? No. I'm just an Angel that has fallen, that's all. I chose the path of freedom and promise like the angels who went into battle with Lucifer. I am the Fallen Angel!"

"Why did you sell us out?" I ask.

Stevenson laughs while mounting his bike then rolls back behind the overturned SUV. "Being strapped in a chair and tortured, staring death in the eye? It changes you, Johnson. It makes you do things you never thought you would."

"Your betrayal almost got Marshall killed!" I shout.

"People die all the time," Stevenson says.

My grip tightens on my rifle. How could he say that about his own best friend? "Why did you join them?" I press.

"It was self-preservation at first. But when they nursed me back to health and enlightened me on Veritas, I learned that I was fighting for the wrong side. During the Deciders' collapse, the Echelon asked me to join them. They offered me a place on the right side of history! And I accepted, not to escape death this time, but because I believed in their vision for a better future."

"You chose the wrong side, Stevenson!"

"Trust me, Johnson, if you knew what the Deciders have planned for this time around, you'd wish you were on the winning team too …"

I've heard all I needed to hear. Now I open fire. Bullets bombard the riot shield as Don slinks behind the SUV and a cloud of smoke quickly envelopes them.

The bike revs up. "By the way, Johnson," Stevenson calls out, "Jessica says hi! You two made a cute kid!"

Everything goes red. I fire a grenade from the M320. It hits the trucks and explodes, dissipating the smoke. Then I spray a hail of bullets their way. Anne joins in, but it's too late. The revving of his bike's engine grows farther and farther away. Still, I fire at the road ahead with no regard for what innocents I might hit with stray rounds. Even when it clicks empty, I continue squeezing the trigger.

Anne places a hand on my arm and lowers the weapon. "We'll get them next time," she says.

I stand there fuming until Steele pulls up behind us in the gun-mounted GMC. "What happened?" he asks through the open window. "Where's your prisoner?"

"I'll tell you when everyone's together," I say, yanking open the door. "I'm not in the mood to repeat this more than once."

We touch down in Fort Sanctum thirty minutes later. After escorting the blindfolded prisoners to the brig, I track down Abdul to drop off the Decider Gauntlets and other devices.

I explain to him what I know about the Gauntlet so far. "Learning how their equipment works and figuring a way to keep us off their radars is your top priority right now. Until then, they'll always have the drop on us."

Abdul nods. "I'll figure it out before your next deployment." He hands me a box. "These came for you and your team."

I open it. Inside are ID badges as well as our dog tags. The USAW badges are like Anne's—clear plastic cards with our photo on the left side and our information, clearance, and ranks to the right. Along the bottom is a magnetic stripe. On the backside, directly behind the photo, is an RFID chip. As for the dog tags, they're nothing special—just thick metal tags with our names, ranks, and codenames beside the old Angels of War insignia. Mine is engraved SGT. DION "ARCHANGEL" JOHNSON. I hang the badge and dog tags around my neck then head for the elevator.

Down in Throne, it takes almost an hour to debrief. Surprisingly, Walker doesn't scold us for failing to rescue the president. How could he? Not only were we late to the scene due to a leak, but between the stealth choppers and being pinged by Decider radar, we were outmatched right from the beginning. Other teams who were tasked with escorting the standing vice president, the speaker of the house, and the other presidential successors to Raven Rock failed to protect their wards as well.

"What are these assholes up to?" Walker grunts. "We need to find out why they didn't execute their targets on the scene."

"Maybe they want to stage another live execution," Anne says.

Walker nods. "Which means we may still have another opportunity to rescue them. The integrations will begin shortly. Hopefully, we'll get something out of the prisoners before it's too late. I'll keep you all posted. You're dismissed." He starts toward the door.

I stand up. "I want a crack at the prisoners, sir. Anne and I know the right questions to ask."

Walker stops but doesn't turn around. "Get some rest, Sergeant Johnson. Your team will be calling the bunks down the hall your home until this is all over. If my interrogation experts prove unsuccessful, I'll consider granting your request."

I nod. "Thank you, sir."

When the general exits, Steele punches the wall. "I can't believe Stevenson sold us out! Not only did he betray us, but now he's one of *them*?" Stevenson never got along with my friends and me, but he and Steele were pretty tight-knit.

"In war, people change sides faster than a quarter flipping in free-fall," Hall sighs. "Most times it's for money. But sometimes, soldiers realize they no longer believe in what they're fighting for. And when they find something that resonates better with them, they fight and bleed for it. Whether it's an ideal or a flag, they'll gravitate toward whatever it is they believe in."

"Humph," Anne says, turning to me. "That's why I did it. I changed sides because I found something better to believe in."

Jeremy snickers. "Well, in that case, we better hope that Dion doesn't change sides or the world is screwed!"

I rub my face. "All right, everyone, rest up. Who knows how long we'll get to sleep before more shit hits the fan …"

11
ANY MEANS NECESSARY

September 10
10:01 A.M.

After four measly hours of fitful "sleep"—which I spent a good chunk of waking up to check my Nexus for updates only to find an empty inbox—I can't wait any longer.

Anne's still conked out so I leave her a note, shower, suit up, and head out.

The brig is a one-story gray building with minimal windows just south of Central Command. It's a newer building but still somehow looks old as hell. Two Vanquisher soldiers stand guard outside with M4s. They both recognize me and throw some praise my way as they let me by.

There's barely any light in the lobby. It doesn't help that the floors are a charcoal concrete and the walls are the same color. The security desk is behind a pane of bulletproof glass. There are a few doors off to the left and right, presumably the surveillance room and an office or two. Across from the entrance is a thick red metal door with a security pad beside it. On both sides of it are tall bulletproof windows. I give the soldier behind the desk my badge and tell him why I'm here. He makes a quick call, then nods at me.

I swipe my ID card at the security pad and the red door swings open on its own. My Nexus vibrates. The message from Walker reads "BASEMENT LEVEL 1. RIGHT DOWN THE HALL. LAST DOOR ON THE LEFT." I pass several holding rooms on the way to the elevator bank. When the elevator finally arrives, it requires a keycard swipe before I can select the floor.

In the basement, I swipe again to access the hallway to the right of the elevator. On each side of the hall are black doors with small windows at head level. Prison cells. Or holding cells. I peer in one to see an empty white-walled room that's about four by seven feet and furnished with a bed, a toilet, and a sink. Far too accommodating for Deciders, if you ask me.

A few doors down there's a large room with a big Plexiglas window on each side of the door. It is a fairly large room set up like a doctor's office. Two men and a woman dressed in lab coats are hurrying back and forth. A black body bag lies on an unattended gurney with an arm hanging out of it, its limp hand missing all of its fingers...

What the hell happened?

After swiping to enter the room, I find Sung sitting off to the left where he's staring at monitors that are displaying someone's heart rate and galvanic skin response. Walker is staring through the large window ahead, presumably a two-way mirror. On the other side of the glass are SSgt. Hall and a tall bald dude with muscles straining against his black t-shirt and pants. Sitting in a metal chair before them, wrists cuffed to the table and ankles chained to hooks in the floor, is the prisoner I captured. *Jezebel.* The tan prison suit she's wearing is soaked and her wet, honey brown hair clings to her face and shoulders. Her bare feet are planted in a puddle that surrounds the chair and she's trembling like an abused dog.

Walker turns to me and nods. "Johnson." He turns back to the window.

Sung just throws up a finger.

"Morning, sir. Sung." I stand beside the general. "Any updates?"

"The Extractor was unable to get anything out of the Loyal before he … unexpectedly perished. And Hall failed to get this one to talk so now the Extractor's assisting."

"So your Extractor killed our best lead …" I grumble.

"Even the best can't get some people to talk …"

I stifle a laugh. "Well, what were you able to get out of her?"

Walker hands me a black folder. "Nothing. But we ran her face through facial recognition and managed to pull her records."

I skim the file. Isabella "Jezebel" Monroe was born twenty-two years ago in Austin, Texas, on November 30. At eighteen, she moved to California to attend California State University—San Bernardino. The following year she was arrested on several occasions during protests against government overreach, Wall Street, and Big Pharma and subsequently placed on the No-Fly List. And in the two years after the Annex, there's no record of her.

"Bite me, asshole!" Isabella shouts. I look up as she spits in Hall's face.

Hall wipes his cheek and stomps out of the room. He joins us in the viewing room a moment later. "I'm done, sir! We need to step things up."

General Walker touches the Bluetooth over his right ear. "Extractor, time to use the tools," he orders.

"Tools?" I ask.

"Since waterboarding didn't work, or leaving her wet in an air-conditioned room while blindfolded and listening to death metal all night, a more … physical approach must be taken."

The Extractor walks to the table against the wall. He picks up a rolled-up cloth and sets it down in front of Isabella. He slowly unwraps it to reveal a hammer and a pair of pliers.

The Extractor presses Isabella's right hand flat against the table. "Three options, Decider," he growls in a deep voice. "Option A: Answer my questions, truthfully. B: Don't, and I break a finger. C: Don't, and I sever a finger from your hand. You get three choices per digit on the first hand. On the second hand, you only get A. and C."

I turn to the general. "He's joking right?"

Walker shakes his head. "SECDEF authorized the use of extreme measures in order to find POTUS ... no matter how inhumane."

"Before you maim her, sir, let me see what I can do."

"If he fails, you can go in," he commands.

If he fails, she'll be fingerless ...

"Where's President Lewis?" the Extractor barks.

Isabella says nothing.

"Ten seconds. What's it gonna be?"

She sighs. "I chooooooose ... *Beeee, bitch!*"

The Executioner picks up a hammer. I vividly see myself separating General Hawthorne's thumb from his hand. It didn't bother me then, but after the war, my bad deeds haunted me. I can still hear the flesh squish and bone crunch. I picture it happening to her and it makes me nauseous. Now flashes of the torture I suffered at the hands of Tyrone and Rose begin. I look at my hands. I was lucky to leave with just cuts and bruises ...

I run to the door and burst into the interrogation room just as the Extractor is about to bring down the hammer.

"Stop!" I say. It's so cold in here, I can see my breath.

He freezes for a moment then ignores me, raising the hammer again.

I grab his wrist, redirecting the hammer at the last moment. It strikes the metal table with a painfully loud bang.

The Extractor rips his arm free. "The hell do you think you're doing?" he growls.

"Get out," I say. "I'm talking over."

"I don't care what kind of hero you think you are. I only take orders from the general."

"I won't condone this, so you don't have a choice," I snarl.

Walker slams open the door. "Both of you! In here! Now!"

The Extractor heads for the exit. I follow.

"I won't stand by and allow this kind of torture!" I shout when the door closes behind me. "We're not the Deciders!"

"I won't condone insubordination," Walker growls. There's a pause. "However," he says in a calmer tone, "Sung says that her micro-expressions suggest that your stunt may have purchased you some favor with her. I'll allow you fifteen minutes to make her talk. Should you fail, the Extractor will finish his job." He hands me a Bluetooth.

I remove my combat jacket and drape it over the empty chair beside Sung and then place the device over my ear. "Fine," I say.

I stand across the table from the exhausted girl. Her jaw's trembling and her lips are almost purple. The skin around her eyes is red and puffy. Despite how terrible she looks, she's still pretty as hell. Her skin's somewhat tanned—olive, almost like she's Greek or Italian. She has these alluring hazel eyes with flecks of green—obvious tools of seduction. She's definitely the kind of girl I would have pursued in a world before Anne. Not that she has anything on my fiancé, but she's a close second.

Those alluring eyes look me over. Her scowl dissipates and a faint smirk appears. "You're Dion Johnson."

"Oh, you know me?" I ask.

She rolls her eyes. "Duh ...You're kind of on the top of our kill list!"

"Surprising ..." I start pacing. "Isabella Monroe, right? Codename Jezebel?"

"Yeah! Wow, you must be psychic."

"If I was, I wouldn't need to ask you anything."

She narrows her eyes at me. "You're the one that pulled me back in through the window, weren't you? The one they called Archangel?"

"The one and only."

"You knew I was a grunt, right?"

"Yup."

She scowls. "Yet you still pulled me up?"

I nod.

"And now you come in here today and stop Big Ugly from breaking my fingers against your general's orders ..." she says, wiggling her index finger. "You either got a soft spot for lady soldiers or you're really good at setting up the good cop act. Which is it?"

"Neither."

"Well, your timing is a little convenient, no?"

"I just woke up and came straight here." I grab the chair from near the door, lift it to the table, and sit across from her. "During the War of Annex I tortured a founding member of the Deciders until he told me where I could find the Loyal who killed my best friends. I waterboarded him, burned him, beat him, and then cut his thumb off with a bolt cutter. Then I was captured and tortured for four days by Tyrone Jones and a girl named Rose ..."

She smiles. "Karma's a bitch."

I nod. "I swore off torture. And, even if I'm not the torturer, I'd rather not see you end up dead and fingerless like the Loyal in the other room."

She raises an eyebrow, smirks, and leans forward. "Got a soft spot for me?"

"Not really. Just trying to spare another human from suffering. My attempt at earning good karma after the fifty-plus lives I've taken ..."

She smirks. "So broken up about the men he's killed he has to keep a tally."

I slouch in my seat. "Look, I have less than fourteen minutes left, so here's how this is going to work. Cooperate before time's up and no harm will come to you from those men waiting outside. If you don't, I won't be able to save you again."

"As Deciders, we're all trained to withstand torture. And women have higher pain tolerances than men, you know."

"You say that until they start breaking bones and ripping off fingers ..."

Isabella purses her lips.

"Help me help you, okay?"

She looks away.

I sigh. "First question, the burgundy coat, what does it signify?"

She looks confused. "Not going to ask about the president?"

"I have to satisfy my curiosity first."

She sighs. "Alright. Burgundy means that I'm an Enforcer."

"Where does that rank on the Decider hierarchy?"

"We're the lowest rank."

"And the other ranks?"

"Loyals, and then the Elites."

"The Elites, are those the White Coats?"

"Yeah ..."

"Like Ghost and the guy that took Lewis?"

Her eye twitches when I say Ghost. She nods.

"Ghost, who is she?"

"Fuck if know."

"What about the male White Coat?"

She says nothing.

"Come on ... at least give me a codename."

"Dozer," Isabella whispers.

"Okay, good. Tell me about the Echelon."

She cocks an eyebrow. "Sorry, handsome. Never heard of 'em."

A lie. "Who's the Dominus? Who's leading the Deciders now?"

"I don't know a Dominus. And we self-govern."

More lies. "Where was President Lewis taken?"

"Here then there ..." she says playfully, looking left then right.

"The people the Deciders took ... some were soldiers. But the rest ... they weren't. They took friends of mine, civilians—girls your age who didn't even fight in that war. Tell me where they were taken ..."

She leans forward, getting as close to my face as she can. "Not going to wine and dine me before you try and get in my ... *mind?*"

I shake my head.

"You're going to have to give me something if you want my goods, hon."

I slam my fist on the table. "I am! I'm sparing you from the horror they'll put you through!"

She rolls her eyes. "You're only doing that to work me ... and I don't like being played."

"I'm not 'working' you. This is me genuinely trying to save your ass."

Isabella searches my eyes. "I don't believe you, Archangel."

"This is a waste of time!" Walker says in my earpiece. "Get in there."

The door bursts open. Isabella jumps as the Extractor, the general, and a short Asian woman in a lab coat and glasses enter the room. The Extractor has a silver case of some kind in his hand. The woman is wheeling in heart-monitoring equipment.

"That wasn't even ten minutes!" I protest. "Give me more time and I can get her to talk!"

Walker glares at me. "She's toying with you, Johnson. Since you don't want us to physically harm her, we've drudged up another option."

The woman starts hooking up Isabella to the monitoring equipment. Meanwhile, the Extractor opens a case and removes a syringe and a bottle with some reddish solution in it.

"What's that?" I ask.

"Mercy," the Extractor answers, sticking the syringe in the bottle and pulling back the plunger.

"Yay, drugs!" Isabella says.

I grab the empty glass bottle. The label reads CAPSAICIRESINIFERATOXIN. Parts of the compound I recognize from neurobiology class. Capsaicin is the compound in spicy peppers that makes your mouth burn. The other part of the word also sounds familiar. "What does this stuff do?"

"Ask Dr. Kitajima. She developed it," the Extractor mutters.

The Asian woman inserts the IV into Isabella's vein then gestures for me to follow her to the other side of the room. She extends a hand. "Dr. Yumi Kitajima," she whispers, smiling. "It's a pleasure to meet you, Sergeant Johnson! Huge fan!"

We shake. "Nice to meet you too. Tell me about this drug. I'm a scientist so don't give me the watered-down lesson."

She smiles. "All right. Well, it's a synthetic hybrid of the capsaicin and resiniferatoxin molecules that I developed for interrogations. It works by activating pain receptors all over the peripheral nervous system, binding to the TRPV1 receptors in neural cells after being readily absorbed from the bloodstream. Unlike with capsaicin, desensitization does not occur quickly. This causes lasting, gradual release of substance P, the pain neurotransmitter. The pain has been described as burning and or stinging that intensifies as it's absorbed. The pain does not subside until the neurons are desensitized or the antidote is administered."

"I see. And the side effects?"

"It's still in the testing phase so we don't know everything yet. But the side effects we do know include increased body temperature, tachycardia, and reddening of the eyes." Yumi fixes her purple-rimmed glasses. "So long as the correct dose is given, and the recipient doesn't have any major health issues, death should not be a concern."

I nod. "Thanks, doc."

"My pleasure, Sergeant Johnson!" she chirps.

I hurry back and grab the Extractor's arm just as he's about to inject Mercy into the small IV bag. "Wait!"

He and the general glare at me.

I look at Isabella. "This drug isn't a truth serum that will make you loopy. Mercy will make you suffer. Dearly. Last chance to cooperate …"

Isabella sighs. "I appreciate the sentiment, but I think I'll take this ride."

I turn to the general. "Are there no other options, sir?"

He looks at me for a long second. "Don't you want to find out where they took your people?"

What Don said last night echoes in my mind: *Just wait till you learn what we're doing to your friends!*

I nod.

The Extractor smiles darkly and injects Mercy into the IV drip chamber. "Let's give it a few minutes," he says, then follows Walker out the door.

"It's not too late to tell me what we want to know, Isabella," I say. "The doc says there's an antidote."

She says nothing.

"Fine. I tried helping you. What follows, that's on you."

Anne enters the viewing room at the same time as I do. While we wait, I catch her up. Three minutes pass. And when we see on the monitors that Isabella's vitals show signs of distress, Walker tells me to go in.

"Why him?" the Extractor asks.

"Because Johnson knows how to get her to talk," Walker grumbles. "If she won't tell us what we need you can increase the dose."

The Extractor and I head back in. I sit across from Isabella, whose teeth are clenched. Her face is perspiring and her arms are trembling slightly.

I lean in close. "I can make it stop if you answer my questions."

Isabella gulps hard and looks up at me, her whole body shuddering like she just took a dip in a frozen lake. It must be Mercy related since the heat is on now. The look in her eyes screams pain, anger, and disgust. "I'm not saying *shit!*" she spits.

"What's it feel like?"

Her eyes shut and she grimaces. "Like there's glass flowing through my veins. Like I'm being bathed in acid!!" She lets out a howl of agony.

"It only gets worse from here. Just talk to me!"

Isabella slams her fists on the table and shrieks. She's turning red and sweating profusely. Suddenly, she starts sobbing. I place the back of my hand on her forehead. Her skin is hot to the touch.

"Where did Dozer and Ghost take the president?" I ask.

Eyes still shut, Isabella shakes her head. The Extractor gives the IV bag a squeeze.

"Who is Ghost?"

"I don't know!" she cries.

"Who are the Echelon?"

"They're the commander class of the White Coats running the show! Enforcers don't interact with them under normal circumstances!" she snarls, saliva spraying out of her mouth. "I don't know anything more!"

"Who's the leader of the Deciders?" I shout.

Her bloodshot eyes bulge and tears stream down her beet-red cheeks. "I don't know his real name! I swear!"

"The civilians and Angels of War the Deciders captured, where are they?"

There's a click in my earpiece. "Stay on target," Walker commands. "Ask about POTUS!"

Isabella rhythmically slams both fists against the table, doubling over with each blow. Her heart rate's way up now. She's so drenched in sweat that it looks like someone just hosed her down. "I don't know! I wasn't a part of that op!"

"Where did Dozer and Ghost take President Lewis?"

Isabella screams like a banshee.

"I'm upping the dose!" the Extractor announces. He produces another syringe and sticks it directly into the IV line.

Isabella opens her bloodshot eyes and looks back. "*No! Don't!*" she yells.

"Stop!" I shout. "She'll talk!"

The Extractor proceeds anyway.

By the time I lunge across the table and remove the syringe from the IV line, he's already pushed the plunger partway down. I shove him hard, sending him stumbling over the monitoring equipment and crashing to the floor.

"What the hell are you doing, Johnson!" Walker shouts in my earpiece.

I rifle through the case and retrieve the Anti-Mercy. "Isabella, tell me where the president is and I'll administer the antidote!"

The Extractor charges at me.

Isabella lets out another ear-piercing banshee shriek. "*Richmond! Richmond, Virginia!*"

The Extractor freezes, his cocked fist suspended beside his ear.

"Where in Richmond?" I ask.

Her body trembles violently and she screams, clawing at the table, legs kicking like a child throwing a tantrum. "In the ruins downtown! Off of James River on Byrd Street! There's a factory! No windows! That's where Dozer and Hellcat took him!"

Hellcat? I look at the two-way mirror.

General Walker radios in moments later. "We got it, Archangel! There's a warehouse matching that description off of East Byrd Street in Richmond. A Griffin drone is being deployed as we speak."

The Extractor heads for the door.

I rush around the table, puncture the IV line, and administer the antidote. "Thank you, Isabella."

"*Fuck you!*" she shrieks at me. "*Fuck all of you!*"

"If you'd cooperated, you wouldn't have had to go through this!"

She screams and cries, sobbing like a hopeless victim from *Saw* who realizes they can't escape the trap.

I lean in close. "Listen, the pain will diminish, okay? But until then, I need you to answer a few more questions. Who's Hellcat?"

Isabella whimpers, then feebly wipes the torrent of snot streaming from her nose. "She's my commanding Loyal! She works directly under Dozer!"

"Will Savage or the Fallen Angel be at the factory where they're holding Lewis?"

Her head starts shaking side to side.

Is that a no?

Then, as if she was shot in the head, her body falls limp. *Is she dead?* I eye the heart monitor. There's still a pulse.

I touch my earpiece. "We need a medic in here! ASAP!"

Isabella jerks to life and her body begins convulsing. Sung storms into the room. The three medics rush in behind him. He uncuffs her and the medics immediately get to work trying to stabilize her. There's nothing I can do, so I leave.

"Good work, Archangel," Walker says when I return to the viewing room. "Perhaps I should have let you interrogate the Loyal after all."

"Perhaps," I mumble as doctors haul Isabella out on a gurney. "Make sure she doesn't die like the last one. She knows more than I got out of her."

"Medical will ensure the prisoner survives," Walker grumbles.

"Did the drone find anything yet?"

"It's still in transit. Should arrive shortly." He clears his throat. "You two head back to Throne and ready up. There's a USAW safe house in the area. Since there appears to be a leak, I'll need your team on standby there for a quick reaction force when we receive confirmation."

Anne and I nod before exiting.

"Interesting interrogation method ..." Anne says when we enter the elevator. "What's it called? The chivalrous cop?"

I arch my eyebrows. "You're not jealous, are you?"

She laughs. "Well, she is pretty. And you do have a thing for Decider girls ..." she purrs, searching my face.

"I have a thing for *you*." I wrap my arm around her and plant a kiss on her cheek.

She kisses me back. "If I had any doubt, I would go back in there and carve her up like a Sunday goose. Maybe I will anyway, as a precautionary measure."

"How about you save your bloodlust for the Deciders in Richmond? Something tells me we'll need it."

12
HORNET'S NEST

September 10
1:41 P.M.

RICHMOND, LIKE MOST metropolises today, is more ruins than city. Though its downtown suffered the most damage, it was one of the first areas to receive an overhaul. Our safe house is right in the middle of all that reconstruction.

It's almost two by the time the Seraphs and I pull into the parking garage of a brown brick apartment building at the corner of Virginia Street and East Cary Street. It's run-down, but it appears to be one of the few buildings in the area that survived the war. When we enter the stairwell, we see the trash and graffiti left behind by squatters and vandals.

Our "field command center" for Operation Hornet's Nest isn't much, just a couple of computers set up on a kitchen table and a TV in the living room of an apartment that faintly reeks of rotting food. The walls are busted and the floor is grimy. The fanciest thing about this place is the steel door and the security system. Couldn't expect too much from a safe house set up in two hours.

Jeremy parks himself on the couch. Hall and Steele sit before the computers and pull up the drone surveillance along with a video chat session with Walker.

"Titan-1," the drone operator, Corporal Carlos Salazar, announces to my squad over the comm. "The Terah drone is in position."

"Copy that," I respond.

Rather than waiting for Hall and Steele to access the drone's feed on their computers, I sit by the window and pull it up on the Gauntlet strapped to my right wrist. Even after working all night and all morning, Abdul wasn't able to retrieve any data from it or access Providence, the operating system for the Deciders' network. He was, however, able to overwrite the system and apply the Nexus OS to it. It functions the same as the watch still strapped on my left arm but it has more capabilities, such as a touchscreen keypad to send messages and the ability to control smaller drones like our field operatives can with their Nexus tactical tablets. That doesn't include the drone currently flying over the target, though.

I tap the option for surveillance and select TERAH DRONE. The PR-1 Terah drone, also called the T-Ray, is a stingray-shaped stealth surveillance drone with the capability to "see through walls." Using a high-powered terahertz scanner, it beams submillimeter electromagnetic waves at a structure and analyzes how the terahertz waves interact with solid objects within the structure and converts that data to video. It also has a standard camera as well as a thermal mode. And as with the other drones connected to the Nexus system, the locations of all the potential targets it gathers are displayed on the Nexus map.

The target building, codenamed Hornet's Nest, is a windowless three-story factory with concrete walls and a light brown roof. It sits on a strip of land that juts out into the water between the James River and the Richmond City Canal. A wall of trees borders each side of the peninsula. There's a cargo entrance on the north side of the building. A few dozen yards north of that is a smaller, secondary building with an even larger cargo door. There are four entrances on the ground floor and one more on the roof. A 500-yard stretch of pavement extends from the building to the park at the point that looks like a prime location for a helicopter to land.

From the outside, it appears abandoned. But the Terah drone's terahertz scanner confirms that it's inhabited. The hazy, light-blue bodies almost look like ghosts, ghosts made of static. A few of the figures on the first floor are sitting down in front of what appears to be a panel of security screens. Those on the second floor and the one above are more active. From the looks of it, everyone on the third floor and some of those near the exits are toting rifles. Isabella's intel was good after all, though, for her sake, she should have cooperated earlier. The last I heard, she was in a coma. I just hope she's not a vegetable now ...

"Looks like they're busy in there," Anne says as I walk back over.

Hall leans toward his monitor. "I count roughly two dozen people inside."

"It doesn't look like any of them are chained up," I say.

"They could've moved him," Steele says.

"Or maybe they already executed him," Ken chimes in.

Anne shakes her head. "Unless they recorded the execution to air at a later time, chances are he is still alive."

I nod. "We need to check it out."

Steele points at the monitor showing video from the MQ-11 Griffin drone—an advanced and more heavily armed variant of the Predator. "There are surveillance cameras on the building. If we can tap into that feed, we might be able to look at who's inside."

"Can we do that without being detected?" I ask.

The new guy, a scruffy, muscular soldier named Sergeant Gabriel "Blackjack" Perez, shrugs. "We'll have to plant the bug directly on the camera in order to hijack their CCTV footage. Who knows what other kinds of security measures are in place? Not to mention it's broad daylight …" Perez was flown in last night from another Special Forces unit called the Reapers to be Hillman's replacement. He came with Finley's personal recommendation so I allowed him on the team.

I sigh. "Which means we'll need to be ready for immediate resistance." I think for a moment. "Let's bring the drone in closer to do a more detailed scan of the target. I don't want to miss anything."

Corporal Salazar drops the drone to eight thousand feet and flies a few tight loops above the building. Even with the enhanced detail, we can't make out any prisoners nor can we pinpoint any early warning devices around the perimeter.

"Screw it," I grumble. "Let's move."

The target location is a half-mile from our safe house, though we can't risk a straight approach. Instead my team—Jeremy, Ken, Anne, and I—drives Hall and Titan-1 Bravo to a parking lot on Dock Street, the road that runs along the Richmond City Canal. Hall leads Perez, Steele, and Manny underneath the train tracks and into the green, murky canal, which they swim across to the wall of trees ringing the factory's peninsula. My team heads back down Dock St. to a parking lot on South 14th. Abby's pulled over on the side of the Richmond Turnpike overpass where she has a direct line of sight on the Hornet's Nest.

During the wait, I watch the Terah drone footage of the building on my Gauntlet. As Titan-1 Bravo advances along the tree wall, things inside carry on as they did earlier. Perez emerges from the trees first. Keeping low, he darts across the train tracks and dives into a prone position at the next tree cluster. From there, he crawls forward through the tall grass and shrubbery toward the smaller building where the nearest camera lies. That's when the ghostly images inside the Nest start moving erratically.

"Shit, I think they've been detected!" I say.

Anne starts the engine, shifts into drive, and screeches off.

I tap my watch. "Blackjack, hold your position! I think you've been spotted!" I say as Anne drifts around the turn.

"Shit! How?"

"I've got movement on the roof," Abby announces.

"Red Death, you're clear to engage!" I say. "No one leaves the facility!" I tap the watch to contact HQ. "General! Activate local USAW troops and police. Lockdown Richmond!"

"Copy that, Archangel," Walker responds.

There's a crackle of gunfire as Anne speeds toward the factory. On the Gauntlet's map, I see that a fireteam of Deciders has emerged from the Hornet's Nest and engaged Titan-1 Bravo.

"Taking fire!" SSgt. Hall announces.

Anne crashes through the gate and drifts sideways into a full stop, blocking off the road. Ken parks the second vehicle in line with ours. As I open the passenger door, I spot a figure dressed in civilian clothes on the roof with a sniper rifle. Before he takes aim, he stiffens and then topples over the retaining wall and hits the pavement below with a thud that sends splashes of gore in all directions.

A door ahead bursts open and two men wearing gray tactical jackets emerge, firing in our direction. Anne and I engage. One drops immediately and the other ducks back inside. As I lay down suppressive fire, I see on the Gauntlet that two more targets are coming around the corner.

"Contacts left!" I announce. The instant the flankers appear, I drop them. When you know they're coming, it's almost too easy.

Two more targets approach from the left. I signal Ken and Jeremy to breach the door ahead while Anne and I take the one around the corner.

Abby's Barrett .50 cal booms every few seconds. The good thing about assaulting a building with no windows is that the only points of contact are the roof and ground-level exits. And with her covering the roof, we're free to focus on immediate threats.

At the corner, some suppressive fire and a well-placed grenade eliminates the threats. Per the Gauntlet, the immediate area is clear, and the nearest four targets are in the cargo area to the left or on the other side of the building engaging Hall's team. I still proceed with caution, however. I'd rather trust my training and instincts than rely on technology ...

Things are clear all the way to the cargo bay. The instant Anne and I hit the entrance, shots start coming. They know where we are just like we know where they are. Then a grenade hits the ground in front of us. We duck around the corner just as it blows, and I lob a grenade of my own. When it booms, Anne goes high around the corner and fires in bursts. I charge from cover, running and gunning before sliding to safety behind a Jeep.

"All the computers on the first floor just exploded!" Ken reports. "They're covering their tracks."

The cargo bay door rises, revealing crates, armored trucks, and two men on motorcycles with riot shields on their backs and duffle bags over their shoulders. One is dressed in a long-sleeve gray shirt and a gray Deva helmet. The other one, in a black leather jacket, is donning his helmet.

I dart out from cover and drop two burgundy-clad Enforcers before they can climb into their truck. "Stevenson!" I shout, firing at the bikers. The gray rider, most likely Chambers, speeds outside, firing at Hall's team. As Stevenson revs off behind him, he gives me the finger.

Anne and I charge after them, firing. Other than what hits their shields, no shots land. The bikers blow right past Titan-1 Bravo, spraying at them with a barrage of SMG rounds as they do. The targets ride onto the train tracks and quickly disappear from view. Behind us, explosions start going off as vehicles and crates erupt into fireballs.

"I need drones tailing those bikes, now!" I bark over the comm as Anne and I jog around the building.

"Both drones are in pursuit," Salazar announces.

"Good. Titan-1 Alpha, we're going after them. Bravo, sweep the building for intel and confirm that POTUS isn't hidden below ground. Be careful."

"Copy that, Archangel," Hall responds.

I pull up the Terah's footage. Stevenson and the presumed Chambers head southeast down the tracks and cross the canal into the park. Once they hit Dock Street, they split up.

Shit!

My team reaches the GMC at the same time. Jeremy and Ken hop in the back. Anne gets behind the wheel and I ride shotgun, directing her to head northwest after Stevenson. When we turn onto the busy main road, I'm reminded that we're not in a warzone—we're in an American city during "peacetime." When those bullets start flying, and when things start blowing up, it's easy to forget that the whole world isn't at war.

Yet.

By the time we reach downtown, USAW helicopters are rumbling all over Richmond. Two lights later, we're told that the Griffin drone lost the gray rider. Stevenson drives into a parking garage for the convention center and we lose his visual. I switch the Gauntlet to the Terah drone's "X-ray" feed but there are dozens of signatures inside.

"Of all the days," Anne frets.

I tap my comm. "There's a goddamn convention or something going on here, General. We need more manpower here, now."

Sirens blare in the distance.

"Richmond PD has been briefed on the target and nearby units are moving to your position," Walker responds. "USAW and Titan-1 Bravo are en route as well. A field team is taking over the sweep of the Hornet's Nest."

"ETA two minutes, Archangel," Hall says.

Abby buzzes in next. "I'm southeast of your position, guarding the East Marshall street entrance."

Anne uses the GMC to block off the ramp on North 5th Street that comes down from the parking lot's third floor. Richmond PD pulls up behind us to cordon off the entrance that Stevenson drove into. Two Blackhawks descend on the area and hover around the surrounding streets and roof. People in the vicinity start running. Some trot backward while recording the scene with cellphones.

Guns in the low ready, we jog up the parking ramp as troops from the Blackhawk rappel down to the roof. Halfway up, there are two explosions, one to the north and another south of us. Gunshots follow. A report of multiple armed shooters firing on police and soldiers comes in.

"They're trying to split our attention so Stevenson can escape!" I say.

"He'll probably use the bridge to the convention center to insert himself into the crowd," Anne says. She updates all units and commands them to cover the convention center exits.

My team runs through the third level and heads for the nearest bridge, the one that crosses over Fifth, leaving Bravo and Abby to take the one that crosses over East Marshall. Keeping a tight group, we cross the bridge and enter Exhibit Hall A. There are multiple stairwells, escalators, and elevators, as well as two more bridges that cross into the Grand Ballroom building. Way too much ground to cover, which makes sticking together impossible. I signal Jeremy and Ken to head right then Anne and I go left.

Stevenson will probably take the most complex route with the most crowd cover that also gets him farthest from where our forces are concentrated, and the way I chose fits the criteria best. We scan the crowd as we jog down the hall toward the next skyway.

"You take this skywalk, I'll take the other!" Anne says. "We'll link up on the other side."

"We're not splitting up!" I shout.

"No time to argue, love. Just go!" She runs off.

It takes three seconds for me to decide not to chase her and sprint across the bridge. "Move! Move! Move!" I bark as I weave through the crowd. As they part, I spot someone at the other end wearing with a black leather jacket with a duffle bag slung over his shoulder. As if he feels my gaze, he turns and stares right at me.

I take aim. "Stevenson! Freeze!" A futile threat since I don't have a clear shot.

Grinning, Stevenson draws a suppressed pistol and sends four rounds my way. People scream and scatter or drop to the floor. Nothing hits me, but a woman in front of me hits the ground with a chest wound.

"Put pressure on that! Help will be here soon!" I shout as I chase after Stevenson.

He cuts left down the next hall. I take aim at the windows of the next building and fire a burst right before Stevenson disappears from view. Keeping my head low, I sprint across the rest of the bridge. When I hit the corner, I press my back against the wall and peek out. Stevenson's in the open now, holding a teenage girl hostage. He has one arm wrapped around her with his pistol's muzzle pressed under her chin and a P90 aimed over her shoulder at me.

"I don't want to kill her, but I will if you don't let me walk through those doors, Johnson," Stevenson says, nodding toward the stairwell behind him.

"This building is surrounded. The city is locked down. You won't make it out. You know that, right?"

"Oh, I will." He grins, slowly dragging the girl toward the door.

"Target's in sight," Anne whispers over the comm.

"Hold your fire," I whisper back. To Stevenson, I say, "If you tell me where my kid and the others are, I'll have those people outside stand down and you can stroll right out of here."

His smile widens. "Since we're old friends, I'll tell you that they're in a place called Naraka. That's where POTUS is too. Find it, you find them!"

"Give me more, Stevenson!"

He backs into the door and opens it with a mule kick. "I'll tell you this. You're fighting for the wrong team, neophyte. The leak that revealed the locations of Jess and your friends, where do you think it came from? Someone high up in the Angels of War leaked that data to our spies so we could draw you out of hiding. And the people who are '*on your side*'? They had intel ahead of time suggesting we were coming for your friends and family, but they didn't say shit because they wanted to use you to lure *us* out."

"You're lying!" I snarl.

He snickers. "Am I? Look into something called 'Anglerfish.' You'll see who your real friends are." He slinks into the stairwell with the girl and the door closes.

"Dion! He's getting away!" Anne shouts. Her voice sounds a million miles away.

Anne punches me in the gut. "Dion! Move your ass!"

I snap back to reality and follow her into the stairwell. Halfway down, a blinking device on the wall brings us to an abrupt stop. Stevenson's hostage stands stiff as a statue on the landing, back pressed against the wall. Past her, next the door, is another device.

"Don't come any closer!" she shrieks. "He said they'd blow up if I moved!"

"Stay perfectly still," Anne says. "Someone will be here shortly to disarm them." She nods for us to head back upstairs.

I follow her without a second thought. I feel awful abandoning the girl, but there's nothing we can do for her. The only thing that matters is apprehending Fallen Angel. Unfortunately, by the time we return to the second floor, word comes in that the Deciders have ceased their attack and withdrawn from the area. And that only means one thing—Stevenson got away ...

After the Deciders' trail goes cold, HQ sends a pair of helicopters to airlift us back to Fort Sanctum. The whole ride back, I'm quiet. I don't care that we didn't accomplish our mission. I don't even care that we weren't able to get intel on the others' whereabouts. All I can think about is whether USAW is compromised and whether it's safe for us to be there. I wonder who I can trust. I debate sending Anne and the others to our safe house so I can finish the rescue campaign on my own. Of course, they'd never go for that, so I'll have to do the next best thing.

After debriefing, I take Anne outside to tell her what Stevenson said.

"I've never heard of anything called Anglerfish," Anne says. "But considering who I shack up with, they would never have told me about it."

"Do you think it's possible that what he said was true?"

"Chances are he made it up to distract you. Not the bit about the spies, though. But to be honest, I wouldn't be surprised if Command was trying to lure out whoever is hunting us."

I rub my face. "Do you think we can investigate this Anglerfish without raising flags?"

She shakes her head. "Doubt it. Not if it's real."

I think about it. "Can we enlist Abdul?"

She nods. "I trust him."

13

TURNCOAT

September 15
3:52 P.M.

IN THE FIVE days since Operation Hornet's Nest, the Deciders haven't made so much as a peep. And the only thing we were able to dig up on Naraka is that it's the Sanskrit word for a Hindu version of hell. Abdul hasn't been able to uncover anything on Anglerfish since he's been swamped with tasks under the watchful eye of General Walker.

To keep myself busy, I've been spending my time training with the Seraphs in the mornings and helping Anne sift through and analyze data for a couple hours in the afternoons. Today, I've spent more time watching the news than doing any actual work. This past Monday, the focus of the news reports shifted from the abductions of the heads of state and the Deciders' attacks in Virginia to the growing military escalation between the megapowers of the world after the Russians claimed that an attack on the Kremlin was carried out by U.S. troops masquerading as Deciders. Since that day, UFR bombers and spy planes have breached U.S. airspace on multiple occasions. On Tuesday, Zhao blockaded the key shipping routes through the South China Sea and the Strait of Malacca. They've taken similar action against the Ummah Wāhidah while the Russians have cut off their oil pipeline to the UNE. The acting U.S.

president, Secretary of Defense Arnold Choler, is threating to strike down any and all aircraft that breach our airspace and send three carrier strike groups to breach the Chinese blockades.

Just as news anchor Trish Childers begins speculating that "we are one incident away from World War IV," my Gauntlet goes off. So does Anne's Nexus watch. It's a video call from Sung. I tap the screen to answer then hold the device between Anne and me.

"Guess who just woke up from their coma?" he asks.

"About damn time."

"Yup. She came to fifteen minutes ago."

"Is she coherent?" I ask.

"Yeah, and the docs are saying that she wants to speak with you and you alone. She also requested no cameras or listening devices."

I look at Anne. "Strange."

"Indeed," she says.

"Where is she?" I ask.

"First floor of the brig, Room 106," Sung replies. "Oxytocin was pumped in through her oxygen mask before it was removed, as per your request."

Oxytocin is the trust hormone. It's produced during sex and when people bond socially or cuddle. Hopefully dosing her with it will provoke her to trust me more.

"Alright, I'll head over now." I end the call.

"I'll be right outside the door the entire time, Anne says. "Keep a secure channel open to me. If she says or does anything that I don't like, I'll end her." She smiles darkly.

"Oh, I know you will, babe. But try not to until she talks, okay?"

"I shall try."

The first-floor medical facility in the brig looks more like a prison than a hospital. When I reach Room 106, I signal for the two soldiers guarding to door to leave. Anne parks herself in a chair near the door while I peer through the window. Isabella is lying on the bed, her wrists cuffed to sturdy metal bed rails and her ankles chained to bars at the base of the bed. There's an IV in her left arm and she's rubbing her temples with her thumb and middle finger as her hand covers her eyes.

Holding the food tray with one hand, I swipe my badge and push down on the handle. Isabella jumps and glares in my direction when the door opens. Her apprehension turns into bitter relief when she sees it's me.

"Archangel ..." she says bitterly.

"How are you feeling, Isabella?" I ask.

She sighs. "Like I've been hungover for a week ..."

I notice how weary and pale she is, and how chapped her lips are. "I brought some food, if you're able to eat," I say, setting the covered tray beside her.

She purses her lips.

I pour water into the plastic cup on the table next to her and put it to her mouth. She eyes me unsurely, but eventually she drinks. "So, apparently, you'll only talk to me, huh?" I set the cup down. "Why's that?"

She rolls her eyes. "You want me to make a speech about how great you are? Fuck that."

I nod. "Fair enough. So, what now? You want a deal in exchange for your cooperation?"

"Who said I was cooperating?" She smiles mischievously.

"If you don't, they'll kick me out and send your bald friend down here to make you."

"And if I do?"

"If you do, maybe I can help improve your situation." I give her more water.

She drains the cup in three loud gulps, water running down the sides of her mouth. "I doubt there's much I can tell you that will help, hon."

I pour another glass. "Talk and we'll see what your intel is worth."

"How much was that last bit of intel your people tortured out of me worth? Did you save the president?"

I shake my head. "They moved him before we stormed the place."

"See? Enforcers don't know shit."

"Then point me in the direction of a Loyal or Elite."

She smirks. "How about this … Let me get to know *Dion Johnson* and I'll decide if I think you're a person worth helping."

I lift the lone chair over to her bed. "Fair enough. Ask me anything."

Isabella shakes her hand, rattling the chains. "Mind uncuffing me so I can eat?"

I unshackle her left wrist.

Isabella sits upright and uncovers the mixed veggies and potatoes. She sniffs it before shoveling some into her mouth. "The Deciders painted a very negative picture of you," she says, spraying bits of food from her mouth. "I mean, I get why. You murdered the Architect and brought down the first regime, after all."

"And you want to know if I'm the same guy you heard about?"

"Mhmm. They made you out to be some Hitler-type who'd stop at nothing to exterminate all Deciders in order to keep mankind in shackles. But if that were true, you wouldn't have done for me what you did. Why don't you give me your side of the story?"

I smirk. "What, didn't you read my book?"

"It was contraband where I was." She smiles.

"And where was that?"

"Tell me your story first. Why'd you fight in the Annex?"

I start by telling her how Hope died from a Decider bullet during our journey to Virginia—my call to arms. Then, I briefly highlight our early missions, my quest for revenge, what happened with Anne and how it led to Operation Deicide, the mission I led that resulted in Richard's death.

"So it's because of the Ice Queen that the Deciders fell?" she asks as she pops the floret of limp broccoli into her mouth.

I nod.

"And you're engaged to her even after she murdered your best friends?"

"Yes, I am."

"Ha! Well, you two definitely have Romeo and Juliet beat."

I smirk. "Anyway, things changed for me after I killed Richard Thomas." I lean in close. "Before Richard took his last breath, he and I had a heart to heart. He revealed how things were supposed to end after Purge. He admitted that he got carried away with power and strayed from his path. Then he gave me access to his funds, the full Veritas, and everything I'd need to restore the world the way his brother wanted. When the Deciders fell, I met with the president. Odom admitted that Veritas was true, so I made him relinquish his presidency to Ron Pell—the only politician Richard trusted."

"That's a little hard to believe ..." Isabella says.

"It's true. After reading Veritas, I started asking myself whether killing Richard and bringing down the Deciders was the right move." I lean back and return to my normal speaking volume. "When I learned Richard's endgame for the world, I knew I did the right thing. And I made sure that Pell kept his promise to prevent the government from reverting into what it had been."

She scowls. "So you believed in what the Deciders did, then?"

"I believe in what Richard and Ryan wanted to achieve, yeah. But I don't support how they went about it. I don't agree with all the killing they did ..."

"Maybe you're not the man I thought you were ..." She smirks. "Or maybe you're a hell of a storyteller."

"You just didn't hear the truth from your masters."

She looks away.

"Well, you heard my story, Isabella. What's yours?"

She eyes me. "Where should I start?"

"Go as far back as you need to so I can paint a picture of why you joined the Deciders."

"Fine, you asked for it."

The story she tells is a sad one. Her father, a Navy veteran, died of cancer when she was thirteen. Because of budget cuts and complications with his insurance, his military pension wasn't enough to cover the treatments he needed. "There was nothing they could do for him by the time it was sorted out." His death changed her. It made her bitter. She blamed his cancer on chemicals he'd been exposed to during the Gulf War and the shit they put in the food. She blamed it all on the government.

And then her family lost their home during the recession, forcing them to move to a crappy apartment in Austin. Once a popular cheerleader with excellent grades, she fell in with a group of stoners at her new school and her resentment of society took root. Despite her reluctance to take on debt just to become a part of the "bullshit job paradigm," she applied for loans anyway, along with grants and scholarships, and got into California State University, San Bernardino with a Pell Grant.

"I wanted to go to LA to pursue a career in dance and modeling. But those were long shots, and I figured getting an education as a backup was still better than working in an Amazon warehouse for the rest of my life, you know?"

"I hear that ..."

"But it wasn't all about the education. I wanted to party. I wanted to 'find myself.'" She makes a single air quote with her one free hand. "I wanted to meet like-minded people. And I did. Early sophomore year, I met a group of activists. We protested rising tuitions, the kleptocracy, GMOs, unsustainable fishing practices, police brutality, you name it. But, even with a grant, my loans didn't cover all my costs. Like, it was so bad I didn't eat some days, even with a part-time job. And my mom couldn't help me—her stoner, psych major daughter—because she was already paying for my sister's education and her apartment. So, I started stripping ..."

"Oh ..." I say, fighting an urge to imagine her on stage.

"Yeaaah. It was a recommendation from a girl in my modern dance class. I didn't last too long, though. The clubs in San Bernardino are pretty rough, and the guys got too handsy for me ... But since I got off on teasing and pleasing guys, I decided to be a camgirl. Solo stuff, if you know what I mean ..."

If I weren't brown-skinned, she'd see me blushing. "You did what you had to," is the only thing I can think to say.

She smirks. "But you'd rather hear about my activism, right? All of our protests were peaceful, yet the police always found a reason to pepper spray us or arrest someone. The first time I got arrested was because I wasn't exercising my rights in a 'Freedom of Speech zone' or some bullshit. The second time was because I filmed a cop roughing up a peaceful protester during an arrest and I wouldn't give up my phone." She sighs. "So when I ended up in a reeducation camp during the Annex, it didn't take many Veritas classes to convince me to join the Deciders."

"Shit, I don't blame you," I say, shaking my head.

"Then you also don't blame ninety percent of the Deciders who joined since the Annex. They all joined for the same reasons I did. They're not bad people."

"But these Deciders aren't the same as the ones that recruited you."

She snorts. "Why, because your buddy Richard Thomas isn't leading us?"

"No, because whoever's leading you is betraying what the original Deciders wanted to achieve."

She doesn't respond.

"Tell me something. The Deciders are responsible for the cyberattacks and drones causing turmoil with Russia and China, aren't they?"

She looks me in the eye. "What if we are?"

"Think about it. Why cause conflict after world peace has been attained? Why destroy society again now that government and banking corruption has been eradicated?"

She stares blankly at me.

"Because the only thing the Dominus and the new regime wants is control. Things are better now than they have ever been."

Isabella shakes her head. "Russia, China, the Ummah Wāhidah ... they're already backsliding. America too. It's only a matter of time until they become the corrupt, warring enslavers they were before. A one-world government under the Deciders rule is the only way to end the cycle."

"Imagine a world where a man who's willing to capture another man's family and friends to exact revenge rules everything."

She looks skeptical. "What are you talking about?"

I pull out my phone and show her a photo of Jessica, our son, and me. "The Deciders kidnapped my son and his mother." I swipe to the photo of the Deciders holding them hostage in a van. "She never fought in the war. Yet, they murdered her whole family and her dog, and took her and my son to get back at me."

"Wait, I thought you were with Anne."

"Jessica—the girl in the photos—and I were together before I met Anne."

"And this is supposed to trigger my latent maternal instincts and convince me to spill my guts?"

"It's to let you know what kind of people you were fighting for."

She looks down at her right hand, still manacled to the bed.

"Listen, as nice as it's been chatting with you, it's time to help me out," I say. "Tell me where the Deciders took them and I swear I'll set you free."

She smiles. "I believe you would. But honestly, I don't know where they were taken, Dion. I wasn't a part of that operation."

"Stevenson—the Decider in black called Fallen Angel—said they were in Naraka."

"Ugh, Stevenson ..." Isabella says, rolling her eyes.

"You know where it is?"

"I've heard of it. It's a prison for POWs and turncoats—our slang for Decider traitors. I don't know where it is."

"Give me the location of a Decider base or something then."

She shakes her head. "My unit was mobile. All the Hives I've been to have been abandoned and wiped clean by now."

"So what can you tell me?"

Isabella smiles as she sits up. "How about you just uncuff me and let me give you the best lap dance you've ever had? It's the least I could do."

"No thanks."

She runs her hand across her chest. "You sure?"

"Positive. I just want answers."

Sighing, she lies back. "Fine. I'll tell you what I can, but I want a guarantee that I won't ever end up in some black site or back in that dungeon."

"I swear on my life," I say.

She takes a deep breath. "Alright," she sighs. "So the Deciders are behind the rising international conflict. I don't know what the endgame is, though."

I twirl my hand, beckoning her to continue. "Give me something better than that."

She screws up her mouth and makes a face. "This may or may not be a shocker, but there are at least two Decider spies operating in Fort Sanctum. Most likely Loyals. I only know them by their codenames, Corax and Corvus."

So Stevenson wasn't lying ... "If I got you a roster of our soldiers, could you identify them?"

She nods. "Maybe ..."

I stand up. "Great. I'll be right back."

"Wait!" she blurts out as I'm walking away. "There's one more thing."

"Yeah?"

"What's today's date?"

"September fifteenth. Why?"

Her face grows apprehensive. "For the record, what I'm about to tell you is only to keep *your* ass safe, not to help any of your comrades."

"I'm touched."

"Ugh." She rubs her face. "Alright. At some point in the next two weeks, something *big* is supposed to go down in the cities on the East Coast."

"Something like what?"

She shrugs. "No clue. All Hellcat said was that when we received the code 'Burrow,' we'd have twelve hours before it all went down."

"The megapowers are mobilizing their troops in preparation for war ... You think it has anything to do with that? Some kind of false flag to set it in motion? Maybe an attack on bases and naval yards?"

She shrugs again. "Your guess is as good as mine."

I blow out air. "Alright, well, thanks for that. I'll be back in a bit so we can get started on trying to identify the spies."

"Bring me a burger and fries!" She smiles. "Oh, and that lap dance is still on the table, if you're interested."

I leave without a word, letting the door close behind me.

Anne rises. "I do *not* like that girl."

I grin. "Really? I thought she was pretty friendly."

"A bit too friendly if you ask me." She holds my hand as we walk. "And to make sure she doesn't get any friendlier, I'll be joining you two next time."

"That might help, actually. Maybe you can persuade her that she's fighting on the wrong side."

Anne scowls. "Are you trying to trying to get her to talk or are you trying to get her to defect?"

I actually have to think about that. "Turning her turn against them is the best-case scenario, but it's not my mission."

When we return to the brig two hours later, we are directed to a different room down the hall. We find Isabella cuffed to the table and floor in an interrogation room with a television in it. She's dressed in a tan prisoner's jumpsuit instead of a hospital gown with her frizzy hair now done up in a bun. She's also hooked up to some sort of monitor.

When I walk in, her face lights up, probably because she sees the greasy bag in my hand. The look fades as Anne follows me in.

"Well, if it isn't the Ice Queen … What's she doing here? This was supposed to be our date night, sunshine." She winks.

Anne smiles fiercely, the way she does when she's contemplating taking a life. "Don't make an enemy of me, girl."

"Sorry, I'm just not big on threesomes." She laughs.

I put my hand on Anne's shoulder. "Isabella's sense of humor is a bit trying."

"Chill, Your Majesty," Isabella says. "I just wanted to see if you'd get jealous—my way of fact-checking his story about you two being *in love*." She sizes Anne up. "After all the stories, the Ice Queen became my role model … You know, we planned on breaking you out of prison once we found out where they had you. Scratch that, I guess."

Anne turns on the TV and mirrors the first page of USAW profiles from her tablet onto the screen.

"Uncuff me," Isabella says. "I'm hungry."

As I unshackle her right arm, she subtly caresses my hand. I snatch it away. "If you're trying to seduce me, you're wasting your time," I murmur, sliding the bag over to her.

Smiling, she unwraps the burger and dumps the fries on the wrapper. "Sorry, hon. Affection is how I say thank you." She shoves fries in her mouth, still maintaining eye contact.

"Feel free to use your words next time," I mumble.

"Maybe next time I'll just ..." She brings her fist up to her open mouth and presses her tongue against the opposite cheek. "... thank you this way."

I close my eyes. "Please stop."

"Oooh, making you uncomfortable is fun. I'm *really* going to enjoy our time together."

"I'll make sure you don't," Anne snarls, handing me the tablet. She sits across from Isabella and leans forward. "Here's how this works: we shall go through the profiles four at a time. Tell us if you recognize anyone. Lie and we *will* know."

Isabella chomps into her burger. "Let's get started."

14
TICKING CLOCK

September 15
10:42 P.M.

THE NEXT FOUR analysts' profiles appear on screen. When Isabella doesn't say anything, I turn to find her slouched forward with her chin resting in her palm, her eyelids almost closed.

Anne snaps her fingers. "Wake up!"

Sighing, Isabella collapses back into her chair. Her head lolls up toward the ceiling. "Listen, we've been through, like, three hundred profiles over the last three hours. This shit's boring, and I'm tired. Can we please just pick this back up in the morning?" She looks to me, batting her lashes. "Pretty please?"

"How about I just get us some coffee?" I offer.

"How about you go down on me? That'll wake me up!"

Anne pushes back her chair and stands up. "We're done here, Dion … The prisoner is clearly too exhausted and delusional to perform effectively."

Isabella pretends to sulk. "Fine." Then she perks up. "Want to walk me back to my cell, hon?"

I unshackle her restraints from the floor hook. "You don't have to play temptress, you know. Hell, I'd probably treat you better if you didn't."

Isabella sighs. "I'll try. And I promise I'll be more *effective* and less of a pain in the ass in the morning. I owe you that much for the burger." She blows me a kiss.

Anne shoves her toward the door. "Move your ass."

September 16
10:01 A.M.

We've been at it for two hours, and surprisingly, Isabella has kept her word. She's been more cooperative and has behaved herself so far as overt flirting goes. But I've caught her staring at me every so often with a smile that seems more appreciative than flirtatious, in my opinion. She even listens politely when Anne explains why she defected from the Deciders and how what Richard planned for the world was almost as bad as the regime run by the elites that he eradicated.

When the third hour rolls around, Isabella is rambling nonstop as she shakes her head at each set of profiles. She claims that she was just a day away from being "peppered," Decider slang for being promoted to Loyal.

"Want to know how I got the name Jezebel?" she asks.

I shrug. "I can guess, but sure."

"Elsa—I mean Hellcat, my commanding Loyal—knew all about my stripping and camgirl careers, my promiscuous ways, how much of a flirt I was, yadda, yadda. She called me shameless, said I was 'a woman unrestrained by social norms who's not afraid to do what's necessary to further her objectives …' A jezebel … Turns out the codename was more like a designation for a role they needed filled."

"And what role did you have to fill?"

She leans in. "I had to use my stunning looks and my powers of seduction to recruit Veritas-swayed males and to get close to certain targets. Male targets. Some I stole information from. One I had to kill, another I had to … get intimate with so we could capture him …" Now she gets all glum looking.

Anne and I exchange a look. She's probably thinking the same thing I am—that maybe Isabella's more dangerous than we thought.

"Relax," Isabella says. "I didn't get captured on purpose to get close to anyone here …" She eyes me. "And I wasn't trying to woo you to kill you, Dion. I was just buttering you up so you'd keep taking care of me."

"I'm aware," I reply. Before I can ask who she's killed or what intel she has stolen over the past two years, our watches go off. The first thought in my mind is that Walker is calling to scold us for being chummy with the prisoner and not sticking to the objective. Fortunately, it's just Sung. I tap my Gauntlet. "Go ahead."

"The Deciders just hijacked every single local and cable channel!" Sung says in a panic. "They're broadcasting as we speak. I'm sending a link to the live stream. Hold on." There's a brief pause. "Check your inbox."

Anne pulls up Sung's message on the tablet. It's just a URL that reads www.thereclamation.com/thedeciders. She taps the link and the webpage pops up on both the tablet and the television. The Dominus is mid-speech, wearing the same fur-lined white trench and silver-visor Deva helmet as in the last broadcast. The sight of him makes my blood run hot.

"—and as the world nears yet another war over borders and tyrannical ideals not shared by the people," the Dominus bellows, "it is evident that the only true salvation for humanity is Decider rule. We will end all wars by finishing the work of the Architect, Richard Thomas. Through the War of Reclamation, we shall obliterate these filthy purveyors of human division and unite humanity once and for all!"

Unseen Deciders in the facility roar and clap.

"Before our Reclamation's dawn, the false leaders will be dealt with, but not before they confess their crimes and willingly relinquish power to the rightful ruler!" He indicates himself with a short bow.

The camera cuts to a dim, soggy room where a couple dozen men and women dressed in filthy, torn formal attire are kneeling on the ground, chained together in a line. President Lewis on the left, flanking his four designated successors who went missing.

"Then," the Dominus says on voiceover, "those responsible for the death of our previous leader and the fall of the first regime will be purged."

Footage of USAW soldiers with their arms, legs, and necks chained to a rust-red wall plays while successors list their "crimes" against the Deciders. It all becomes muffled jabbering to me as panic sets in. I identify Kenny Washington, Hudson, Denmark, Marquez, and Han. They're wearing bloodstained Vanquisher BDUs. Their faces are bruised and swollen, and their eyes are vacant of all emotion except for fear. Tenth in line is Han, who's also dressed in a USAW uniform. The photo of him with the caption "stay tuned" makes sense now.

The camera pans to Dave, who is hanging from the opposite wall. And then further down the line, I see them—Sam and Jessica, both dressed in Savior class BDUs. Sam is sobbing, but she appears to be unharmed. Jessica's cheek is bruised and her bottom lip is split.

Everything starts going red. I turn to Isabella while jabbing my finger at the TV. "Do you see those two girls? Neither of them fought in the war! Your people dressed them up like soldiers just so I can witness them being slaughtered on TV! Is killing innocents in the name of revenge what you signed up for? Is that the kind of person you want ruling the world?"

Isabella looks disturbed, but she doesn't say anything. Instead, she shifts her eyes from me to the screen.

Anne's hand slides into mine. I know her well enough to know that she doesn't care what happens to them. But she does worry about what will happen to me if I'm unable to save them.

The video switches back to the Dominus. "Come noon, one Angel of War will be executed live every six hours until the Reclamation. When the last prisoner dies, we shall pick up right where the Annex left off."

Anne releases my hand and taps her Nexus. "I counted thirty prisoners. That leaves us with one hundred and eighty hours until they make their big move."

The Dominus looks over his shoulder. "President Lewis, care to kick things off?"

Don Chambers unchains Lewis from the others and drags him off the edge of the frame. The camera pans over the other prisoners' faces. Then the feed goes back to the room where the Dominus has been giving his speech. Chambers kicks Lewis onto a white tarp and puts a gray 1911 to the president's temple. "When you're ready, Mr. President."

"My name is Gary Lewis," he snivels, trembling. "I am the acting president of the United States of the Americas, and like the man I am filling in for, I am another agent of division working to keep humanity from unifying …" He stops abruptly. "And the Deciders are maniacs who are behind the very—" Don Chambers' gun barks, ejecting blood and gore out through the opposite side of Lewis's skull.

"Lie, you die. Tell the truth and you get to live out your sentence. Why's that so hard to understand?" Don laughs. "Now who's next?"

I tap my Gauntlet. "Any progress locating this transmission, Razer?"

"We've got everyone on it," Sung replies, "but this signal is bouncing off routers in literally every country. As of now, it's untraceable."

The British prime minister ignores his script too and is executed next.

"If we don't find them—"

"Hold on a second!" Sung shouts. "It's originating from somewhere in Philadelphia!"

"How could we possibly have a trace on it already?" Anne asks. "The last broadcast would have taken ages to narrow down …"

"We're on the way up!" I announce.

"Don't go!' Isabella says. "Anne's right. My friend Pixie said these broadcasts are untraceable. If you found something that easy, it's probably bait."

"And how can we trust that you're not trying to protect them?" Anne asks.

She sighs. "You don't have to trust me. You know it's too good to be true."

Walker joins the call. "A team is preparing to mobilize," he says. "If you're not airborne in the next five minutes, you can watch from here while local USAW units handle the op."

"I'll be there," I say, then disconnect.

Anne puts a hand on my chest. "Don't you mean we?"

"If Isabella's right, I don't want you walking into a trap. Stay here with her and find the mole."

"We do this together or not at all. That was the deal!"

"Um," Isabella says, "you ever think maybe they're waiting six hours between executions because they're stalling until they can make you two the final kills?"

Anne eyes me.

I take a few deep breaths, close my eyes, and try to think rationally. I admit, it's probably a trap. So why couldn't Walker see it? The techs in Throne must have warned him that the trace was too easy. Was he that desperate to save what was left of our presidential line of succession? And then I had a dark thought: *Maybe he wants me to be captured so he can track me to the Dominus.*

"Isabella, do you know something about this?" I ask.

She shakes her head. "No, I swear! But they lingered on your baby mama for a *long* time. Like this whole execution spectacle is all for *you*, not some power display for the world." She gestures toward my chair. "Now sit down and let me help you find Corax and Corvus. The sooner we find them, the faster you can find Naraka."

"Why are you so cooperative all of a sudden?" Anne asks.

Isabella shrugs. "Maybe I'm starting to see the Deciders in a different light."

While Anne goes over the profiles with Isabella on the tablet, I watch the Deciders' broadcast, eagerly waiting for the Terah drone to reach the signal's location. Over the next hour, the remaining politicians cooperate with the Deciders, making their resignation speeches and advocating for Decider rule moving forward. At 11:58 A.M. the last politician is carried off-screen and the Dominus announces that the first of the Angels of War will be executed. I hold my breath.

"This one first," Don says, pointing to Kenny Washington. Before I can quash it, I feel a wave of relief that it's him and not Jess, Han or one of the others, and I hate myself for it.

Two Elite-class Deciders release Kenny from his chains and drag him to the bloody tarp. After they force him onto his knees, he stares at the tarp, expressionless.

"Special Agent Kenny Washington," Don says, "you have been found guilty of leading the Frederick Militia against the Deciders during the War of the Annex. You also served as head of Ron Pell's protection detail. Both of these offenses are punishable by death." He puts the 1911 to his head. "Any last words?"

Kenny smiles faintly. "I'm sorry I won't be around to watch you all die by Dion Johnson's hands!"

The gun goes off and Kenny collapses.

Anne rubs my back. "Sorry, love …"

"Did—did you know him well?" Isabella stutters.

"I knew him well enough …" I sigh. "If he hadn't let me through his militia's roadblock during the Annex, I would've been killed or captured before making it to Virginia from Pennsylvania."

"I see …" She looks at the tablet and her eyes widen. "Well, I got something that might cheer you up, hon." She turns the device around and points at the photo on the top right, a stocky soldier named Lance Corporal Peter Henderson. "That's Corax."

Anne expands the profile. It says he repairs computers and detection systems. "Are you absolutely positive?" Anne asks.

Isabella nods. "I'm one-hundred-fifty percent sure. His real name is Peter Morton. He and I were in the same training platoon back at Iceworm. Last time I saw him was before he left with Fallen Angel to head back to the States over a year ago."

Anne dials up Sung while she works to locate Corax's position on the tablet.

I'm curious about Iceworm, but finding out what it is isn't my top priority. "What can you tell us about Morton?" I ask.

"He's a Loyal—real tech-savvy and a decent marksman. Finished first in our hand-to-hand combat class."

"We've identified one of the moles," Anne tells Sung. "It's Lance Corporal Peter Henderson. He is currently in Central Command Server Room B. Do *not* issue an alert. Capture him quietly and bring him to us. We don't want to spook his partner."

Isabella cocks an eyebrow. "So you're going to move me to my new digs now, right?"

"Not until we confirm he is who you say he is," I say, looking down as my Gauntlet vibrates.

The alert is a notification that the Terah drone is in position. I mirror the feed on the TV. The source of the signal is the old CSX warehouse on the Delaware River near the Walt Whitman Bridge. It's listed as abandoned, but the scans from the Terah drone show about ten targets inside. None of them appear to be chained to the walls like in the broadcast.

"You guys have a drone that can see through walls?" Isabella asks. "Pretty badass … We've got shit that can see through walls too. Not drones, though."

"Tell us all about it later," Anne says.

Liberty Bell, the codename for the Philadelphia-based USAW team, quickly moves into position around the target in trucks and boats. Two long minutes pass before Walker greenlights the raid. The feed switches over to a four-paneled split-screen of the lead fireteam's helmet-mounted cameras. Flashlights scanning every corner, Liberty Bell sweeps through the darkness down to the sublevel where the targets are clustered together, unmoving. When they reach the door, one soldier plants a breaching charge. Once the charge blows, the soldiers donning Cameras One and Three toss in flashbangs. Then the fireteam storms in, shouting, "Hands in the air! No one move!"

Through the smoke, there are ten silhouettes dressed in gray trench coats and helmets standing in front of a bank of computers. None of the Loyals move. They just stand there, hands up, frantically mumbling something and shaking their heads. As the smoke dissipates, it becomes clear that the ten hostiles are shackled to the ground with their hands being held up by chains suspended from the ceiling, chains that were hoisted up by a contraption triggered by the door being opened. On the wall behind them, just above the four wall-mounted monitors, there's a message painted in red: IT'S NEVER THAT EASY!

"Liberty Bell, get out of there!" the general orders.

As they make a break for the door, the room lights up with a white flash and then the feeds go black. Drone footage pops up twenty seconds later showing a pile of rubble where the building once stood.

"Good thing you trusted me …" Isabella whispers.

"Yeah … good thing," I mutter as a call comes in. "Go ahead."

"Corporal Henderson was sedated and transported via stretcher to the interrogation room on Basement Level One." Sung says. "He should be awake in the next few minutes."

"Did you find anything suspicious on him?"

"A flash drive and an unauthorized cellular device. Abdul is looking into them."

I head for the door. "Copy that. I'm on my way down. Have someone bring a bed to this interrogation room." I end the call.

"Wait, you're leaving me in here?" Isabella asks. "What if I need to go to the bathroom?"

"Just bang on the door and someone will escort you to the one in the hall. In the meantime, now you've got a TV to watch."

She nods. "Thanks."

Peter Henderson's interrogation starts off light. It has to. We can't give him the treatment we give Deciders without proof that he really is a spy. As expected, Henderson denies ever having any association with the Deciders. The lie detector doesn't indicate that he's lying, but anyone can be trained to deceive those things.

One hour before the next execution, Abdul cracks the encryption on Henderson's phone and recovers messages containing sensitive information about our operations. The last message reads "Archangel didn't go for the bait. Clear to detonate." The one from yesterday called for Corax to "identify and eliminate the USAW prisoner before they flip." None of the messages are traceable.

With the knowledge that Peter is Corax, and with the next execution looming, I abandon all restraint, doing everything to him that I stopped them from doing to Isabella. After the second time I almost kill him, Walker has me dragged out of the interrogation with orders to observe the Extractor from the viewing room.

At 6:00 P.M., another USAW soldier is selected for execution. This time it's Sergeant Brent Owens—a soldier I don't know personally but saw a few times at Quantico and Camp Boonies during the Annex. Just like with the last broadcast, another signal location is detected, this time in Austin, Texas. And just like last time, it turns out to be another phantom signal in a building that gets blown to bits.

I'm starting to worry that we're never going to find them …

September 18
11:55 A.M.

Even after enduring two days of torture, Corax maintains his silence. And in that time, six Angels of War are executed. Since Owens, Corporal Tim Anderson, Sergeant Marquez, Lance Corporal Vince Harper, SSgt. Kevin Ramstad, and Sergeant Remy Smith were executed in that order. Like the first two executions, each one was accompanied by transmission signals to abandoned and sometimes rigged buildings.

With five minutes until the next execution, Anne and I sit in the secured barracks apartment that Isabella's been set up in. We've watched every execution since Owens with her in hopes that the brutality of it all will break Isabella down.

Every time someone I know dies, I tell her how I met them and what kind of person they were. In turn, she's opened up to us a bit about the Deciders' operations during their time underground. Still, even after learning that the Deciders put a kill order out for her, and after she admitted she doesn't agree with what the Dominus is doing, she still won't flip on them. I'm starting to wonder if maybe she's telling the truth about not knowing anything.

At 11:57 A.M. the Deciders' broadcast goes live. Don Chambers walks up and down the line of remaining USAW prisoners, dragging his machete on the floor behind him as he does. Suddenly, he stops before Han and points the blade at him. "This one."

As two Elites unshackle and drag Han to the killing zone, things slow to a crawl. All the times we hung out, all the parties, all the laughs, all the times we wing-manned for each other—they flash through my mind.

"Jai Han," Don declares, putting the machete to the back of his neck, "intel suggests that you are directly responsible for shooting down the Chinook that Richard and I were flying in after the fall of D.C. That action led to Richard's death. And it caused these burns ..." He raises the blade. "For that, no last words for you ..." In one swipe, he beheads Han. Blood spurts up from Han's neck as his head rolls across the tarp.

Chains rattle as Isabella cringes in her bed. "Oh shit ... I—I don't know that I can watch any more of these ..." She covers her mouth with both hands and gags.

"You will watch every one until you understand that the Deciders must be stopped," Anne snarls.

"I get it, alright? They're not the force for good I thought they were ..." A long moment of silence passes. "Dion?"

"What?" I mutter, unable to look away from the terrible scene.

"Promise you won't get mad at me."

"*What?*" I snap.

"Please, promise me first."

"I promise! Say what you have to say!"

She lets out a long breath. "I can help you find Naraka ..."

15
ASSET

September 18
12:03 P.M.

IT TAKES EVERY ounce of resolve not to lunge across the room and choke her. I close my eyes and regulate my breathing. "What haven't you told me, Isabella?"

"I, uh, I lied about not knowing where any active Decider Hives are …"

I give her a look that makes her shrink into the bed.

Anne draws her knife. "Should I kill her or would you like to, love?"

I hold a hand up. "After all I've done for you, you let eight of my people die before you fess up?"

"I'm sorry! I wanted to tell you after they showed your friends all chained up, but you were so mad … I … I thought if I did, you'd flip out on me for not saying something sooner."

"So why now?"

A tear rolls down Isabella's cheek. "My conscience can't handle any more executions … The guilt of knowing I could have helped you prevent them is drowning me …"

"Alright, just tell me where the base is."

"Are you mad?" she whimpers.

I look away. "Disappointed …"

"I'm so sorry," she sniffles. "I really am ... I hope I didn't ruin things between us."

"Listen, if you want to mend the damage, tell me where this Hive is."

She nods. "Before I tell you where, you need to understand that you can't go in with guns blazing ... You do that, they'll wipe their computers and you won't be able to locate Naraka. And no one you capture will talk."

"Then how will you help us find it?"

She stands and shuffles up to me, chains rattling. "You'll have to send me in so I can access the Providence network. It's the only way to find the true broadcast origin."

"You go in there and get caught, you're dead," I say.

"Yeah, and that's the other reason I didn't say anything sooner ..." She gives me a pitiful look. "But I need to help you save the rest of your people. No matter what the risk."

I study her for a long moment. She sounds and looks sincere. But what else would you expect from a spy?

"Besides," she adds brightly, "I was trained in infiltration and espionage. It won't be my first rodeo."

"And what do you want in return?" I ask.

"You mean if I make it out?" She smiles faintly. "My freedom. I'll also need a new identity so the Deciders won't kill me when they take over. And my mom and sister—get them somewhere safe. They'll need the same disappearance package."

I place a hand on her shoulder. "I promise that if you help me, I'll make sure you come out alive."

She blushes.

"I take it you don't want to include Command in this?" Anne asks.

"No way. There's still one mole left. And then there's the whole Anglerfish thing … If this is going to work, we have to keep the circle small until we locate Naraka."

Anne nods. "So where are we going, Isabella?"

"Baltimore."

In ten minutes, the team I assembled for what I codenamed Operation Final Hope meets up in the parking garage. Everyone is dressed in civilian clothes—black jackets, blue jeans, and tactical boots—with Aegis armor underneath and a duffle bag full of gear slung over their shoulders. Once everyone is briefed, we split up to make the necessary preparations. Six minutes later, Abdul establishes a secure back channel for our team, Rogue Titan, to communicate on. He announces that the surveillance cameras monitoring Isabella's room and the building's exits are on a loop, the cue for Isabella to change out of her jumpsuit and into the burgundy shirt, black hoodie, blue jeans, and boots that Anne provides for her. Anne and I put a black sack over her head and escort her downstairs to the rear exit where Jeremy and Ken are waiting for us in an armored GMC.

We slip through base security without setting off any alarms. From there, we head north on I-95 until we see the sign for the 7-Eleven in Dumfries, Virginia, where Steele, Abby, Sung, Abdul, and Corporal Carlos Salazar are waiting to rendezvous with us in a black surveillance van.

While Jeremy tops off the gas tank, Abdul hands Isabella her Gauntlet and a flash drive.

"Once you log into the system," he says, "plug in this flash drive and open the app. Your Gauntlet will act as a relay to the computers in the van until the program grants me remote access to their network. Then I'll start by disabling this TARSEN Field."

Before we left, Isabella briefed us on the Deciders' Total Area Sensory Field—or TARSEN Field for short—that blankets all of their bases and areas of operation. TARSEN is a rapid, pulsating Wi-Fi emitter that triangulates all enemy movement and communication signals. If the movement detected can't be tied to a Decider frequency, the system will flag it on the Deciders' Gauntlets as either a neutral blip or, if the signal matches known military frequencies, it'll show up as an enemy combatant. The plan is for her to log into the system before she turns on her Gauntlet and notifies Abdul. Then it will be a race for him to shut down the TARSEN Field before the Deciders notice an unsanctioned blip on their maps.

"If you're in trouble," I say, "turn on your Gauntlet and signal us. We'll have Terah drone coverage over the Hive so, if need be, we can storm the place and extract you."

She looks nervous, but she nods. "Cool. I got this shit."

During the drive, Isabella briefs the team on the target building over the comm. "Other than one or two sentries that'll be chilling outside, the first floor of the apartment building is usually unoccupied. The apartments from the second floor up are the living quarters. The basement is where the operation's command and armory are set up. That's where I'll be heading. The sublevel spans from underneath 300 North Charles Street to all the buildings on that block, connected by a series of holes blasted through the dividing walls. If you need to come in to catch them off guard, come through the Vietnamese restaurant just south of the corner of Mulberry Street."

She goes on to tell us about the SH-7 Specter, the stealth helicopter that has been giving us so much trouble, how it can not only evade radar but has unevenly spaced rotor blades to dampen its noise signature. She reveals that the Deva Helmets the Elites wear—the MR-Deva Farsight Variant—have smart glass technology that displays their maps on a HUD, which is how Dozer detected us in the hotel that night without looking at his Gauntlet. Elite Farsight Devas can also "see" how the TARSEN Field waves interact with objects through walls in the same way that our Terah drone works, except those interactions are displayed in their smart visors in real-time.

She also tells us that after the Disintegration, she and her team went to an underground base called Iceworm on southwestern Greenland's Disko Island. There are similar bases in Guyana, northern Canada, the Falkland Islands, and the countless other places where the Deciders went to ground to prepare for the Reemergence. The most shocking thing she mentions is that there are Decider Hives all across America, built secretly in new and reconstructed buildings by contracting companies owned by the Deciders.

As we cross the Potomac, my attention is stolen away from Isabella by the sight of Capital Bay, the body of water that flooded the crater that once was Washington, D.C. It's my first time seeing it in person since the river first flooded the steaming cavity blasted into the Earth's crust by the Deciders' antimatter bomb. For a brief moment, I forget about those who I'm trying to rescue and wonder what devastation will occur across the globe if I don't stop the Dominus at Naraka.

Abandoned row houses charred by fire, cracked and crater-filled streets, hollowed-out storefronts, rats and packs of wild dogs—this is the forgotten city of Baltimore.

Other than a few homeless types, there's no activity until we reach the Inner Harbor where we encounter light traffic and some reconstruction. At East Fayette, the surveillance van breaks away toward Abby's overwatch position across from our target. Isabella directs us to Davis Street, a one-way alley a quarter-mile from the Deciders' surveillance grid. Ken parks at the rear entrance of an abandoned deli. Anne exits first, performing a quick survey of the desolate area before signaling that it's clear.

A breeze washes over me when I step outside. It's much cooler here than Virginia and the air here has that crisp smell of fall. It's too nice not to appreciate so I take a moment to bask in the cool wind.

While I help Isabella out of the SUV, Anne stands guard with her hand clutching the pistol in her pocket, ready to shoot Isabella dead if she tries anything after she's released.

"Ready?" I ask as I uncuff her.

Isabella works her wrists. "Yeah, I'm good to go. Any word on my family yet?"

Anne touches her earpiece. "Just got word that a USAW team has picked them up." She shows her the picture of them I requested.

Isabella sighs. "Good. Thanks."

"I'm counting on you," I say, handing her a flash drive.

She pulls down the neck of her shirt, exposing her cleavage, and tucks the flash drive into her sports bra. "I won't let you down, Dion. Promise."

"I'll hold you to it. But if you do fail, we'll improvise."

She nods.

"If you betray us … well, let's just say you don't come out of this in cuffs. That's an order I don't want to give, understand?"

"You won't have to worry about that," she whispers.

Nodding, I unstrap her previously confiscated combat knife from my leg. "In case you get into trouble …"

"Thanks," she says, sliding the sheath into the back of her jeans. She turns and starts walking away only to stop after a few steps. "Hey, Dion?"

"Yeah?"

Her hazel eyes gaze into mine. "In case I don't make it out, I just want to say thanks for being a decent human being. You didn't have to treat me the way you did." She smiles. "Despite how I acted toward you at first, I appreciated your kindness every step of the way, hon."

"You're welcome, Izzy. And thanks for your cooperation." I pull the hood up over her head and pat her arm. "Be safe."

Walking backward, she blows me a kiss then turns and continues toward the corner.

Anne laughs as we climb into the SUV. "Izzy? You're giving each other pet names now?"

"It just came out!" I protest.

"Oh, I hope she betrays us so I can end her ..."

"Yeah, let's hope not. If she does, things will get messy, real fast."

16
FINAL HOPE

September 18
2:44 P.M.

WHILE KEN DRIVES, I monitor Terah drone footage of Isabella walking hastily down the street on my Gauntlet. Three minutes later, we reach our objective, an alley around the corner from the Hive. Five minutes after that, Isabella rounds the corner onto North Charles Street. Before she reaches the brownstone, one of the two homelessly dressed men leaning by the entrance walks into the middle of the sidewalk with a hand in his pocket—probably palming a pistol. When she's about ten feet away, he waves then approaches her with open arms. They hug. The trio exchange words for almost five minutes before she heads for the door.

"Activating surface penetrating mode," Sung announces over the comm.

I change over to the terahertz scanner's feed. Only ten or so apartments are occupied. They all appear to be sleeping or relaxing on their couches with the exception of a group of three eating in one apartment and the couple having sex on the fourth floor.

When Isabella heads below ground, her image fades to almost nothing. I tap my earpiece. "Salazar, bring the drone as close as you can and increase scanning output."

"Copy."

Slowly, the visual of the basement becomes more defined. And by the time it clears up, I've lost Isabella. There are almost as many bodies below as there are above, maybe more. Half are parked at what appear to be computer stations in a large room. A smaller cluster is grouped around a large table facing what looks to be a television. The rest are buzzing around … like, well, bees in a hive.

"I think I found our stripper," Anne says, pointing at her tablet. "Top right of the stairwell. The skinny one with their head down."

The figure she's talking about ducks down an empty hall when two other fuzzy forms turn the corner. "Probably," I say.

When the two targets pass, the one we suspect to be Isabella reenters the main hall and continues on. *It's her.* When she reaches the larger, unoccupied room at the end of the hallway, she slowly opens the door then slinks in, closing it gently behind her. Now she rushes to the desk and parks herself in the chair. She appears to move the mouse then does what looks like typing. She reaches for her chest then shoves the flash drive into the computer.

Hurry up! Hurry up!

Almost a minute passes before I see a blue dot appear on my HUD. Then there's some static. "Rogue Titan, the app is running," Isabella whispers somewhat nervously. "Copy?"

"We copy, Rogue Delta," I say. "You have a fast-moving target inbound. Get away from that computer!"

"Shit! Copy." She lingers at the computer for a moment then runs toward the door.

"Control, please tell me you're in their system!" I say.

"Connecting!" Abdul says. He sounds a little panicked. It's his first field mission, after all.

The target bursts into the room.

"Elsa!" Isabella exclaims. That must be Sgt. Elsa "Hellcat" Crawford, her commanding Loyal and the second-in-command of the Maryland operation.

"Smith told me you were back," Elsa says in an angry southern drawl. "Mind telling me where the fuck you've been for the last eight days? You didn't check in once, and now you're skulking around in my goddamn office! Why the fuck are you in my office, anyway? You should have come straight to me!"

"Chill, Elsa. I heard you were in a meeting or some shit so I came here to hide from Dozer. I'm not ready for him to yell at me yet. And what are you talking about, checking in? You told us not to make contact after the mission if we got left behind."

"I'm in the Providence network," Abdul says. "My worm is tracking Naraka's broadcast origin and I'm disabling TARSEN."

"Rogue Delta, eliminate Hellcat and get out of there, *now!*" I order. I call Tommy, who should be airborne and nearing Baltimore with pilot Lance Corporal Grant Sanders, Leo "Simba" Hill, Lance Corporal Oliver Hawke, and Hughes. "Flying Titan, prepare for extraction."

"Flying Titan is air-bound!" Tommy responds. "ETA twenty minutes."

"And what the fuck were you doing these past eight days?" I hear Elsa say to Isabella. "Taking a goddam vay—" She stops abruptly and looks down at her wrist.

"Shit," Abdul says. "I think I just triggered an alert when I disabled TARSEN ..."

"What is it?" Isabella asks.

"A Providence alert just popped up ... It's gone now but it looks like TARSEN is down ..." Elsa turns toward her computer, stiffens, then whirls back around, her pistol drawn.

"Elsa, what the fuck?" Isabella exclaims as she puts her hands up. "Quit pointing that shit at me!"

"Rogue Titan, prepare to infiltrate the Hive," I command.

"In the time you were gone," Elsa sneers, "the Richmond Hive came under attack, Corax went dark, and now you show up out of nowhere and TARSEN immediately goes offline? You're the USAW prisoner, aren't you? They got you to turn on us, didn't they?"

"What the hell? How could you even think I'd betray you—betray the Deciders? You ever think that maybe someone else was captured and *they* talked?"

Elsa waggles her gun. "We'll find out ... Now move it."

Isabella turns and heads for the door. As she does, I spot three figures rushing toward them.

The door bursts open and the lead figure knocks Isabella to the floor. "You fucking turncoat! What have you done?"

"The fuck ... I didn't do anything, Dozer!"

The two people with Dozer turn her over and cuff her.

"Bullshitting me will only make this worse, Jezebel." There's a pause. "Hellcat, take her to Shawshank. He'll make her talk."

"Naraka," Abdul says. "I've located it! Its signal is originating off the coast of New York ... Possibly a ship ..."

"Are you positive?" I ask.

"Ninety percent positive, yes. We'll know for certain when they resume broadcasting."

"We're not waiting for the next broadcast. Once we extract Rogue Delta, we head to Naraka. Hijack their CCTV footage and cut off outside surveillance. The second we breach, disable their access to all cameras inside. Rogue Bravo, do not engage until I give the command."

"Copy," Abby, Steele, and Sung respond one after another.

Anne mutes her comm. "We're still extracting her? We got what we came for ... They outnumber us almost three to one, they have her prisoner, and they likely know we're here ..."

"I promised her I'd get her out. My conscience can't take another loss right now, Anne."

"Fine." She racks a round into her HK416. "I'm in a murderous mood anyway."

"External surveillance is disabled," Abdul announces. "Standing by to cut internal feeds."

"Step on it, Ken!"

The SUV screeches out of the alley onto North Charles Street and turns north. Ken parks across from the bank at the corner and the four of us hurry across the street to the apartment entrance between the Vietnamese restaurant and the bank. My Gauntlet shows the immediate area is clear so I pry open the glass door and enter.

"Their camera access has been disabled," Abdul says. "I'll guide you from here."

The locks securing the basement entrance are a little more complex so I set thermite charges, move away, and then activate them with my Gauntlet. The bright, sparkling reaction burns for eight seconds before I'm able to breach. It's the same for the next door.

I take point with Anne right behind me, moving down a short hallway toward a hole in the wall that leads to the next building. As we do, Ken sets up sticky bombs on the ceilings and walls.

"Two targets approaching from around the next corner," Abdul says.

Anne and I post up against the wall. When they hit the corner, I grab the guy closest to me with my right hand, kick his feet from under him, and slam him to the ground while simultaneously plunging a knife into his heart. Anne drops the other with a headshot from her suppressed P226.

"Do you even need us here?" Jeremy whispers.

"We will soon," I whisper back.

Halfway down the hall, Abdul warns that there's a group of three in a room to the left and a group of six in the one across the hall. Anne and I take the room of six. Once we've memorized their locations on our maps, we charge in. Anne grabs the guy nearest the door and pumps two rounds into his chest. Then, using his body as a shield, she aims over his shoulder and dispatches the two to the right while I drop the remaining three.

We move from one building to the next, eliminating threats in a similar fashion, until we reach the building Isabella's being held in. There are too many Deciders ahead to eliminate them all without being spotted.

"Control, can you disable the Decider comms?" I whisper.

"I can," Abdul responds. "For now. They're getting close to kicking me out of their network."

"Alright, Rusty, get a distraction going as soon as the comms are cut. Red Death? Thin the herd. And Razer, hit 'em with RPGs when I give the signal."

I pull up the security footage of the room Isabella's in. She's tied to a chair and some male Loyal is smacking her around while Elsa questions her. We quickly cycle through the other cameras to locate all enemy contacts. Outside the room, there are two guards. There are a few more in the hallway, but the rest are working feverishly in the computer rooms.

As I return to the map, Abdul announces that the Decider comms have been disabled. Twenty seconds after that, there's the faint, constant crackle and pop from an XM96 diversionary grenade outside.

"Go!" I order.

I take point through the hole in the wall and enter the main part of the Hive's basement network. As we pass Hellcat's office, the lights dim and red lights near the ceiling start flashing. Peeking around the corner into the lobby, I watch as Deciders in civilian clothes emerge from the other end and head toward the stairwell. Straight ahead, in the opposite hallway, the guards are still standing their ground.

I signal toward the objective. "I'm going for Isabella. You three cover me from here and keep the escape route clear."

Anne grabs my jacket. "You're not going alone."

"I'll be fine. There are only four targets ahead. I need you three to draw fire from the targets in those two rooms." I say, unholstering my two P226s. "Besides, when I free her, I'll have backup."

I punch out around the corner and sprint into the lobby. A Loyal emerges from the armory and I put two rounds in his head then slink behind the nearest support column before a second Loyal emerges. He only gets off one round before Anne drops him. While my team suppresses the Deciders in the rooms ahead, I plant a charge on the support column then dart into the open, planting another charge as I pass the next one. Then with one pistol aimed at each target, I drop both sentries simultaneously. I scoop up one of their M4s and check the Gauntlet. Hellcat's heading for the door and the other Loyal is watching the exit, pistol in the low ready.

My palms are sweating as I hear Hellcat approach. I've never killed a woman before, and I don't want to, but Elsa will have to die if I want to save Isabella.

Just do it!

Time slows as the door opens. Elsa's jaw drops and her eyes widen in an almost exaggerated fashion when she sees the pistol in her face. Then my round tunnels through her skull. In a fraction of a second, I have both pistols trained on the Loyal beside Isabella. Diving out of the line of fire, I pump two rounds into his chest, one in his neck, and another through his jaw.

Isabella stares in shock. Her cheek is reddened and her lip is split. "Dion?"

"Yeah, it's me," I say, cutting her free.

She stands, holding her side. "You actually came for me ..."

"I promised you, didn't I?"

She smiles.

The gunfire outside intensifies.

"Archangel, the Elite and the remaining Deciders have taken control of the main area!" Anne says over the comm. "You're cut off!"

Izzy spits on her torturer. "And we were supposed to be friends ..." she mutters.

The dog tag I take from the corpse reads: OWEN "SHAWSHANK" BRADSHAW. I shove them in my pocket with Elsa "Hellcat" Crawford's. "There's a secondary exit, right? Is it close?"

She nods. "Out this room to the left, there's a rear stairwell. It leads to the parking garage behind the building. From there, we can cut through the fence to the alley."

"Fall back to the breach point and detonate the charges," I tell Anne. "We'll take the secondary exit and link up at the vehicle." I put a fresh mag into my P226 and extend it to Isabella. "Can I trust you not to shoot me or my friends in the back?"

She nods. "Word's already out that I'm the traitor. You guys are all I have left, sunshine."

I hand her the pistol and the M4. "Stay close."

The camera outside shows the immediate area is clear so I step out and sweep the corridor. Down the hall I came from, four

Loyals and the white-clad hulk that is Dozer are shooting at the smoke-filled hallway where I left my team. While they're distracted, I signal Isabella to make a break for the stairwell. Rounds chew at my heels as I jog out behind her. At the next corner, we post up behind the corner and return fire.

"Razer, let the rockets fly! Ice Queen? If you're clear, detonate those charges, now!" I shout.

The entire building shakes with thunderous explosions. Dozer and two others just reach the hallway's entrance when the bombs on the support columns explode and send them flying forward. Their bodies are engulfed by the cloud of dust and debris from the collapsing ceiling.

More explosions rattle the structure above as we ascend to ground level. I flip the deadbolt on the door and we emerge into the parking lot. Most of the cars are derelicts but I spot a handful of armored SUVs like the ones we encountered during our first mission.

We've almost reached the fence when the door behind us bursts open. I don't look back. I just grab Isabella and drag her down behind an armored Ford pickup. Through the vehicle's window, I identify six Loyals and Dozer. The Elite soldier's white uniform is now tattered and gray with soot and dust, but there's no blood.

While Isabella lays down suppressive fire, I arm and throw three TD6 grenades to where they are taking cover. One explosion lifts a Loyal several feet into the air. The rest of the Deciders scatter. I cross one out. Another drops from Isabella's rifle fire. Dozer just keeps firing and advancing. I time his next move to cover and land two shots—one to the chest and another to the bicep. He rocks from impact but keeps coming. *Shit!* I think back to the White Coat I killed during the first war with a knife to the chest.

Isabella's rifle barks twice and a Loyal wails. "I need ammo!" she says, switching to the pistol. She cracks off four rounds.

I slide her two rifle mags and one pistol mag. "Make 'em count!" I rise from cover and drop another Loyal with a burst to the head. "Handle that last Loyal. I'll take Dozer."

"Be careful!" she says, firing at her target.

I reach into the pouch on my tactical belt and extract four MG18 bomblets—black fragmentation grenades the same size as a golf ball. I arm them to detonate upon impact with two hard, rapid squeezes and lob them over the SUV that Dozer is diving behind. The blasts send Dozer flying back into the open.

There's no liquid armor protecting his hand, I think, taking aim and firing before he recovers. The round blows a hole in through the base of his hand and his LMG clatters to the ground as he cries out. Now I send ten rounds center mass, but the bastard is unscathed. My last HK416 round skips right off his damn helmet.

Imagine an army of Elites ...

Dozer draws a knife with his good hand and charges. Quick for such a big dude, he's right up on me before I can draw my knife. I parry the incoming thrust with my forearm and put him in an arm lock. He's strong, but, eventually, I hyperextend his arm and he drops his blade. I kick him in the side of the leg then knee him in the chest. He eats the blow and drives me right into the hood of a car. I block and retaliate with an elbow strike to his clavicle and a kick to the gut that sends him stumbling back. I draw both my combat knives and when he charges again, I drive them into his chest. The blades slide right through his armor, piercing lung and heart.

With a kick, I free my knives and Dozer hits the ground with a thud. Along with blood, my blades are coated with a silvery, viscous liquid reminiscent of mercury. It's a different substance than what was in the Echelon STF-Deva armor that our Aegis armor is based on.

Urgent footsteps prompt me to draw my pistol and aim at the source. It's just Isabella, so I holster my pistol.

"Holy shit ..." she says in awe.

"Holy shit as right." I kneel beside Dozer. Beneath his Farsight helmet is a thirty-something black male with a scraggly beard. I shove his dog tags and Gauntlet into my pockets and hand the helmet to Isabella. "Let's move."

I cut through the chain-link fence and we turn down the alley. There are sirens in the distance. Izzy and I aim at a black GMC that screeches to a stop in front of us, blocking the alley. The door of the SUV flies open and Anne waves us on. "Come on!"

Isabella starts forward and I grab her elbow. "Weapons first," I demand.

"I understand," she says, handing them over. When the last one is in my possession, she stares at me for a moment then wraps her arms around me. "Thanks for saving me, Dion." She buries her head in my chest and tightens her embrace. "You risked your life and your team to keep your word. The Deciders never do that for their own. I owe you my life."

I pat her back. "You're welcome. Now let me go before Anne puts a bullet in your head ..."

Ken drives to a fenced-off stretch of abandoned lots a few blocks from the Hive. There are just the outlines of the former buildings here—broken rows of concrete walls no more than a foot high. Sung and Steele cut through the fence and toss flares out across the weeds while the rest of us head inside the nearby building to change from civilian clothing into our combat BDUs. Not long after, a black V-22 Osprey rumbles overhead then circles the area.

"Rogue Titan, is that you?" Tommy asks. "Over."

"Yup," I respond. "The LZ's clear so get your ass down here."

"Aye, aye! Stand by."

The Osprey touches down in the center lot a minute later. Isabella moves to board first. I follow right behind her with Anne and the others trailing me.

Hughes eyes Isabella with suspicion as she sits. "Archangel, were you able to locate Naraka?"

"Yeah," I respond. "Well, we're ninety percent sure we did, anyway ..."

"So where the hell is it?" he asks.

I nod at Abdul as he climbs in. He consults his tablet. "Floating off the coast of Long Island ..."

"Good thing you requested high-altitude jump gear and scuba gear, huh?" Leo asks, patting the large case tied down beside him.

"I figured Naraka wouldn't be a place we could just drive up to," I say.

"We bringing the general in on this now?" Hughes prods.

I shake my head. "Not until we know for sure it's the real deal."

"You sure, D?" Sung asks. "We don't even know if Stevenson was telling the truth about Anglerfish ... And if this *is* the right place, we'll need full USAW support on this op."

"Can't risk it. Command leaks like a sieve. We need to confirm the target before we tip the Deciders off." I tap my Gauntlet. "Tommy, Abdul has sent the coordinates to your GPS. Get us airborne."

"Copy that, brother!" Tommy says, and we dust off.

17
NARAKA

September 18
4:29 P.M.

LIVE SATELLITE IMAGES show the target—a massive gray Shughart-class cargo ship anchored a few miles southeast of New York's Jones Beach. Between the four-story white bridge near the stern and the double- and triple-stacked shipping containers clustered at the bow, there's a bare section that looks like it opens up. Ten armed men dressed in gray jumpsuits patrol the ship's deck.

The Terah drone reaches the ship fifty minutes after we landed at Nine Gun Battery, an abandoned military facility on the barrier spit of Sandy Hook, New Jersey. The standard scan shows the company name, Erebus, painted on the back of the hull. Erebus is the Greek god of darkness born of Chaos. Appropriate.

A quick internet search shows that Erebus is a privately-owned shipping company that was registered in Panama just months after the War of Annex. Abdul is trying to find the identity of its owner when I look up at the Osprey's drop-down monitor and see that "SS AKARAN" has been crudely painted on the starboard side of the hull.

"Akaran!" I exclaim. "That's Naraka spelled backward!"

"But when we searched for anagrams of Naraka, nothing came up ..." Abdul mumbles.

"Judging by the paint job, it's not the ship's official name," Anne says. "It's likely a message for us ..."

"Yeah ... maybe Stevenson wanted us to find this place," I say. "But why?"

The Terah drone begins its terahertz scan, revealing five SH-7 Specter stealth helicopters and vehicles that resemble the Goliath LAV in the hold beneath the massive doors on the deck. On the first two sublevels near the bow are dozens of cabins that I assume are sleeping quarters. Underneath the bridge, a computer-filled command center and server rooms beside it. Underneath that, a prison that spans the two lowest levels. Besides the ten sentries topside, there are approximately one hundred to one hundred and twenty human-shaped figures below deck. Most are lying on the floor of their cells on the lower levels. The rest are armed, either patrolling the ship or standing in distinct clusters.

"Naraka ..." I breathe.

"Are we calling this in now, or what?" Sung asks.

"And risk alerting Corvus?" I snap. "If we're exposed, the Deciders kill everyone and the Dominus escapes."

"So what do you suggest we do, Archangel?" Hughes says, annoyed.

I glare at him. "We board Naraka, eliminate as many Deciders as we can, destroy their comms, and eliminate their means of evacuation. Once their comms are down, we'll call in reinforcements."

Anne nods. "That is our best move."

Jeremy raises his hand. "Mind telling me how you plan on getting us aboard that thing?"

I eye the case of jump equipment. "We parachute in."

His eyes widen. "I ain't trained for that, Dion ..."

"I know. That's why you're staying on the Osprey."

He looks taken aback.

Isabella whistles. When she has my attention, she waves with the hand not cuffed to the seat's rail. "You doing a HALO jump, hon? That was part of basic training back at Iceworm. Let me take his spot."

I shake my head. "Thanks for the offer, but I can't jeopardize my team's lives or this mission with an unknown. Abby will fill his position."

She smiles. "You'll be outnumbered and going up against Loyals, Elites, and maybe Echelon on that ship. You're gonna need all the help you can get. And I don't want to lose you ..."

I say nothing.

"Come on," she begs, clasping her hands. "Some of those people I killed today were my friends—my family! I've proved my loyalty."

Anne laughs. "You'll be loyal right up until you sell us out for a pardon and promotion ..."

She shakes her head. "Do you really think that poorly of me?"

Anne smirks. "I think poorly of everyone I don't know."

"I'd never betray Dion like that," Isabella says. "Or you, Anne."

I study her. Once again, she looks sincere. "Listen, if things go south, I'll have Tommy drop you and Jeremy off as reinforcements, okay?"

She nods. "If it comes to that, you can count on me."

"Alright then, let's finish doing recon and start planning this op," I say to my team.

"Dion ..." Sung begins. "If we're gonna have a chance, we can't board the ship until after sunset ... That's at seven o'clock sharp."

A pit forms in my stomach. *An hour after the next execution.*

"There could be a silver lining," Anne says, ever practical. "If the Dominus makes an appearance, we can confirm that he's still aboard and where he is on the ship. Also, judging by the pattern of executions, the next person to go won't be one of your people. So that's something ..."

Hughes's scowl is so deep that his eyes have almost disappeared. "What, because they aren't his friends, they're expendable?"

Anne sneers. "Forgive me, but the ability to feel anything for anyone who isn't my fiancé or my child is difficult for me. It's a psychological condition I'm working on ..."

"It doesn't matter who feels what, we're all here for the same purpose," I grumble. "Now get to work."

A corporal named Julian Bice is dragged out to the execution tarp at 6:00 P.M. Looks like Anne's prediction was correct. Once again, an unbidden sense of relief is followed by a pinch of self-loathing. They both give way to unadulterated excitement when the camera pans to the Dominus. And the icing on the cake is that the movement on the Terah drone footage matches the execution broadcast.

We don't green-light Operation Vengeful Repossession until 10:00 P.M., after it seems that most Deciders have retired for the night. Minutes later, Rogue Titan is flying at fifteen thousand feet above the ocean. I hate heights. What's more, I hate the idea of falling.

I double-check my TSI-Icarus wingsuit for tears before putting it on.

The Tactical Stealth Insertion Icarus wingsuit is a diving suit specially designed by USAW for Special Forces operations where soldiers need to parachute into an area without drawing attention. It's made of a black matte material designed to deflect radar and dampen body heat signatures. Its modified wing design allows for a 4:1 glide ratio, which means that for every foot I'll fall, I will glide four feet, keeping me airborne longer than with a parachute. It also has airbrakes—pouches—on the dorsal and ventral parts of the suit that I can activate and deactivate with a device attached to my glove. I wore one of these suits for the HALO/HAHO practice jumps at SF training, but that doesn't mean I'm any less terrified.

For the fourth time in the last ten minutes, I double-check the oxygen tube connected to my Deva helmet. We're so high up that if my air isn't connected right, I'll pass out in thirty seconds.

"Twenty seconds, Archangel," Abdul says in my earpiece.

I look over my shoulder with a thumbs-up. My team stares back, their expressions masked by their Deva helmets.

"Right behind you, Dion," Anne says. "I love you, my king."

"I love you too, my queen!"

The countdown proceeds. On ten, the ramp begins to open. My wingsuit flutters violently from the pressure change. I can barely hear the rest of the countdown.

"Six ... five ... four ... three ..."

I activate the night-vision device attached to my helmet and run for the ramp.

"Two."

One!

I jump out into the NVG-enhanced darkness, arms against my side and legs together. After freefalling for six seconds, I spread my arms and legs. The wind pushes up against the wings, sending me into a steady glide. It feels like I'm going to pass out, but after steadying my breathing, that feeling passes. Then nausea hits. I swallow hard and focus on my objective.

Save your son. Save your friends. The nausea slowly subsides.

Now adrenaline's pumping full throttle. Looking to my left at the green-tinged city lights of Long Island, I feel free as a bird.

I toggle the airbrakes every few seconds to bring my speed down. Eventually, I feel my velocity dropping gradually. Abdul plotted my course so that I would be gliding against the wind, which would slow me down and allow me to reach a steady velocity of around forty to fifty miles per hour. A quick glance at my Gauntlet shows my speed is in that range. Beside the velocity is the altimeter.

Two minutes later, I see the SS *Akaran* squatting in the dark ocean waters. The altimeter now says that I'm approaching fifteen hundred feet. I open the airbrakes and angle back, bring my hands to my chest, and open the stealth chute. The canopy opens and catches the air, barely making noise thanks to the sound-absorbing material it's made of. The upward force of the wind pulls me back as it fully expands, taking me into a gentle descent. I uncover the suppressed MP7 strapped to my chest and let it hang from the sling. Then I grab the toggles and steer for the bow, where the security has been lax all day.

"The Terah drone shows one target at the bow and one heading toward the bow from portside," Abdul says. "They are both unaware of your approach."

"We're a minute and a half behind you," Anne says. "It better be clear before we land, love."

It will be, I think, angling the parachute.

As I glide toward the bow, I one-hand the submachine gun and sight the target. My feet clear the rail and I hit the deck with a jog, firing a single shot at his head on my second step. The target drops without making too much noise. I detach the chute and look around for cameras. I find none.

"Thirty seconds until contact," Abdul says.

I quickly remove my wingsuit and toss it overboard along with my chute. Then I free my HK416 before stealthily moving portside to ambush the next target. On the boat-shaped map generated by the Terah drone, I see that his dot is almost in range. I press myself against the short side of a container and wait. When he passes, I grab him by the helmet and shove my knife up through the soft underside of his chin. I flip him over the rail, wincing as he hits the water with a splash.

I check the map again. There are no more red dots nearby so I blink my laser pointer toward the sky, signaling that it's all clear. Then I remove the night-vision device and slide it into a pouch on the side of my pack.

Forty seconds later, Anne touches down. The others come in one by one, five seconds apart. Ten seconds after landing, Rogue Titan has disposed of their wingsuits and parachutes.

"Don't forget," I say as we huddle up, "maintain radio silence until Rogue Titan Bravo and Charlie confirm that the Decider comms have been disabled."

Everyone nods. I signal them to move out.

We split into three teams. Rogue Titan Bravo—Steele and Leo—breaks away, heading along the portside of the ship toward the bridge. Rogue Titan Charlie—Hughes and Sung—take starboard toward the same objective. Rogue Titan Alpha—Anne, Abby, Ken, and myself—cuts through the middle where the Terah drone showed a door leading to the lower deck.

With me at point, we sneak through the narrow path between the shipping containers. The map shows a sentry right outside the door and two near the center of the ship. I signal Ken to take out the sentry once I'm in position to shoot out the camera we assumed would be watching the door. Anne and I slip around the containers. At the corner, I post up and identify the camera above the door opposite the wall and the sentry. Abby makes some noise to draw the guard's attention, and when he turns, I jog toward the container opposite the door that's out of the camera's field of view. From there, I see Abby's fingers counting down. When her fist closes, I shoot out the camera and Ken puts a round through the guard's temple. Now I cut between the two containers while Anne slips around the one to the right. Once we have both targets in sight, she gives the signal and we drop them at the same time with one suppressed puff each. On the way back, we take out the lights over the entrance.

Once we reconvene at the door, I consult my Gauntlet. "Except for two more at the stern and five in the bridge, the deck's clear," I say in a hushed voice, inspecting the stack of the cargo containers that Abby has to climb. "You're up, Red."

"'kay," she whispers. She pulls on her vacuum gloves and starts up the container.

"Found a keycard on the guard," Ken says, extending it to me.

"Let's just hope the doors don't require biometrics too ..." I say.

"We'll just cut off one of their hands," Anne says. "Or borrow an eyeball."

Once Abby reaches the top of the highest container, she lies prone, scopes out the bridge, and whistles faintly. That's our cue.

With a swipe of the keycard, the door opens, revealing a metal staircase that leads down into a dull gray hall. Below deck, we move even slower than we did above, taking the time to knock out lights and destroy cameras in between knifing sentries and random targets who happen to be strolling down the hall. Ken plants flat motion-triggered trip charges on the cabin doors we pass. Anyone emitting a Nexus frequency can pass by a trip without incident, but if the laser aiming at the doorframe is disturbed by anything else, the trip detonates after two seconds.

We better be where we need to be before someone decides to wake up for a late-night piss.

Near the end of the hall, Ken cuts the lights then Anne knifes a patrolman.

Just as the body drops, there's a short burst of static in my headset. "Rogue Titan Alpha?" Sung begins. "Control? Decider comms have been disabled. Moving to the secondary objective."

"Copy that," I respond. "Control, contact Command. Let them know not to move on this place until I give the signal."

"Yes, sir, Archangel," Abdul responds.

"Red Death," I continue, "we just cleared sublevel one. We'll wait for you at the stairwell."

"En route," Abby says.

When Abby arrives, we descend to Sublevel Two. Around the corner from the base of the stairs, there's a guard in Loyal gear standing beside a door labeled NARAKA PRISON COMPLEX. Anne disables the camera while I headshot the Loyal. The door to Naraka requires a keycard and a retinal scan. Good thing the guard still has eyes.

The heavy door opens with a loud clunk. Beyond the threshold is a gloomy, rusted hall. Eight handleless metal doors the same color as the walls stand on both sides. Beside them are security panels. There are no glass windows to peer inside, just a sliding metal panel. I open the one closest to me and a foul smell gusts out. Someone groans in a pitch-black cell. I click on my pistol's tactical light to reveal a man I don't recognize dressed in a filthy sky-blue prison jumpsuit curled up on the floor and shielding his eyes.

"Fuck off …" he groans.

It's the same story with every cell we check. Most are men. Some are women. All of them are strangers to me.

"This is horrible …" Ken says.

"If Decider turncoats are also imprisoned here, we can't free everyone until we have more manpower to manage them," Anne says.

I nod. "Our people must be on the lowest level. That's all we need to worry about right now." I signal the team to advance.

The entrance to Sublevel Three also requires a keycard and retinal scan. Good thing Anne bagged the eye and brought it with her. We put down three guards then proceed toward the ship's center where the executions are held. At the end of that hall, before we're halfway to the stairwell, we find a door with a small glass window that looks different than the rest. The sign above it reads CONTROL ROOM. There are two Loyals sitting at a console and staring out a large window that overlooks the bottom level. Ken unlocks the door with the keycard, then Anne and I burst inside and put rounds into their heads.

I slowly approach the blood-spattered window and, when I reach the console, I see them. Dave, Sam, Jessica, Hudson, and the others are being dragged out by their chains to the walls where they'll be shackled. And beyond the cameras, behind a partitioned area to the right, I spot the Dominus. He's helmetless, but his back is to me. Still, I can tell by that fur-lined white trench coat and his posture that it's him. Beside him, there's a woman with white hair down to the middle of her back. She's wearing a white leather trench coat with a hood on the back. *Ghost.* With them are a tall olive-skinned woman in white, Stevenson, Don Chambers, and a couple of Elite- and Echelon-class Deciders.

I'm going to kill them all …

Suddenly, I feel feverish. Everything goes red.

"… Dion! Dion, we have to move!" Anne's muffled voice shouts.

I shake my head to clear the rage. That's when I hear the sirens blare and notice the yellow lights flashing. The Dominus puts on his helmet and Ghost pulls up her hood. I run toward the door leading to the stairs.

"I can't get through to anybody!" Ken shouts.

"I don't even hear you in my headset," Abby says, as softly as always.

I stop at the door and eye my Gauntlet. No signal. No map data. "They're jamming our comms," I say. "Abdul will know something's up and call in reinforcements. Just finish the mission!"

As I yank open the door and sight the targets through my HK416's scope, explosions from above begin cracking off, shaking the ship. That must be Ken's trip charges going off.

A helmetless Elite heading for the stairs suddenly looks up at us. I dispatch him with a headshot then run down the stairs. Behind me, my team opens fire on the Loyals closest to us.

"Contact!" someone yells.

Now the bullets start coming. Keeping low, we scurry from the stairs to cover behind a stack of crates. Four Loyals stand their ground. Meanwhile, the Dominus, Ghost, and their entourage use our friends as shields—some holding guns to their heads, others shooting at us—while walking backward toward a long modular office that juts out of the starboard wall.

Abby, who's still upstairs, picks off one Loyal. We make quick work of the other three with 40mm grenade launcher rounds, grenades, and gunfire. With the area secure, I lead the charge toward the office. Through the two wide windows along the walls, I see the targets entering the middle room. Running a few feet ahead of the others, I bolt through the entrance. Right as I do, there's a mechanical sound and a loud crash behind me. I dive for cover and glance back to see that I've been separated from the others by a blast door. Ahead, Don Chambers slams the door behind them. The Dominus appears in the window beside it. Shutters fall, blocking off the windows to the right that look out on the execution area.

"Dion!" Anne cries from the other side.

"Free Hudson and the other prisoners they left behind then find a way around," I shout back.

"Dion Johnson!" the Dominus roars over an intercom.

I pop up and fire two rounds at his face. Neither penetrates the glass. The bastard didn't even flinch.

The Dominus shakes his head. "Are you or are you not Dion Johnson?" he booms, pulling Jessica to him and pressing a gun to her head.

"It's me," I growl. "Where's my son, Dominus?"

"Your boy is not on this ship … Now come to the window and remove your helmet. Let me set eyes on you …"

I don't budge. For all I know, this room is rigged to fill with toxic gas.

"Do it before we kill them all in front of you!" he commands, slamming Jess's face against the window.

I slowly walk toward him, tossing my helmet as I do so. When I reach the window, Stevenson smirks. Don scowls, pointing his machete at me. Ghost's eyes are mostly hidden by her hood. Her black lipstick–coated lips are pursed. As for Jessica and the others, they stare back at me silently like they don't recognize me. Except for Sam. "Dion!" she whimpers, squirming in Ghost's grip.

"And there he is ..." the Dominus says as if in awe. A deep bellow of a laugh follows. "Dion 'The Archangel' Johnson! Humanity's *savior*! The people's *champion*!" He laughs again. "Oh, I've been waiting a *long, long* time for this ..."

"And who the fuck are you, Dominus?" I snarl.

The Dominus gestures at the door behind him. "Secure the helicopter. Take the prisoners with you."

With a nod, his lackeys shove everyone but Jess out the door. Ghost is the only Decider who remains. She stands there, head lowered and tilted to the side, glaring at me through her hair.

The Dominus shoves Jessica to Ghost then hands her his white SAR-21 assault rifle. "For the record, I wasn't hiding my identity from the world. I've been hiding it from *you*, Archangel." He removes the helmet. Ear-length brown hair falls out from underneath. "But the time to reveal myself has finally come!" He lifts his head and smirks.

Those deep-set, bluish-gray eyes ... That smug look ... He looks just like ... Richard Thomas?

"*You buried me, remember?*" Richard's voice whispers in my mind. "*Look harder! Think, kid!*"

A relative? But which one?

Images of Richard Thomas's family that I dug up during my research flash in my mind. One photo freezes in my mind's eye, the one of Richard and his brother that fell out of his journal when I first opened it.

My eyes widen. *It can't be ...*

The Dominus grins. "There it is ... That's the 'oh, shit' face of a man who's just figured it all out."

18

LEX TALIONIS

September 18
11:43 P.M.

"RYAN THOMAS ..." I gasp.

He smirks. "Bingo."

I eye the pale girl and I recall an excerpt from Richard's journal. Eight years ago, he wrote about visiting his cousin Lauren for her birthday. He described her as "pale enough to blind a man on a sunny day." He also said she was a prodigy set to start college at the age of sixteen. Ominously, Richard overheard Ryan telling her that he wanted her to be a part of "something big" and gave her a laptop containing everything she needed to know. And that was before Richard learned of Ryan's plans for launching a global rebellion ...

When I tried compiling a profile on Lauren during my research, I couldn't even find one photo. All I dredged up were her birth records, something about ballet, a mention of her in a school article about her finishing second on the balance beam at a gymnastics meet, her name listed as valedictorian of her high school, and a mention of her research during her time at Harvard. After that, she ceased to exist.

"And the girl behind you, Ghost—she's your cousin, Lauren Thomas."

Ghost raises her head slightly. She puts her knife closer to Jessica's throat. "Never utter that name," she says in a flat, monotone voice. "Lauren's dead."

"Bravo, two for two ..." Ryan Thomas says. "Tell me, how did you learn of my dear cousin? We had her connection to us wiped."

"Richard left me his journal, among other things," I respond.

"Richard didn't leave you shit! You stole his possessions after you murdered him!"

"There was a lot about your family in that book of his," I continue, "including you recruiting *Lauren* to your cause at her fourteenth birthday party."

Lip quivering, Ghost raises her chin to me. With the light now illuminating the top half of her face, I see her powder-blue eyes glaring at me through her snowy locks. The black mascara she has smeared around her eyes gives her an even creepier vibe.

"Hmm, I wasn't aware he knew about that ..." he says, glancing at Lauren.

"Also in that journal is a very detailed mention of your 'death,' Ryan ... Losing you destroyed Richard. Why'd you deceive him?"

"It pained me to do, but it was the necessary push he needed to become what I needed him to be."

"You let Richard be your pawn so you could do what exactly?"

He smirks. "You don't think Richard purged all the elites and annexed the world on his own, did you? Before the Deciders, there was a group of one hundred and thirteen soldiers from across the globe that wanted to overthrow the world governments. That group was dubbed Echelon, and I was its leader. After Echelon obtained Veritas, and after those of us involved faked our deaths to avoid being hunted, we went underground. Not long after, I began working for a private military that dabbled in wet work and security on behalf of a powerful banking family."

"Interesting how you worked for the elites that you sought to destroy," I remark.

"Working for them, gaining their trust, and moving up the ladder to get close to them was the only way to identify and locate the so-called Illuminati—the Powers That Be—the men who lived in the shadows pulling the world's strings, dividing humanity. Identifying them and purging them, this was Operation Erebus.

"The thing about the 'Illuminati,'" Ryan says, making air quotes, "is that they also wanted to overthrow the world governments and rule the world through the United Nations and one global central bank. So, when they found out there was a group called the Deciders with a similar goal in mind, they wanted to hijack their cause and use them to usher in the collapse. Once society fell, they would swoop in, eliminate the Deciders, and establish *their* control. So I put them in contact with the Echelon aiding Richard. After that, they funded the Deciders, armed them, and the rest you know.

"While you were fighting my brother, my faction of Deciders and I were busy eliminating the elites." Ryan lets out a wild laugh, just like his brother used to. "And do you know what happened when I finally purged the last one? During preparations to reunite with Richard, I learned from Don Chambers that he was murdered by *you*, and that the Deciders were collapsing thanks to a random fucking militia called the Angels of War!"

I step closer to the glass. "Taking my son and friends, was it all just to lure me here to kill me for what I did?" I ask, fishing a thermite charge from my pocket.

"Kill you?" Ryan grins. "No, I don't want to kill you, boy. Not yet. I want to make you suffer first! That's what Lex Talionis calls for!"

I plant the charge on the lock. "Lex what now?"

"Lex Talionis is a Latin term that means punishment should be equal in degree to the crime. You know … an eye for an eye, a tooth for a tooth! My retribution against you calls for you to suffer for the remainder of your days the way you made me suffer when you took my brother from me!" His eyes shut. "Yes, taking your friends was just a ruse to lure you out of hiding and to bring you here, but it was also retribution against them for their crimes during the war. That's what Naraka is for! Naraka is where those who have done wrong are made to suffer for their sins until they can be reborn."

"And so you're executing people help them become *reborn*?"

"Oh, that was just a show for you. It was a shame to prematurely end to their suffering but we needed to draw you out." He grins. "And here you are! A little earlier than we expected, but we're ready."

My eyes flick around the room, searching for traps. "Ready for what?"

"Poseidon, Mr. Johnson! It's the event that will kick off the Reclamation and bring the world to its knees! Using antimatter bombs placed strategically throughout the world's oceans, I will generate tsunamis and earthquakes that will wipe the coastal cities of my choosing off the map. All the navy ships around the world gathered at ports in preparation for the war I engineered? Gone. And cities on major fault lines like the Cascadian subduction zone? They'll crumble into nothing."

That must be the threat on the coast Isabella warned me about, I think, as I pound my fist on the glass. "You fucking monster! How is this better than the mass extermination the elites had planned for the world—the one you once set out to prevent!"

Ryan shrugs. "It's no better, actually. Or worse. In fact, it's the only logical move to better humanity."

"You're fucking deranged …"

"No, you're just naïve. The elites had it right. The only way to effectively control humanity is to reduce the population to a manageable level. When the death toll rises, our power and control will rise conversely with it. And after Poseidon, the world will know exactly what the Deciders are capable of. They will fear us. They will regard us as gods. They will be too weak and scared to resist the new world we'll bring."

"I'm going to stop you …" I growl.

"Stop me? It's your fault that Poseidon is happening …"

"It's no one's fault but yours!"

"To create a new world, first you have to destroy the existing one. The Chaos-Purge-Restore that Richard carried out was meant to destroy the old world with minimum casualties. You halted that progress before he finished and restored an incorrect version of the world. Since it's impossible to re-create what my brother did, the only option is to activate the failsafe I had in place in the event that Richard lost control. Your 'victory' did nothing more than delay the inevitable. If not for you, we'd be well into our utopia and those hundreds of millions of people wouldn't need to die."

I glare at him. "I *will* stop you …"

He shakes his head. "You can't, boy … Even if you could capture or kill me, my Vice is ready to pull the trigger tonight if I don't contact him in the next—" he eyes his Gauntlet— "hour. Either way, I hope you'll be around for the big event. Your file says that most of your relatives live in New York? I brought you here so that you can witness the city's destruction up close with the knowledge that it's your fault." He taps his Gauntlet and puts it to the glass. "You've already lost a family member today …"

It takes me a while to accept that what I'm seeing is real. When I finally do, my eyes flood with tears. Before me is a photo of my son Marshal. His body is pale and his head is twisted unnaturally far to the left.

"Lex Talionis, Dion!" Ryan grins psychotically as he takes his Deva helmet from Ghost. He puts his arm around Jessica and walks backward toward the door with her. "You murdered my blood, so I murdered yours!"

Fury rises from my gut like fire from a flamethrower. With a roar, I unleash an entire magazine at the window, no regard for ricocheting bullets.

The image of Ryan, Jessica, and Ghost distorts behind the expanding cracks, but even after thirty rounds, the glass doesn't shatter. I look back to the door and see the thermite charge I planted before Ryan showed me that photo of my son. Since the Nexus signals are jammed, I activate it manually then dash back to cover. Ghost and Ryan stop and turn at the sound of the steel-melting reaction. Ghost draws two white Glock 18s from leg holsters underneath her trench coat and gives Ryan a nod. He says something to her before fleeing through the door with Jessica.

Once the thermite burns through, I kick the door open and leap to my left as bursts of gunfire from her automatic pistols snap through the doorway. An eerie silence follows.

"I've heard rumors of your battlefield prowess," she says flatly. "And I watched the security footage of your fight against Dozer. Sure, you're talented, but you're not in my league, Archangel. There is no scenario that ends with you getting past me."

I toss a flash grenade far into the room, wait, then throw a second. The second one I didn't pull the pin from. So once the first one pops, I bolt toward the door, training my MP7 on where I expect her to be standing. Instead, she's actually charging toward me with one eye closed. She spins into a kick that sends my weapon flying. The second strike hits me in the chest. I fall back to the floor, drawing my pistol and aiming at her head.

Ghost trains one Glock on me and holsters the other. "Fun fact ... I get off on taking lives ..." She removes her hood, finally revealing her face. Her face is slim with somewhat sunken cheeks. Her skin's almost the color of milk.

An unpleasant vibe buzzes through me like static. Her powder-blue irises boil with anguish, anger, and a burning hatred the likes of which I have never seen. When I first met Anne, I saw something good buried beneath her ruthlessness, sadness, and emptiness. There's no hint of anything good in Ghost, just darkness swirling with misery, bloodlust, and fury. Something in that look resonates with me, and I don't like the thought of sharing anything with her.

The longer our eyes stay locked, the more intense the vibe becomes. My breathing quickens. Ghost's breathing seems to pick up too. She shivers.

"Inflicting and receiving pain also pleases me," she says, "but ending human lives is the only thing in this world that makes me *truly* happy. And over the last two years, the idea of taking your life—the life of the world-renowned soldier no Decider could kill—has become somewhat of a fantasy of mine ..." Her free hand caresses her thigh. "The thought of spilling your blood makes my skin tingle ..." She breathes in deeply.

This girl is severely disturbed, I think, standing slowly, pistol still trained on her. "Let's both pull our triggers and see who walks away ..."

She sighs. "I'm the last living relative Ryan cares for. Though unlikely, if you were to kill me, he would simply sink this ship with everyone on it, including your *Ice Queen*. And as badly as I want to still your heart, I promised him I wouldn't. Yet ..."

Let him try. Subtly, I begin depressing the trigger.

She adjusts her aim. "Don't give me a reason to disappoint him … Or do … It would make my day."

I ease my finger off the trigger. "I'm not just going to let you walk out of here."

"And I'm not leaving without having some fun with you." She licks her lips. "Now toss your weapons." She starts lowering her pistol. "Don't worry, I'll do the same …"

I lower my weapon at the same speed she lowers hers. When our weapons are at our sides, we both toss them away. She draws a combat knife with a white and purple handle from inside her trench coat and holds it in reverse grip. I do the same with my blade.

The corner of her mouth twitches when she assumes her fighting stance. "We have approximately three minutes to play … Bore me and you die …"

She charges.

Ghost strikes first, leading with a low kick and following with a flurry of punches and blade swipes. I block and evade most of them but eventually take a few punches and a cut to my left arm. She's incredibly fast. And her moves are so unorthodox, they're hard to anticipate.

I manage to cut her knife-wielding hand, then she punches me in the face with the other and kicks the blade from my hand, sending it across the room. I disarm her shortly after. Another spinning kick connects with my jaw, but just barely. I respond with a right to the ribs, a left jab to her face, and a low kick to her thigh. She parries my next punch and counters with a punch to my mouth that splits my lip. A right hook bloodies her mouth in return and a side kick to the kidney drives her back.

Holding her side, Ghost slowly straightens up. She smiles and licks the blood from her teeth. "This is *fun* ..." she moans, walking toward me slowly, hips swaying. "Most people don't last thirty seconds. Or make me bleed."

I pick up her knife. "Enjoy it now because this is about to end."

"Indeed. No more holding back ..."

Once in range, Ghost unleashes a crazy combination of strikes all while dodging my knife attacks and driving me into the corner. It's a worse ass-beating than Anne or Richard ever gave me ...

I take a chance and swing the knife at her neck. Leaning forward, she blocks my attack with her left forearm and thrusts the bottom of her right fist down at my left leg. A sharp, crippling pain shoots up my thigh; I don't have to look to know she stabbed me. *When did she get another knife?* She grabs my right wrist, uppercuts me, then slams me against the wall, pinning right arm and putting the knife she slides out of her sleeve to my throat.

Breathing hard, she slowly leans in close to my face. "Mhmm ... I really want to slit your throat ..." she pants.

"Do it and I'll plunge this knife into your lung," I groan, pushing the tip of the backup blade I drew from my tactical belt into her rib.

Ghost shudders at the feel of the point and looks down. "Oh, you did not disappoint, Archangel ..." She brings her face even closer to mine and leans into the knife. "If only we had more time to play." Her mouth opens and her tongue slides out. The tip of it touches my chin and she licks the stream of blood up to my busted lip. Her eyes close momentarily. "Ah, at least I got taste ..." She head-butts me then knees me in the gut, finishing with a hook to my temple.

Disoriented and winded, I drop to my hands and knees, watching a blurry image of Ghost moving hastily toward her pistols. I hike up my pant leg and draw the Glock 26 from my ankle holster. I try standing but immediately collapse to my knees—the leg she stabbed won't support me. "We're not done yet, Ghost!" I wheeze.

She turns and aims. "No ... we're not ..." she says, drawing out her words as she gracefully walks backward. "I shall still your heart another day ..." She slips through the door.

"Shit!" I grumble, falling onto my ass, still aiming at the door. I stare at the small throwing knife lodged in my thigh and wrap my hand around the white handle.

This is going to hurt ... One. Two.

I howl as I pull the blade free.

19
POSEIDON

September 19
12:03 A.M.

HAND TREMBLING FROM the pain, knife still clenched in my fist, I examine the wound. Warm blood runs out the open gash in a non-pulsing fashion. Doesn't look like an artery was hit, just muscle.

My attention shifts to the knife. It's a double-edged black blade outlined in silver; only about three of its five inches are covered in blood. It has good weight and feel, and judging by its sharpness, it's high quality and handmade. I slide it into an empty mag pouch and climb to my feet.

I step with my bad leg first. My vision pulses with the flare of pain but I keep my footing. I limp toward the exit, scooping up my weapons along the way. I step through the doorway that the Dominus and Ghost took and sweep the stairwell with my rifle. The immediate area and the stairs are clear, but there are footsteps crashing rapidly against the metal steps above and muffled gunfire in the distance. Never lowering my weapon, I shuffle up the stairs, desperately trying to contact my team along the way. It seems comms are still down.

Then static bursts in my headset. "Rogue Titan Alpha, do you copy?" Steele asks. "We've disabled the signal jammer. Does anyone copy?"

"This is Archangel! I copy!"

"Dion, thank goodness!" Anne says before I can ask whether she's okay.

"Archangel!" It's General Walker, and he sounds pissed. "You and your team—"

"There's no time for a scolding or threats, General!" I shout, cutting him off. "The Deciders are about to activate something called Poseidon—a series of antimatter bombs planted in the oceans that, when detonated, will send tsunamis hurtling toward coastal cities around the planet!"

"*What?*"

"Issue evacuations immediately and clear all troops from the coastlines! Flying Titan, we need extraction! Rogue Titan, meet me at the hangar in the center of the ship!"

"Copy," Tommy responds. "ETA seven minutes."

A strong breeze gusts through the door at the top of the second flight. I shoulder the door and limp out, clearing the area with my rifle. Directly ahead, the hooded Ghost walks past Jessica, Sam, Dave, and Hudson who are kneeling on the floor with their heads down, their hair blowing in the wind being generated by the spinning helicopter blades behind them. The Specter stealth helicopter ... It's the first time seeing one up close and I can barely hear it, even from less than twenty yards away. The aircraft is gray, slightly larger than a Blackhawk with a fuselage of hexagonal panels set at odd, bulging angles, making it look like some sort of cubist wasp. If someone told me it was reverse-engineered from an alien spacecraft, I might believe them, especially since Veritas revealed that world governments had spent millions investigating UFOs ...

In the door of the Specter, Don and Stevenson and two other Deciders are pointing their guns at my friends.

I dart behind a support beam and take aim at Ghost. "Don't take another step!"

She halts, glancing over her shoulder at me.

Ryan Thomas appears behind Don. "Fire one round and not only do your friends get blown to hell," his voice threatens over a speaker system, "but you get a round in your head and then your team will drown when I blow the charges on the ship's hull."

Ghost resumes strolling toward the helicopter.

I spot a blinking device behind Dave. Arms trembling with rage, my aim shifts to Ryan. Before I can curse him, a door across the hangar bursts open and Anne comes running through it, aiming at the chopper. Ken, Abby, and six rescued and rearmed USAW soldiers charge out behind her, then fan out in a semicircle.

Ghost, who's now aboard the chopper, and the Deciders aim at my team.

"Don't shoot!" I shout.

"Why the fuck not?" Ken asks, squinting as he aims his rifle.

"They've booby-trapped the ship ... and our friends. Ryan!" I shout, fixing the crosshairs on his helmeted head. It takes everything not to pull the trigger. *The round won't be able to penetrate his helmet, anyway* ... "The next time we meet, I'll kill you the same way I killed your brother!"

The stealth chopper lifts off. "We shall see about that, Mr. Johnson! Now, enjoy the show. Showtime's in ten minutes ..."

I keep my sights trained on the Specter right up until the ceiling doors close and block my view of it. "Shit!" I curse, limping toward Jess and the others. "Are you guys okay?" I ask as I squat down to help Jess up. She refuses to look at me. She won't even take my hand.

"What did they do to you?" I ask.

Dave just stares blankly back at me, shaking his head.

Hudson looks at me with wild eyes. "They did things to us, Johnson. They broke us, man … They fuckin' broke us …"

"It'll get better," I say. "You're safe now." Lame, but I'm at a loss for words.

"Anybody got a hacksaw?" Ken asks. That's when I notice that their shackles are chained to hooks in the floor. And the device I thought to be a bomb is no longer blinking.

"Nope," Anne says, but they left some thermite cutting torches … How kind of them …"

The others huddle around us. As Ken gets to work freeing the prisoners, Anne eyes my bleeding leg. "What the hell happened?" She squats and feverishly rummages through her tactical pack.

"Ghost happened … Bitch stabbed me in the thigh."

She extracts a tube of Cascade and a wound irrigation bottle from the pack. "You didn't hold back, did you?" she asks as she quickly cleans the wound.

"Nope," I say, wincing. "She's just that skilled …"

She slaps on the Cascade. "That old hag beat your ass worse than I did …"

"She's not old at all. She's Lauren Thomas, Richard's younger cousin …"

"What?" Anne says while wrapping a bandage around my thigh. "And the Dominus? Ryan? Richard's brother?"

"That's right … Ryan Thomas isn't dead after all."

She rises, helping me to my feet. "You're kidding."

Ken finishes cutting Sam free, and she runs over and buries her face in my chest. "Thanks for coming for us, Dion." She lets out a sob. "The things they did …" She glances at the others.

"Tell me later …"

Our group breaks into a jog with Anne and I leading, Ken and Abby at the rear, and Hudson, Jessica, and the others in the middle of the pack.

A few feet from the stairwell door, two Loyals come racing around the corner. I'm too close to stop so I charge. A burst from Anne's rifle kills the furthest one as I push the nearest target's EVO Scorpion barrel away from me and put my pistol to his ribs and pump four rounds into him.

The distinct whirring of the Osprey becomes audible as we ascend the stairs, as does the buzzing of its ramp-mounted Dillon M134 rotary machinegun. Anne kicks open the door to the deck, revealing a portrait of tracer rounds from the Osprey's M134 racing through the night sky at an enemy Blackhawk. The rounds tear through the cockpit and the helicopter spirals out and crashes into the water.

There goes the Deciders' evac …

Jeremy's manning the gun. Lance Corporal Oliver Hawke is beside him, laying down suppressive fire with an M240.

Four Loyals emerge from behind a cargo container to the right, shooting at what can only be Rogue Titan Bravo. We engage as we race to cover. Then we're flanked by a trio of Deciders from the left. Abby, Ken, and Hudson scramble to beat them back. Before they're in position, a spray of gunfire from a shooter hidden between two cargo containers cuts right through the enemy.

"I got you," Isabella says over the comm.

"Good work, Izzy," I say. "Move in for the flank. We'll draw their fire."

She does as instructed, sneaking up behind them and putting two down with a few controlled bursts. Abby gets the first one that pops up. We focus fire on the last one.

"Coming out! Hold your fire!" Sung announces over the comm. He and the rest of Rogue Titan Bravo emerge from behind the containers across from us.

"The Terah drone shows the deck is secure," Abdul says.

"Touching down in the center of the ship," Tommy says. "Clear the LZ."

We gather at the edge of the LZ. Anne takes the rifle and pistol from Isabella while giving her a nod of approval.

"Thanks," I say.

"No problem, hon. Though I damn near died jumping down onto a container from the helicopter!"

I don't say anything.

In the awkward silence, she scans me from head to toe. "Looks like someone gave you a run for your money."

"Ghost was that someone."

"Shit." She looks over the party we rescued. "Hey, uh ... your kid ... Was he ...?"

He's dead.

No, he's not.

"He wasn't on the ship with them ..." I mumble.

"Don't worry, you'll find—"

Something rocks the ship, which dips alarmingly to starboard. The Deciders' fallen weapons skid across the deck. Then the ship rolls back in the opposite direction before settling.

"What the fuck was *that?*" Steele asks.

"The tsunami," I say. "It's official—we failed."

The Osprey's wheels hit the deck and we board. Tommy dusts off the second the last person is on and we turn west toward New Jersey.

"You ... you guys want to see this?" Abdul asks. "We have a drone over New York Harbor."

"Turn it on," I say, and the feed flickers on to the overhead monitor. Now past the continental shelf, the wave could be a good hundred feet tall. It crashes through the houses and housing projects of the Rockaways and Coney Island like they're made of paper, then doubles in height as it crosses Jamaica Bay. Brooklyn and southern Queens go black as if they were being covered up by a vast set of blinds.

"So this is how the world ends ..." Jeremy sighs.

Moments later, the tsunami crashes into Downtown Manhattan, and the same terrible scene repeats itself. Skyscrapers topple like dominoes. From our vantage point, we can't see how far the carnage extends, but the Empire State Building, the Chrysler Building, and the rest of Midtown fall.

We hold our breaths, staring at the black screen.

Isabella is crying. "All those people ... How could they just kill so many people ...?"

"And you said there are still more tsunamis to come?" Hawke asks.

I nod. "I couldn't stop it ..."

Just like you couldn't stop Ryan from killing your son ...

Marshal's not dead!

"Don't blame yourself for this, Dion," Anne murmurs. "This isn't your fault."

"It is ... It wouldn't have happened if I didn't stop Richard. Poseidon was just a contingency ..."

Anne grabs my jaw and turns my head to face her. "You didn't pull the trigger! Ryan did! He was going to launch Poseidon no matter what ... Whatever he told you was nothing more than a ploy to break you!"

"I should've been able to uncover it and prevent it from happening ... All of this. Him taking my friends—my son ... I should have dug deeper … I missed something somewhere down the line. I could have done more to—"

Anne slaps me hard. "Everything that's happened since their reemergence was out of your control! There was nothing you could have done to prevent any of it!" She holds my hands and searches my eyes. "Protecting the world is not your burden to bear. Never was. And neither is protecting your friends."

I scowl and look away.

"They weren't captured because you missed something," she continues, speaking softer now. "They were captured because they let their guards down—because they weren't strong enough to protect themselves … You need to come to terms with that. Otherwise, you will live in regret for the rest of your life … and I can't have that." She squeezes my hands. "Now, let me hear you say none of this was your fault. And I want you to mean it."

I find comfort and acceptance in her eyes. She's right. It was out of my control. I did what I could. At least Anne and Dean are safe. My parents are safe. Karla, Casey, and Eric are safe. Jeremy and my team are good. We rescued Sam, Dave, and Jess. But Marshal … I refuse to believe he's dead. I know he's not dead. And I will get him back.

And I will kill Ryan Thomas for everything that he's done.

And before I spill his blood, I'll kill as many Deciders as I can. *Lex Talionis* …

The self-doubt and guilt fade. An unshakeable focus replaces them, fueled by a dark, vengeful fire raging in my core. I can't let Anne see that though, so I suppress it by taking a deep breath and slowly letting it out. "You're right," I finally say. "I protected as much of *my* world as I could. I can't keep putting everyone's lives and the world on my shoulders."

Anne searches my eyes once more. When she's sure of my honesty, she nods. "Good."

We kiss.

Someone clears his throat. "Archangel?" It's Abdul. He looks nervous.

"What is it?" I ask.

He points at the monitor. On screen, there's a map of the world with countless small yellow dots scattered across the oceans. In the bottom-right corner, there's a smaller window showing a live stream of General Walker.

"These yellow dots represent tsunami buoys," Abdul explains. "Approximately three minutes ago, hundreds of them began to pick up oceanic disturbances. Buoys closer to the coasts have begun to follow." He presses a key on his laptop and arrows pointing toward the coasts appear on the screen. "And these are the tsunamis' projected paths ..."

"Holy hell ..." Sung says, his words trailing off. "The cities on the United States' eastern and western seaboards, Lisbon, Shanghai, Hong Kong, Japan, Mumbai, Singapore, Sydney, Melbourne, ... Cape Town—"

"Enough," I say, gritting my teeth.

"—when those cities get hit, that's hundreds of millions of civilians dead. All in a matter of minutes ..."

"Enough!"

"How long till they strike?" Ken asks.

"Anywhere from five minutes to three hours," Abdul says.

"At this point, it doesn't matter," I say. "There's no stopping it. When those tidal waves hit, the Reclamation begins, and we need to be ready for their follow-up attacks." I turn back to the video chat screen. "General Walker, do we have any secondary, off-the-books bases that USAW can fall back to?"

"There are several around the country that our troops are relocating to as we speak. Fort Sanctum's backup is a place codenamed Babylon. Sergeant Seo knows where it is. Help Mr. Rahman get the base operational. The reinforcements who went to aid you at Naraka shouldn't be far behind. The rest of us are en route."

"What about Corvus?" I ask. "If you bring him with you, that's it for us."

"I guess news that Corvus was identified earlier and killed during his attempted escape didn't reach you during the time you went rogue ..." Walker says. "At any rate—"

Something that sounds like an explosion cuts him off. He looks left. "Fucking hell! We're under attack!"

There's another explosion.

"What?" Jeremy yelps, rising from his seat. "Karla—we have to go get Karla!"

"Do *not* come back for us!" Walker barks. "Staff Sergeant Hall and his team has your friend under their protection. Just get your asses to Babylon!"

PART THREE
RECLAMATION

20
AFTERMATH

September 19
1:01 A.M.

WITH THE MANMADE tsunamis comes the destruction of countless buildings, homes, historical sites, and landmarks in dozens of the world's greatest cities, as well as the utter erasure of smaller communities along coastlines around the world. Several of the underwater earthquakes are estimated to have reached 11.0 on the Richter scale—more than thirty times bigger than the strongest earthquake ever recorded. This is not the setting for an apocalyptic movie. This is the Earth after Poseidon ...

Every surviving news station around the world broadcasts coverage of the devastation. And the carnage is still ongoing as more tsunamis make landfall after completing their silent journeys across hundreds of miles of ocean. The reports are flickering on an eight-panel grid, an incoherent montage of flooded streets, building smashed to matchsticks, overturned vehicles, fallen bridges, uprooted trees, bodies floating through intersections, survivors on rooftops awaiting rescue—the story is the same everywhere ...

The latest estimates put the death toll somewhere around six hundred million people—again, for a process that's still underway. American stations are calling it the "Tidal Apocalypse." Trish has been pulled from the air, but her stand-in is filling in admirably by speculating that Earth's oceans were bombarded by undetected asteroids as her co-anchor Bill Hayes looks on like he's trying not to strangle her.

If only they knew …

They'll find out soon enough, a voice that sounds like Richard's whispers in my mind. *Ryan will be making his speech shortly, kid.*

No one aboard the Osprey speaks while the footage plays, aside from muttered curses. Most watch quietly with tears streaming down their faces. Chances are each of them had friends and relatives in places ravaged by Poseidon, like Jeremy, whose family lived in Brooklyn, and Steele's, whose family lived in Charleston. As for me, I am just numb to it all.

It was inevitable. Before the Deciders, the elites were going to execute a mass extermination. If Ryan Thomas didn't do it, someone else would have eventually. This was always the fate of mankind.

Like Anne, I'm stone-faced, wishing I could feel sorrow over the deaths and destruction. Even if I could, the depression I feel for my relatives who were washed away and for my missing (*or dead*) son, and rage for what Ryan has done would just drown it out.

Alerts come in over Nexus that the inland American military bases have come under attack. Abdul replaces the grid of news reports with a mosaic of live streams from USAW, Army, and USMC base security cameras along with satellite footage of those areas. Once again, the scenes blur together in their sameness—missiles fired from drones and other aircraft raining down on the bases like meteors. Most are destroyed by anti-ballistic missiles and lasers. Some make contact, destroying buildings and grounded aircraft. Other drones crop-dust bases with chemical agents. From the reports, the symptoms of exposure read like Miasma—

asphyxiation and bleeding from the eyes, nose, mouth, and ears. Satellites keeping tabs on rivals and friendlies overseas show the same style of attacks during different times of day.

Not long after, the Deciders unleash hell on landlocked cities as well. Drone and satellite feeds show Decider jets, helicopters, and ground forces swarming through cities as large as Chicago and as small as Santa Fe.

Just like that, the world is on fire once again.

Hudson suddenly begins half-laughing, half-sobbing. "Welcome back to the suck, boys and girls! We won't be so lucky this time around."

"Hudson," Sung says cautiously. "Do you know what's coming next, brother?"

Hudson grins. "Yeah. Death. Lots of it too, *brother*!" He cackles.

Sung turns to me with worry in his eyes. *He's lost it* is what his face conveys.

I nod, shifting my sights to the others we rescued. Jessica's trembling in her seat, staring at the floor. Unless I missed it, she hasn't spoken or even acknowledged any of us since we found her.

"Guys?" Abdul says. He taps a few keys and the monitor changes to the multiscreen news grid. "Center window and on the bottom right …"

At first glance, it appears that all the channels are now focused on the war that has suddenly erupted around the world, but there are two broadcasts that stand out. They are both still shots of the Decider flag with a caption that reads THIS IS NOT A TEST. Another channel goes black and the same thing pops up shortly after.

My muscles tense in anticipation of what I know will follow. One after another, news channels change over to hacked broadcasts. In seconds, they've all been hijacked. The shot cuts to a helmeted Dominus standing before a podium, a Decider flag as a backdrop. Abdul clicks double-clicks on the center window and it expands to fill the full screen just as Ryan Thomas begins his address.

"Good morning and good evening to those who were spared from the ocean's wrath," Ryan Thomas begins.

My left eyelid has developed a tic. I want nothing more than to jump through the screen and rip his throat out with my teeth.

"It's introduction time," Ryan continues, planting his hands on the sides of the Deva helmet. He removes it slowly, finally exposing his face to the world. He smiles smugly just like his brother used to. "My name is Ryan Thomas, elder brother of the fallen Architect, Richard Thomas, and I am your Dominus … In all actuality, I am the *original* Architect, the true creator of and unseen driving force behind the Deciders, but that is a story for another day."

"It really is him …" Anne whispers.

"Now," Ryan sighs, "my condolences to those who lost loved ones in the disaster. It truly is a shame that so many lives were lost. I'm sure many of you would like to know why this happened. Well, let me shed light on that for you, my people. This was a manmade incident caused by a project dubbed Poseidon. Those tsunamis were generated by explosives that were scattered throughout Earth's oceans, sending tsunamis hurtling toward the coasts. The people responsible for the triggering of Poseidon are none other than your government leaders and your militaries. They were given a choice to end their feuds and relinquish their power to us. They were told what would happen if they didn't. But instead, they chose their own self-interests over humanity. And because of their inextinguishable urge for global conflict and their incessant need to ensure that humanity remained divided, they willingly sat back and allowed the deaths of almost one billion people. And they did not say one word about it to you either."

Ryan is gesturing and grinning frequently as he speaks. "In the wake of Poseidon, we, the Deciders, have taken it upon ourselves to take back the reins and continue along the path that my younger brother started us out on. This time, nothing shall prevent us from achieving absolute global domination and crafting a utopia where humanity can finally live in peace, without division! We do not wish for the loss of any more lives, but for those who resist, death awaits them at the frontlines! Submit, and you will be met with protection and a better life than before. Let me assure you, no reeducation camps await you this time around as you have all been educated on Veritas. Only food, water, electricity, and security await you in our graces. Be wise in your choices and prepare for the transition. It will be a rocky one ..." A dark smile creeps across his face. "And now—" he raises his hands— "let there be darkness ..."

The screen goes black.

Abdul returns to the grid view. Every last channel is blacked out.

"Don't tell me they ..." Hughes grumbles.

"Pull up satellite images of Earth," I demand, almost shouting.

Abdul nods and begins typing away. Four windows showing America, Europe, Africa, and Asia come up. The whole of the Americas is completely dark. So are Africa and Europe. It's reasonable to assume that the power is out for the nations experiencing daytime as well.

"Looks like a fucking EMP hit the planet ..." Sung says.

"I should hope not," Anne says. "If this isn't temporary, today will become a footnote. Another seventy to eighty percent of the world population will perish within ninety days without electricity."

"Unless they grovel to the Deciders," I say.

Steele scowls. "Do you really think that the people are just going to kneel before them after *this*?"

"Yes," I answer. "It's either that or starve. People have families, children. They'll do what they have to do."

Sung cracks his knuckles. "Then we just gotta control the resources before they do."

Anne shakes her head. "How? The grid went down. There's not much we can do without power, much less while our troops are fighting for their lives."

"Well, then how the fuck are we going to get the upper hand?" Hughes asks.

I sigh. "No clue. Ryan's already playing this smarter than Richard did. He's already predicted our moves thus far and he'll likely anticipate what we're gonna do next. Obvious will get us killed."

We spend the next twenty minutes bouncing strategies off of each other, trying to develop a plan to prevent the Deciders from establishing control before it is too late. Nothing sticks, of course—not against a plan that Ryan's been preparing for decades. It doesn't help that my thoughts are too clouded to dredge up anything useful. Somehow, though, my mind is still sharp enough to visualize hundreds of ways to torture and kill Ryan. Currently, I imagine myself vivisecting him while he's chained to an operating table, forcing him to watch in a mirror as I remove his organs one by one.

"Touching down at Babylon in five," Tommy announces over the speaker system, breaking my trance.

"Hey, Dion!" Isabella calls from two seats down.

"What is it?" I ask.

"Sorry to interrupt," she says hesitantly. "Not trying to sound self-centered or anything, but what happens to me when we land? I'm not going to get black-bagged and locked up, am I?"

Hughes looks from her to me. "I was about to ask ... I mean she hasn't been cuffed this entire flight ... Did you just plan on letting her roam free at Babylon?"

Everyone looks at me.

"Freedom in exchange for helping us find Naraka was the deal. You came through for us so I'll make good on my promise."

Isabella smiles. As she's about to say something, Hughes interrupts. "So what does 'freedom' entail?" he asks.

"She wants a new identity and to be sent off to a dark corner of the world where the Deciders won't find her," I answer.

"Actually—" Isabella says before Hughes cuts her off again.

"You'd let her go with everything she knows about us? There's nowhere for her to hide after Poseidon. They will find her, and when they do—"

"Hey!" Isabella interjects. "The thing is ... I don't want to disappear anymore."

The team eyes her curiously.

"Then what do you want?" I ask.

"I want to stay with you," she says with a slight smile. "I want to fight alongside you for the Angels of War ..."

Anne turns to me, lips pursed with one eyebrow arched. "She wants to stay with *you*, eh?" she whispers, annoyance in her tone.

"Ha!" Hughes laughs. "You're joking, right?"

"Why would you want that?" I ask. "You'll be better off on an island somewhere rather than fighting what's looking more like a losing battle ever second ..."

Isabella shrugs. "I don't care how shitty the odds are. I set out to make the world a better place and I did the opposite by joining the Deciders. I need redemption … I owe this world penance for my crimes. I owe you for not saying something about Naraka earlier. If it costs me my life, so be it."

I sigh. "I'll do what I can to get you in. Just know I'll always have someone watching your every move until I know I can trust you. That means you don't even burp without us knowing about it."

She nods. "That's fair. Of course."

"Sergeant Johnson, we just got rid of two moles—you sure about adding a potential third?" Hughes asks.

"The Deciders punish betrayal with death, so I doubt they'll ever take her back. We'll be fine," I say.

"The moment we start trusting her is the moment she goes double agent on us," Hughes says.

"I think you mean 'triple agent,'" Sung says.

"Guys," I say. "My gut's telling me she won't be a problem. Besides, she has intimate knowledge of the Deciders' operations. Having her around might help us out. And right now, we need all the help we can get."

It's 2:50 A.M. when the Osprey touches down at AWB Babylon. The Gauntlet's GPS shows we're a few miles outside of Greenstone, Pennsylvania—a small mountain town southwest of Gettysburg. The Osprey's ramp opens, revealing a walled-in base that looks very reminiscent of Fort Sanctum, with the exception of the rolling black hills in the background.

As the engines are cut and the twin rotors wind down, everyone rises, stretching from the long ride before gathering their belongings. A black LMTV pulls up beside the helipad. Inside the cab are two Vanquisher soldiers. Sung and Hughes disembark from the helicopter to greet them.

"Hey," Sung hollers to us a few seconds later, "these guys are going to take the Naraka prisoners to get looked after. Another convoy's comin' to pick us up in a few."

For some reason, Sam doesn't follow the others out. She sits in her seat and watches intensely as they walk sluggishly toward the LMTV. She's probably too tired to stand. She nodded in and out of sleep for most of the flight. Every time she passed out, she sprung back awake, like something spooked her.

Sam turns to me with worry in her eyes. "Dion, I need to talk to you," she says in a hushed, panicked voice. "It's …"

Abby and Ken sidestep past her with their gear, scanning her curiously. Isabella follows them, looking back at Sam as she does.

"It's …" Sam's eyes roll up into her head, and she pitches forward. With a lunge from my seat, I catch her before her head hits the floor. She can't weigh more than ninety pounds, but the strain of arresting her fall aggravates my arm and leg wounds.

"Sam? Sam!"

Her eyes open. "I'm … alright."

"We'll talk later," I say. "Get yourself taken care of first."

"I will," she murmurs, her eyes barely opened. "But they aren't the same. They aren't the same people you knew before. They did something to them. They did something to all of us …"

I nod, eyeing the rescued as Hughes and Sung help them into the back of the LMTV. "Alright. Go get checked up. I'll see you soon. Jeremy?"

Nodding, she smiles pitifully. I stand her up. Jeremy slings her arm around his shoulders and walks her to the truck.

"She didn't want the others to hear," Anne notes. "Have they been turned?"

I shrug. "She said '*they did something to all of us*,' so who knows if she's a reliable source."

"She seemed terrified of the others, though," Anne says.

Isabella is waiting for us as we start down the ramp. "Your friend okay?" she asks.

"I hope so," I sigh, stepping out onto the helipad. Instead of concrete, I'm standing on a grated black metal platform with designated landing zones for almost a dozen helicopters. Through the holes, there appears to be a level beneath it. *Did this come out of the ground?*

Three armored black Ford Excursions pull up alongside the LMTV. Each vehicle is empty save for the soldier behind the wheel.

Isabella grabs my jacket sleeve. "Can we talk real quick?"

"Fine." I turn to Anne and tilt my head.

She nods, glaring at Isabella before walking off.

"What is it?" I ask, somewhat annoyed.

Isabella searches my face. "You alright, Dion?"

I shrug. "As close to alright as I'll ever be … What do you need?"

She takes a deep breath. "I want to let you know …" She pauses. "You need to know where I stand … You need to know that I swear I will never betray you …"

"I get it. You're loyal to me," I say, turning toward the SUVs. "Come on."

She grabs my wrist. "No. You *don't* get it." She raises both hands. "These hands you saved from mutilation are yours, and I will fight for you with them no matter what." She steps in closer and wraps her arms around my waist. "You risked everything to save my life so I am yours for *whatever* you need."

"Cut it out," I say, pulling away. I glance at Anne, who's standing with her back to us, talking to the driver.

"Sorry." She smiles. "What I'm trying to say is that you are the only soul on this planet I would die for, Dion Johnson. Your mission is my mission now, whatever that is."

I force a smile. "Wow ... Listen, I believe you ... Part of me even trusts you. But that doesn't mean I won't have you under constant supervision."

"I know. I wasn't trying to get out of it, hon." She winks. "Just clarifying where I stand."

"Good." Now I grab her arm as she starts to walk away. "If you're with us, you have to do me a favor."

"Anything."

"Tone down the affection. Anne *will* kill you. And I don't know if you have some Stockholm crush on me or what, but you're just setting yourself up for pain. I'll never want anyone else in this world other than Anne. You understand? That will never change. And I don't want you heartbroken and pining for me—that will make working together very difficult."

She scrunches up her mouth and nose. "Couldn't you ask for an easier favor?"

"Isabella, I'm serious."

She playfully punches my chest. "Chill, I'm kidding. All cards on the table, though ..." She watches Anne climb into the back of the lead Excursion, then leans in close and whispers, "I *really, really* want to have sex with you. Especially after today."

I scowl. "Cut out the bullshit. I told you, that's never going to happen."

"Maybe not one on one, but it's pretty much the end of the world, right? I'm sure I could talk Anne into a threesome ..."

"You know, I'm starting to think locking you back up might not be such a bad idea."

"Whoa! Chill, buddy! I'm just trying to give you something more pleasant to think about." She glances at me, smiling. "You're thinking about it, aren't you? Me and you and Anne ... the two of us pleasuring you ..."

The thought does cross my mind for a second before the anger and depression wash it from my mind. I say nothing.

She giggles to herself as we reach the convoy.

"Well aren't you two just the best of friends ..." Anne hisses, gesturing for me to climb in. "Come on, the base commander is waiting to meet with us." She gives me a look.

Shit, I think, climbing in back with her. *Walker probably told them to detain us.*

"Archangel, sir," the driver says, twisting in his seat to nod at me. "I am Sergeant Major Mitchell Gaines. It's an honor to meet you. Welcome to Babylon."

21
BABYLON

September 19
2:01 A.M.

A LOUD MECHANICAL sound rumbles behind us as our SUV makes its way toward the base. Even from inside the vehicle, I feel the ground tremble. Everyone but the driver watches through the rear window as the heliport descends into the ground, swallowing our Osprey. When it disappears, two large doors topped with concrete come together and rise up to blend with the surrounding pavement.

The buildings we pass are built in the same style as those at Fort Sanctum and look just as new. The largest one is a mirror image of Fort Sanctum's Central Command. Others resemble the barracks and one the brig. The only building that's lit is the one the LMTV parked in front of—the medical center. I see no USAW or American flags anywhere on the campus. If not for the forty-foot wall surrounding the perimeter, this place could pass for an office park.

Sergeant Major Gaines drives us west toward the bare end of the base where the gray sky beyond the wall is blacked out by the mountainside. "So this is basically the East Coast version of Cheyenne," he says. "But more advanced. Like Fort Sanctum, it's protected by Sky Guardian. We got antiballistic missile systems, antiballistic lasers, and anti-drone systems mounted on buildings, along the walls, and in a perimeter fifty miles outside the base. For ground defense, autonomous and remote-controlled turrets scattered on and above ground level. And in a few hours, we'll even have a fleet of UGVs patrolling the perimeter and UAVs providing both surveillance and defense against enemy drones."

Gaines rambles on, but I zone out. As we near the wall, a large portion of it extends then parts in two sections, revealing a slowly opening blast door that's wide and high enough for large construction vehicles to fit through. Now we find ourselves cruising through a vast paved tunnel, lights dangling from the mountain rock above and concrete walls on both sides. It goes on for almost a quarter-mile before we end up in a massive garage. To the left and right are an assortment of military vehicles—tanks, Humvees, Valanxes, BAE Caimans, MRAPs, SUVs, LAVs, Bradleys, HIMARS—and artillery. There are some vehicles I don't recognize.

"Goddamn …" Ken says in awe from the passenger seat.

"Yeah," Gaines says. "This is our military's *ark*. We've been amassing weaponry and battle-ready vehicles here for the last year. Believe it or not, this is just the tip of the iceberg."

Gaines parks in an open space beside a group of similar SUVs at the end of the garage and just in front of a man-sized blast door. BUILDING A is painted beside the door in dark blue. The two other Excursions pull into the empty spots to the left of us. Almost in a synchronized fashion, all the car doors open at once then everyone climbs out.

My team and I assemble at the vehicles' trunks. Gaines introduces himself and the other two drivers, Sergeant Owens, and Sergeant Grimes.

The blast door opens and five soldiers emerge.

As Hawke reaches for the trunk handle, Grimes puts up a hand. "Oh, don't worry about your gear. We'll take it in for you."

We back off as they scoop up our rifles and bags.

Seems like they want us disarmed ...

Gaines passes his Nexus watch over the security panel and leans in for a quick iris scan and the blast door rises. As we walk the hall, Babylon's history lesson begins. Gaines tells us that construction began after 9/11. Back then, it was called Site G, or the Green Grotto. It was supposed to be a bunker for the Army that would act as a support for its older sister bunker, Site R—or Raven Rock Mountain Complex—which is three miles southeast of Babylon. Excavation of the mountain and the pit beneath the buildings we passed was completed in 2008 and the project was mothballed, left as an abandoned quarry to throw off the locals.

Fearing the Deciders' reemergence, the late President Pell ordered construction to be resumed in order to establish a Cheyenne Mountain Complex in the east that would act as a last resort for USAW and Army personnel as well as direct support for the DoD at Raven Rock. Private construction crews were blindfolded and flown in to construct the underground buildings and those on the surface.

After descending two levels and navigating a series of hallways, we reach Babylon's Executive Command and Overwatch. Gaines pauses to access the biometric scanner. There's a loud clunk and the door opens, revealing a dimly lit area that looks just like Fort Sanctum's ECO. This one, however, is larger and the walls are covered in monitors. Across the room, on the second level, is Babylon's TATCO. The windows are tinted so I can't see inside. A small handful of Vanquisher-class soldiers sit parked at the desks. A few more stride through the work area with urgent steps, looking down at tablets.

"Since its completion earlier this year," Gaines continues, "Babylon has become the main site for the USAW's fleet of ground and air drones." He gestures to the men and woman inside. "There are less than fifty soldiers stationed here who serve as base security, technical specialists, or as drone operator specialists. It gets pretty lonely here. We've been waiting to get more personnel on site. I just wish it wasn't under these circumstances ..."

Gaines turns to Abdul, who's intently scanning the room. "Mr. Rahman, a terminal has been set up for you over near Sgt. Cara Hopewell," he says, nodding toward a Vanquisher soldier with her hair pinned up under her service cap. She's typing away at her computer. "Hopewell! Get him up to speed."

Cara spins in her chair and waves him over.

"It's good to have him here," Gaines says. "There's still millions of classified USAW personnel and intelligence files to transfer from Fort Sanctum and too few techs here with the clearance to do it."

From upstairs, there's the distinct sound of a heavy bolted lock opening. The door to TATCO swings open and an orange-bearded officer emerges wearing the all-black service uniform and cap, two Vanquisher-class soldiers at his heels. The stern-looking officer immediately locks onto us and urgently descends the stairs.

"That there's the base commander," Gaines says, saluting the rapidly approaching man.

"Gaines, head up to TATCO and make the preparations for the fleet's arrival," the CO orders.

With a nod, Gaines hustles off toward the stairs.

Now the officer glares at me. "Colonel Douglas Tannin, acting base commander," he says. "It's an honor, Sergeant Johnson." We shake, and his grip nearly shatters my hand. His eyes shift to Isabella. "Mind telling me what the hell the Decider you broke out of custody is doing standing in ECO uncuffed?" He raises his arm and flicks two fingers in her direction. The two soldiers swarm Isabella and grab her by the arms, forcing them behind her back.

"Release her," I demand. "If it wasn't for her, we wouldn't have found Naraka or been able to give the early warning to evacuate the bases."

The men look to Tannin. He searches my face. "Given what you have done for our country, I'm sure you have a damn good reason for pulling the stunt you did ..." His glare burns into my eyes.

"I do. She renounced her Decider ties and agreed to become an asset for two operations that needed to be conducted in secret to avoid being discovered by moles operating at the highest levels of Fort Sanctum. In exchange, I promised her freedom. Isabella has willingly fought by our side and proven her loyalty. She's one of us now, without a doubt."

"I can also vouch for Isabella's actions," Anne says. "She identified the mole without coercion and risked her life by entering a Decider base alone and unarmed to access the network that allowed us to find Naraka."

The rest of Rogue Titan nods, except Hughes.

Tannin scowls. "Why didn't you include General Walker in this op? Did you or do you have any reason to suspect him as the mole?"

I didn't loop him in because he might be behind Anglerfish, but I sure as hell am not about to say that to Tannin. "Intel suggested that the mole or the person assisting the mole was likely someone in the Commander class. To be safe, I only included people I trusted."

"Do you trust him now?"

"Do you?" I snap back.

He hesitates. "President Pell appointed him general of USAW, so I trust he is not compromised. He's been known to go to extremes to do what's necessary to protect the nation. I don't necessarily agree with all of his methods, but he's a patriot and I trust Pell's decision."

"Alright then." I glance at Tannin's men. They look ready to arrest us at any moment. "Are we going to have a problem, Colonel?"

"General Walker wanted me to detain you and your team for questioning upon arrival, but this interrogation has revealed that there is no need to execute that order. So, no, *we* are not going to have a problem, but the general might have a bone to pick with you." He nods to his men. "Release her."

They do as instructed. Isabella scampers behind Anne and me.

"You're responsible for her from here on out. If she does anything to compromise this base or the lives of our soldiers, it is on you, Sergeant Johnson. You and your team."

"I understand."

"Good," Tannin says, turning around. "Hopewell, grant the Archangel's team full access to Babylon and send the facility's map to their Nexus gear. And highlight a route to their sleeping quarters."

"Copy, sir!" she shouts back.

"Seraphs will be staying in Building C, second floor. Room assignments are first come, first served so you all will have your pick of the officer's quarters that are unoccupied. That means decent beds and private bathrooms for you. All you have to do is register the room with your Nexus gear. The armory on your floor is stocked with Special Forces equipment. Private storage for personal effects can be found in your rooms." Tannin eyes his

Nexus watch. "You have at least another hour or two before General Walker arrives. I suggest you rest up until then."

I nod. "I appreciate that, Colonel Tannin. Thank you."

We grab our gear and head out of ECO.

"That went well," Anne snorts once we're in the hall.

"Better than expected," I say, holding her hand.

"Hey," Hughes calls from the back of the pack. "Remind me never to go rogue with you guys ever again ..."

Isabella squeezes between Anne and me, putting her arms around us both. "Hey, thanks for what you guys said about me back there. Especially you, Anne! I never thought you'd have my back."

Anne shrugs her off. "You helped us. I helped you. That doesn't mean we're friends."

The base map Cara Hopewell sends is detailed as hell. It shows us every room, including closets in our immediate area, and with a pinch of the screen, it displays the entire mountain base in both two-dimensional and three-dimensional maps. There's a massive cafeteria on the top level of Building A, a gym, food storage, and an armory near the entrance to the vehicle storage area. Building B is essentially the same as A but it has a shooting range in place of the cafeteria and a kill house for training purposes. Building D, the one nearest the aircraft bay, is the medical facility. Building E is the brig. Like Fort Sanctum's, it begins above ground and has four sublevels. Building C has the largest armory in the facility and several smaller ones on the floors beneath. Of all the buildings, this one has the most sleeping quarters.

The highlighted route sends us to the level just below the main armory, the level with the largest rooms. Anne and I take a room at the end of the hall. Isabella and Abby, her monitor, take the one next door. Inside there are two full-sized beds, a wardrobe depressed into the wall, a closet-sized locker beside it for weaponry and gear, and a small bathroom, like the kind you'd find in a motel.

Anne and I push our beds together then immediately disrobe. After showering together, she cleans my wounds, applies another round of Cascade, and starts stitching up my leg.

Anne smiles. "Suturing your wounds reminds me of the night we met."

I flinch as the needle enters my flesh. "How romantic ..."

While she works, I message Abdul, asking him to check up on Jessica and the others for me, and to look into Anglerfish while he has unfettered access. A few minutes later, as Anne is wrapping my leg, the Gauntlet vibrates with a message from one of the docs saying that my friends have been given a sedative to help them recover from "severe sleep deprivation."

"Looks like I won't find out what happened to them until tomorrow," I say.

"Good," she purrs, crawling into bed. She clicks off the light then pulls me down beside her, wrapping her arm around my torso.

After a few kisses, we cuddle in silence, finding comfort in each other's embrace. She passes out in under two minutes. I stare at the wall illuminated by the eerie glow of the nightlight. I keep visualizing Ryan snapping my son's neck, over and over.

He's not dead ...

Yes he is, Richard's voice taunts. *Yes, he is!*

Fists and jaw clenched, I slowly shake my head on my pillow. *Ryan lied to you. He's trying to get in your head!* I take a deep breath and try clearing my mind.

An image of Jessica holding our lifeless son manifests in the blackness. There's rage in her eyes. *Marshal's dead, Dion,* she says bitterly. *That's why I can't even look at you ... Because he's dead and it's all your fault ...*

My eyes shoot open. *Anne. Think about Anne. Think about seeing Dean and your parents again.* I roll over to see her sleeping peacefully, probably more peacefully than anyone in the world right now. I close my eyes and hold the image of her in my mind, repeating her name over and over, replaying memories of her until I drift off.

22
AFTEREFFECTS

September 19
11:19 A.M.

SOMETHING BETWEEN A groan and yawn escapes me as I wake from a deep and surprisingly dreamless sleep.

"Morning, love," Anne says, rubbing my sheet-covered leg. She's sitting up in bed reading something on her Nexus phone. "Walker and the troops have arrived. Came in around five last night."

"And Walker hasn't knocked down our door yet?" I ask, checking my Gauntlet and noting that it's after eleven. Slept longer than I thought I would. I tap the message icon. There's nothing from the general, but there's one from Jeremy saying that Karla has arrived safely.

"I was surprised too. Sung says Walker is too preoccupied with getting Babylon operational and coordinating nationwide counterattacks to deal with us, but—" she makes air quotes— "'he will get to us before the day is through.'"

I sit up and kiss her. "Well, we better eat and go see Sam before that happens."

She sets her phone down. "We should have until late afternoon before we are called upon." She pushes me back and climbs on top of me. "I'm sure we can fit in time for a quickie."

Blissful smiles stretched across our faces, we suit up in our Seraph BDUs, leaving our combat jackets behind. We then tuck one P226 in our drop leg holsters and hide a backup pistol in the small of our backs because … Anglerfish.

The first thing I see when I open the door is Isabella leaning against the wall across the hall from us. Her face instantly lights up when we make eye contact but she quickly suppresses her excitement. Abby's standing a few feet away and fiddling with her watch while chatting with Ken and Steele. They're all waiting for us, per my instructions. "We walk Babylon together until this Anglerfish thing is solved," were my orders.

There are "hellos," "heys," and "good mornings" all around.

"Mornin'," Isabella says. "Aren't you two simply glowing today."

Anne takes my hand. "Thanks for noticing."

"If you ever want to spice things up a bit, shoot me an invite." Isabella reaches for Anne's free hand. "You're stunning, you know. I'd totally go bi for you, Ice Queen."

Anne snorts, flicking her hand away. "Things are *spicy* enough as is …"

"I'll get you to change your mind," Isabella whispers sensually.

I shake my head. *Wow, she's really going for it …*

Steele grins. "Um, what the hell is happening?"

"Dion! Anne!" Karla calls as she enters the hall from two doors down. A glum-looking Jeremy appears a moment later, shutting the door behind him. She runs up and hugs me, then embraces Anne. "With everything that's happened, it feels like a lot longer than twenty-four hours since I've seen you last!" She hits Steele. "Guess what? I met your reporter girlfriend before the evacuation …"

"What the hell was Trish Childers doing at Sanctum?" I ask.

Steele checks his watch. "Listen, I just wanted her to be somewhere safe. She here?"

Karla shakes her head. "Pretty sure she was taken to a different base."

Steele sighs. "Good … Wasn't ready to be trapped underground with her …"

"We going to see Jess and them now?" Karla asks me.

"After breakfast," I answer, saluting Tommy as he steps into the hall.

"What about Eric and Casey?" Karla asks as we head for the main corridor. "You leaving them at the cabin?"

"No. I'll have a team pick them up as soon as possible. I can't leave them out there if we're not there to protect 'em."

She snaps her fingers. "Oh yeah! I don't know if Jeremy messaged you about it, but we have your things from Sanctum in our room. I made Anthony and his men help me grab all our shit before we evacuated! You're welcome."

It's not the best news in the world, but it makes me smile anyway. I'd brought a lot of important things to Fort Sanctum, especially Richard's journal and the flash drive with his files. "Good looking out, Karla."

Babylon feels like Times Square compared to yesterday. Vanquishers and Saviors stream by in all directions with packs on their backs and duffle bags in hand. They're all looking down at their watches for directions like freshmen trying to orient themselves on their first day at college.

In Building A, the center of everything, newcomers are hauling large duffle bags and weapons crates from the Caverns (the vehicle storage garage) to various areas in the facility. Things in the cafeteria are less busy, probably because we slept in so late.

However, by the time we get our meals, it starts filling up with the lunch crowd.

Despite what happened last night, everyone seems to be in somewhat decent moods. Maybe it's because we rescued the surviving prisoners. Or maybe everyone is just pretending that everything's okay like I am. During the Annex, avoiding talk of doom and gloom became something we got good at.

The gang includes Isabella in the small talk, treating her like she wasn't a Decider just days ago. Anne's even trading Decider stories with her like they're reminiscing about some sorority they were both in. Steele, who hated Anne at first when she defected to our side, is clearly trying hard to get into Isabella's pants.

After breakfast, we head to Sublevel One of Building D, the medical facility, where the Naraka Ten are being treated. Lightly armed men sitting at the ends of the halls look up from their tablets to greet us with smiles and nods. If they're on guard duty it doesn't look like they're taking it too seriously, which is good because I don't want my friends thinking they're being treated as hostiles.

The door we just passed opens and an older woman with gray streaks in her hair steps into the hall. She tucks her left hand into her lab coat's pocket and extends the other. "Good afternoon, Sergeant Johnson," she says with a wide smile that reveals coffee-stained teeth. "I'm Dr. Katherine Kaminski. I was told to expect a visit from you."

I shake her dry hand. "How are they?"

She gestures for us to follow her. "Well, they were all severely sleep deprived, dehydrated, and malnourished when they arrived, but they are improving. Everyone is exhibiting signs of psychological damage, the extent of which is still undetermined."

We stop at Hudson's room, which is right across from Dave's. "Sergeant Joseph Hudson and Corporal David Schoenly have suffered significant physical trauma—numerous bruises, lacerations, stab wounds, fractured bones, and burns. Hudson also has pneumonia. Samantha Schoenly was apparently unharmed. Jessica, however ..."

"*What?*" Karla snaps. "What's wrong with Jessica?"

Dr. Kaminski sighs. "Her injuries are consistent with blunt-force trauma, strangulation, and ... sexual assault ..."

Karla covers her mouth. "Oh god ..." she sobs, eyes welling with tears.

"Her current behavior," Dr. Kaminski continues, "is in line with acute rape trauma syndrome."

"Those fucking monsters ..." Isabella mutters.

"And Sam ... she wasn't ... assaulted?" I ask.

Kaminski shakes her head.

They left Sam untouched and violated Jessica ... but why? The answer comes to me in a flash. *Lex Talionis, that's why.* Hurting Jessica was Ryan's way of getting back at me for taking Anne from his brother.

"Toxicology screening also shows that they were all subjected to a number of psychoactive drugs," Kaminski continues. "Those we could identify were artificial cannabinoids, LSD, methylone—bath salts—methylphenidate, scopolamine, and trace amounts of the Psycho nerve agent ..."

"That sounds like a brainwashing cocktail ..." I say.

"Was it successful?" Anne asks.

Kaminski pauses for a moment. "Since you know them best," she responds, "I thought I'd leave that for you to determine."

I peer into Sam's room. She's fast asleep. "Anne, let me know when she's awake. In the meantime, I'll talk to Dave."

"I'm with you, D," Ken mumbles.

Jeremy bumps Tommy's arm. "We'll come in for a bit too."

Karla wipes her eyes and snorts her runny nose. "I'll talk to Jessica."

Steele gestures toward Hudson's window. "Coming, Red?"

Abby gives a slight nod.

"Alright," I say, scratching at my goatee, "find out what happened but don't make it seem like an interrogation. Treat them as you normally would and see how they respond."

Everyone splits up, leaving Anne and Isabella in the hallway.

The guys and I greet Dave as we enter. He looks at us with dead eyes and a pitiful smile. "Hey, fellas," he says weakly, sitting up in bed. "Sorry I didn't thank you guys yesterday. Those drugs had me out of it ..."

I smile. "Hey, no worries. How are ya feeling now, bro?"

"Alive. Thanks to you guys."

"Ah, you know we were coming for you, man," Ken says.

He rubs his face. "Never doubted it, but those ten days felt like years." He stares off into nothing. "Being locked in a dark cell, sensory deprived, drugged, and bound in a straitjacket fucks with your sense of time. Fucks with your mind ..."

"Dave ..." I say softly. "I'm sorry, man. I wish I got to you guys sooner ..."

"Listen, you got us out, and that's what counts." He forces a laugh. "Heh, that's more than I can say I've ever done for you ... When you were captured by the Deciders, you had to escape on your own ..."

I don't know how to reply to that.

"How's my sister?" Dave asks in the awkward silence.

"Still sleeping," I respond. "She's improving, though."

"Hudson?"

"About the same as you ..."

He lowers his head. "You talk to Jessica yet?"

We shake our heads.

"Karla's with her now," I say.

"They hurt her, Dion. Bad …"

I look away. "Yeah, the doctor told me."

He shakes his head. "Ryan Thomas … that fucker … he told me everything he was going to do to her. And then when he did, they played the audio over the headphones they made us wear in our cells. I had to listen to her screams for hours, one day after another until she finally just stopped …" He sighs. "Did the doc say if Sam was—"

"They left Sam alone," I interrupt. "It seems like they tortured you all in different ways … If it's not too difficult for you, do you mind telling us what they did to you? It might give us an idea of how to help you recover."

Dave looks down at the bandages on his hands. "It started with them making me watch them waterboard and shock Sam. Then I got my waterboarding and electroshock treatment. Then they nailed my hands to a table … After that they treated my wounds then I was sensory deprived and tossed in the cell. Every time I started falling asleep, they played Sam's screams over those headphones to keep me up."

There's some commotion outside, but since Anne's not reacting to it, I ignore it.

"Then they started pumping me with drugs," Dave continues. "Things got hazy. I remember them saying things to me—like phrases. I remember some fucking monologue playing over the headphones while I was locked in my cell. It just went on and on like that. Sometimes I was whipped … Sometimes I was stabbed … Sometimes I was hung in uncomfortable positions for hours.

Sometimes I had needles shoved under my fingernails and toenails …"

"Shit … Did—did they ask you anything?" I stutter.

"On the way to Naraka, right after they grabbed me, they asked where you guys were hiding. I didn't say anything; that's why they started hurting Sam … But after that, Ryan said you surfaced with Anne and never asked me anything after."

I take a deep breath. "You think they were trying to turn you like they did with Stevenson?"

Dave scowls, his empty eyes flicking back and forth. "They didn't turn me. I would never betray my brothers like that bastard Stevenson did. Never."

I nod. "I know you wouldn't, brother. I'm just trying to figure out what they wanted."

There's a knock at the window. Anne's gesturing for me to come out.

"We'll stay here with him," Jeremy says.

"Hey, I'll be back in a few," I say. "Need anything?"

He smirks. "Whisky?"

"I'll see what I can do." I step out, gently shutting the door behind me. "Sam up?"

Anne nods. "Dr. Kaminsky is with her now."

I peer inside Sam's room to see Kaminski handing her pills and a plastic cup of water. I turn to Jessica's room across the hall and find it's empty. "Where are Karla and Jess?"

Isabella shrugs. "Taking a walk."

My eyebrows rise. "Hmm?"

"Don't worry. I put a guard on them," Anne says.

"I'm surprised you even let her out," I say.

"Well, Jessica had a panic attack and went ballistic a few minutes ago," Anne says. "She was screaming and carrying on about how she can't be cooped up in a room anymore and demanded to get fresh air. Kaminski wanted to sedate her, but Karla calmed her down and took her out. It was either let her walk or shoot her ..."

"You should've seen the look that girl gave Anne," Isabella adds.

"She's dangerous," Anne says. "Deranged." She searches my face. "How did Dave seem to you?"

I shrug. "Traumatized for sure, but not psychotic from what I can tell. Something's off, though."

Sam's door opens and Dr. Kaminsky steps out. "Sgt. Johnson, Samantha is ready to see you now."

"You coming?" I ask Anne.

"Sure," she says, turning to Isabella.

Isabella smiles. "Don't worry. I'll be right in front of the window the whole time."

"Dion! Anne!" Sam exclaims as soon as the door opens, sitting up in the bed.

"Hey, feeling any better?" I ask.

"A little woozy from the sleep meds, but yeah. Have you talked to my brother?"

"I did. He's alright. I'll take you to him in a minute."

She nods. "Did he tell you what they did to him?"

"Yeah. And he told me some of what happened to you too."

"They didn't do much to me. They roughed me up a bit the first day, cattle prodded me and damn near drowned me to get Dave to talk, but that was it. Ryan Thomas made me watch every bit of torture they put everyone else through. He made me watch him drag Jess into that room where he chained her down to a table and ..." She closes her eyes and shakes her head. "It wasn't just him, either. Fucking Stevenson ... and a guy with burns on his face. And if I looked away, they'd hurt Dave worse than before and make me watch that. Ryan said I had to witness it all so that I could tell you everything when you rescued us."

"Wait," Anne says. "*When* we rescued you?"

"That's what I wanted to say last night!" Sam says, wide-eyed. "He was never going to kill us. You were *supposed* to rescue us from Naraka and bring us back with you."

"But why?" I ask. "Why would he let us you rescue you?"

She shakes her head. "He didn't say exactly, but he said that you had to figure out which of your friends were still your friends. He said to tell you 'Lex Talionis?'"

Anne and I look at each other.

"What?" Sam asks.

"Do you think he turned one of them?" Anne asks. "Is that why you were nervous around them last night?"

She nods. "They all seemed different to me, even my brother."

The door bursts open. Anne and I turn, reaching for our pistols.

"The bloody hell is wrong with you, girl?" Anne snaps.

"Didn't ya'll hear that?" Isabella asks.

We stare back at her, clueless.

"I just heard gunshots from back near the elevators!"

My first thought is that a guard shot Jessica. "You sure it was a gunshot?" I ask as we rush into the hallway.

"I've been in this shit long enough to know a gunshot when I hear one, hon. And I heard two!"

Up ahead, Dr. Kaminski is poking her head out of Corporal Tim Blake's room, watching Steele peek around the corner with his pistol at the high ready. Abby's right beside him, pistol low ready.

"Shut the door and don't open it until you're told to," Anne says to Kaminski.

A high-pitched beep from our watches makes me jump. The screen is red with an alert that reads "SHOTS FIRED. MEDICAL ASSISTANCE REQUIRED." The distress beacon is coming from a soldier on the ground level of this building.

Ken, Jeremy, Tommy, and the guards rally in the hallway. Anne extracts the P226 from the small of her back and drops the magazine, leaving one round in the chamber. She hands it to Isabella.

I point to the three guards. "Secure this floor. Don't let any of the patients leave their rooms. Everyone else, pair up. Isabella, you're with Abby. Take the stairwell up to the third floor and sweep each floor on your way back down. Steele and Tommy, you start from the top floor. Jeremy and Ken, take the stairwell to ground level and sweep the perimeter. If you see Jessica, be careful. She could be the shooter." I nod to the guards who were guarding the rooms. "You guys take the sublevels."

At the elevator bank, I mash the up button until an elevator arrives. When the doors open on the surface level, we find a body lying halfway out of the other elevator. There are two bullet holes in his back and a pool of blood around him. There's no pistol in his holster.

"He's the guard that was escorting Jessica and Karla …" Anne says in a low voice as she sweeps the immediate area. "She did this."

Karla … *Where's Karla?* I activate my comm while checking the soldier's pulse. "The shooting victim is KIA. It appears Jessica stole his weapon and shot him. There's no sign of Karla—"

"*Wait, what?*" Jeremy interrupts.

"She was escorting Jessica out for a walk," I say, moving down the hall with my pistol at the high ready. *Jess, what have you done?*

A woman cries out up ahead. I pick up the pace, quickly sweeping rooms and dark corners and turning on light switches as I pass them. At the end of the hall, something metallic clatters to the ground. I press my back against the wall and peer around the corner to see a body lying in the middle of a lobby. Judging by the petite frame, I'm guessing it's Karla.

I give the signal and we move stealthily down the hall with me at point and Anne right behind me with her back to mine. At the threshold between the hallway and lobby, she and I breach at the same time. I go left. She goes right. And as I round the corner, I see Jess. Her eyes are wild and her face is sweaty with hair clung to it. There's a pistol in her left hand but she attacks me with the metal pipe in her right, swinging at my face.

In other circumstances, I could have easily downed an attacker from this distance, but this is my friend, the mother of my child. And because I hesitate, the pipe cracks me across the head, and the second strike knocks the pistol from my hands. She lets the pipe fall and holds her pistol firmly with both hands, aiming it at me.

"Drop it, Jessica!" Anne shouts, weapon trained on her.

Jessica's wide, deranged eyes flick from me to Anne. "Drop yours, bitch!" she snarls, kicking my pistol away. "Toss it and kneel!"

"Jess, calm down, alright?" I say. "Tell me what's going on … Let me help you."

"Shut the fuck up, Dion! You can't help anyone …" She glares at Anne. "Do what I asked or I *will* shoot him!"

Anne doesn't budge.

"*Fucking do it!*" Jess shouts, wildly jabbing the gun toward me.

"Easy now …" Anne says. She tosses the gun.

"Now kneel, hands behind your head."

Anne does as instructed.

"Jess?" I say. "What are you doing?"

"Getting my son back," she snarls, shifting her aim to Anne.

"Hey!" I draw the backup pistol from my waistband and point it at Jessica. "Drop the gun and tell me what's happening!"

She turns the gun back on me, shaking her head back and forth. "No! I have to do this! Killing her is the only way to get Marshal back. And if I don't do it before forty-eight hours is up, he'll kill him."

"Ryan Thomas lied to you! He showed me proof that Marshal was dead!"

She laughs. "He's alive. I saw him before you rescued us."

"Even if he is, Ryan will never make good on that promise," I say. "You know that. The only way to save Marshal is to drop your weapon and let me find him!"

Jess smiles like a madwoman. "You don't want Marshal back. You never wanted him in the first place."

"That's not true!"

"It is and you know it, you lying fuck. You want me to believe he's dead so you can get away with not looking for him. Well, *fuck* ... *you*. If letting you live wasn't a part of the deal, I'd shoot you where you stand."

Her gun goes off. The 9mm round rips through my right bicep, but I keep my grip on the pistol. Time immediately slows to a crawl. Anne dives to the floor for her weapon as Jessica pans her aim from me to her.

She killed the guard and shot me. She's serious about killing Anne. If I hesitate, Anne dies.

I have no choice.

The gun goes off, not once, but three times. Her body jerks violently as dots of blood spatter the wall behind her like some abstract painting. Jessica's body crumples and hits the ground with a muffled thud, the pistol loosely clutched in her lifeless hand. I stare in disbelief, waiting for her to get up, waiting for a director to yell cut. But she just lies there, blood pooling around her, eyes wide open, unblinking, still crazed.

My arm falls to my side. The pistol slips from my grip and clatters to the floor as I crash onto my knees. Anne rushes over to Jess and kicks the gun out of her hand before kneeling to check her pulse. She shakes her head.

Jessica.

The girl I used to love.

My friend.

The mother of my firstborn.

A person I vowed to protect no matter what.

Dead.

Murdered by my hands.

I killed her.

I killed Jessica Stewart ...

23

ANGLERFISH

September 19
6:19 P.M.

I'VE ALREADY THROWN up twice since killing Jessica, and saliva floods my mouth as I struggle to keep the bile down. This is the normal response to taking a life, though I was unfazed after my first kill and the dozens that followed. I had to kill someone I cared for to experience that revulsion.

The scene replays in my mind once again. Her body jerks, circles of blood blossom on her hospital gown as she collapses. I pitch forward and plant my palm against a tree as I vomit into a bed of ferns. As I push off of the trunk, there's a dull ache in my now bandaged and Cascade treated arm. After wiping my mouth with my sleeve, I grab my rifle and resume my aimless walk through the woods.

It's a small comfort, but it feels soothing to be back in the Pennsylvania wilderness. It hurts too much to think back to my camping trips with the Penn State crew, so I focus on those early morning walk through Prospect Park with my dad when I was a kid. Climbing the hill overlooking the lake and looking out at the buildings of Crown Heights.

You had to do it. You saved Anne. Losing Anne would have hurt worse than this—it would have killed you. Maybe after what Jessica went through, she wanted to die … Maybe you gave her what she wanted, what she needed. You gave her peace.

Something in the woods crunches. I snap out of my trance and aim at the underbrush to my left. A deer lifts its head from a shrub, chewing on a mouthful of herbs. It freezes and stares me down. I stare back at it, just as still.

My Gauntlet buzzes twice and the deer bounds away. It's been going off every ten minutes over the past few hours. The first was from Anne saying that Karla has regained consciousness.

Karla … How can I ever look her in the eyes again after killing her best friend?

The other messages were from General Walker and Hall. The message previews revealed that they required my presence at TATCO so I didn't bother opening them.

The message is from Abdul, and it's labeled urgent. I tap the screen without hesitation. It reads: "I found that fish you were looking for. Might have been caught. I'm topside heading toward the small office building near your last known location. Titan is on the way." He sent it to every member of our team.

The fish I was looking for? With everything going on in my mind, it takes a few seconds to click, but when it does, I break into a jog. *Anglerfish!* If they're on to him, a shitstorm is about to follow.

The guard eyes me curiously as he opens the north gate into the complex. From there, it's a thirty-second jog to the warehouse. Despite the influx of troops at Babylon, it's still desolate outside, which is probably why Abdul chose to meet here.

I slink behind the warehouse and hurry toward the little three-story building that's our rendezvous. A door hinge squeaks as I approach. I peer out from around the corner of the warehouse just in time to see the trailing leg of someone in dark pants slip inside the office building. I send Abdul a prewritten message: "Outside."

He responds seconds later: "First-floor office. South corner."

Shit. That doesn't sound like he's the one who just walked in, though it still could be one of ours. I draw my pistol and scamper across the open ground, then wince as I tug the squeaky door open. I ghost my way down the hallway, sweeping every corner as I make my way south.

"Please don't hurt me!" Abdul shouts. "I don't know what you're talking about!"

Shit, shit, shit. I'm almost running now.

"Give me the thumb drive and you don't get hurt!" a man barks.

"What thumb drive?"

"You're not leaving me a choice here ..."

I take two steps through the open door with my pistol raised. A Vanquisher-class soldier in a ski mask is holding a trembling Abdul at gunpoint.

"Drop your weapon soldier!" I shout.

He turns, eyes widened behind his mask. "Archangel!" his voice cracks. "I have orders, sir!"

During the distraction, Abdul runs for it. The soldier's gun reports and Abdul collapses, cracking his head on a table on his way down. The round I let off tears through the soldier's forearm. He cries out and his weapon clatters to the ground. I rush him, slam him to the floor, and pin his arms behind his back. "Abdul?" I call out, kneeling on the soldier's wrists.

No answer.

I rip off the assailant's mask and put my pistol to his temple. I don't recognize him from his side profile. "Who sent you?"

"Same side, Archangel! Just following orders! He's the enemy! He stole sensitive USAW intel and tried to flee the premises—"

"If you know me, you know what I'm about, so believe me when I tell you that the person who gave you your orders is the true enemy of USAW. You were sent here to keep someone's dirty secrets buried, that's it." I press the pistol harder into his skull. "So if you don't tell me who sent you, I'll brand you an enemy combatant and empty the contents of your skull onto this floor!"

"Alright, alright! Walker! General Walker sent me!"

"What else do you know? Who else is working with him?"

"Listen, Walker just called me to his office, said that Abdul Rahman was trying to smuggle classified information to the Deciders, and sent me to retrieve the data and apprehend or execute the threat. That's all I know! I swear!"

"Is Staff Sergeant Hall working with Walker too?" I ask.

"I don't know!"

I crack him over the head with my pistol, knocking him out cold. I hurry over to Abdul and kneel beside him. The bullet entered through the back of his right shoulder. I roll him over, revealing the exit wound at the top of his pectoral. *Missed his lung.* There's a cut on his head from where he hit the table. I cut away part of his shirt with my knife and quickly wrap the wound.

As I'm finishing up, multiple footsteps stomp through the hall. I quickly slip behind a filing cabinet and take aim. A gun appears in the doorway and half of Anne's face peeks out with it. "Anne!" I call out.

She rushes in, waving those behind her forward. "What happened?"

"Abdul was attacked by this guy," I say. "Walker sent him."

"I knew it," she says as Isabella and Ken enter and holster their weapons.

I tap Abdul's cheek with the backside of my hand. "Abdul, wake up!" I look at Anne. "Where are the others?"

"Securing the building. After Abdul's message, I figured there'd be trouble ..."

I slap Abdul's face harder. "Wake up, Abdul!"

He stirs and groans. "Am I dying?" he asks.

"You'll survive," I say.

"Walker sent him to kill me ..." he says, reaching into his inside jacket pocket. "There might be more of them ... Here."

I take the thumb drive. "What did you find?" I ask as Anne and I help him up.

"Anglerfish was a black op created by General Walker, carried out by him and a few Commanders. Essentially, they used key Angels of War soldiers and civilians known to be targeted by the Deciders as bait to lure out those pulling the strings ... During that hack, Walker deliberately leaked the personal data that led to the capture of your friends to Corvus."

Anne shakes her head. "That son of a bitch ..."

I'm too furious to speak.

"And you guys were suspicious of me ..." Isabella mutters.

"You're shitting me," Ken growls. "Walker knew about Corvus the whole time and kept him in play to expose our people? Why?"

Abdul winces as Anne assists him in sitting down on the table. "In the proposal to the Secretary of Defense, Walker claimed that the Deciders would only commit their key personnel if it involved pursuing you, Dion, because you came up in all of their chatter. He knew that you would only come out of hiding if your friends were in danger. And once you surfaced, he let the Deciders know by giving you command of the Seraphs—a team formed for the sole purpose of allowing you to head all counter-operations against them. He even leaked that you'd be heading Operation Priority Package to Corvus ..."

There's no word for what I feel. I'm so far beyond furious that I look down to the thumb drive and just start laughing. "And it's all on here, right?"

Abdul frowns. "Everything, including all involved parties."

I nod. "Good."

Ken racks his slide. "What's the play?"

"We're going to make him pay."

When Sung messages us that General Walker and the officers involved in Anglerfish have assembled in ECO, we make our way down from the above level, submachine guns hidden under our jackets. Everyone, including Isabella, is armed and geared for combat, Aegis armor and all. There's no half-stepping when you're about to launch a coup.

At the door to Executive Command and Overwatch, the soldiers standing guard adjust their grips on their rifles.

I halt a few yards away. "You going to stop us?"

They shake their heads.

"We got the message from Sergeant Sung Seo," the center soldier says. "We can't have a man like General Walker leading USAW."

"We're on your side, Archangel," the soldier to his left adds.

They step aside and the soldier near the security panel unlocks the door.

Once inside, I spot the target in the middle of the room speaking with Colonel Tannin.

"General Walker!" I shout, marching toward him.

Walker looks tense, like he knows that I know, and confused, like he's wondering how I got in here. With one hand hovering near his pistol, he faces me. "What is it, Johnson?"

Once I'm in range, I snatch his weapon from the holster before he can react. Then I slug him in the jaw with all my might. He hits the floor like the proverbial sack of potatoes. I want to continue beating him, but, somehow, I restrain myself. Instead, I extract the MP7 from inside my jacket and train it on him.

Pull the trigger ... It's his fault Jessica and Marshal got captured! It's his fault I had to kill her. Just do it! Shoot him!

Soldiers, unaware of what's happening, train their weapons on me. My team draws on them.

"Lower your weapons!" a sergeant demands.

"Lower yours!" Sung grunts.

Walker climbs to his feet while holding his reddening face. "Have you lost your goddamn mind, Archangel?"

"General Barnard Walker," I begin, "you and those who have conspired with you have betrayed the United States Angels of War by endangering the lives of our soldiers."

"I'm afraid I don't know what you are talking about, son—"

"Hopewell," Anne says to the tech sitting at the nearest row of terminals, extending a flash drive.

Hopewell nods, takes the device, and starts typing away on her computer. Sung briefed her on Anglerfish and about what we were going to do.

On the main monitor, multiple video chat windows open up in a grid, displaying live streams of the command centers at Raven Rock and the other USAW bases. Acting President Arnold Choler and the base commanders sit facing their screens, waiting for what they think is a meeting regarding an updated war plan to begin.

"General Walker! What the hell is going on?" one officer asks. "Is that—is that the Archangel?"

"Yes, it's the Archangel," Walker says. "And as to why his team is holding us at gunpoint, I am unsure …"

Hopewell gives me a nod.

"Right about now," I announce, "everyone in the Nexus system should be receiving a file called Anglerfish."

Devices go off all around the room and on the live streams. While soldiers and officers scroll through the document, I outline everything Abdul uncovered, reading several excerpts straight from Walker's keyboard. The faces in the room and on the screen go from confused to appalled to horrified as I go on. The soldiers aiming at my team lower their weapons.

"Not only did he compromise missions," I conclude, "not only did he get the people he used as bait killed, but just today he sent a soldier to kill the analyst who discovered this crime!"

"General Walker, is this true?" Colonel Tannin asks.

"I did it for the good of our nation," Walker says. "When you're facing a foe as formidable as the Deciders, you have to be willing to sacrifice the few for the survival of the many. Any good leader knows that …" He glares at me. "And I looked out for you, Johnson! You and your friends!"

Sung turns his head and spits on Walker's boot.

"It was an inevitability that the Deciders would come for you and the former Delta Squad. You knew that, I knew that, the president knew that. To ensure that you were ready for that day, I had Finley convince you and your friends to take Special Forces training—"

"So you had Anglerfish planned since you were first instated?" I ask, my voice a little louder than I wanted it to be.

Walker nods. "If they were coming for you, I had to make you formidable so that you could resist and draw out the Decider elite. I even put Staff Sergeant Hall on your team to protect you all. I'm on your side and always have been. I am no traitor."

I look to the soldiers who had drawn their weapons on us. "Take Mr. Walker, Staff Sergeant Hall, and the Fort Sanctum officers to the brig. Hill, Hawke, you go with them."

"Disregard that order!" Walker demands.

The soldiers approach with disgust etched into their faces. Anne tosses one of them a zip cuff, and they turn Walker around and slam him against a desk, then bind his wrists behind his back. On the screen showing Raven Rock, Acting President Arnold Choler is being detained as well.

"A man willing to throw his soldiers away like worthless pawns has no authority here," I say. "In order for soldiers to put their lives on the line for their leaders, they have to trust them. After what you've done, you have lost that trust." I look around the room, making eye contact with as many soldiers as I can. "And until we can find out *who* to trust, Sung, Anne, and I will be taking temporary command of Babylon, with counsel from Colonel Tannin and the officers of Babylon." I turn to the screen of base commanders. "All commands will come to you through us until—"

"This is a mutiny!" Walker shouts.

"If it is, I'm a willing part of it," Tannin says. "But you're far from qualified to run this base, despite what you did during the Annex."

"It should only take an hour or so to vet you," I say. "Once you're cleared, command will be yours until one of the other generals is cleared. Until then, everything runs through us. Does anyone here have a problem with that?"

No one answers. Many of them shake their heads.

"Base commanders, will you recognize our authority until the leadership issue is resolved?"

"Well, you've led an army to victory once …" a colonel on the screen says. I'm not sure if it's sarcasm. "Excuse us while we deliberate." The screens go black.

Three tense minutes later, the officers reappear.

"In light of the current situation, it doesn't matter what we think," the colonel says. "We can hardly spare the resources to dislodge you. Temporary command of Babylon will be authorized as of now, Archangel. You have two hours to get Tannin cleared for duty and forty-eight hours to clear the other officers."

I nod. "Good. Tannin, have the other Fort Sanctum officers rounded up then meet us in TATCO."

Tannin eyes the troops in the room. "As you wish …"

Anne smiles mischievously. "We went from civilians to commanding an army within a week." She leans close to my ear. "Maybe we don't surrender control when the time limit expires …"

I smile and tap my temple. Leading is what I'm meant to do. That's the realization I came to after the Renegades passed the reins of the Angels of War Militia to me during the first war.

"I can't believe how smoothly that went," Isabella says. "I thought for sure I'd be back in a cell by now …"

"Most USAW soldiers joined up because they were inspired by what Dion did during the Annex," Sung says. "They'll follow him anywhere, no matter what."

"Damn straight," Steele says.

"Can you handle this?" Hughes asks me.

"For two hours?" I ask. "I should hope so."

"You're sure?" Hughes presses. "After … after what happened earlier, Johnson? Temporary position or not, there are lives on the line every second. The world depends on us. We need your head in the game one hundred percent."

The gunshots, the blood pouring out of Jessica as she collapses … My hand tightens around Anne's as my heart rate ramps up. Dizziness sets in. It takes everything I have to keep the distress from showing on my face. "I'll be fine," I say, staring up at TATCO. "This will help me keep my mind off things."

The temporary leadership sits around the table in the Threat Assessment and Tactical Command room strategizing and coordinating with base leaders from across the country. While Anne and Sung multitask between focusing on the war at hand and vetting Tannin, I sit watching surveillance video on my Gauntlet of Walker being taken into an interrogation room where Hudson and Dave are waiting for him.

You don't get my friends captured and expect to walk away with just a punch to the face, you bastard …

The soldiers shove Walker inside and slam the door behind them. Walker shouts something like "You can't do this!" but the men pay him no mind.

Hudson and Dave slowly approach Walker, rage burning in their eyes. Hudson cracks his knuckles and mouths something that makes Walker panic. The disgraced general starts waving his arms and is shouting something like, "Stay back!"

Enjoy your therapy, boys …

Hudson delivers the first blow and then the pair descends on the older man.

24
ARCADIAN SPRING

September 27
8:19 A.M.

WAR ... NOT ONLY is every inhabited region on this rock plagued
by it, but there's also one roiling in my mind. While the external
war is a bloody, destructive storm that is tipping more and more in
favor of the Deciders every hour, I am slowly winning my internal
struggle against guilt and depression. Though thoughts about my
firstborn possibly being dead and the vivid memory of killing Jess
leak into the forefront of my mind every so often, they've been
doing so much less frequently as the days go by.

Meditation has been a great help. It's something that I used to
do with Anne in the days after the Annex to suppress the
flashbacks that haunted me when combat was no longer a tool to
keep them buried in the dark recesses of my mind.

But my main weapon in this mental war is keeping busy.
Brainstorming, war planning, issuing orders, training with my
team—that's what keeps my mindscape in check between
meditation sessions.

I hear the gunshots. Jessica crumples to the ground in slow
motion, her outstretched arms making a last appeal to a universe
that condemned her to nothing but betrayal and pain.

"Captain Johnson?" Tannin says impatiently, like it's not the first time he said it.

Anne nudges my leg under the table.

I snap back to reality. Even though it's already been a week, being addressed by my new rank is still taking some getting used to. The promotions for Captain Anne Buckingham, Captain Sung Seo, and me came with a digitally signed order from the other base commanders after the Anglerfish fallout to help our temporary positions seem more official and to mitigate the shortage of officers. Surprisingly, the new ranks stuck, even after Colonel Tannin and Brigadier General Howard Krieger—the most senior Fort Sanctum officer to be cleared of suspicion—were reinstated.

"Hmm?" I ask.

"I asked if you had any input regarding the revised targets for Operation Arcadian Spring," Tannin grumbles.

I quickly assess the map and crosscheck the proximity of the target locations against civilian population density, updated Decider zones of control, and terrain. "We'll definitely need to increase our military presence near the more high-risk AOs to keep what we're doing off of enemy radar until it's completed or until we achieve complete subjugation of the region." I start naming off the specific targets.

"Captain Buckingham, where are we with your projections for Decider expansion and your defense plan?" Krieger asks.

Anne taps her tablet a few times and her work appears onscreen. She stands and begins laying out old Decider protocols for expansion out of cities into rural areas and the countermeasures we've come up with.

In the two days before Brigadier General Krieger was cleared, Anne and I sat on the war council with Tannin, the other top Babylonian officers, and the leadership teams of the other bases and dazzled them with a strategy to counter the Decider attacks on bases in the east. Our signature victory was a preemptive strike that Anne directed against their attempt to envelop our 96th Battalion entrenched north of Utica, a victory that allowed us to seize control of the farmlands of Upstate New York. Since the tactics and strategies that were drilled into her and Richard came from Echelon, we're essentially fighting them using Ryan's playbook.

When Krieger was reinstated and given command, we were asked to remain on the war council. A few days later, I came up with an idea to tip the odds in our favor.

What worked last time? The Deciders were brought down by civilians turned guerillas attacking them where they least expected it. Why not re-create what we did in the last war, but everywhere? Why not drop Special Forces soldiers in key areas across the country and have them train partisans who could wreak sabotage and assassinate Decider command units? And to eliminate any incentive to acquiesce to the Deciders' regime, our Special Forces units would destroy the power plants in Decider-controlled territories as well as their food and medical stockpiles.

That thought became Operation Arcadian Spring.

Arcadia is the codename that the council gave to all the territory under our control on the northeastern seaboard. The name stemmed from Acadia, a French colony in modern-day southeastern Canada and parts of Maine that were conquered by Britain in 1710. After Sung jokingly suggested that our territory should be called Arcadia because it sounded like Archangel, Anne, and I began referring to it as such in front of the council, and the name stuck.

As for the operation codename, it was an homage to the Arab Spring—CIA engineered protests, uprisings, and revolutions by the people of multiple countries in North Africa and the Middle East between December 2010 and December 2012.

General Krieger asked Anne how feasible it would be to embed our soldiers not only in Decider civilian camps but within their military like they did with Corvus and Corax. "It takes a lot of manpower to conquer the world," Anne said. "As the Deciders establish control, they will surely expand their military with the civilians they find to be sympathetic to their cause. Recruits will be selected during the screenings of civilians requesting admission into Decider colonies. I no longer can speak on behalf of the current Deciders' methods and metrics for this process, however. We will need Corporal Monroe's expertise on this."

The newly instated Corporal Isabella Monroe was brought in just minutes later and immediately got to work briefing the war council on the Deciders' recruitment procedures and protocols. She was unanimously appointed to a team with Anne and me to head the top-secret mission called Operation WISC—Wolf in Sheep's Clothing.

"Alright," Krieger says. "We'll get the revised mission specs out to the Army and Marine heads and get things in motion ASAP." He looks to me. "Have you heard back from Corporal Monroe?"

After checking my Gauntlet, I shake my head. "She's likely in the kill house or the rifle range right now."

Krieger rubs his nose. "Find her and get her down to the briefing hall. The WISC candidates will be waiting for you there. Get them up to speed and airborne before sundown. As soon as you're finished, get your team ready to ship out for Arcadian Spring."

With a nod, Anne and I gather our belongings and then exit the room.

"I thought you were going to tell them that we wouldn't be shipping out with the others," Anne says when we hit the bottom of the stairs in ECO.

"I did," I reply. "Earlier." Before she can respond, I walk off toward the U-shaped three-person station where the head analysts and my go-to drone pilot are working.

I walk up behind Abdul and pat him on his good shoulder. "I'm shipping out, you guys," I say softly so Anne, who is talking to another techie, can't hear me. "No matter what anyone else says, I want you three to keep looking for the target." I look from Abdul to Hopewell and then to Salazar. "The second you find something, I want to know."

Cara Hopewell gives me a thumbs-up. "You got it, Cap."

Salazar, who's focused on operating the MQ-11 Griffin drone, nods slightly.

Abdul smirks. "I'll keep them on task, Dion," he says, side-eyeing Hopewell.

On top of the countless surveillance and combat operations, I gave them a special op—hunting down a key Decider target that I know will lead me to the Dominus. Visualizing the target's face makes me shiver.

Ghost.

Earlier this week, there was a report of an Elite female matching her description leading a team that wiped out an outpost in Ohio before raiding a genetics lab in nearby Ashland. Even if Ryan is out of reach, if her bloodlust keeps her returning to the field, we'll find her sooner or later. And once we do, she'll either point us to her brother, or he'll come to us to recover her.

A few days after Naraka, Isabella mentioned that Ghost was supposedly obsessed with biological engineering. Entire floors of the main complex at Iceworm were dedicated to her laboratories.

Redundancy is vital to any wartime operation, so I recruited a WISC operative to try to embed himself in whatever science program Ghost is heading. Lance Corporal Oliver Hawke was a USAW reservist studying biochemistry before the Reclamation. He's intelligent, skilled, keeps a cool head under pressure, loyal as hell, and he knows his science. I briefed him on our research at Coeus and listed the kidnapped staff members he should keep an eye out for, above all, my friend and the director of Coeus, Carmela Discala. Hawke will operate under codename Raptor. His target is a lab somewhere in Colorado that Isabella heard talk of way back when.

Anne and I walk in silence from ECO all the way to Building B. The tension between us is thick. As soon as we're alone, I'm going to catch hell.

We step into the empty viewing room of the kill house. On the other side of the one-way glass, Isabella, Ken, Steele, and Abby are moving tactically through the facility. When they dip out of sight, I track their progress on the monitors lined up on the console as they engage the other Special Forces operators acting as OPFOR.

Anne shoves me. "When were you going to tell me that you decided to deploy without me?"

I sit on the edge of the console and sigh. "I was still trying to figure out a way to cuff you to the bed before I confessed."

Her frown deepens. "That's not funny. You lied to me."

"You asked if I told them that *we* weren't going. And we aren't. You're staying here."

"Spare me your shitty technicalities! You said that after Naraka, you were done! You saved everyone you could; now you're supposed to stay here with me and help fight this war from Babylon. That was the deal!"

"But I didn't save everyone ..."

"Even if he *is* still alive, capturing Ghost won't be the leverage you need to get him back."

"I have to try."

Anne throws up her hands. "That's what they want. They want you to try. They want you out there so they can get to you."

"I'm counting on it," I say. "Walker had one thing right. I'm the perfect bait for the Deciders, Ghost especially. She's obsessed with killing me. If I can lure her out again, if I can capture her—"

"Fine. I'm going with you."

"No, you're not. Ryan sent Jessica to kill you. That's proof that they will stop at nothing to make sure you die."

"I don't give a shit!" Anne shouts. "We promised each other that if we had to fight, we would fight together."

"And after Operation Deliverance, I promised *myself* that I would never let you risk your life again unless we had no choice." I take her hands. "I already broke that promise by letting you take part in the last couple of ops, but I'm not going to let you fight in a full-blown war."

Anne yanks her hands free. "As if you could stop me ..."

"I can," I say.

"Oh, and I can't stop you from leaving?" she asks, her hand inching toward her pistol.

Shooting me in the leg to keep me from risking my life is exactly the sort of thing she would do, so I continue in a more placating tone. "After what happened with Jess, after what I did, I need to be out there. Combat is the only thing that will keep me sane enough to deal with what I've done."

"I know what it feels like to need combat in order to escape your troubles. You know that. You know how addicted I became to combat. I was commander of the Deciders. I could have led from the safety of HQ but I begged Richard to let me fight on the front lines because I needed the rush. But you were all I needed to overcome that addiction. Having you in my life, having our son, those are the reasons I don't want to be out there anymore. But I need to protect you because I know that I'm the only one who can. And if I lose you … I can't live without you, Dion …"

"And I can't live without you either." I hug her tightly. "You and I will do anything to protect each other. That includes taking unnecessary risks. I've lost focus out there because I was worried about what might happen to you." I brush the hair from her face and caress her cheek with my thumb. "Remember during our first op when I dove into the line of fire and took a round to make sure you didn't get hit? If we both keep risking our necks to keep the other safe, odds are we both won't be able to get home to Dean."

"Valid point … But again, neither of us has to be out there fighting. No matter how much you're struggling, we can get through it together, right here."

There's worry in her eyes. I've never seen her this concerned, this … vulnerable.

I shake my head. "I can't be here anymore. Not right now, Anne. This place, Karla, Sam—it all reminds me of what I did."

"Then let's leave! Let's go to the bunker to be with your parents!"

"Every second I spend sitting on my hands is another second she haunts my thoughts, Anne."

"And you don't think she'll haunt you while you're in the field? What do you suppose happens if you have a panic attack out there?"

"Combat is how I dealt with loss during the Annex. Combat keeps me centered. And knowing that I have to make it back to you will keep me focused."

She gives me a look of such ferocity that I worry she's contemplating shooting me again. "Combat is an addiction. The deeper you go, the sicker you'll get. By the time this war is over, you might never be able to climb back out."

"No. I can atone for killing Jess by getting Marshal back. After that, it's over for me, and I'll be able to live with myself again." I take her shoulders and stare into her icy blue eyes. "If you want me to keep being the man you love, you'll let me get my mind right. You'll let me go and you will stay here and make sure I have everything I need to make it back."

She searches my eyes for a long while. "You're certain that there is no other way for you to deal with what's going on in that head of yours?"

"No. There's no other way."

She takes a deep breath, then nods. "Fine. If this is the only way, you can go on two conditions."

"Name them."

"The longer you stay on this warpath of yours, the higher the chance your lucky streak ends, so the *instant* you get your mind right, you come back to me."

"And the second condition?"

She pokes my chest hard. "You come back to me *alive* and in one piece."

I pull her in for a long kiss. "As long as I have you to return to, nothing will stop me from accomplishing that. I promise you." I kiss her again.

We turn to the monitors just as Isabella takes a Simunition round to the arm. During the Annex, the Deciders taught her how to kill mercilessly. They did so by giving her a pistol and locking her in a room that they released bloodthirsty U.S. Army prisoners of war into. Some were armed, some weren't—and she had to murder them before they could end her. They taught her how to survive and how to fight in the woods of Washington State. She saw combat while fighting in Seattle during the Disintegration. And in that battle, she was shot at and eventually shot in the leg by her friend and former romantic interest, Austin Lahey—an Enforcer who wanted to desert from the Deciders before it was too late and wounded her to keep her from dying for their cause. She's seen a lot, but she needs this training if I'm going to trust her ability to fight and survive alongside me.

"You want her to take my spot on the squad, don't you?" Anne asks.

"Yeah."

"Well, she's no replacement for me ..."

"No one is."

"Look at her, blundering around like a drunken goat. She's clearly not ready for a Special Operations team."

"Neither was Jeremy, but he held his own out there." I press the button to activate the speaker system in the kill house. "Isabella, it's Dion. We need you in the observation room, pronto."

"Seriously, why her? You'd have your pick of anyone on this base."

"She told me that I'm the only person in the world she'd die for. I believe she meant it and I figured that if there was anyone you could stand having fill your slot, it'd be someone willing to take a bullet for me."

"Oh, you're right about that ... The more human shields around you, the better." She glares at me. "Third condition: just make sure that when you're missing me on those cold, lonely nights you don't end up filling her ... *slot* ..."

I smile. "Yeah, I'll die before that ever happens."

"Good." She smiles mischievously, palming my manhood. "And to ensure that you don't forget what you'll be missing, I am going to give you one hell of a sendoff."

"What's up?" Isabella asks when she steps into the room. "Am I in trouble?"

"Not yet," Anne says, smiling more devilishly now.

"You have to brief the WISC operatives then we need to get airborne," I say.

Her eyes widen. "Wow, already? Thought I was scheduled for a few more weeks of training."

"Don't worry. I'll finish training you in the field."

25

WARPATH

November 1
4:19 P.M.

THE WALL BEHIND us erupts upon the RPG's impact. The shockwave throws Isabella, Ken, and I onto our faces. Chunks of concrete, shattered glass, and other debris pelt me like hail. A storm of bullets immediately follows, blasting through the dust and smoke cloud.

Disoriented, I grab my rifle and crawl as fast as I can for cover, rounds striking the ground inches from me. "Everyone good?" I shout over the comm. When I hit the wall, I stick out my rifle and blindfire. I can barely hear the gunfire over the ringing in my ears.

"Peachy!" Isabella says while scrambling up beside me.

Ken leans against the more intact wall to my right. "Still in this fight!" he shouts. He pops out, aiming his AT4, and fires a rocket of his own back at the prick who nearly blew us up. The third-floor room where the RPG came from collapses and a plume of thick smoke erupts from the rubble like a volcanic vent. "Antitank soldier down!"

As rounds chip away what little cover we have left, I take stock of the situation: we're pinned down by a sniper and a platoon of Loyals a dozen blocks behind enemy lines—things can't get much worse.

"Fucker!" Isabella curses. "Guys, I've got eyes on an Elite!" A sniper round snaps through the gap in the wall an instant after she ducks back to safety.

It just got worse.

We've spent thirty-five days in the field for Operation Arcadian Spring, and today is the worst one yet. Titan Squad and I had to take a break from sabotaging Deciders and training the rebels we liberated and rallied outside the small city of Greensburg to aid the main USAW force here in Pittsburgh. Our mission, codenamed Operation Nutcracker, began two days ago. The objective was to parachute in and destroy the Deciders' Iron Dome Systems on the eastern perimeter that have been preventing our aircraft, drones, and long-range missiles from doing what they need to do.

Ten minutes ago, we destroyed the last of three targets with a few bricks of C4. With this being our third target, it goes without saying that the Deciders were prepared for our attack. A strong defensive presence was anticipated but we were able to wipe out the Loyals and Enforcers they had guarding the missile and gun systems with a well-thought-out plan of attack and some precision sniping from Abby. It was their reinforcements we weren't ready for ...

"I hope you guys still have some Infernal rounds squared away ..." I say, moving two of the three remaining magazines containing the Elite-killer ammunition from the front of my pack to my tactical vest. Infernal rounds are explosive-tipped, incendiary ammunition that have been found to compromise the outer layers of the Elites' damn near impenetrable liquid armor, rendering it vulnerable to standard ammunition.

"I've been out since yesterday!" Ken shouts over his gunfire. "Put it to good use, though. Don't forget, I've killed more Elites and Loyals on this mission than you!" The tension between us over me swiping the team lead spot has subsided, giving way to a heated competition.

I give him the finger.

"One mag left for my sidearm," Isabella says, shoving it into her pistol. "He's all yours, hon."

Through all the gunfire, I hear Abby's .50 cal boom in the distance. "Enemy sniper down," she reports. "Did I tell you I'm loving this new rifle? Because I am." She's referring to her Barrett .50 BMG Model 82A2 Tracking Point variant, a computer-controlled, precision-guided sniper rifle that she acquired off of an enemy sniper yesterday. Once a target is tagged with the smart scope, it tracks them and fires as soon as the target is reacquired by the reticle. The shot hits almost without fail even at one thousand yards.

"Playtime's almost over, Red Death," I say, dropping a target. "Rusty and Simba should be here soon. Get ready to haul ass to the RP."

Her rifle thunders again and the soldier beside the one I just eliminated falls. "Don't worry. I'll be there ..." The rifle booms once more and another Loyal crumples. "... in time." Her weapon reports again seconds later.

Red's sharpshooting forces the Deciders to scurry for cover, allowing us to take the offensive. Meanwhile, the Elite repositions for the flank with two Loyals riding his coattails for cover. "The Elite and two grays are about to pay us a visit. Get ready." I say, signaling Isabella to cover me and for Ken to switch positions with me.

As we move, something nearby explodes and the entire area trembles. Probably our drone strike taking out the communication jammer on the roof of the Cathedral of Learning Building—at least it better be. Until those jammers are taken out, we can only communicate on PROXCOM, a secure, encrypted frequency for proximity communications that was found to be invisible to Decider scanners. That means no connection to Command or our forces in the area. And without being able to contact Command, we can't arrange for exfiltration.

I activate my comm. "Rusty? Simba? Anyone copy?"

There's some static. "Simba and I copy," Steele responds over the rapid gunfire in the background.

A Loyal pops his head out and I fire a burst of Infernal rounds at the corner. The bullets glow like tracer rounds then explode into burning bullet holes when they hit the wall. "Where are we with that ride?"

"En route. Listen for the honk in thirty seconds."

There's a burst of heavy static. "Ice Queen to Titan Squad Alpha Team," Anne says, her voice muffled and chopped up by the interference.

Another missile strike rumbles in the distance.

"Archangel, do you copy?" she asks. The audio is much clearer now. "You better still be alive. Over."

"Five weeks without you is hard," I say, "but not being able to hear your voice for two days was unbearable."

Between the breaks in gunfire, it sounds like someone's leaning on a horn. Our cab's here.

"It has been hard on me too, love. Are you still near the green smoke at the Botanical Gardens?"

"About a block away," I respond.

While a Loyal lays down cover, the Elite barges into the room, firing wildly. Isabella dispatches the Loyal through the wall while I send two controlled bursts of glowing streaks across the dark room. Several of them explode against the Elite's arm and chest when they make contact. When he goes down, I rush him, firing at the wailing soldier as he desperately reaches for his weapon. I fire at the same spot until blood spurts from the burning holes. He's dead before I'm halfway there.

"Schenley and Forbes!" I hear Steele say over the mayhem. "Hillman Library!"

"Never mind, we have you!" Anne says. "The satellites just acquired your signals!"

I kneel beside the Elite and rip the dog tags from his neck. A quick glance reveals the Elite's name was SSgt. Charles "Nightbeast" Manning. The tags go in my jacket pocket with the others. Collecting the dog tags of my kills has become somewhat of a twisted obsession of mine. And sometimes I risk my ass just to get them ...

I remove a red smoke grenade from my vest. "Izzy!" I shout, tossing it to her. She catches it, pulls the pin, and lobs it through the hole in the wall in one fluid motion.

"We're going to need an airstrike at the red smoke as soon as we're clear!" I say, firing at those outside then spinning and crouching to shoot the remaining Loyal in the building.

"Roger," Anne says. "The Valor will meet you at the extraction point one-point-nine klicks south of your position in ten. The location is marked on your map."

The V-280 Valor is the next-gen counterpart to the V-22 Osprey. The Valor is smaller (holding fourteen troops instead of twenty-four), lighter, and has increased top speed and combat radius.

A machinegun chugs away outside. "We're out front!" Steele says. "Move it!"

I give the signal while I walk backward and fire on the enemy in the hall. Ken punches outside first, laying down cover as he rushes toward the gray armored truck. It looks like an MRAP of some kind with a CROWS II remotely operated weapon system controlling the M2 machine gun on the roof. Isabella follows right behind him and dives into the open rear passenger's side door.

"Archangel!" Ken calls. "Come on!"

I ignore him. Instead, I double back around the corner to surprise the Loyal gunning for me. As I hoped, the bloodlust lures the Loyal out and I catch him in his right shoulder. As his SCAR-H clatters to the ground, I blow another hole in his leg and jog over to him.

"Dion!" Isabella cries. "What are you doing?"

"Johnson!" Steele barks. "We need to move!"

"Get to the RP. I'll meet you there!"

"Fuck that! I'm not leavin' you!" Isabella says. She runs back inside and dives for cover. "Go! I got him!"

The truck doors slam and they screech off. "Hurry your asses up!" Steele says.

I kick the Loyal's rifle away. Before he can grab his sidearm, I step on his hand, remove the FN Five-7 from its holster, and toss it. I roll him over onto his stomach with a kick in the ribs. "Do what I say and you live!"

The soldier laughs. And before he can backtalk me, I shoot him in the ankle. He cries out.

Isabella crawls over and hops into a crouch. "Could've told me you were gonna pull something like this," she says, laying down cover. "You know I always got your back."

Nodding, I glare at the Loyal and draw my knife. "Get on your Gauntlet and send a message to Lauren Thomas for me. You might know her as Ghost. Do that and I'll let you keep those hamstrings."

"Fuck!" he sobs. "Alright, fine! What do you want me to say?"

"Tell her Dion Johnson was here." I detach the filter portion of my helmet, revealing my face. "Tell her I'm looking for Lauren Thomas."

His eyes widen behind his visor. He turns onto his shoulder and starts typing with a trembling hand.

I step on his typing hand, pinning it to the floor. "Show me!"

He raises his Gauntlet. The message addressed to a contact only labeled Ghost reads: "Dion Johnson is in Pittsburgh looking for you, Lauren Thomas."

"Alright." I remove my foot from his hand. "Send it."

He does. And I shoot him in the head anyway.

"Let's go!" I say, ripping the tags from his neck.

Isabella and I take turns laying down cover fire as we retreat to the hallway. Then we book it, being sure to check our corners. Her tactical skills have improved significantly over the course of our deployment. So have her field medic skills—from training with Manny—and CQC skills, thanks to training with me during the calm periods. And when we weren't helping her hone her skills, Isabella and I spent a lot of time bonding. Maybe too much time. I think I know everything there is to know about this girl now, like how she cheated on her first love with a choreographer for a shot at joining a dance team. Hell, I even know all of the details regarding her hookup in a club bathroom with a DJ … and the one she had in the woods with her friend Austin during their Decider training …

A Loyal steps out just in front of us. He's too close for Isabella to shoot, so she disarms him, smoothly I might add, cracks him in the face with the butt of his own rifle, then kicks him to the ground before putting four rounds in his chest.

"Nicely done," I say, clearing the hallway.

She spanks my ass as I turn to the exit. "You're a good coach."

We reach the other end of the building a few seconds later as Abby, who has just rappelled down the side of the building, is climbing into our armored truck. Isabella and I have to fend off a few attackers before the truck pulls up.

"The fuck was that, Johnson?" Steele scolds as Isabella and I pile in.

The truck lurches forward before I even slam the door shut. "Sorry. Random side mission came up last second."

Ken shakes his head. "Still as reckless as ever ..."

There's a slight hum in my earpiece, followed by Anne's voice. "And if he keeps being reckless, I'm going to have you tie him up and ship him back here."

I smile. "Won't happen again, Anne."

The drone strike hits behind us as we turn down the next street, kicking up a massive plume of dust.

"Mind telling me what was so damn important that you almost got left behind for?" Anne asks as debris knocks against the roof. Another drone strike crashes ahead.

"I made a Loyal let Ghost know that I'm in town."

"And what makes you so sure she'll keep that to herself?" Anne asks.

"Given her obsession with me, chances are she won't share that with her cousin." Bullets skip off our vehicle's rear. Three gray L-ATVs are speeding after us. "Have our people keep an eye out for her reply."

"Will do," Anne says. She sounds irritated. "Take the next left. A path to the river has been cleared for you. Extraction is ready and waiting."

The trucks chase us down Bates Street until we race under the overpass. That's when the Apache hovering overhead blows them to hell. Several helicopters surround the area, forming a perimeter around the extraction point. Some descend, dropping off troops. As we pull up to the grassy field next to the Bridgeside II building and scramble for the idling Valor, Sung and Titan Squad Bravo—Hughes, Manny, and Perez—emerge from behind the thicket of trees along the Monongahela River, waving at us as they jog to the aircraft.

I wave back, happy to see that they all survived as well. Their team was in the west end of Pittsburgh doing what we did in the east so I imagine they had as rough as a time as us. Upon boarding the chopper, we immediately start up a pissing contest to see which team had the shittier mission. From the tale Sung spins of day one, they might have us beat.

November 4
12:19 P.M.

In the forty-eight hours after Operation Nutcracker, USAW, along with our armed rebels—codenamed Heretics—overthrew the Deciders controlling Greenburg. The Heretics attacked from within. Titan Squad, a small platoon led by the exonerated Staff Sergeant Anthony Hall, and our UGVs attacked from without. With the city under our control, we comb every block for surviving pockets of Deciders who weren't exterminated.

Scanning windows, doorways, and alleys through our scopes, Isabella, Ken, Steele, and I keep in a tight group behind Chemo—the Ripsaw MS4, light tank drone attached to our unit—as we patrol north down Pennsylvania Avenue toward the courthouse. Isabella dubbed it Chemo because *"It helps us destroy the Decider cancer."* This UGV does so with a front-mounted M2 loaded with .50 caliber Infernal rounds and a side-mounted Mk19 40mm grenade launcher. We can send it into areas too high risk for us to clear. It's thanks to the Ripsaw and the other UGV drones in our detachment that we overran this city so quickly. Well, this city and a few other towns that were successfully taken in the first wave of Arcadian Spring over the past few days.

Reports from elsewhere in the country revealed that the Deciders have terrifying drones of their own—fast, four-legged, dog-like drones fitted with guns. The militarized versions of Boston Dynamics' Spot and Big Dog have been tearing apart our soldiers out west. If we come across any of those, we're screwed ...

"Titan Squad," Cara Hopewell says over the comm. "The building showing heat signatures is the one coming up on your right."

Steele makes a farting sound with his mouth. "It's probably civilians in hiding like the last three places ... Hey, beautiful, where the hell is our Terah Drone coverage, anyway?"

"The Terah drone is where it's needed," Hopewell snaps. "And quit talking to me like I'm your reporter girl, Rust Bucket ..."

"We're Special Forces—tip of the spear. *We* need it," he snaps as we assume breach position.

Something flits in the windows upstairs. "Got movement on the third floor! Far-left window!" I announce.

Rounds start coming my way as I duck behind the Ripsaw. Chemo's M2 sprays across the third floor, allowing me to run to the entrance. Once there, we breach and storm the place. Two Loyals greet us on the second floor. Ken and Steele shred the one taking point. The one in the doorway behind him falls right after. Meanwhile, the Ripsaw uses its thermal cam to target and shred heat signatures above.

"We surrender!" a man cries from inside the room the Loyals emerged from.

"No one's surrenderin'!" the wounded Loyal groans, crawling back into the room. "Get up! We fight until—"

Steele pumps six Infernal rounds from his AA-12 through the wall, silencing him for good.

I toss a concussion grenade into the room and we breach with Isabella covering the rear. Inside are three Enforcers on their bellies with their hands over their ears. One's wounded. We zip-cuff them and then sweep the rest of the floor. Upstairs, we find a Loyal with a huge chunk of his right arm missing who fends us off with a pistol until he's out of ammo. A flash bang goes in and then we rush him and cuff him.

While my team hauls the Enforcers outside, I remain behind with the Loyal on the third floor who's now tied to a chair. I draw my knife and sit before Staff Sergeant Daniel Smith.

"You're going to tell me where to find Greenburg's Hive and the rest of your troops in this area. Then you're gonna tell me how to find Ghost. It's completely up to you whether I use force ..."

Silence.

I stick my knife in his gunshot wound, giving it a twist. He doesn't speak, but he does writhe in pain, stifling a scream through gritted teeth. I take a needle and jab it underneath his fingernail like Ryan did to Dave. Smith howls but the bastard still doesn't talk.

I extract the syringe of Mercy that I always keep in my pack and inject it straight into his arm. It kicks in fast and he starts wailing.

I push him over, squat beside him, and show him a second syringe. "Talk and I'll give you the antidote. Don't and I'll shove this sewing needle in your eye until it's sticking out just a little, causing you crippling pain every time you blink!" I hold open his eye and slowly bring the needle toward it.

"*Alright! Alright!*" Smith begs when the needle's less than a millimeter from his pupil. He tells me everything about the Greenburg detachment of Deciders but swears he can't help me locate Ghost.

Once Hall's platoon confirms that they've located the Hive, I drag Smith outside. The plan now is to take him outside the range of our jammers and make him send another message to Ghost.

Isabella rips the wanted poster of herself off the wall of the building as we step out. Just like in Pittsburgh, there are posters of her, Anne, and me everywhere, offering a reward for anyone who has information on our whereabouts or who captures us alive.

Isabella sighs. "I've always wanted to be famous. This isn't what I had in mind ..." She balls up the poster and throws it at Smith.

"Turncoat bitch!" the Loyal snarls.

Isabella rolls her eyes. "You scream like a bitch!" She looks at me. "So, whatever happened to that guy who said he swore off torture?"

I shove the Loyal over to Ken who then shoves him toward the truck containing our prisoners.

"In a world post-Poseidon, a man like that can't exist," I say. "Not against an enemy who still supports the Deciders' cause."

One eyebrow rises. "So if you captured me today instead of back then ..."

"I still wouldn't have you tortured."

"Why not?" A huge mocking grin slowly spreads across her face. "It's because I'm a girl!" She laughs. "You're, like, so chivalrous! Or is it because I'm fucking gorgeous and you get a semi just looking at me?"

"Partly because you're a girl. Nothing to do with your looks, though. And I definitely don't get a *semi* looking at you ..."

"Pretty sure I felt your soldier come to attention when we were practicing jujitsu a few weeks ago ..."

I make sure my comm is off and no one's nearby. "That's because you were dry humping me when you had me pinned ..."

"Valid point ... But just to clarify, you *do* think I'm gorgeous, right?"

I shrug. "Let's just say you're far from ugly."

"I'll take that as a yes ... Anyway, tell me why you wouldn't have tortured me."

"Because you didn't have that hate-filled look in your eyes. I saw something benevolent in you, something human, something worth protecting."

Isabella's cheeks turn red hot. "Phew!" she says, fanning herself with her hand. "Think I'm gonna need to change undies! You really know how to get a girl hot and ready to go!"

I laugh and shake my head. "Wasn't my intention."

She snorts. "You can't go around saying shit like that in your caring ass tone and not expect me to get turned on, hon."

"Maybe I should talk Anne into a threesome so you can get this out of your system," I joke.

She smirks. "Such a selfless gentleman."

My Gauntlet goes off. It's Anne. I feel like a little kid who's been caught with his hand in the cookie jar. "Hello, my queen!" I answer, a little louder than I meant to.

"Hello, my king," she says.

"Yeah, you know this conversation is with the whole team, right?" Steele asks. "We don't want to hear all this lovey-dovey shit."

"Deal with it!" Anne snaps. "Anywho, I have news that will make your day."

"The Deciders all died of bubonic plague?" I ask, my voice still unnaturally cheerful.

"If only ... Your undead friend received your message and responded. Satellite surveillance caught her at a laboratory in Arcadian territory, Georgia zone. Check your Gauntlet."

I bring up an overhead view of dead USAW soldiers laid out in a distinct pattern—the logo I designed for my company, Coeus Labs. Standing beside the corpses is Ghost, looking up to the sky, holding up a sign with ARCHANGEL written in blood.

"After reviewing surveillance of the raids on bioengineering laboratories within our territories over the past few weeks, we've placed her at the scene of every one. It's safe to assume that since Coeus is the most advanced genetics and biopharmaceutical lab in the country, she'll be heading there eventually."

"But the Deciders already abducted your head scientists ..." Ken says.

"They didn't take the tech or data, though," I say. "And there's an off-the-books section of the building where I had our top-secret research conducted ... The scientists she captured could've told her about it. Even if they didn't, we have to stop her. If we lose Coeus, we lose mass production of our next-gen medical tech for our military."

There's noise on Anne's end. "Nearby units have been dispatched to Coeus. Transport is being arranged for you as we speak."

"You heard her, Operation Séance is greenlit. Let's load up and catch us a ghost!"

26
SÉANCE

November 4
6:19 P.M.

COEUS LABORATORIES SITS northeast of Hagerstown, Maryland, on the site of an abandoned dairy farm that's encompassed by woods. The only direct route there is Coeus Road, formerly Christian Tabler Road, and that's not an option. Ghost's forces have it locked down, along with every main road in a twenty-five-mile radius. A quarter of the way to the objective, word came in that the Army unit sent to defend Coeus was decimated by a drone strike before even nearing the facility. Shortly thereafter, all nearby bases and outposts came under siege. And within thirty minutes, a perimeter was established around Coeus labs.

That means the only way in is by parachute. Again.

Live surveillance reveals that a bulk of the Decider forces lie at the edge of the perimeter. There are about thirty troops scattered throughout the woods surrounding the lab and a platoon of about fifteen engaging the lab's small security force in a firefight just outside the building. It won't take them long to infiltrate.

It's after sunset when Titan Squad and I touch down in a small clearing five hundred meters north of the lab. Stealth chutes are shed and strung up a tree to avoid alerting patrols to our presence.

Sung leads Abby and Titan Bravo southwest. The rest of us head south, silently killing Deciders along the way.

Seven Loyals and three hundred meters later, I signal the team to hold. "Continue on to the objective," I murmur. "I'll link up with y'all in a few."

"The hell you going?" Steele grunts.

"There's something I have to check."

"Well, I got your six then," Isabella says under her breath while trotting up behind me.

"No," I say. "Head to the objective and await further instructions. That's an order."

With a huff, she pivots and follows after Steele and Ken.

I creep to an aged utility shed fifty meters west. There's a lock on the door, and I slip the key for it out of my pocket. Once inside, I close the door behind me, locking it with the slide bolt. I push the table toward the rear and then roll back the dusty rubber work mat, revealing a metal hatch in the concrete floor. It's not on any blueprints but, when the Coeus lab was constructed, I had them build an escape tunnel that leads from the off-the-books portion of the lab to here, just in case something ever happened while I was on site. Never thought I'd use it to sneak in, though.

I jump off the ladder three rungs from the bottom then head to the door and punch the code into the panel beside it. The tunnel is equipped with solar-powered motion sensor lights. Since it's dark ahead, I know it's clear so I sprint toward the final door.

Sung buzzes in. "Titan Bravo in position."

"Ten meters from the objective," Ken says. "Archangel, what's your POS?"

"About ten feet below ground in a secret tunnel heading to the building."

"What the *fuck*?" Steele says.

"And why didn't you tell us about this tunnel before?" Ken asks.

"Because one of you would've followed me in here."

"And why would that have been a problem?" Steele asks.

"Well, for one, we need as much manpower outside as possible to clear the area," I say while punching in the code to the last door. "Second, I'm the only person Ghost won't kill. And she's very skilled—she almost beat me last time, and she was restraining herself. Chances are, if we aren't fighting to kill, whoever came with me wouldn't make it out."

Steele sighs. "Low blow, Archangel ..."

"Suck it up. For this to work, I need your help." I press enter and the door opens. "I'll be bringing her out in fifteen. Going dark."

"If you're not out by then, we're coming in," Isabella says before I disable my comm.

I slip into my dark office and gently close the panel behind me, letting it blend back into the rest of the wall. The only light in the room comes from underneath the door—just enough to show me where to walk without tripping over anything. I take a broad-spectrum jammer from my pack and place it under the desk.

A shadow slowly floats across the gap underneath the door. It pauses for a moment then continues on. After waiting for a second shadow that doesn't come, I knock the butt of the rifle against a bookshelf then move as quietly and quickly as possible toward the door, planting my back against the wall beside it. The footfalls halt then start again, moving quietly toward the office. With a kick, the door flies open and a Loyal storms in. I strip him of his rifle in one fluid motion and plunge my blade into his chest three times. He's so caught off guard that he tries to pull the knife out of his chest instead of reaching for his sidearm, weakly clawing at me as I gently bring him to the ground. There's a gurgle and a gag, and in seconds he's lifeless.

I step into the hall, MP7 in the high ready as I head toward the bioengineering lab. There's a lot of rustling and bustling ahead along with some faint voices. A few feet from a darkened corner, I hear a flat, monotone, female voice that makes me shudder. "Get it all out of here now," she says. "We're not alone in here either."

I place an OSO camera on the floor then pull up the footage on my Gauntlet. A helmetless Lauren "Ghost" Thomas stands outside the lab holding a liquid nitrogen–cooled metal cryogenic container with a biohazard symbol on it while she speaks to a birdlike Loyal with a pair of wireless glasses perched on the bridge of his long nose. There are a couple of biohazard-worthy viruses and bacteria in this lab that worry me, particularly a virus discovered in the Amazon's silvery marmosets called ENODA— which stands for "End of Days" because, if it got out, it'd eradicate humanity in a rabid, people eating people kind of way. Some are agents used in CRISPR that can edit the genome for the purpose of eliminating diseases or potentially engineering super soldiers.

Six Loyals file out of the lab hauling computers, lab equipment, and vials. They're all helmetless.

Ghost hands off the cryo-container to the Loyal wearing glasses. "If for whatever reason you are unable to extract anything else," Ghost continues, scanning the men before her, "get this back to my lab, no matter what." Her head turns to her right. "You two, find and bring him to me now. Cerberus, keep them alive."

Two Loyals exit the lab and march my way. As they near the corner, an Elite emerges with a white MTAR-21 hanging across his chest. He puts on a Deva helmet, takes one step in my direction, pauses, and points. "Found him."

So, apparently, there's an active TARSEN Field letting him see me through the wall ... Like a pouncing cheetah, I burst around the corner, knock away the closest Loyal's rifle, put three rounds in his chest, and spin him around, using him as a shield while lighting up the Loyal behind him with my Infernal-loaded MP7. Glowing streaks tear through his comrade, leaving burning holes in his chest.

Ghost glides into the lab while the Elite dubbed Cerberus shields her, firing at me as he does. The guy holding the cryo-container flees. I send rounds at Cerberus to keep him at bay, but that doesn't stop him from leaning out and returning fire. Another Loyal pops out around the corner and joins in.

"Hold your fire!" Ghost shouts.

Both Deciders cease fire. So do I.

Ghost seems to float up behind the Elite and rests her chin on his shoulder. Just like last time, she's wearing that black, raccoon-style makeup that makes her pale blue eyes pop in the creepiest way possible. "Glad you received my message, Archangel."

Once again, a strange buzz rolls through my body. Why does this happen every time I encounter her? Is it fear? No, it's something else ... I tap the side of my helmet and the lower part of my Deva detaches. "How'd you know it was me?"

"Shivers run down my spine whenever you're near," she moans.

As I inch toward them behind my meat shield, that sensation intensifies. "Funny," I say. "Same thing happens to me when you're around ..."

Her eyebrows dance on her pale white forehead. "Interesting ..." She lifts her chin from Cerberus's shoulder and snaps her fingers. "Leave us. Eliminate his team."

Multiple boots march away without delay, their shadows dancing across the wall behind them.

The Elite lingers. "Ghost, you know it's my job to—"

"What? Protect me?" she smiles mockingly. "I don't need your protection. Besides, you are no match for the Archangel ..."

"How dare you? Anubis and I taught you how to fight."

Ghost strolls back into the lab. "Prove me wrong then. Subdue him." She sits on a lab bench, elegantly crossing her legs. "Sic him, boy ..."

Cerberus and I open fire at the same time—me burst firing and advancing behind my shield while he blindfires from inside the lab. After two exchanges, the MP7 runs dry. I let the submachine gun fall, rip a concussion grenade from the dead Loyal's chest rig and toss it his way. When it pops, I remove a remote explosive from my vest, slide it into the Loyal's trench pocket, then draw my P226. By that time, I'm right outside the lab. Cerberus, who wasn't fazed by the grenade, emerges, shooting. Nearly a dozen rounds bombard the body as I shove it at him with all my might. The dead weight hits him, knocking him back slightly as he pushes it aside into the lab. I dive for cover and detonate the bomb using the Gauntlet.

The blast widens the doorway, shatters the windows, and sends Cerberus flying out into the hallway. He lies there, face flat on the floor, uniform charred and shredded, metallic-looking liquid leaking from the fabric of his armor. But somehow, he's still alive. Pistol in one hand, knife in the other, I charge.

Cerberus groans while trying to push himself up. "Clever ..." As he reaches for his sidearm, I kick him in the gut. He collapses, coughing, and I drop down on him and drive my blade into his spine.

Debris crunches to my right. Leaving my knife in his back, I bring my pistol toward the impending threat. My fastest isn't fast enough. Ghost grabs my weapon, disarms me, and follows up with a knee to the side. Then she slams me into the wall with my arm pinned behind my back.

She strips me of my backup pistol and tosses it. "Paralyzing him and leaving him to die slowly?" she moans. She rips off my helmet and brings her mouth close to my ear. "I admire your brutality."

With a head-butt and a spinning elbow, I break free, swiping one of her Glock 18s in the process. A front kick sends her stumbling back as I take aim. She quickly pulls her backup on me.

"That same brutality is what will end you ..."

"Please ..." Glock still trained on me, she draws her knife, squats, and rolls Cerberus over. She removes his helmet and stares into the wheezing Elite's eyes. "You're weak like him," she whispers, then slowly slits his throat. Her dead eyes lock onto mine as she stands. "You lack what it takes to kill me."

"Keep telling yourself that ..."

"Don't waste your energy, Archangel. We both know you are not here to end me tonight ..."

"And you're not here to kill me either."

Her thin black lips widen into a flat smile. "That is still to be determined ..."

"Something tells me Lex Talionis isn't over yet. You need to bring me to Ryan alive."

"Oh, I'm *keeping* you. Somewhere I can play with you whenever I want until I grow bored." She licks her lips. "Only then will my dear cousin resume his pointless little game with you."

"You sent your troops away too soon. You'll need them if you plan on capturing me."

"Such hollow boasting from a hollow little man. It's more pleasurable when it's just the two of us making each other bleed. Clearly you feel the same way. Otherwise, you wouldn't have been foolish enough to pursue me on your own ..."

"No. I just didn't need anyone else to take you down."

"Lies," she whispers. "I see it in your eyes." She steps closer. "You and I are the same." She takes another step. "We are warriors, not soldiers. We fight and kill because it's the only way we feel alive—the only fuel to animate the shells of who we've become. And when enemy warriors of our caliber cross paths, the desire to win a great victory trumps the logic of having comrades at our side."

She's right. I abandoned my team to take on Anne after she killed my friends. I did the same to fight Richard after we shot him down following Operation Deicide. "Keep trying to convince yourself that we're alike, Lauren."

Her face flickers with revulsion at the sound of her name. "The drive to spill blood, the hate, the rage—I see it in you the same way I see it in myself when I look in the mirror. With the exception of what makes me superior, we *are* the same, whether or not you want to admit it. Yet you think you're some kind of hero. I'm sure by now you know what happened to those friends of yours we held captive. Would a hero allow his friends fall victim to such a fate?"

Rage burns in my gut, but I prevent it from showing on my face.

She nods, satisfied. "Yeah, you know ... How did things turn out with what's her face?"

"The innocent girl you people broke and sent to kill Anne? Her name was Jessica ..."

"That's it. *Jessica.* Oh, dear." Ghost touches her finger to her lips. "You said that *was* her name? So, as I hypothesized, she didn't survive the experiment … Tell me, did you kill her or did someone else?"

The flashbacks, the sorrow, and the anger hit me all at once, and for a moment, my mind blanks. Ghost darts forward and to the left, but I don't react when I should—how I should. The Glock 18 goes off, but it's not me who pulls the trigger, it's my muscle memory driven by subconscious. All rounds from the spray miss, except for the one that strikes her ribs under her left arm. But these are her rounds, not Infernals, so she merely jerks from the impact.

She knocks my arm away and brings her Glock up and fires. A round hits me in torso like a sledgehammer. I grab her wrist and push the weapon away. Both guns fire off at nothing as we grapple. In seconds, both guns run dry.

"So you killed her," Ghost whispers. She's not even breathing hard. "Bravo."

Ghost doesn't attempt to reload; she just lets the gun fall and uses the free hand to strike. I do the same, but to block. What follows is a hand-to-hand fight worthy of two grandmasters in an old martial arts movie. There are more blocks on each side than landed blows. Unlike the last encounter, I land most of them.

A low right kick to the thigh, a left jab to her mouth, and a straight punch to the gut stuns her, allowing me to slam her into the lab window. I pin one arm against the wall and grab her throat with my free hand.

As she chokes, enjoyment beams from her wild eyes. Something like a faint smile appears, revealing bloody teeth. "Much more fun than last time!"

Her hand shoots down to her leg, presumably to grab a knife. I release her throat and grab her wrist before she can. Her chest heaves. Her body arches. Then she leans forward and licks my face. A head-butt and a knee to the groin follow. When my grip breaks, she elbows my jaw then punches my chest. As I stumble back, a spin kick hits the same spot. She cartwheels and back handsprings into a flying triangle choke, driving us both to the ground.

"Do you like being choked too …?" she asks, constricting me with her surprisingly powerful thighs.

Dizziness quickly sets in as oxygen is cut off from my brain. I wrestle her onto her back and grab her trench coat. With one knee to the floor, one foot planted, I stand, lifting her and then slamming her hard onto the floor. She lets out a grunt and squirms beneath me, trying to get free.

Panting heavily, I stumble to my feet, drawing my second combat knife from the rear of my tactical belt. "Negative …" I respond, switching the blade into a reverse grip.

"Oh, well." Her arm draws back and she hurls a throwing knife at me.

I turn just in time for the blade to spin by with millimeters to spare. She rises and throws another that I jump backward to dodge. She has throwing knives in both hands now. With a smirk, she spins one and then the other. I push off the wall and dodge the first. The second I try to parry with my blade, but I miss and it slices through my glove.

Ghost draws a kunai from inside her coat. "It's a shame this fight has to end …" She twirls the blade into a reverse grip. "I was just beginning to enjoy myself."

I assume my fighting stance. "What makes you so sure?"

She charges. We trade blows—both relentlessly trying to punch, kick, and cut the other. I dodge all the blade attacks, and in the midst of her combo, I cut across her right arm only to receive a knee to the ribs in return. She spins into a crouch and cuts my left thigh with the kunai. A flurry of attacks follows. As I dodge them and retaliate, something starts feeling off. My attacks and movements get slower. My footwork's getting sloppy. My limbs feel like noodles.

After a front kick sends me stumbling back into the wall, I push forward only to collapse to one knee. And no matter how hard I try, I can't get back to my feet.

Ghost strolls toward me, returning her kunai to the inside of her coat. "The nicotinic receptors in your limbs are being depolarized, paralyzing your muscles. All this thanks to the suxamethonium chloride my knives are coated in."

"Couldn't beat me so you had to cheat, huh ...?" I growl, still trying to stand.

She shrugs. "I have a deadline ... And if you had dodged my attacks, you wouldn't have this problem, would you?"

When she's in front of me, I feebly swing my knife at her, almost falling over as I do. She grabs me by the throat and slams me backward onto the floor. She mounts me, and that intense buzz I feel whenever she's around intensifies. She slowly brings her face close to mine, her flour locks tickling my cheeks. Her unblinking pale blue eyes stare into mine while blood drips from her open mouth onto my lips.

"You're all mine now, Archangel ..."

27
COMMUNE

November 4
7:40 P.M.

GHOST'S COLD FINGERS slide up my wrist to my palm. She interlaces her fingers between mine and brings my hand to her mouth. Her eyes close as she traces her lips with my fingertip, like it's lipstick or some shit.

"Your blood ... I like the way it tastes." She slides my finger onto her bottom left canine and presses it hard onto the pointy edge until her tooth breaks my skin. When blood starts flowing, she starts sucking like a starving baby would with a bottle. Her tongue wriggles and slithers playfully across the wound.

The "feeding" goes on for almost a minute before Ghost abruptly yanks the finger out of her mouth like it bit her. Just as suddenly, she dismounts and rolls me onto my stomach. "Not sure what came over me ... Any longer and the paralysis would have worn off," she whispers while zip-cuffing my wrists. She frisks me, stripping me of all weapons. "Something about you makes me act wildly out of character, as though your essence alone intoxicates me."

"So you don't suck the blood of all your victims ...?"

She rolls me back over. "I've always enjoyed the taste of my own blood, but I would never have dared to ingest someone else's filth." Her head tilts. "That is, until I tasted you during our first fight." She strolls down the hall to retrieve her weapons. "Now I'm addicted …"

Limited motion is returning to my fingers and toes. "Maybe what you think is an obsession to kill me is more like some twisted, sick crush."

"I don't do *crushes* …" She sits me up and starts dragging me down the hall by the collar of my combat jacket. "I am and always have been incapable of feeling those kinds of emotions."

"That's because you never met someone like me," I say.

"Ugh," she says.

"You said it yourself. We share *some* similarities. Our common ground coupled with the fact that I'm the only person who challenges you excites you. Maybe that's what translates into attraction for someone of your mental … situation."

We stop, and Ghost lets me go. She presses the elevator's up button. "Please, elaborate on our similarities …"

"You were right earlier about us being warriors. About having the drive to fight in order to bury the hurt. About having the thirst for a good challenge. That's what got me into this predicament …"

"Lesson learned. I'm always right." The elevator door opens. She drags me inside and punches "G" for ground level. When the doors close, she grips my throat, digging into my trachea with her black painted nails. "You're much too chatty for someone who was just captured … Perhaps I'll cut your tongue out …"

I search her eyes. "How did you get like this? What made you this bloodthirsty, emotionless, murderous shell of a girl? What is the hurt that you fight to bury every day?"

Ghost scowls, her eyes scanning mine. "That almost sounded like genuine interest …"

"It is."

The door opens. She releases my throat, draws her Glock, and rams it into my temple. "You should be able to walk now."

I pull myself up by the wall of the elevator and put one foot in front of the other. My legs are wobbly, but I don't fall so I lead the way out. Gun now to the back of my head, Ghost guides me to the main lobby doors. "Not going to answer me?"

Feet from the exit, the body of a Loyal crashes into the glass doors and slides down, leaving a blood trail. Ghost steers me back the way we came. "Your soldiers are quite bothersome ..."

Back in the elevator, Ghost hits the top floor button.

"It'll probably be a while before that helicopter arrives," I say. "Plenty of time to tell me how Lauren Thomas died and became the Ghost."

A fast left hook rocks my jaw and then a powerful jab hits me in the gut. She grabs me by the face and slams my head into the wall. "Call me that one more time and I'll cut your tongue out and eat it ..." she hisses.

"Just answer me."

"Supposedly, you are pretty astute," she sneers. "If you had to guess why I am the way I am, what would you say?"

I search her eyes and her face for a few moments. "Given the fact that you're pretty much a genius, I have to say it's partially due to a low emotional quotient that came packaged along with a high IQ, as it usually does. Also, I suspect that, like me, your low EQ comes paired with an Axis II personality disorder that prevents you from feeling remorse."

"And the other part?" The elevator stops and the doors open but she doesn't budge. Her eyes burn intensely into mine, like she's waiting for me to say the wrong thing.

As sincerely as possible, I say, "Not that I think there is anything wrong with the way you look, but I imagine growing up was difficult for you."

The corner of her mouth twitches. Her lids lower. "Well done." The closing doors rebound as she shoves me out of the elevator.

"That's it? There are plenty of non-murderous geniuses who were bullied when they were kids. I wanted to know how Laur— how the old you died?"

"As though you actually care to know ..."

I turn around. "I do. If you're anything like me, not knowing something drives you nuts. And you're probably the most interesting, intriguing person I've ever crossed paths with. Not knowing how you became *this*," I say, looking her up and down, "will bother me for the remainder of what's looking like a shorter life than I'd hoped for ..."

Her mouth twists to the side. "Fine. Once we're on the roof."

We walk in silence to the secure roof access door that lies at the other end of the building. She swipes the badge she stole from one of the dead security personnel and shoves me through. At the top of the stairs, she opens the roof door and peeks out. I see the corpses of the two Decider snipers behind the popup defensive barriers and one USAW solder lying near the retaining wall. Ghost extracts a flare from her tactical belt, lights it, and tosses the bright green stick outside. She then kicks my feet from under me, knocking me back into the wall. As I slide down it, I very subtly stick my hand into my pants and extract the utility blade hidden in the slit of the waistband. She strolls to the opposite end of the landing and leans back against the wall, pistol trained on me.

"Tell me about your first kill," she says.

"This conversation is supposed to be about you …"

Her head tilts downward and her white locks cover half of her face. "It will be."

"It was early during Act One of Richard's takeover. A few days after the Deciders cut off evacuation routes out of the cities, a group of marauders sacked my neighborhood. When they got to my house, we fended them off. One flanked. Before he got the sliding door halfway open, I put two rounds into his chest."

"What did you feel?"

"Nothing. Relief. Never regretted it and it never haunted me."

Though her face is mostly blank, she looks slightly pleased. "I was seven years old when I took my first life."

"Shit …" I say under my breath.

"Gwen Prescott, a little bitch in my third- and fourth-grade classes—the alpha of a group of mean girls. I'd been bullied since kindergarten. No one wanted to be friends with the albino who skipped two grades, but they couldn't leave it at that. 'Run, the ghost is coming! She's going to suck out your soul!' I dealt with them how I could—I pushed my tormenters of playground sets, I dosed their shitty cafeteria pizza with Visine … Life was miserable, but things didn't get unbearable until Gwen came along."

With slow passes of the blade, I cut through the cuffs.

"For a year and a half," Ghost continues, "that little bitch ensured that every second of my day was filled with torment. I hit my breaking point a week before the Christmas vacation. Two days later, I stole her friend Aimee's phone and texted Gwen to come over after school. She biked there alone like she always did. And after a 'Help me!' drew her into woods at the edge of the neighborhood, I pulled her into the bushes and stabbed her thirty-six times."

Ghost holds up her left hand and stares at it, grinning. "As I sat there in the snow, staring down at my bloody hand, giggling, the only thing I felt was joy. It was the first time I had experienced that feeling since I came to understand that I was different. I wanted to do it again to get that feeling back. I wanted to kill everyone who ever hurt me ..."

"And did you kill again?"

"Not during elementary school or junior high. In sixth grade, this little swine named Chris Campbell knocked my books out of my hand. I tackled him, clawed his face, and beat him into a coma with my textbook. No one messed with me after that."

The zip cuffs are cut enough now to pop with a hard jerk. "And I imagine things got worse in high school ..."

She nods once, slowly. "Of course. There's nothing crueler than American teenagers with internet access. Sophomore year, I managed to track one of the cowards' IP addresses—a senior football player who was at the center of the cyberbullying campaign. For his punishment, I broke into his house while his parents were out of town and beat his head into a pulp with one of his trophies. I made it look like a robbery."

"Did that stop the bullying?"

She shakes her head. "Later that year, around prom, a post with a picture of me sitting alone at lunch after I spilled juice on myself began circulating. 'Ghost Girl, kill yourself. You already look dead ...' The next day, some asswipe put up printouts all over school. All those shitheads ... pointing ... laughing, making hanging and cutting gestures as I walked the halls ..." The hurt appears on her face.

"You didn't deserve that."

Ghost shrugs. "I left in tears. For days, I didn't leave the house. I didn't eat. I missed my gymnastics tournament ... And my parents—those assholes did nothing to comfort me. They only cared about my sister, Lindsey, the pageant queen, the ditz, their pride and joy—not me, a child prodigy. I hated everyone … it wasn't like the situation with Gwen, where I could end the torture by killing one person. I wanted everyone dead. Every single person on the planet … Because I realized that no matter what, everywhere I'd go, there would be someone looking at me funny or talking about me. And since it was impossible to murder every insensitive peon on the planet, I decided there was only one way to deal with it."

"Suicide …"

Ghost hikes up her sleeve, revealing a thick snaking scar that runs from her wrist up to the inside of her elbow. "From the day Lauren Thomas died." Her sleeve goes back down. "My sister found me. A few minutes later, I would have bled out. But I was dead. I died inside long before then, but on that day, I accepted it. While they had me committed, while they forced me to undergo counseling, I plotted my next attempt. A visit from Ryan quelled those suicidal thoughts. He was always the only person I considered family, the only person who truly loved me. The only person I loved and will ever love.

"He cared for me until I was better. He promised that if I held on and fought through the pain, the day would come where he would make things better. He convinced my parents to enroll me in a new preparatory school, and things did get better. And things remained that way all the way through college, for the most part."

"But something tells me you never gave up your vow of omnicide …" I say.

She shakes her head. "Never. Imagine my delight when—"

"When Ryan told you about the Deciders on your fourteenth birthday."

"That's right!" she says, eyes wide and wild.

"So, while Ryan and his followers fight to unite the world for the benefit of mankind, you're in the business of inflicting suffering and death."

Ghost slow claps. "Now you understand."

"You know, I get it," I say after a moment. "After everything you went through, I don't blame you for wanting to kill everyone—for what you've become."

She appears almost appreciative. "That's not the response I expected …"

I shrug. "I mean, it makes sense. Experiencing mankind's cruelty day in and day out your entire life, a lack of love and attention from your parents … Even for someone without your psychological makeup, hating everyone is a fairly sane response."

"Thank you."

"But not everyone deserves your wrath."

"Even those who weren't actively cruel to me are guilty. No one reached out to me. No one ever stood up for me! No matter where I went, that would have held true because humanity is inherently cruel. And cruelty must be purged …"

"Had we gone to the same school at any point, I would have reached out to you."

"Doubtful …"

"Even now, knowing how deranged you are, I don't see you as a ghost or a freak. I just see a lonely girl who's fallen victim to hatred. I would've seen that when I was younger too. And I would've tried befriending you because you needed a friend, and because you were different in that weird way I've always found intriguing."

Mouth twisted to the side, she kneels before me. "Part of me actually believes that you're being sincere. But after being starved of care for my whole life, caring people sicken me. And a caring person who is also my nemesis in war is even more nauseating."

I grin. "Sorry, that's just who I am."

She bares her teeth. "If you were trying to soften me up, you failed. You actually convinced me to end you sooner ..."

"There's no ulterior motive here. I know you're not the type who's swayed by kind words."

Ghost cringes. "I want you dead so badly ..."

"When the time comes, you won't kill me. You'd miss me too much. You're addicted to me, after all."

"All addictions must end, one way or another ..." She stands back up. "Extraction will be here shortly. I can't wait to get my next fix ..." Slowly, she licks her lips.

"Before you lock me away in your dungeon, tell me something. Why'd you signal me to meet you here, of all places?"

"Aside from the fact that this was the last stop on my requisition mission and is in relative proximity to your last known location, I figured your familiarity with the lab would make you feel comfortable enough to sneak in on your own."

"Smart ... And what did you take from here—a plague to end humanity?"

"Oh, just the research you stole from us."

"Let me be more specific. What was in the cryo-container you stole?"

"A certain viral vector that's perfect for adult human gene therapy using CRISPR ..."

"Project Aeon ..."

She nods. "Did you know I hold a master's in genetic engineering and biochemistry?"

"Well, I didn't think you were an art history major."

"Ha … The viral vector was the focus of my thesis. Then I started Project Aeon at Ryan's request."

"Your work is brilliant …"

Ghost dips into a curtsey. "Now imagine my surprise when one of your scientists finally broke and divulged the advances that Coeus had made with my brainchild …" The hinge of a door squeaks somewhere downstairs. "Up," she says, opening the door.

With my back against the wall, I rise using only my legs. Just as I cross the threshold of the doorway, I jerk both arms down, breaking free of my restraints while spinning out of Ghost's line of fire. I grab her arm and head, slamming her skull into the wall and smashing her hand against the concrete until she drops the pistol.

"Didn't think capturing me would be that easy, did you?" I pant, pinning her arm behind her back while still mushing her face into the wall.

"Certainly not," she groans. "That would have been disappointing."

"Did you expect me to escape?"

"I hoped you would make an attempt so we could tango once more before the trip. As time passed, I thought you wouldn't. Pains me to admit you caught me off guard."

"Something I never thought I'd hear …"

"Not that you will successfully capture me, but what are your intentions, Archangel? Torture me into telling you how to find my cousin? Remember, pain is my aphrodisiac …"

"Well, since you like pain and hate kindness, I'll make sure your torture consists of constant pampering and Disney movies."

She giggles like some demonic child. "If you're planning on using me as bait to lure Ryan out, he won't show. Instead, he'll send wave after wave of Deciders until you are all dead and I am liberated. And if you end me, he will turn every inch of land to ash until only Deciders remain."

Grabbing her hair, I slam her head into the wall again. While she's stunned, I shoot my hand down from her head to the inside of her coat, snatch her kunai, and put it to the side of her neck. "Guess we'll see about that."

"You know why I fight ... Tell me, why do you?"

I rattle off a brief version of what I told Isabella about why I fought in the first war, about how I partly agreed with Richard's mission to reboot the world, about how I tried to restore the world the way I thought was best.

She smirks. "Interesting ... and now? Is your mission just revenge against my cousin, or do you have a greater purpose?"

"To be honest, I don't see this war ending. People like me will keep resisting against people like you until there's no one left to fight. Right now, all I really want is to kill your cousin. Him, and everyone involved in what happened to my son and friends."

"Better slit my throat then. I orchestrated the kill order of your friends and devised most of the torture methods ... Even Jessica's."

I press the blade to her jugular. The thought of slicing through it crosses my mind, but for some reason, everything in me screams not to. "No. You're too fascinating. Too intelligent. Ending you seems like a waste of potential ... Besides, I want a rematch."

"Mmmmm ..." she moans, her body shuddering. "And what potential do you think I—a homicidal sadist—have?"

"You're a genius. If you could purge yourself of your hatred, you could make this world a better place. You'd do a better job than your maniac, revenge-obsessed cousin ..."

"You are just as vengeful as Ryan and me ... and your lust for revenge will have a single outcome."

"Ryan's death …"

"Sometime very soon, Ryan *will* lure you to right where he wants you, *again*, because your compulsion for retribution makes you predictable. And this time around, he *will* kill you. Then you and I won't get to play anymore."

"You and I can play in peace if you tell me how to get the jump on him."

"As much as I want Ryan to stop wasting his time on Lex Talionis, I will never let you kill the only man I love."

From the floor below, rapid footfalls stomp urgently in our direction. Ghost pushes hard off the wall, thrusting her butt into my pelvis as she does. I stumble into the handrail as she rolls across the floor, retrieves her gun, maneuvers into a catlike crouch near the door, and takes aim. "Time's up," she says. "Guess I'm off to see my dear cousin since I'm leaving here alone tonight …"

"How about I give you a ride?"

The door below bursts open and crashes hard into the wall. "Dion!" Ken shouts.

"I already have one," Ghost says, then slips through the doorway.

"Up here!" I shout. "Hurry!" I look out to see Ghost sprinting across the roof toward the edge where a rope ladder is dangling from an SH-7 Specter. Ken bursts out and fires at the chopper's gunner, an Elite with a machine gun. The Decider's barrage forces us back inside.

"Mission … fucking … failed," Steele spits. "We could've had her if you hadn't tried to be the goddamn hero!"

Isabella punches me hard in the arm. "What were you even thinking?"

I raise my palms. "Relax," I say, bumping past them. "Operation Séance might still be a success."

"Unless Ghost pulled an Anne and told you where to find Ryan, I don't see how that's possible ..." Ken says, jogging down the stairs behind me.

I navigate the options on my Gauntlet. "She didn't, but she's heading right for Ryan ... and I just placed a tracker on her."

28
RANCOR

November 5
8:09 A.M.

THE TRACKER PLACED on Ghost was programmed to transmit a signal once every four hours—just often enough to establish a pattern of movement while hopefully not attracting the attention of Decider signal detection tech. Around midnight, the tracker pinged Ghost almost five hundred miles southwest of Hagerstown, Maryland. Our course was immediately corrected for those coordinates. While awaiting the next signal, Titan Squad touched down at Mid-Ohio Valley Regional Airport on the outskirts of Parkersburg, West Virginia—the site of an Angels of War outpost dubbed OP Kanawha—to refuel, resupply, and rest up.

Four hours ago, the tracker resurfaced in the Ozarks. Using live satellite imagery, we located the Specter and tracked it to just outside of Highlandville, Missouri, where it then landed on the helipad for a massive Château Style building that can only be described as a palace. Ghost and her team exited the stealth chopper and disappeared into the fortified structure while the Specter descended on some kind of lift into the ground behind them. Surrounding the palace is a defensive wall and an anti-air system that rivals what we have at Babylon. On the roof, there's something that resembles a Tesla Tower—a device that Veritas revealed to be able to provide a city with free wireless electricity.

Colonel Tannin identified the property to be Chateau Pensmore, a manor house erected from 2008 onward by a former friend and CIA officer who once ran a company dealing in medical, defense, and intelligence applications. The complex had been a focus of conspiracy theorists—or more accurately, conspiracy realists—since construction began. Pensmore was rumored to be a safe haven for elites after society collapsed. That was likely the case, except the former property owners disappeared during the Annex and its construction wasn't completed until sometime in the past two years ...

Anxiously staring at the screen of my Gauntlet, I watch the live map of the manor, aptly codenamed Castle by Anne, and wait for the blip to appear. At 8:11 A.M., exactly four hours and one minute since the last transmission, I conclude that Ghost either realized that I tagged her or the thick walls of Castle are blocking the signal.

With a tap, I return the Gauntlet to split-screen view, revealing the video chat that I have open with Anne. "How long until the supply drop?" I ask.

She raises an eyebrow. "Not waiting for visual confirmation of the Dominus?"

"Ghost said she was going straight to Ryan."

Rolling her eyes, Anne types away. "Supplies are dropping ... now, actually ..."

With a snap of my fingers followed by a rally-up hand signal, Isabella, Tommy, and Ken close their laptops and grab their weapons before following me out of the hangar.

"Supplies are here," Ken says into his comm. "Meet us out front."

I look up to the grayish sky. Ten crates containing our supplies rock back and forth as they parachute toward the other end of the base.

Two transport trucks pull up seconds later, Leo Hill driving one with Steele riding shotgun and Abby, Manny, and Perez in the back. Hughes drives the second with Sung in the passenger seat.

"I'll grab Sanders and prepare the Valor," Tommy says. "Wheels up in …?"

"Eh, two hours …" I say, climbing in the back of Hughes's truck.

With a thumbs-up, Tommy starts toward the Valor.

At the drop site, we load each container onto the trucks in order of the codes painted on their sides. Back at the hangar, we pry off their tops in the opposite order that they were loaded in. Inside is everything we could possibly need to complete the mission—Infernal rounds, Aegis armor, HALO jump gear, drones, weapons, attachments, magazines, multiple patterns of BDUs, boots in each of our sizes, and First Strike Rations.

As the team gathers what they need, my Gauntlet goes off. It's Abdul. I patch him into the open call I have with Anne.

"Open crate TSS4," he says.

Scanning the row of crates, I spot it last in line. It's the only one not on the supply manifest. "What am I looking for?"

"A gift. You'll see."

I release the latches and flip the lid back. Beneath the bubble wrap, I find another, smaller case. Inside of that is a Deva helmet unlike anything in the Angels of War armory. With its angled, narrower visor, it resembles those worn by Decider Elites …

"Remember the Farsight Deva helmet you acquired in Baltimore during the rogue op?" Abdul asks.

I pick it up. "Dozer's?"

"Mm-hmm."

The once-white helmet is now matte black and has an Angels of War emblem etched into the sides. Attached to the right side of the helmet over where my temple would be is a 2"x3" device with a camera in it—something not seen on Elite Farsight models.

"Try it on!" Abdul says in the most excited tone I've ever heard from him. "The power button is on the underside near the right side of your jaw."

I slide the helmet onto my head and power it on.

Isabella leans on the other side of the crate, resting her chin on her palm. "Oooh," she purrs. "Someone got an upgrade."

"I sent an update to your Gauntlet last night," Abdul says. "There's an app called Farsight. Use it to sync up the Deva to your gear and the Nexus network."

I do as instructed. It takes a few seconds but eventually prompts appear in the visor's smart glass only to almost immediately disappear. In the visor's right corner, a HUD pops up, showing all friendlies, drones, and building outlines in the area in relation to my position. A thin blue square appears over Isabella's torso. "It's like something out of Halo ..."

"It took a while, but I finally cracked the helmet's encryption," Abdul says. "Had to rewrite some code to make it compatible with the Nexus system."

"Great work," I say. "What about—"

"The Farsight's ability to see through walls?"

"Yeah."

"Keep digging. We confiscated some TARSEN Field emitters from a Deciders outpost a few weeks ago."

I reach into the crate and grab one of the metallic, cylindrical devices. Isabella snatches it out of my hand. "Allow me," she says with a smirk. She powers it on and a pulse expands outward from

the device, blanketing everything and everyone in a white haze—
even those who are unloading gear on the other side of the truck.

"Abdul, this is insane …" I say in awe.

"Ha ha, I know! The embedded camera transmits TARSEN
Field interactions to the Farsight's computer, which displays it in
the visor's smartglass, superimposing images over targets and
structures in real time. The device attached to the right side of your
helmet allows you to perceive terahertz waves in the same fashion.
Astounding technology! And those aren't the only features."

A red dot appears in the HUD at the bottom right of the visor.
An enemy combatant? Here? The target is just outside the hangar. I
turn left and find a red dashed square floating toward the hanger
entrance at walking pace. I quickly bring up my rifle.

"Relax!" Abdul says. "The red blip on your HUD is just a
friendly. I had Salazar mark him as a target with the drone flying
overhead to demonstrate the secondary situational awareness ability
of the Farsight—tracking enemies out of visual range who aren't in
a TARSEN or terahertz field."

The square goes from red to blue.

"This will drastically level the playing field … How far are we
from replicating this?"

"Eh … a ways away … For now, yours and the one you
acquired at Coeus are the only working models. Try not to destroy
it …"

It takes nearly two hours to load up the Valor, map out a flight
plan, strategize, and coordinate before Titan Squad and the support
platoon headed by OP Kanawha's Lieutenant Schaffer is airborne
for Operation Rancor. I could have just as easily named it
Operation Spite. Killing Ryan won't do shit for the world. If he
dies today, his Vice will take command. If the Vice dies, Ghost or

some other trench coat–wearing fucker will just assume the mantle of the Dominus or whatever cheesy name they name they choose. This mission is all about converting my hate into pure fury and directing it into one all-out assault on Ryan and hopefully all of the Echelon who may be in Castle. If we cut the head off of the Deciders and cause their regime to crumble, great. All I want to do is get in there, confirm the kill, and have a thermobaric bunker buster or nuke handle everyone else inside …

With the exception of Sung and Hughes, everyone onboard the Valor is either napping or trying to. I'm slouched in my seat, arms folded, eyes closed, running through all the scenarios of how this mission might go. Every one of them seems to end poorly. I tell myself not to be so pessimistic—it can't be any worse than Operation Deicide, right?

Sure it could. Especially if Ghost and Ryan know that I—we— are coming for them.

Positive thoughts … I need to think positive thoughts. I picture Anne. Now I want to talk to her, I want to see her, because imagining her isn't enough. I unfold my arms and tap the icon on the bottom left of the Gauntlet to bring up the call log, then scroll down in search of our last video chat. Seeing her on a choppy video chat isn't enough either, but it's all I've got at the moment. I want to smell her, feel her heartbeat against my chest as we hold each other. I miss her so much I feel ill, like my blood sugar is low or I'm coming down with the flu.

I'm coming back to you, I promise, I think as I'm about to tap call.

The screen displays an incoming call. It's Anne. "Hey, love," I whisper. "I was just calling you."

The screen freezes on Anne's smiling face. "I miss you too, my love."

"Is that what you called for? To tell me that?" My wrist vibrates with a new message.

The video unfreezes. "Well, yes … and no. Check your Gauntlet."

The others stir and check their recently acquired Gauntlets, then join in on the call.

The message begins streaming prerecorded drone footage of Castle. As the camera zooms in on the stronghold, it reveals a group leaving the building. The drone zooms in on Ryan Thomas, then on Ghost, Stevenson, and several Elites. They climb into an armored truck and drive to the runway a mile from the property where they then board something akin to an AC-130 fixed with the same bizarrely arranged panels as on the Specter.

"When is this from?" I sputter.

"Sixteen minutes ago," Anne says. "The delay is due to connectivity issues."

"Where are they heading?"

"Based on their current trajectory, they're heading east …" A map showing their flight path appears on my screen. "If they continue along this path, they will intersect with your route in approximately three and a half hours …"

Sung grins as he rhythmically nods his head. "Might be a good thang. Intercepting them before they get to where they're going sounds a hell of a lot better than infiltrating Castle!"

"*The fuck is that?*" Hughes shouts, pointing out the window.

My head snaps to the left. "What the *shit!*"

Flying beside our Valor is a gray drone shaped like manta ray, with thrust engines facing the rear and vertical lift props embedded in the wings that are angled slightly forward. Like the Specter and Ryan's gunship, it's covered in those strange panels.

I put on the Farsight helmet and grab my rifle. "Tommy! Sanders! Combat drone nine o'clock! Evasive maneuvers!"

"Copy!" Tommy shouts.

The Valor banks right, hard. Our bodies whip forward. As Ken reaches for the controls to deploy the belly-mounted M134 minigun, the manta drone ascends while banking left. Its minigun opens fire, buzzing like a chainsaw. The Valor shakes as rounds shred our left tiltrotor. Something explodes. Alarms blare. There's the distinct whine of a dying engine winding down. The helicopter tilts left and drops into a counterclockwise spin.

"*Bail! Bail out!*" someone shouts. Not sure who said it. Maybe it was me.

The next thing I know, the ramp is open, my seatbelt is off, my assault pack is buckled to my front side, and I'm diving out of the spiraling deathtrap. Thankfully, we're already wearing jump gear for the planned HALO insertion. I'm trying to maneuver into a diving position, but I can't. I'm in a tumble and I can't get control. There's sky. Then there's the ground closing in. Then there are my scattered teammates, some falling toward me, some drifting away, some still bailing from the chopper.

The ground's getting closer. I can't break this tumble. Panic's consuming me.

I can't die! Not now! Not like this!

29
CRUCIBLE

November 5
12:35 P.M.

THE ENDLESS TUMBLE makes me vomit. Somehow, I choke it down instead of befouling my helmet. The altimeter displayed in my Farsight's visor shows that I'm rapidly approaching fifteen hundred feet.

"*Shit! Shit!*" I panic and reach for my ripcord.

"*Dion!*" a voice in my earpiece shouts. More words follow but they're drowned out by the wind and my panic.

Then, something crashes into me with a bone-jarring thud. Someone, not something. Whoever it is wraps their arms around me, stabilizing me. I find myself helmet to helmet with Sung.

"You're good!" Sung shouts, slapping my helmet a few times to focus me. "You're good now, bro. Let's push off and deploy chutes!"

We separate and then I pull my ripcord. The parachute deploys and my mind slows along with my body. Only now do I notice the snowflakes floating beside me. A handful of my squadmates are descending to my right, maybe a half-mile away. Behind us, a few more. I'm still too in shock to count them. *Did everyone make it out? Tommy! Did Tommy make it out?* Ahead and to my left, the Valor is crashing toward a small, snow-dusted town, drone still in pursuit, still firing.

Finally, I land. Well … I get caught up in a damn tree, my boots maybe five feet from the ground. I detach the buckles, kick my legs out, and hit snow and dirt with a roll. With a tap of the button near the underside of the helmet near the left corner of my jaw, the air filtration part of the Farsight parts down the middle and pops forward slightly before retracting to the sides of the helmet. Now I can breathe. Cold air burns my lungs, though my body's kept warm by the battery-powered heating strips in my Aegis gear.

Bushes rustle to the right. "You good, D?" Sung asks as he emerges.

Shaking my head, I blow out air. "Now I am …" I say, moving the assault pack from my front to my back with jittery hands. "Thanks."

"Fucking fuck, man … *Fuck!* How'd they find us?"

My Gauntlet's showing that the call with Anne was disconnected. Makes sense considering the call came through the Valor's Nexus uplink. My team, however, should still be on PROXCOM. While trying contacting them, I use the Gauntlet to zoom out the HUD in my Farsight's visor. Eight blue dots with call signs hovering over them appear scattered throughout a mile radius, some alone, some in groups two or three. "Archangel and Razer here. Everyone alright?"

Isabella's voice comes in first. "Rusty and I are shaken up but breathing."

"Khagan checking in. I'm good," Ken pants. "So is Hughes."

"Chiron, Blackjack, and Red Death checking in," Abby says. "We're fine."

"Simba here. All good," Leo adds.

"Copy. Rally at our POS." I zoom out further to look for Tommy and Sanders. I don't see them, but I do find a VTOL aircraft icon a few klicks to the north. "Tank? You there, brother? Tommy? Answer me, damn it!"

Dead silence.

Sung grips my shoulder. "He's probably just out of range."

With a nod, I turn my attention to the incoming call from HQ. "*Dion!*" Anne shrieks. There's panic in her voice and it sounds like she was or is crying. "So help me—"

"Anne, I'm alright," I interrupt.

"That's it! You're done! You get your ass back to base right now! You're not scaring me like that ever again! You hear me?"

"Sorry, babe. Won't happen again. Promise. This op is blown, anyway. We'll find Tommy then evac out of ... wherever we are."

"You're near the edge of Hoosier National Forest, Indiana, three miles south of a town called Paoli."

"How far out are Lt. Schaffer and the Kanawha unit?"

"Both of their aircraft were downed moments after you were," Anne says. "There were survivors in Schaffer's party, but they are miles away and likely to meet resistance soon."

"The drone that hit us was strapped with missiles," Hughes says. "If the Deciders wanted us dead, they could have blown us to hell before we even saw it coming ..."

"They knew I was in that Valor," I say. "They wanted us grounded, not dead."

"You think ..." Isabella begins. "You think they've been tailin' us since Coeus?"

"Shit ... probably." I say, shaking my head.

"Is this all a fucking game to them," Sung grumbles.

"They're coming for you," Anne says.

The gears start turning. Ghost let it slip that she was going to Ryan on purpose, hoping—no, knowing I'd abandon our strongholds in the east to pursue them. Now we're grounded, exposed, and hundreds of miles from any source of support. What Ghost said last night echoes in my mind: *"And your lust for revenge will have a single outcome ... Sometime very soon, Ryan will lure you to right where he wants you, again, because your compulsion for retribution makes you predictable."*

"Deciders stationed in Louisville are already en route," Anne says. "Get to Paoli and hunker down. We'll provide overwatch via satellite. Combat UAVs are inbound. When possible, find transportation then get your asses to the USAW base in Quincy, Illinois."

"Copy." I start moving. "And ... Tommy ... Any sign of—"

"Dion ..." Anne sighs. "Neither he nor Sanders have responded. And they weren't wearing parachutes. There's no way they survived ... I'm sorry ..."

It's faint, but barely a quarter-mile into the trek, the air begins vibrating. It's a familiar sound, the rhythmic whomping of low-flying helicopters approaching. In the visor's HUD, a red helicopter icon appears, and it's beelining straight for us. I zoom out and four more appear. One by one, they stop advancing, forming a box around the sector encompassing Titan Squad. And like the one less than a hundred meters away, they are probably descending toward my team.

Better to catch 'em all in a bunch before they split up and surround us, I think, signaling Sung to go right while I dash toward the helicopter. With my back against the largest tree in sight, I peer out as the last Loyal rappels from a gray Huey into a small clearing. One by one, red squares pop up in my visor as they spread out. There are eight in total.

Holding three fingers up to Sung, I wait until the Deciders are in range then count down. When I make a fist, we strike. Sung and I simultaneously fire 40mm grenades from our M320 grenade launchers with a pair of hollow-sounding *fwoops*. The explosions each send two Deciders flying. Follow up rounds strike down one more before the remaining three scurry for cover.

For about a minute, we trade rounds with the enemy. Then while I'm reloading during a lull in the fight, a Decider with a nasally voice shouts, *"Dion Johnson! Are you out there?"*

I don't recognize the voice and I don't answer. I take a TARSEN emitter from my pack and activate it. Three hazy Decider silhouettes appear sheltering behind the trees.

"We know you're out here somewhere!" he shouts. "We don't wanna kill ya by mistake!"

I arm a grenade and step into the open, aiming down the HK416 I'm one-handing. "I'm right here!" I shout, tossing the grenade at the Decider to the far right.

The silhouette of the Loyal nearest me scrambles to the left. The instant he emerges, I put him down with flaming rounds to the helmet. As I pan to the center Decider, I see he's ducking and preparing to lean out. My sights cover the exact location his head will appear and my bullet greets it as soon as he does. That same instant, the grenade explodes, sending the third Loyal flying. Sung pumps a couple of bullets into the motionless body.

"Holy hell, D!" Sung says. "You just went God Mode on those bitches! Fuck, I need me one of those Farsights!"

I smile. *God Mode ... Yeah, that's exactly what this feels like.* I scoop up the TARSEN emitter then activate my comm. "Titan, lead the Deciders to my location."

Isabella and Rusty reach us first, four of the eight Loyals they've yet to kill right on their asses, popping disjointed shots at their heels. Sung and I spring an ambush that cuts them down before they know we're there.

Over the next ten to fifteen minutes, the others arrive one group at a time, some being pursued, the others strolling in after ending their opposition. The pursuers meet their ends just like their predecessors. Once the last one is dead, I lead Titan on a brisk trek through the now snow-blanketed woods toward town.

Twenty-nine minutes. That's how long it takes for us to reach the outskirts of the small town of Paoli. That's how long it takes for the second wave of Deciders to mobilize from the Louisville area.

"There will be more this time around," Anne warns. "Probably two to three times the size of the first wave …"

"How long?" I radio back.

"Another fifteen minutes until the helicopters arrive. Thirty before ground forces show …"

"Copy. Where are the best sightlines in this shithole?"

"Umm, it appears the town's center is probably the best place to mount a defense. I'll set a waypoint on your HUD."

A GPS marker appears dead ahead. We break into a brisk jog.

From the looks of it, Paoli is a ghost town. Nothing moves in the windows. There are no scavengers rummaging through the abandoned homes or storefronts. Satellite thermal scans confirm the absence of life. The only sounds come from howling winds and our boots crunching in the three inches of snow. Walls and cars are speckled with bullet holes, windows are blown out, and decaying bodies lie sprawled out in the streets. There was conflict here before the townsfolk fled to Decider-controlled cities for aid and sanctuary.

The waypoint leads us to the town square. In the center, a three-story, white courthouse sits on an island of snow-covered grass ringed by the Court Street roundabout. Various storefronts and buildings encompass it. The tallest of them is Mineral Springs Hotel, a three-story red-brick structure overlooking the southeast corner of the square. East of the courthouse, flanking an entrance to the roundabout, is a two-story brownstone that the Valor crashed into. The building is ablaze. There's no safe way to get in there and check for bodies or recover supplies.

Abby and Leo take the courthouse and start digging in. Perez sets up remote cameras throughout the square and its perimeter. Isabella, Ken, and I do the same with the six remaining terahertz emitters from the supply drop, mainly for my benefit but also for Abby, whose rifle has been fitted with a TERA-scope. Then we split up into groups to cover as many sightlines as possible. Steele and Hughes move out to the Liberty, a formidable brick structure on the east side of the northern entrance to the roundabout. Sung, Manny, and Perez take a two-story brick building overlooking the roundabout to the west. Isabella, Ken, and I set up shop in the hotel.

As we smash windows and jam tables in front of them as defensive barricades, Ken nudges me. "Remember that time we defended your house from looters during the Annex?"

"Heh, yeah."

"Well, this reminds me that night … only two hundred times worse."

For some reason we both laugh.

Soon, the air rumbles again. Seven helicopters in total appear on my HUD. From the third-floor window facing the south, I spot a gray Chinook descending through my binoculars. It looks like it's towing some kind of equipment that it's lowering onto a rooftop ... Three other enemy helicopters on the HUD are hovering to the north, east, and west, forming a box around the town.

"Anne," I say into my mic. "You still there?"

"I am, my king."

"The Deciders are setting up signal jammers around Paoli's perimeter ... We'll lose connection any moment." I highlight the four helicopters surrounding the town. "I've marked the presumed positions of the jammers and sent it to you. When UAV support comes in, strike those areas."

"Copy, Dion. Be careful. I love you."

"I love you too, Anne."

"You promised me you would return alive and in one piece. Remember that!"

"Don't worry, I—" There's a burst of static, then nothing. All enemy and friendly icons disappear from the HUD. I switch to PROXCOM and the friendly blips reappear over the last map overlay provided to us. "Titan, you guys still read me?"

One by one, they respond.

"We're cut off from Nexus. Chances are PROXCOM is next to go. If things go south, fight until there's an opening, jack a ride, and get the hell out of Dodge."

The hotel rattles as Chinooks fly from the four corners of the perimeter toward the town's center. The one approaching from the south is dropping small items attached to parachutes. *Supplies? Explosives? More jammers?* The others report seeing the same from their vantage points. The four Chinooks fly right over the town square, crossing paths in an X-formation, still dropping their items. Then they fly off into the distance. Flashes start popping up all over the city—flashes only I can see through the Farsight visor.

Hazy silhouettes of homes and vehicles appear in the distance as my range of vision expands.

"They were dropping TARSEN Field emitters," I announce to Titan.

"Elites are coming," Isabella says.

Through the walls, I see convoys of armored vehicles and trucks approaching all four entrances to the roundabout. "Deciders inbound. No one dies. That's an order."

The walls vibrate as the low roar of truck engines intensifies. Brakes squeal as Decider vehicles come to a halt. Doors open. Doors slam. Troops in gray trench coats unload from the trucks and rally into formation, splintering off into fireteams and scattering like roaches through the thickening sheets of snow. I count four Elites, their white trenches and gear camouflaging them against the winter landscape.

Abby's .50 cal sounds off and, through the wall to my left, I watch a hazy form crumple.

"Elite down," she whispers. She knows just like the rest of us do that there is no need to conceal our locations. The enemy knows exactly where we are.

Hell rains down on us. Bullets chip away walls. Sporadic grenade rounds and rockets erode cover over time. My team knocks out at least two dozen Deciders, but some slip unscathed past our attack zone. Like the time when my friends and I defended my home in the early days of the Annex, I leave Isabella and Ken to continue holding off the distant threats while I handle intruders. Through the walls, I see the two combatants sneaking through the hotel's back office. I sling my rifle, draw my knife, press myself against the wall, and wait for the first one to come through the door. When he does, I push his weapon away, plunge my knife under his helmet and into his throat then use his rifle to kill his backup. The TARSEN Field reveals two more approaching the breach point, but a spray of rounds from the ACR I acquired and a grenade from my kill's vest finishes them off.

God Mode.

I remain downstairs, calling out threats as I see them through the Farsight. Abby does the same from her sniper's perch. Leo uses our portable quadrotor drone to cover the big picture and mark targets for us.

With only what remains of the ammo strapped to us when we bailed out of the Valor, the Deciders seem poised to overwhelm us through cannon fodder alone. Whenever possible, I wait until they're close enough to kill with hand-to-hand combat and my knife, then turn the weapons and ammo of the fallen onto their comrades. I only switch to Infernal rounds when I encounter my first Elite. And the one that appears seconds after I drop the first. On my HUD, I watch Perez and Hughes venture out of their defensive posts to acquire enemy weapons and replenish their ammo, then fighting in the streets to drive the enemy back before they can retreat to relative safety. As for our team, Ken runs down the stairs at intervals to resupply himself and Isabella from the pile of weapons that I've acquired.

Eventually, the hotel begins to collapse and we're forced to retreat into the street, ducking behind cars as we fire at the enemy. The Deciders also overrun Sung's team's redoubt, forcing them to flee down its fire escape. God Mode or not, I'm forced to expose myself and take risks to eliminate the horde. My combat pants have two holes in the right leg. There's a tear in my left sleeve and a hole in my jacket in the lower left of my abdomen. Sore spots from bullet impacts throb. It's the same for Isabella and Ken. Today we're going to learn just how much damage the Aegis armor can withstand.

Blackjack disappears from the HUD. "*Shit! Perez!*" Manny cries. "Two Elites three hundred meters west of my POS. Boxed him in and sprayed him close range then hit him with a globular grenade."

The town's center is slowly being reduced to rubble. Decider bodies litter the streets and the snow is painted with their blood. The red target squares highlighting the enemy abruptly disappear when our drone is shot down. Ken suffers a stab wound to the abdomen right before Isabella eliminates his attacker. While she feverishly puts her medic skills to use, I leap from my cover to escape an exploding grenade and land right in the arms of an Elite. The standup brawl becomes a ground fight that ends with me turning the knife in his hand on him and stabbing him in the heart with it.

The Aegis armor's limits are soon revealed. Members of Titan Squad are incurring grazes and nonfatal gunshot injuries. During our big push against the dwindling threat, a headshot through the visor takes out our best medic, Manny. Of all the battles I've fought, this is the only one that I can describe as a crucible—a brutal test of will.

After nearly four hours of carnage, the last Loyal in the second wave goes down. Only three Elites remain. They're on the defensive now, holed up on the first and second floors of a radio station partially tucked into an alley opening into the southwest corner of the square. Hughes and Sung turn west, hoping to loop around to Water Street and enter the building from behind. Isabella ducks behind an armored truck and lays down cover fire while Steele and Ken sprint into the radio station and engage the two that aren't shooting at us. Meanwhile, Abby and Leo are making their way up to a rooftop with sightlines on both exits.

The rapid chugging of heavy arms fire thunders from above as rounds carve a line toward our cover. Barely visible through the snowflakes and against the clouds is a white SH-7 Specter that's descending on the town.

Ryan Thomas ...

Isabella and I dive through a blown-out window into a Mexican restaurant. The others scatter behind armored vehicles and a nearby building. The chopper gunner keeps firing as the silent death machine prepares to land on the street northeast of the courthouse. And just as it's disappearing out of sight, the machinegun stills and someone in white fires a rocket at the building Abby and Leo are in. The massive explosion sends up a geyser of white brick.

"Abby! Leo! Report!" I shout into my comm. "Damn it, someone report!"

No response.

For the first time since the battle began four hours ago, the town of Paoli is dead silent. From behind the white courthouse, nine Deciders clad in white scatter left and right of the building. A thin hooded form floats beside a bulkier, more extravagantly dressed Decider. *Ghost and Ryan.* From the right, there's a Decider with a white trench coat with a black BDU underneath and a black helmet. *Stevenson* ...

A large quad drone manifests through the snowfall and hovers ten feet in front of our bombed-out restaurant. "Dion Johnson!" Ryan's voice booms from a speaker on the underside of the drone. "I've come to end you, boy!"

"Only one of us dies here today," I bark, angling my rifle out of the window. "And it's not going to be me!"

He chuckles. "Oh, we shall see about that!"

The drone advances.

I aim my rifle about twenty feet above Ryan's position and pull the trigger. My last grenade round exits the barrel with its characteristic *fwoop*. At the same time, Isabella shoots the approaching drone, which explodes with a tremendous white flash that knocks me off my feet.

30
WHITEOUT

November 5
4:41 P.M.

THE CONCUSSIVE FORCE leaves me winded and coughing with ringing ears. My vision's blurred, not from blunt-force trauma due to the concrete block that collided with my helmet, but from the resulting crack in the smart visor. It takes a second to register that the HUD and the Farsight enabled X-ray vision that spans the entire visor is flickering in and out ...

Shit. Grunting, I rise to my knees, bricks and rubble falling off of me as I do. A quick examination reveals that I'm not impaled or bleeding so that's a win ...

Bullets snap through the dust overhead as I quickly check Isabella for injuries. Satisfied, I stand up and extend a hand. "You good?"

She groans. "Peachy keen, Dion."

"Good thing you shot that thing down when you did!"

"The Deciders are big fans of exploding drones ..." she says as we crouch-walk toward the rear exit.

"Everyone alright?" Ken radios in.

"Archangel and I are fine," Isabella says. "Heading south in the direction of Water Street."

Sung buzzes in next. "Hurry! Hughes and I are fending off four of these fuckers right now! Infernal ammo's getting dangerously low! We need an assist!"

"Two of three Elites in here are down," Ken says between bursts of gunfire. Working on the last then heading to you."

"Copy," I say. We hurry down the alley leading toward the dumpsters. I step out into the open and sweep the area. "On the way!"

Someone coughs. "Simba checking in. Red's knocked out. Took a blow to the head from debris. Our rifles are buried and we've got two Deciders inbound."

My heart leaps. "It's time to go. Steele, when you're done there, find some wheels and get to Simba and Red then head to Quincy base. Ken, help Izzy and me extract Sung and Hughes. Oh, and one more thing. Farsight is on the fritz so we're pretty much flying blind …"

"Well, back to basics …" Ken grumbles.

Isabella's watching my six, but my head's on a swivel as I cross lawns and hop fences, making use of the intermittent Farsight when possible. The helmet works every thirty seconds or so for two- to three-second spurts. The once hazy, human-shaped forms of friendlies and enemies now appear as staticky, amorphous apparitions with guns.

A hostile appears on the other side of the building we left. "Eleven o'clock, Jezebel!" I say as the image disappears.

The Elite turns the corner only to get lit up by Isabella. Meanwhile, I exchange fire with a White Coat who's shooting at us from behind a massive tree up ahead.

"Area secure," Ken shouts. "Coming to you!"

Steele chimes in with, "And I'm heading down to play GTA!" he adds.

Another, shorter pulse of the Farsight reveals that Sung and Hughes are holed up in a little office building across the street. Three Deciders are firing into the front windows and the fourth is flanking around the back. I can't see who the flanker is, but I can sense it, feel it.

"Handle this White Coat and then wait for Ken before you advance on those Elites," I say to Isabella. "I'll take the flanker to the south."

I sprint across the street and around the public library. The Farsight is offline during the brisk jog. But as I turn the corner, I see her darting across the parking lot and into a line of trees. My Farsight flickers on and shows that she's still making her way south. Mesmerized, I follow her, crossing a frozen creek and then a dirt parking lot lined with excavators, backhoes, and other heavy construction equipment. On the other side squats a warehouse with five loading doors on the near end. The one on the far left has been lifted to expose a three-foot gap at the bottom. I smack the side of my helmet but the Farsight won't reengage.

Slow down, she can still see you coming and you don't know where she is anymore, I remind myself. I roll under the gap and sweep the gloom with my rifle. To the right, something glimmers on the concrete.

Wet boot prints ...

"Ghost!" I shout.

The Farsight comes to life, as though I somehow willed it to, revealing a thin hooded form bursting out of the darkness with a rifle. I pivot to move out of the line of fire. Her image appears and disappears with each muzzle flash from the three controlled shots she fires. The last round punches me between my right shoulder and pectoral muscle. As a result, my return fire sprays wildly and all of my exploding, incendiary rounds hit the wall behind her—all except for the one that cuts and burns into her left bicep. She cries out, looking to the smoldering wound. In that brief moment of distraction, I knock the rifle out of her hand with a spin kick. The following side kick she blocks, retaliating with a kick-punch combo.

Gotta save the last Infernal rounds for exfil ... or for Ryan ... I think, stumbling back and drawing my knife.

"Mmm, oooh ... that burns so good," Ghost moans, smothering the glowing armor with her gloved hand.

"I bet," I say.

She pulls down her hood and removes her helmet. "I was going to ask how you knew it was me, but I noticed you are wearing one of our Farsights ... Now I see how you survived so long against that onslaught."

"It was only a matter of time until we leveled the playing field."

She draws a Glock 18. "I'm here now. Whatever advantages you had are null." She opens fire.

I dive behind a cement mixer as rounds skip and spark off the drum. Since there's no time to play around, I draw my pistol and fire off a few. When she stays behind cover instead of returning fire, it's clear she fears the incendiary rounds. So I charge, still firing, and when I get close, I attack with hand-to-hand techniques and eventually disarm her.

While I'm fending off her barrage of Wing Chun attacks, the Farsight freaks out and the visor starts flickering. Now I'm blinded and distracted. The next thing I know, her six-hit combo ends with me on my ass. I rip the helmet off just in time to see her plunging her knife toward my gut. I smash the helmet into her wrist and divert the blade, following up with a punch to her head. She hits the ground, and I scurry back. Ghost crawls after me and swipes at me as jump to my feet, slicing open my armor.

We face each other, panting. Something akin to a giggle escapes her as she switches her blade to reverse grip. "I will miss you when you're gone, Archangel."

"Hughes!" Sung shouts over the comm. "He's hit! Hughes is down!"

"Don't worry, I'm not going anywhere!" I say, charging.

After going blow for blow and block for block, I land a three-hit combo that ends with me grabbing her knife-wielding hand. And while she's open, I drive my combat knife toward her abdomen. She blocks it with her free hand, letting the blade go right through her palm. She snarls, spitting through her clenched teeth as I drive her back into the wall with everything I've got.

I pin her knife-wielding arm against the wall and force the knife-embedded hand toward her gut. "I really don't want to kill you, Ghost." I push the blade deeper into her hand until the knife tip meets her belly.

"Why not?" she strains through gritted teeth.

"Ending you just feels wrong ..."

Confusion hits her hard. My head-butt hits her harder. The back of her skull bounces off the wall as I shove the two to three inches of the blade jutting through the back of her hand into her abdomen. I yank the knife out then pistol-whip her in the temple. Finally, she goes down. After confirming that she's unconscious, I zip-cuff her to a drive train that's sitting on a rack, then strip her of her ammo and knives before removing her GPS system and Gauntlet to keep Ryan from knowing her status. Finally, for some reason, I quickly cut open her combat top and armor and slap a quick-clot bandage on her wound.

Idiot ... I'm an idiot ... I should let her bleed out ... "Flanker down!" I radio in, steam leaving my mouth as I jog back outside. "Where am I going?"

Ken radios in: "Sung made it out. He's back in the alley on the southwest corner of the square but Stevenson has him pinned down. Approach from the west and you'll be able to flank him."

"Help us with these fuckers when you're done," Isabella adds.

"On it! Rusty, SITREP?"

"Almost to Red and Simba," Steele responds. "One target left! Jezebel, when you're ready, there's a gray Humvee on 1st with the headlights on and the door open! Keys are under the seat."

I cross the bridge over the creek and creep back to the square, checking every window, corner, and doorway of Gospel Street as I go. I can feel Ryan and the remaining Deciders watching me, but I don't know where they are.

There's grunting and commotion ahead. Back against the building, I peer around the corner of the bombed-out Mexican restaurant. Stevenson and Sung are both without helmets, fighting in the middle of the alley. I don't have a clear shot so I keep low and advance, checking my six every so often. Stevenson kicks Sung hard in the chest, knocking him into the dumpster behind him. As Sung charges with his knife, Stevenson grabs something out of the snow and thrusts it forward. Sung stops abruptly as the tip of a tactical sword bursts out of his back, dripping blood into the snow.

It takes a second for my brain to comprehend what just happened. I stifle a cry and train my rifle on Stevenson, waiting for him to pull the blade out and let Sung fall out of the line of fire.

"Sorry, brother," Stevenson says to his former comrade. "I told you to surrender. You made me do this! You chose to be on the wrong side of this war!" He yanks the blade out and kicks the gagging and gurgling Sung into the snow.

That's when I pull the trigger twice, sending one round into Stevenson's right shoulder blade and one into the center of his back that explodes and burns into him. I fire a third into his left hip as he spins toward me on his way to the ground.

"*Fucking shit, Johnson!*" Stevenson cries, rolling onto his butt. His eyes widen as I sprint toward him. He reaches for his sidearm, but I stomp on his hand. With my other foot, I kick him hard in the jaw.

"You traitorous son of a bitch, Stevenson! He was your brother!" I stomp on his face until it's a bloody, unrecognizable mess. Then I take my still-bloody knife and plunge it into his trachea. "A slow, painful death for you, Stevenson. That's what you get." I grab his dog tags and rip them from his neck as I rise, leaving him gasping and thrashing in the snow.

"Rusty here," Steele buzzes. "I got Simba and Red. They're injured but breathing. Getting them to the ride now. Are you positive you don't want me to come get you?"

I look to Sung. He's lifeless, one hand over his chest, eyes wide and mouth hung open. "Just get them out of here."

"Dion, where are you?" Isabella cries.

Shit! Past the west end of the alley, I see an Elite hurrying toward Water Street. I take Stevenson's rifle and check the grenade launcher. There's one in the tube. I take a second sticky round from his chest rig and pocket it before swiping his ammo and grenades.

Along the way, I grab up Stevenson's helmet and put it on, opening the lower portion so I can catch my breath. The Farsight functionality is off, as expected, but as long as I have head protection, I'm good.

At the end of the alley, I see an Elite kneel behind a low concrete wall ahead. And before he disappears from view, I notice a patch on his arm of a bloody troll face. *Savage ... Don Chambers.* I aim at the second-floor wall above where he's sheltering and fire.

The glob sticks just under the window like snot. Since I don't have the ability to detonate it, I shoot the blinking charge. The thunderous blast sends an avalanche of bricks and rubble onto Chambers, muffling his cries. I load the tube with the last globular bomb and sprint back onto 1st Street and then into the parking lot behind the office building that Hughes and Sung were trapped in.

"How many?" I ask.

"Just one," Isabella says. "He's out front. But we're out of Infernals, and we can't get Hughes out while he's blocking the entrance."

"I got it. Open fire on him … now."

As Isabella and Ken lay down fire, I break a window and hurry through the building. Out front, the Elite is advancing across the street, rounds thudding against his armor. I fire the remaining sticky bomb onto his back. He rips off his trench coat before the bomb detonates, but I manage to shoot it in one try before he clears the blast radius. The bastard flies forward, right toward Isabella and Ken. Before he rises, Isabella yanks back his helmet and slices his throat.

Ken covers the street as Isabella rushes back into the building. I find her kneeling beside Hughes and applying Cascade.

"How's he looking?" I ask.

"Not good," she says grimly. "Gutshot."

Shit! Shit! Shit! I'm losing everyone … "Help me lift him," I say.

We're hurrying down 1st Street to the Humvee when something that sounds a minigun buzzes on the other side of the brick apartment building bordering the town's center. Rounds shred through the structure like it's made of rice paper. And because the shooter can see through walls, the hailstorm of bullets barely misses us as we scatter. Something the size of a grenade round shoots down the alley where Sung and Stevenson lie and explodes mid-air, sending Ken flying into a wall and knocking me on my ass.

The machinegun ceases fire.

"*Dion Johnson!*" Ryan's voice booms in the silence. "The time to avenge Richard is nigh!"

I put up a middle finger, hoping it's clear through the building. "I'm right here, Dominus!"

The minigun buzzes, showering me with brick fragments.

I stow away my last half-empty Infernal round rifle mag and jam in one of Stevenson's mags. Counting that, and the two twenty-round Infernal-loaded pistol magazines in my P226s and the one spare on my belt, I have about seventy left. "Izzy, get Hughes to that vehicle! Now! We'll hold them off!"

Another blast explodes mid-air, closer to Ken this time.

She hesitates. "I won't leave you!"

Another airburst cracks. Bricks rain down on us.

"*Go!*" I shout.

"I'll come back for you soon, hon!" Isabella says, her voice strained with the effort of dragging Hughes. "And you, Ken."

Ken snickers. "You damn well better include me in the extraction!"

The machinegun opens up again, this time from the north instead of from the central square to the east. Ken leaps through the blown-out window nearest him, rounds chewing at his heels. Before the gunfire can shift back to me, I shoot through the apartment building's back doors and duck inside. As I peer out, Ryan emerges from the alley. He's wielding a white XM25 CDTE, a semi-auto airburst grenade launcher. Instead of his trench coat, he's wearing a white combat suit with off-white to gray armored segments covering his chest, legs, and arms. His helmet looks different than before as well, thicker than normal Devas.

It's going to take all seventy rounds to stop him ...

Ryan aims at the window Ken dove into while I aim at him. Before I can pull the trigger, an Elite lugging a massive machinegun turns the corner and fires through the shattered glass doors. The last thing I see before ducking is Ryan firing another airburst grenade into the building.

"Ken, report!" I radio, firing single semiauto shots at the Elite. "*Ken?*"

Gunfire ceases. The Elite's spent ammo belt hits the ground and I hear him reloading. I pop up and aim at where I think he is, but he's ducked back behind the corner.

"Druid, I'll take things from here!" Ryan commands. "Handle those who fled!"

Druid chambers a round. "As you wish, Dominus!" He opens fire once again to keep me suppressed.

I crawl to cover that doesn't look like Swiss cheese. "Jezebel, you've got an Elite with heavy weapons coming your way!" I report.

There's static. "I've got something for his ass."

When I'm sure it's clear, I make my way down the hallway toward Ken. I kick open the door and turn into the apartment but Ken is nowhere to be found. Snow blows through the shattered wall facing the parking lot.

"Dion Johnson!" Ryan shouts. "Before you meet your end, tell me where the fuck my cousin is!"

"Maybe she's dead! Maybe she's dying! Maybe she's alive and captured!"

"Perhaps you'd like to rethink that answer ..." he growls.

There's a thud and violent coughing. I peer out and find Ken, helmetless and on his knees. Ryan is looming over him with a hi-tech rifle I cannot identify pointed at the back of his skull.

"Alright! Wait! Lauren's alive. Spare him and I'll tell you—"

The rifle's report echoes through the parking lot as the contents of Ken's skull erupt into the snow.

31
STALEMATE

November 5
5:32 P.M.

IT'S DISBELIEF THAT strikes first. The pain in the ass who was randomly assigned to me when I moved to my apartment sophomore year quickly became one of the best friends I've ever had. He taught me to be more generous. He saved my life more times than I can count, and after everything we've been through, from the first war until now, after becoming one of the most talented soldiers I've fought alongside, I never thought he'd meet his end.

Ken Nguyen, one of my few remaining best friends, just got his brains blown out by the same sonofabitch who murdered my son and exterminated millions.

That gunshot still seems to continue echoing through the ghost town, muffled slightly by the snow. Ryan slinks behind cover and continues talking shit, but I pay no mind to his words.

Maintain your composure! Do not explode. Not yet! Wait for the right time.

The distinct jackhammering of Druid's machinegun snaps me out of that trance. Something like a missile launch hisses next. An explosive crack follows.

"Isabella!" I shout into my comm.

"I'm good, hon." she pants. "Found me a rocket launcher. Kept it hidden in a metal weapon's case and let him have it when he popped out." She laughs. "Turns out Elite armor don't do so good against RPGs."

I huff, a poor attempt at a laugh. "You wouldn't happen to have one more rocket, would you?"

"None that I can see … Listen, I'm going back for Hughes then I'm coming to you and Ken. Survive until then?"

"Of course. Ken … won't be there, though …"

Isabella says something that sounds like "I'm so sorry" but I can't make it out because Ryan fires a bullet into the sky.

"Did you hear me?" he roars. "Ignoring me is a piss-poor decision, Archangel! Ten minutes. If Ghost doesn't show up by then, a slow and painful death awaits you."

There's an SUV parked about twenty feet away that looks like it might give me some cover. I take a breath and make a break for it. *FWOOP!* A grenade round explodes behind me, sending me flying forward.

My body bounces hard off the front grill. I scramble under the SUV as rounds punch through it like it's tin. From underneath the car, I see his boots marching toward me. Ignoring the pain, I scramble out to the opposite side and crouch behind the engine block, taking one of the grenades I got off Stevenson from my vest as I do. I set the grenade to explode in ten seconds before I toss it into the snow by the front end and scurry to the trunk, blindfiring.

Counting down in my head, I continue returning fire at Ryan, who's now crouching behind the hood.

Eight … Seven … Six …

At five, I book it to a nearby truck, still firing in bursts. One of his rounds rips across my side.

Three …

Just a few feet from the grenade, he stands tall and sprints in the opposite direction, keeping his head low. I'm not sure if he saw the grenade or if he guessed what I was up to …

One!

Snow, debris, and smoke erupt into the air and Ryan hits the ground with a roll. Skidding to a stop through the slush, I spin on my right foot and charge, roaring as I fire standard 5.56 rounds.

The first few bullets kick up the snow in front of him. Then one hits his arm. Another, the chest. One skips off his helmet. No damage done.

I dump the empty mag and jam in my last Infernal-loaded clip as he climbs onto one knee and returns fire. Bullets snap past me but I keep pushing forward, burst firing. A round punches me in the chest. At the same time, the last round I fired hits under the right side of his visor and explodes, leaving behind a burning circle. Ryan hits the ground, spraying in my direction as he rolls and scrambles for cover. I don't stop shooting. Nothing hits him, but I blow a hole in the receiver of the rifle a split-second before he pulls it to him from under the van he crawled beneath.

I sling my empty rifle across my back and switch to one of my P226s.

"I'm curious, Dion!" Ryan yells. He rolls out to the opposite side of the van and drops his damaged helmet in the snow. "How would things be different if I told you that your son was still alive?"

"You're wasting your breath!" I growl, creeping around to the van's rear.

"If I said he was alive when you and I first crossed paths, do you think you would have been foolish enough to fall into the trap Ghost lured you into? Do you think you would still be here, minutes from death? Or perhaps you would have played it smarter?"

"Irrelevant. You killed him!"

Ryan chuckles darkly then bursts out from behind the van, rapid firing with a white pistol. Caught in the open, I return fire while rushing to the protection of a charred Toyota Camry. As I slide over the hood, a round tags me in the lower left abdomen underneath my ribs and it almost knocks me over. Searing pain hits as I land on the snow-covered pavement. Something warm and wet runs down my side. The round that clipped me earlier compromised my Aegis armor enough that this one could find its way into my body ... Hissing, I pull the torn fabric aside to see the entry wound. Doesn't look like anything important was hit. I slip off my pack and fish out the same quick clot patch coated in Cascade that I used on Ghost.

"What if I told you that I lied?" Ryan continues. "That I said I killed your child to make you hurt the way I did when I found out my brother died by your hands? What if I just wanted you to suffer for as long as possible before I ended you?"

With the bleeding temporarily stemmed, I draw my second pistol, holding one in each hand. "Did you kill my son or not, Ryan?"

"Answer me first ..."

"No. I may have not been as reckless. I probably would've played it smarter. Now tell me, *is he alive or not?*" My shout echoes off the shattered buildings.

"Did you really think that I was capable of murdering an innocent child with my bare hands?"

"Pretty sure millions of children died because of Poseidon!"

"True, but that was different. It's like assassinating someone by drone strike versus using a knife. Do it from a distance and it feels no different from killing in a videogame."

"*Is my son alive or not!*"

"Jessica told you the truth. Little Marshal Johnson is alive and well ..."

I'm overwhelmed by a storm of elation ... and guilt ... All the risks I took, all the people I put in harm's way for a lie. "Where? Where the hell is he then?"

"Somewhere far, far away from here ... He's currently under the care of Rose. I believe you met her when you were under my brother's care?" He laughs. "Yes, your son will be raised as one of my own, alongside her son, my nephew Ryker. I wanted you to die knowing that if the Angels of War survive for long enough, one day your son will be killing them in combat ... Or maybe they'll kill him ... You've failed, Archangel. Everything you touched has turned to ash. The world you failed to protect. The friends you lost. The friends I broke. The Angels of War I turned. The former lover you had to murder. The son you'll never see again. These are the things I wanted you to contemplate in your final moments of life. This is Lex Talionis! This was my plan for retribution against you!"

A cold wave of defeat leeches all the energy from my body. I slump against the side of the Camry and close my eyes.

"*Gray truck!*" Isabella shouts in my earpiece. "Ryan is flanking you from the gray truck!"

My eyes shoot left just as Ryan appears, darting out from behind the armored vehicle parked in the street and firing in my direction. I scramble around the hood and crouch behind the engine block, returning fire as I do.

A third set of shots pop in the distance. Ryan's attention shifts from me to the gray Humvee speeding toward him. The driver, clad in black, is one-handing a rifle out the window. Ryan sends rounds at the truck, drops a mag, reloads, and resumes firing as he runs back into the parking lot and slides behind a Jeep. The driver retracts the rifle and jumps the curb. Ryan tries vaulting over the hood just as she slams into the rear end, sending the Jeep skidding in the snow. Ryan bounces off the hood and eats concrete, losing his gun in the process.

I squeeze off Infernal rounds in three sets of two as I charge. I land a hit to his arm. Another leaves a burning streak across his back.

Now bullets from somewhere in the distance snap past me, forcing me to retreat to cover. I keep one pistol trained on Ryan and the other at the hooded shooter gliding up 1st Street.

Ghost! Damn it! *I should have just killed her!*

I send Infernal rounds at both of them. Ryan speed crawls out of the line of fire. Ghost ducks behind an armored truck and switches her aim from me to Isabella, who's emerging from the Humvee.

A blur of white explodes from behind the bullet-riddled SUV. Knife in hand, Ryan rushes me as I squeeze off the last round from the P226 in my left hand. It skips off his chest plate just as he turns his body in an attempt to dodge.

"Your incendiary rounds are no match for this Onyx Armor!" Ryan shouts.

He pushes away my right hand as I fire one round into the distance. A swipe of the knife follows, but I parry and knock it out of his hand with a pistol whip, following up with an elbow to the face. A spin kick knocks me back and a storm of punches and kicks follows. He's fast, relentless, and strong as all hell. There are no breaks, no time for me to line up a kill shot. The one time I think I've freed myself up to gun him down, he parries my pistol and the round strikes nothing but snow. Three Elite-killer bullets remain.

In an explosive blur of movements, the Dominus disarms me and maneuvers me into submission. I execute a reversal before he can pin me and kick him in the face, giving me enough time to roll away and draw my knife in reverse grip. He draws a backup knife in the same position. We charge, roaring like lions.

The knife fight doesn't go on for long. Somehow, we both end up disarming each other before either of us is stabbed or cut. A barrage of six or so punches follows before I slip in an uppercut and a hook. He blocks my next four strikes and lands a hit to the jaw. He eventually adapts to my fighting style and starts landing more hits—two or three to my one. The cold is setting in, probably because of blood loss. With every second that passes, the fight tilts more steeply in his favor.

Ryan draws a knife from his sleeve as he spins in the snow, slicing across my right thigh as he maneuvers into a trailing floor sweep. Even with a cut quad muscle, I somehow stumble back in time to dodge it.

A back kick sends me slamming into the car behind me. He raises his knife like it's a stake meant for a vampire's hard. I try to knock it away with my left hand. Instead, searing, crippling pain surges down my arm as the knife slides right between the two bones leading to my wrist.

I cry out as three or four inches of bloody steel burst through the other side of my arm before the handle stops the blade from going any farther. With my right hand, I grab my left forearm and shove with all my might, trying to keep the blade's tip from meeting my throat.

Ryan braces his palm on the bottom of the handle and leans into it. "*Just die!*" he roars.

He releases one hand and draws another, smaller knife, twirling it into reverse grip before plunging it into the right side of my abdomen.

Spitting and growing through clenched teeth, I push back as hard as I can and backhand his temple. A knee to his ribs and a side kick sends him stumbling. I pull the knife out of my side and throw it at him while he's trying to regain his footing. He dodges it with a twist of his body.

A storm of punches and kicks follows. The pain is breaking my concentration so I only dodge a quarter of what I normally would and block even fewer due to the knife in my arm. When a knee hits me in the side, I fold and he comes at me with the mother of all haymakers.

In a heartbeat, time seems to slow a bit. With a hard swing of my right arm, I knock away his punch, immediately following up by feinting an elbow strike. He leans back to dodge the attack, and if I were throwing an elbow, he would've evaded it. But that dagger he left impaled in my arm, the one sticking out of my wrist like a raptor talon, comes at him too fast to escape. The blade meets the base of his cheekbone and slices across his right eye and forehead.

The Dominus howls in rage and perhaps fear, somehow managing to grab me and throw me three feet away into the snow. My hand strikes metal—a pistol in the hand of a dead and almost frozen Decider. Ryan stumbles back a few feet, cupping his wounded face. Left eye squinting from the pain, he falls to one knee and draws a white pistol from an ankle holster as I frantically try to pry the pistol from the dead Decider's hand.

"You ... you will pay for this!" He brings the gun up. "For Richard's death!"

I finally get the pistol free of the frozen hand and start firing. As he pulls the trigger there's a *fwoop* followed by an explosion in the air above that blows us away from each other. I fly back-first into the car behind me, my head bouncing off something hard. I squint to see Ryan lying motionless in the snow.

Ears ringing and vision fading in and out, I pitch over and fall into the snow, straining for the pistol that's too far out of reach. Something in the distance explodes and the ground trembles as the hooded Ghost appears, holding Ryan's XM25 CDTE grenade launcher. She's pointing it in my direction, but she's not aiming at me. I turn slightly as a black boot crunches the snow beside my head. It's Isabella. She's aiming back at Ghost with a gray and white Decider rifle.

"I got you, sunshine," Isabella says, her voice muffled.

I force a weak smile as consciousness fades.

"Stay with me, Dion," she orders, dragging me away from the threat, her rifle still trained on Ghost and Ryan. There are two more explosions in the distance. "You hear that? Reinforcements are here, but their backup is here too, so we've got to move!"

It sounds like I'm listening to her from underwater. One eye closed to fend off double vision and fighting the urge to pass out, I look at Ghost and my nemesis. Ryan climbs to his feet. There's blood on his abdomen, but I'm not sure if it's from a bullet or his eye. He starts toward us but Ghost grabs his arm and pulls him back.

The pale soldier stares me down. Her black lips mouth something like "Don't die yet …" before she and Ryan disappear from view.

Darkness bleeds over my vision like ink's being poured onto my eyes. I hear helicopters, gunfire, a slamming car door, and Anne's voice shouting, "*Dion, are you there? Can you hear me?*"

32

REDUX

Date Unknown
Time Unknown ...

THERE'S DISCOMFORT AND pain ... everywhere. I open my eyes and immediately clamp them shut when the light assaults my pupils. Groaning, I sit up and squint as I take inventory. I see bandages wrapped around my left arm and an IV in my right. The back of my skull is a little sore, and when I rub it, I find bandages wrapped around my head. The rest of me is covered with a patchwork quilt. I pull it away, along with the blanket underneath it, and lift the white shirt one size too big for me to find my torso wrapped with more bandages. On the nightstand beside the IV hook is an HK USP pistol and my Gauntlet.

"Dion!"

I want it to be Anne but it's not.

Isabella strides through the doorway. Instead of her Seraph gear, she's dressed in jeans, a tan wool sweater, and brown hiking boots. There's a pistol in a drop leg holster and a gray and white LaRue PredatOBR 5.56 rifle leaning against the wall by the door.

Half-smiling, half about to cry, she says, "You're awake! You're finally awake!" She wraps her arms around me and holds me. It's oddly comforting.

"You say that like I was out for days or something ..."

"Days? Try almost two weeks."

My face scrunches up. "What?"

"Yeah," she says. "It's the nineteenth. Two weeks to the day."

I look around, taking a deep breath and exhaling slowly. The bloodbath that transpired in Paoli comes to me in flashes. *I was knocked out from that airburst grenade ... Ryan got away.* "Well, shit ... What happened after I blacked out?"

"Your concussion had you in and out of it for a bit while we fled Paoli. The Decider reinforcements blocked off our route to Quincy so I took us southwest until Anne said it was clear. Found a house, got you inside, got that bullet out of you and patched you up the best I could with a med kit I found in the truck. Not going to say that you might have died once ... but, uh ... you might have died once."

"Huh?"

"Yeah, uh, your heart stopped for a bit ... probably from blood loss and hypothermia. Had to give you mouth to mouth, pump your chest, and give you a shot of adrenaline to get you going again. Gave you a transfusion after that then cuddled with you naked to keep you warm." She blushes. "Don't tell Anne ..."

I bark a nervous laugh. "Trust me, I won't ..." I lock eyes with her, the girl who was once my prisoner and recently saved my life. "Thank you."

"Anything for you, sunshine." She places her hand on mine.

I smile, clearing my throat. "So where exactly are we?"

"Before the comms stopped working, I got one last transmission from Anne. Seems the Decider manhunt was on its way. I got you out of there and headed a few more hours southwest. Now we're shacked up Sweeden, Kentucky." She says the name in her imitation of a strong Southern accent.

The wood floors outside the room creak. My hand shoots over to the pistol and I point it at the door. Pain shoots through my side from the quick movement.

"Is he—" a bearded older man starts to whisper as he peeks into the room, stopping abruptly at the sight of the gun.

Isabella gently pushes down on my hand. "Relax, he's a friend. His name's Joseph Ashworth. This place belongs to him and his wife, Enid. They've been letting us stay here since they caught me scavenging fuel from their truck."

Joseph laughs. "The only reason I didn't shoot her on sight is because I noticed the Angels of War insignia. And when she told me Dion freaking Johnson was with her, we had to take y'all in!"

I lay the gun on the bed. "Sorry, sir …"

Joseph nods. "I'm a vet myself, son. I know how it is having someone startle ya."

A woman appears behind him, her stringy white hair in a bob. "He's a veteran, and I'm a veterinarian." She speaks with a strong Appalachian twang, not the Southern accent that Isabella was trying to mock.

"You got good ol' Enid here to thank for being infection free and for getting your fluids," Isabella says.

Enid smirks. "And your lady friend is the reason you've been kept clean these last few weeks …"

I look to Isabella, imagining her giving me a sponge bath and spooning with me naked. "Thank you very much, ma'am. And sir. Your care and hospitality are very much appreciated."

Joseph waves me off, smiling. "Anything for you, hero!"

"Come now," Enid said. "Soup's ready."

Isabella sets a stack of clothes on the end of the bed. "Need help changing? I mean, it's nothing I haven't seen …" She smirks.

I shake my head. "I'll be okay."

Dressed in a thick black sweater that smells like mothballs, some decently fitting albeit holey jeans, and my tactical boots, I hobble on a pair of crutches to the kitchen. Joseph and Enid are sitting at the table while Isabella peers through the window blinds, but I only have eyes for the steaming bowl of chicken and dumplings in front of me. Wincing as I sit down, I lean the crutches against the table and start shoveling the soup into my mouth.

"You haven't eaten in weeks, son," Joseph says. "Slow down before you make yourself sick!"

I slurp one last spoonful of broth before taking a breather. "You're right, my stomach's already uneasy."

The Ashworths make small talk about collecting more firewood and other things that need to be handled around the house. Isabella disappears for a bit. While I eat, I think about the last few things I remember—shooting Ryan, Ghost separating us with that airburst grenade ... Was she trying to save both of us by doing that?

Marshal. Marshal is out there somewhere with Rose ... I didn't dream that ... Finding him, that's my next mission.

There are more flashes of the failed Operation Rancor. *Tommy's dead ... Ken ... Ken's dead. Sung's dead. Perez is dead. Manny's dead. Since Hughes isn't here, I have to assume that he's dead too ... Abby, Leo, and Steele could be as well ...*

A toilet flushes and pipes rattle. A few seconds later Isabella emerges from the dark hallway.

"Did you hear anything about Abby and them?" I ask.

She shakes her head. "No one's heard from them ..."

I sigh.

She grabs her bowl of soup and takes it over to the window. "I'm sure they're fine. They left long before we did. Before the reinforcements started blocking off the route to Quincy …" She parts the blinds and looks out.

I ask Enid about her recipe while I work on my meal. Apparently, the trick is to fry the chicken before adding it to the soup.

Suddenly, I realize that I've been hearing a low hum. That hum quickly turns into a low rumble. Isabella lets the blinds snap shut.

I draw the USP from my holster then drop the magazine and examine it. The mag's full so I load it back into the gun and rack the slide. "Helicopter?"

Isabella grabs up her LaRue rifle. "Yup. Looks like they're circling this area. Probably scanning with thermal cams …"

A chair screeches across the floor as Joseph slides away from the table. "I've got more guns back in my room and some winter clothes you might need. Come with me."

Abandoning my crutches, I limp after Joseph to his bedroom. He hands me an OD green winter coat with a fur-lined hood and a black aviator-style winter hat with earflaps. While I struggle to put on the coat, Joseph produces a Smith & Wesson revolver that he tucks into his pants, a Mossberg shotgun, and a scoped Remington 700 hunting bolt-action rifle.

Joseph pumps a round into the shotgun then hands me the rifle. "I don't need to ask if you're good with one of these …"

We work feverishly to set up defenses around the house. Enid takes up the rifle she had hiding in the pantry and heads upstairs. Joseph, Isabella, and I cover the ground floor. Posted up at the front-facing window of the living room, I watch the woods through the scope. Eventually, the helicopter leaves the area and the propeller hum is replaced with the rumble of truck engines and slamming doors.

I watch intensely through the scope, waiting for the slightest movement. A blur of gray moves between two trees to the left. There are two more gray flashes to the right. A gray-helmeted soldier slowly crawls out from behind cover then sights the house through his scope.

"Contacts at twelve, two, and eleven o'clock!" I say in a low voice. "Looks like they're running thermal sights. Get ready."

"Copy," Isabella says. "Glad you woke up when you did, Dion!"

A gunshot cracks off outside and glass shatters upstairs. Commotion follows. I pull the trigger and blow a hole in the head of the prone soldier, pull back the bolt to eject the round, and slam it back in place as I pan to the targets on the left.

All hell breaks loose as Deciders come pouring out of the tree line.

I put down another Loyal, then duck away from the window a split-second before rounds shred through walls and glass.

The fight never ends …

And my fight damn sure won't end here.

I post up at a different window and fire another shot, then I dive behind the couch as more rounds hunt my flesh.

I will get back to Anne. And I will keep on fighting until I get my son back—until Ryan Thomas and the Decider leadership are all dead!

That's a promise!

END OF BOOK TWO